Praise for *The Russian Doll*

'Elena is a delicious villainess, and the compelling dynamic
between plutocrat and protégée makes this an addictive read'
The Sunday Times

'Part thriller, part romance, part social commentary,
this is a wildly entertaining novel'
Literary Review

'Fast-paced and clever, with a pleasing blend of political
intrigue and romantic suspense as well as a whodunnit,
this is perfect entertainment for a winter's evening'
Guardian

'A real page-turner'
Sun

'A sharply observed take on the Faustian
pact – and contemporary London'
Financial Times

'Russian money of questionable provenance is at the
heart of Palmer's novel, with a terrorist strike in London
transforming the life of her struggling heroine Ruth.
Strong on the topical issue of "Londongrad"'
i Newspaper

'A fantastically compelling novel about an ordinary person who
is propelled into the seductive world of Russian oligarchs, where
nothing and nobody is who they appear to be. Tense, twisty and
highly topical, Its skewering of the obscenely rich makes for a
sophisticated treat by a dazzling new star of Cold War fiction'
Amanda Craig, author of *The Golden Rule*

About the Author

Marina Palmer is the pseudonym of bestselling
British author Imogen Robertson used for
her contemporary solo thriller writing.

Imogen was born and brought up in Darlington and read
Russian and German at Cambridge. Before becoming a
full-time writer, she directed for TV, film, and radio. She
is the author of several novels, including the Crowther
and Westerman series and *The Paris Winter*, and has
co-written novels with former Labour Deputy Leader
Tom Watson (*The House*), screenwriter Darby Kealey
(*Liberation* as Imogen Kealey) and the legendary Wilbur
Smith (*King of Kings*). Imogen has been shortlisted for
the CWA Historical Dagger three times and for the CWA
Dagger in the Library Award once. She has also written
for Hampton Court Palace, chaired the Historical Writers'
Association and been mentioned in *Private Eye* twice.

Palmer is Imogen's husband's surname – she is married
to the cheesemonger and author Ned Palmer – and
she chose Marina as tribute to Russian Silver Age Poet
Marina Tsvetaeva. She almost went for Anna, after Anna
Akhmatova, but as her mother-in-law's name is Ann,
that started getting a bit confusing. She, her husband,
and her multiple identities live in south London.

MARINA PALMER

The Russian Doll

HODDER

First published in Great Britain in 2021 by Hodder & Stoughton
An Hachette UK company

This paperback edition published in 2022

1

A CIP catalogue record for this title is available from the British Library

Paperback ISBN 978 1 473 69380 7
eBook ISBN 978 1 473 69378 4

Typeset in Plantin Light by Hewer Text UK Ltd, Edinburgh
Printed and bound in Great Britain by Clays Ltd, Elcograf S.p.A.

Hodder & Stoughton policy is to use papers that are natural, renewable
and recyclable products and made from wood grown in sustainable
forests. The logging and manufacturing processes are expected to
conform to the environmental regulations of the country of origin.

Hodder & Stoughton Ltd
Carmelite House
50 Victoria Embankment
London EC4Y 0DZ

www.hodder.co.uk

For Rowan and James

I

'Miss? Are you all right, miss? Are you injured?'

Ruth heard the words but they were echoing and distant, like when you duck your head under the water at the swimming pool. The light too. Everything bright and blurred and fractured. She felt a hand on her shoulder, shaking her, and the voice got more insistent.

'Miss? Can you hear me? Are you injured?'

Then she saw him, a smear of a yellow hi-vis jacket, short brown hair in a buzz cut, pink skin, a tiny smudge of dry shaving cream behind his ear. She shrugged him off. She felt sick and her head was screaming. As if the worst hangovers of her life had all got together and flash-mobbed her frontal lobes.

'What's your name, love?' he said, leaning so close she could smell the coffee on his breath. 'Can you tell me your name?'

'Ruth,' she said.

He seemed reassured.

'Great, Ruth. Well done. Now, are you injured?'

He kept his eyes on her, waiting for her to reply, but murmuring into the radio on his lapel at the same time. 'Female, early twenties. Conscious and talking.'

'No, I'm OK,' Ruth said, guessing. Someone shouted a little way off, and hi-vis's head flicked up.

'Just stay here. Don't try and move. I'll be back.'

He got up and headed towards the other voice out of her blurred field of vision. That's fine, she thought. Take your time. I don't think I'm going anywhere just yet.

I'm not drunk. I'm not in a hospital. Think, Ruth.

It was like trying to see your reflection in a tiny mirror; you could catch a glimpse of little bits, each fractured image neat and pin-sharp, but they didn't add up to a whole picture. Not yet. One thing at a time.

She was sitting on a black-and-white tiled floor, her legs half under her, leaning against a purple velvet banquette – the sort stuffed very tight with the buttons driven down deep into the plush. Not at home in Brockley then. Not that Brockley was really *home* yet; she'd only been there three months, a baby Londoner still getting used to the commute into Green Park. The weekends she spent walking, trying to learn the city through her feet. She'd done Spitalfields and the West End from Piccadilly to Tottenham Court Road a couple of times; been to the National Gallery, the Tate Modern twice and the British Museum; and round her own patch, in south-east London, she'd covered Peckham and Dulwich. The rest of the lonely city was still vast and uncharted. There be dragons. A memory, a flash, a hot roar and then the sound of shattering glass falling in a thin rain.

She blinked again. She had something in her eyes and her skin felt gritty. Where hi-vis man had been blocking her view, she could now see a chair on its side, one of those bistro ones with a curved back and a wicker seat, and an overturned table with a veined marble top. She tried moving her head; the world lurched and a sudden wave of nausea made her close her eyes again.

Bits of her body seemed to be clamouring for her brain's attention, overloading her. The cold of the tiled floor through her jeans, a slow boom of a headache radiating out like shock waves from the centre of her skull, a metallic taste in her mouth, a pressure in her side. And a sharp concentration of pain in her left hand. She opened her eyes, looked at it lying in her lap, and turned it upwards. Her palm was smeared with cream, and she could see a narrow fissure of blood, a long knife-like swipe from her index finger to her wrist. It looked deep, starting to blossom with blood, so it must have just happened – whatever 'it' was. She fluttered her fingertips and registered they were still working through the resulting lurch of hurt. The flurry of pain flowed up her arm and got lost in the booming ripples in her skull.

Don't throw up.

She needed something to bind up her palm, and found, magically, a scarf, held ready in her right hand, pale blue and patterned with skulls. Such soft, fine material. She tied it closely around the wound and held her arm up across her chest. Keep the wound elevated. She recognised the scarf, but it wasn't hers. Two Ruths in her head now: one who knew what to do with an injury and a silk scarf, then this other dullard still trying to work out where she was. The dullard needed more information. What could she see? Shattered crockery everywhere, spread across the tiles between the upturned chairs, flashes of knives and teaspoons, the glitter of broken glass and food.

The dam broke and her memories came in a rush, a stuttering flood of jump-cut images. A café, that's right. A fancy one on Piccadilly in the West End. She had a flash of coming in here off pavements clogged with weekend crowds and tourists, the road a tight parade of black cabs and double-decker buses, the smell of diesel. It was a Saturday afternoon and London had looked good, pretty, its postcard self. Not hunched and rain spattered. For the first time she'd felt, walking along the street, staring in at the windows, like she might be able to make a home here. Survive the first isolated lonely weeks, find a foothold, a handhold, a bolt-hole, a safe space.

But why had Ruth come in *here*? This grand European-style café with huge plate glass windows, all lined with extravagant fancy cakes, creamy monstrosities in teeth-aching pastels. The waiters wearing white shirts and black aprons. Tea served in silver pots. Not Ruth's sort of place. She was on a bottle-of-water-on-a-park-bench budget.

The scarf. Yes. Ruth had seen the blonde woman looking through a jeweller's window, opposite the Ritz. The blonde was with two dark-haired girls and they had all been pointing out rings and bracelets on the black velvet cushions and laughing, the blonde woman leaning forwards so her face was level with the girls'. Ruth had come to a halt next to them, studied their reflections, and her heart had stopped dead in her chest at the sudden, miraculous sight of them. The scarf was trailing out of the woman's handbag, twitched at by the spring breeze and the passing crowds. Careless.

Ruth shifted her position against the banquette and wondered if she could stand. No. She absolutely definitely could not. Best wait for hi-vis man after all then.

The woman and the girls had moved on. Another image. The loose folds of the scarf in her own hand. She had almost kept it, almost shoved it in the pocket of her jacket, turned round and walked away – it felt so delicious against her fingers. Then she'd turned away from the window to catch up with the woman and the girls, just in time to see them come in here. *Here.*

A new pain, slow and sudden at the same time, was growing out of the pressure in her side. It pulled her back into the now. Ruth pressed her uninjured hand onto her flank and bit back a groan, lifting her head. A woman, not the blonde, as over-packaged as the cakes, was now standing right in front of her among the spilt food and the overturned chairs. Ruth looked up at her. She seemed a bit vacant, as if she was searching for a friend, scanning the crowd, her left hand raised; her Birkin handbag in the crook of her arm.

Not less than seven grand, that bag, Ruth knew that. Her boss had one. Whenever she carried it she had this look of being both faux-casual and eagle-eyed at the same time, like someone at a party who knows their date is way too hot for them and is secretly scared their status symbol will be spirited away by someone who could really carry it off. Someone like this woman. The bag looked right on her arm. She turned slightly and Ruth saw her right side was ruined. The cloth of her top burnt off, the skin showing black and pink. The side of her face was sooty and the bottom part of her right arm was missing. She shook, began to fall. Ruth tried to force herself up; her sneakers scrabbled for purchase on the slippery tile and she tipped over onto her elbow. A fresh barrage of pain came as the woman began to fall. Ruth put out her bandaged hand, but the woman was too far away.

Another hi-vis jacket person, a woman this time, swept in and grabbed hold of the falling woman round the waist, supporting her on her good side, then half led, half carried her out towards the street, shouting for help.

'Table for one, miss?'

That's it, Ruth had reached the *Please wait to be seated* sign, scanning the interior for the blonde, still blind after coming in from the sun. Something in the waiter's tone suggested Ruth had no right to their overpriced cakes. Sod him. She *wouldn't* spend a tenner on a scone, but she *could*. She had a job, a bank card. She'd ignored him for a second, then spotted her. The miraculous mysterious blonde. She was sitting at one of the tables against the wall, on a velvet banquette, staring at her phone with the two girls opposite in high-backed chairs, their dark heads bent together over the menu.

'I'm not stopping, thanks. That woman dropped her scarf,' Ruth said. 'I'm returning it.'

'I can take it for you, miss.' He put his hand out.

She stared him down. 'I can manage. Don't fret, mate. I'm not here to steal your cream jug.'

He had backed off, half shrug, half smile.

The walls were lined with mirrors, so everything – the light, the chatter, the chink of silverware against the teacups and china plates – bounced back and forth in the space. The woman with the two girls looked up. She was beautiful, early forties maybe, but with high cheekbones, lips glossy and eyes dark, her hair salon styled, but not overdone, not like some of the women here and the cakes they were eating. Poised.

She had caught Ruth's gaze and raised her eyebrow in enquiry. Her gold-coloured iPhone went face down on the table. One of the girls got up, menu in hand and stood next to her, pointing out something on the stiff card. The woman put her arm round the girl's waist, but she was ignoring her, still waiting for Ruth to approach.

Pain getting worse. Where was that the blonde now? Had Ruth lost her chance? She rubbed her eyes and felt that strange grittiness on her skin again, then a sweetness on her lips. Christ, sugar. She had sugar in her eyes, no wonder she couldn't see anything. She blinked. Cleared it off with her sleeve. Then she saw the gold iPhone under the table, screen shattered, its light pulsing. And behind that, in the shadows behind the overturned tables, a heavy-looking coat ... That's too warm for spring. No, it's something else.

Ruth had been holding out the scarf, the line about seeing the woman drop it all ready and formed in her head, and then something had made her turn round. A squeal of breaks outside, shouts, the door opening and three men striding in.

They hadn't looked like fancy-cake eaters. Combat trousers, dark hoodies. Their faces were wrong somehow. Masks. Halloween masks. Were those semi-automatics? Were they police? Why would the police be wearing Donald Trump masks? Ruth remembered, re-felt her slow, curious confusion, her bafflement. One man had lifted his gun and fired it into the ceiling; yelps of alarm had turned to screams. They looked at each other and the other two threw tight black globes, passion fruits, grenades. They looked exactly like the ones you see in the movies.

The men had chucked them underarm as if they were throwing tennis balls to a kid with his first racket, one into the back of the room, one – Ruth looked straight at the masked face – towards her. More screaming, chairs tipping over, people scrambling away, plates and glasses crashing to the ground.

Ruth had looked down and seen the ugly ovoid spin to a halt at the feet of the other dark-haired girl. She had stared at it, frozen in fear, and Ruth had ... Her mouth turned bitter as terror finally turned up late and loud. Ruth had dropped to her knees, and grabbed the damn thing, and chucked it away towards an empty table at the end of the counter. God, she hoped it had been empty. She had just needed to get it away from the girl.

Then the explosions while she was still in a half-crouch. The dragons roaring light and heat. She had lifted her hand to cover her eyes even while the shockwave threw her backwards. She felt the neat slice of spinning glass on her palm, then the suddenly solid air cast her down hard among the wreckage. Everything upside down and inside out and her brain shutting down and blanking out.

Hi-vis came back.

'OK now, where does it hurt, Ruth? Can you move? I'm John.'

Bless, John remembered her name – and they say London is unfriendly. Speaking was harder now. Funny, and right when things were beginning to get sorted in her brain.

Ruth looked down at her side and he helped her peel her fingers back from the pressure-pain in her side. A great black stain was soaking her good weekend top now and she saw the red slick around her fingers, the bright edge of a chunk of glass the size of her hand disappearing into her side. She felt her gorge rise.

Nice to meet you, John.

She wrapped her fingers round it.

'No, Ruth, don't pull it . . .'

He made a grab for her wrist. Too late. She yanked it free and let it fall on the tiles beside her. Her vision went swimmy again. Maybe that hadn't been a good idea. The urge to throw up was back.

'Jesus, woman.'

John drew in his breath. He rummaged in his bag while Ruth turned away, stared at the shattered, buzzing phone. And . . . And in its pale-blue light . . . Thinking was hard again. John pulled something out of his bag of tricks, ripped off a plastic wrapping with his teeth. She flinched as he lifted up her shirt and pressed some sort of dressing to the wound. It felt firm and giving at the same time.

'Let's get you out of here,' he said.

No.

'Come on. Can you stand? The ambulances are waiting.'

'Wait, John.'

'Ruth, we need to get you to hospital.'

Some people just won't listen. She punched his shoulder, weak as a cat. Found her voice.

'John, fucking hang on, man . . .'

He paused, primly surprised at the swearing, the sudden Teesside twang in Ruth's accent, the closed-fist punch in all this velvet and crystal.

'Under the table, up against the wall!'

And at last he looked, saw, gasped, reached out with his hand and touched the bare, still leg of one of those two dark-haired girls.

'Keep pressure on that wound,' he shouted at her as he stood up and started dragging the table out of the way. I'll do my best, mate, Ruth thought. But I'm not making any promises. 'Mike, Vera, there's a kid back here!'

Well done, John. The voices slipped away again and a cold peace came down between Ruth and the world like a wall of snow, a wall of sugar and cream.

2

Ruth was eating toast and scrolling through Google Images when the doorbell went. She got up stiffly and shuffled downstairs. Delivery for one of her housemates probably. Or one of those guys who sell dusters door to door.

She'd recovered from her injuries pretty well, coming to in the ambulance, then finally, properly, in a private room at St Thomas'. Apparently the room was a perk of being involved in a 'terrorist incident'. The nurse had told her how many stitches she'd needed in her hand – eighteen – and about the operation to repair the nick on her kidney from the glass, long but successful, then had asked if she was up to seeing the police. They came in an hour later, notebooks at the ready.

Hi. Ruth Miller. Twenty-three. Administrative assistant at Harrison and Partners Wealth Management in Mayfair. Recent arrival in London. Nearly got killed in a cake shop. Picked up a live grenade and threw it behind the till saving three or four lives including her own, so kudos. But bit of a bust after that. Didn't see anything worth seeing, doesn't know anything worth knowing.

Ruth had tried to help, but the three men who'd come into the café with their squall of violence had had the light behind them and those stupid masks on. The detectives closed their notepads with tight smiles and thanked her. Told her not to fret. They had the CCTV, the number plate of the car, the tiny fragments of grenade picked out from the cream and glass, shell casings. The counter terrorism lot were a smart bunch. They'd work it out. If she was sure she couldn't think of anything else? She paused. Then shook her head. Nothing.

Later in the afternoon one of the liaison officers had asked her to talk to the press. There would be a lot of interest in her, the woman explained, her bright blue eyes framed by clumping mascara. Ruth was such a hero, grabbing the grenade like that, saving the kiddies. Ruth shook her head and explained why she couldn't talk to the press. The liaison officer was immediately sympathetic, understanding. Yes, they would keep her name out of the papers, of course they would. Least they could do, she said, choking back her tears and squeezing Ruth's shoulder. Two days later she was back in Brockley, signed off work for eight weeks with a victims' fund cheque which covered rent and groceries. Told to heal. She read. Researched. Ate toast.

Finding the name of the blonde woman had been easy. It was right there in the reports from the first days after the attack, among the calls for action and conspiracy theories. Elena Shilkov, Russian national and philanthropist, second wife of Yuri Shilkov, accountant and financial advisor to the oligarchs. Both resident in the exclusive enclaves of Kensington. A bit more searching, dropping crumbs on a knackered laptop she'd bought from a pawnshop in Bermondsey, and Ruth had arrived at a website for Elena's charitable foundation, with an email address. There were pictures of Elena too, mostly from the *Evening Standard* diary pages; a series of portraits in ball gowns, posing on red carpets, hugging models, designers, actors, all at charity galas and openings. Elena wore a different dress but the same smile on her face each time. It was definitely her. No doubt.

Ruth had written the email: *My name is Ruth Miller, I was in the café that day, trying to return your scarf. I still have it. Can I pop by and give it to you sometime? I don't trust the post.*

Can you even pop by a house in Kensington? Would a Russian even understand what it meant? As soon as she'd sent it, it seemed like a mistake. Ruth fretted, bit her nails. She was bound to get the brush-off, be told to leave the scarf with the doorman or just keep it. Perhaps she should have said she was the girl who had noticed her dark-haired daughter thrown by the force of the explosion into the shadows, but that would have made it look like she was after a reward. And she didn't want a reward.

That had been a week ago.

The doorbell rang again as Ruth got to the bottom of the stairs, ready to exchange nods with an Amazon delivery guy, and opened the door. Not a delivery. Not a duster salesman. It was the woman still splattered all over Ruth's open browser windows. Elena Shilkov herself, in tight stonewashed jeans and Gucci belt, a white shirt, heavy gold chains around her neck and smiling that smile. She offered her name and her hand – smooth skin, firm handshake.

Ruth stared at her for fully three seconds.

She began to look impatient. 'From the bomb? I have come to see you. Is it convenient?'

'Yes. Sorry. Of course.'

She took a step back to let Elena in and took her into the living room.

'Tea?'

The Russian woman nodded. 'Tea is good.'

Ruth headed into the kitchen and clicked the kettle on, all the conversations she'd practiced whirling round her head like dead leaves in the wind. They'd all begun with Ruth arriving at Elena's place, not Elena storming into the house in a cloud of expensive perfume and her designer jeans. She opened the cupboard. Why had she never bought decent mugs? Every one of them had some logo on them, or a funny-not-funny slogan advising calm and gin. There were a couple of plain-blue Ikea ones at the back. Not fancy, but not so infantile either. She brushed toast crumbs off her hoodie as the tea brewed. She hadn't noticed how worn the cuffs were getting. It doesn't matter. It doesn't matter.

When Ruth came back through to the living room clutching the mugs, Elena was peering at the bookshelves, a collection of tatty paperback thrillers. She turned back into the room and flashed that smile again. She was too bright, too glossy for this room. A stadium floodlight in a forty-watt-bulb house.

'How are your girls?' Ruth asked, putting down the tea mugs on the coffee table (did nobody ever wipe that thing?) and sitting on the edge of the sofa.

'All good.' Elena picked up an empty vase on the mantel piece, looked at the bottom of it, then set it down again with a bored sniff. 'Katerina's arm was broken, though I think that was because the fat waitress stood on her, and Natasha had to have three operations.' She held up three fingers. 'But now she is good. They are back at boarding school.'

She said it all so offhandedly it was almost funny.

'And you, Ms Shilkov?'

Elena plonked herself down on the sofa, nearly bouncing Ruth off it, then shuffled up very close to her and looked at the ceiling, pointing with one manicured fingernail to a tiny mark at the edge of her eye.

'Call me Elena. See? Only this! One inch different and I would be wearing an eyepatch now, like a pirate. My plastic surgeon is an artist. Urgh, any other man would have left me looking like a monster, but he is a master. Very expensive. Very excellent. He made sure I stayed quite perfect. Oh and *concussion* . . .'

She made an exploding gesture next to her head and shrugged. Ruth caught a breath of her perfume again, musky and citrus.

Elena scooted further away, picked up her tea and sipped it, then made a face and put down the mug again.

'Sorry, did you not want milk?' Ruth said. 'Sorry, I just added it without thinking.'

'Tea!' Elena said, rolling her eyes. 'It is like everything with the Russians and English. We think we like the same things, but we like them different. In Russia we make our tea very strong, very dark, then add a little lemon, a little sugar. I cannot like these *tea bags* . . .'

Elena said it with a rich disgust and Ruth laughed. Elena grinned back at her.

'And this "sorry sorry"! I was in a shop yesterday, the woman in front of me wants to buy wine, the man behind the counter, he wants to sell her wine, so why did they have to say sorry to each other seven times? I *counted*.'

She didn't seem to expect an answer. Instead she just stared round the living room again with frank curiosity. A bland painting of flowers over the empty fireplace, the bookshelves, the TV. The decorations had all come with the house. Ruth thought it looked great when she took the room here, but it all seemed a bit drab and shabby now. She tried to remember if she had brushed her hair this morning. Probably not.

Her housemates were all at work. She shared with a junior lawyer, a video editor who wanted to direct and a woman who worked in advertising, who came home pissed three times a week and constantly claimed to have 'a bit of a cold'. Then Ruth. Ruth had got the job at the wealth management place through an agency, so the company sent flowers and a bath oil gift basket to the hospital, and the agency sent them another girl. The housemates had visited her while she was recovering and had kept asking if there was anyone they could call, kept asking till it had got embarrassing, telling them again and again to their concerned smooth faces no, there wasn't anyone. She could have called the Cunninghams, her final and favourite foster family, but didn't. Pat might have thought she needed to come, or send Mike, and they both feared and hated London with a passion.

'I am glad I still have my daughters. That is because of you.' Elena reached out and patted Ruth briefly on the knee. 'It is good I dropped the scarf.'

Then she took Ruth's hand. Ruth tensed up. Elena put her free palm against Ruth's shoulder, like she was holding her in place. It wasn't violent, but still Ruth felt herself go still, like an animal being controlled. Elena was examining the scar on her palm.

'You, I see, had a shit plastic surgeon.'

Ruth pulled her hand back.

'My fingers work, that's all I care about.'

Elena gave her a side-eye but Ruth meant it. Seriously, burn scars on the face or your nose sliced off would have been grim, no mistake, but a mark like that on her palm? She honestly didn't care. She had worse scars than that when she walked into the bloody cake shop.

'So you can still type. Good. And this?'

Elena pointed at Ruth's side.

'It's fine.'

Which was true too. Just a bit of stiffness now.

'Do you still have the scarf?' Elena asked after a pause.

'Yes, I do.' She went to fetch it from her room. Taking it to the dry cleaners had been her task of the week when she got out of hospital. When she went to pick it up again the woman behind the counter had returned it to her with a sort of reverence, in a little package of tissue paper. Ruth had looked it up online. Alexander McQueen, £300.

She handed it over. Elena didn't even undo the tissue paper.

'I think they managed to get rid of the bloodstains,' Ruth said.

'Good.'

'Elena, I . . .'

'Come and work for me.'

'What?'

Elena chuckled and wagged her finger close to Ruth's face. Her nails were neatly manicured, but short and unpolished.

'You didn't say "sorry"! Maybe you are not that English after all!'

Ruth blinked. 'Did you just offer me a job? I don't understand.'

Elena nodded. 'It is not difficult. I need you. You are a secretary, I am told. I need a secretary. A person. You will live at my house, with the girls when they are at home and my husband and my stepson, Andrei. You will do things I need doing and I'll pay you five thousand pounds a month. Are you still too sick? You don't look too sick. Just like a person with no job.'

'In your house?'

'Yes; housekeeper, head of security and you live in.'

'No nanny?'

'We send the girls to school. Nanny only in holidays, sometimes.'

She pulled her phone out of her pocket, checked a message and made a tutting noise at the screen before shoving it back. Gold again, like the one she had had in the café. Ruth's heart jumped and steadied.

She touched her hand to her hair. Definitely unbrushed. Did she say five grand? A month? That's what, sixty a year?

'So you didn't come because of my email?'

Elena lent back in the sofa, put her feet up on the coffee table and thrust her hands in her pockets.

'Email? I do not do email. That is why I need a secretary. A nice policeman told me your name and address.'

That was helpful of them. Ruth shook herself, told herself not to be so touchy. What did it matter? Elena was here now, they were having a conversation and that was what she had wanted. The job thing had to be bullshit. Ruth couldn't do anything worth five grand a month. Was it charity? A thank you for the grenade? No, she might have unbrushed hair and a cheap rented picture on the wall, but she was not a bloody charity case. 'I'm signed off until next week, then back to the agency. They'll find me a job.'

Elena tutted under her breath. 'A stupid job. For less money and ten per cent of that, they keep.'

Ruth had an image of being able to press the 'See balance now' button on the ATM screen without a spasm of fear. Of buying the supermarket 'Finest' products and not even adding up her purchases as she went. Of walking into Jigsaw or L.K.Bennett and not heading to the sales rack at the back. God it was tempting, just like she'd been tempted to stick the scarf in her pocket and walk off on the day of the attack . . . but no. She shook herself. Sod it. She'd worked way too hard to take handouts and she wanted to talk to Elena, not just doff her cap and get a fistful of cash. Nothing else mattered. She could get another job; she could keep on managing with the discount stores and the small bedroom at the back of this house.

16 *Marina Palmer*

'And I will give you clothes, because . . .' Elena waved at Ruth's ensemble. 'Because you need clothes. I'll give you phone and iPad and if I fire you, you get a payment of ten thousand pounds but you can't sue me.' She lifted a finger again and put her head on one side. 'I do fire people sometimes. They are irritating. The lawyers made me put that in. Ten thousand, but no suing.'

Get thee behind me, Satan. This is not for you, Ruth. Don't be daft. This is just a rich woman's whim. Even if you wanted this job, it's just an illusion. She'll forget she offered it to you tomorrow. You'll get dropped again.

'But aren't there agencies for that sort of thing? For executive assistants for people like you? And how do you know I'd be any good at the job?'

Elena pulled on one of the gold chains round her neck. Ruth saw that between the links were woven little enamels of doves and red berries. A short impatient sigh.

'There are no "people like me". After the nice policeman told me your name, I had people look at you. They spoke to the money place you worked. They said you were a good worker. Thorough. Careful. You have no boyfriend. No family so no reason you cannot live at my house. And best of the best: you saved my life. And my girls. I do not need an agency to tell me what I want. Agencies are irritating.'

Not a whim then. Ruth wanted a minute to let her brain unscramble, restart this whole conversation.

'I'll need to think about it. And I need to ask you something.'

'Ask anything.' Elena got to her feet and dusted off the front of her jeans. 'But go dress, come to my house. See your room. Ask there.' She looked at her watch. 'I need to go home.'

Ruth stared at the cooling tea. She could go and visit the house, couldn't she? That would be a way to restart this conversation. And she was . . . curious. She wanted to see behind the money walls, just for a minute. How often had she wondered, walking around London over the long lonely winter, how the other half lived? Or the other one percent, the ones who got to eat those mad cakes. Carry those bags, shove those scarves carelessly into those bags. Now she had been given an invitation to go and have a look. She could ask there, in the house. Elena had to go, so she had to go with her. Simple as that. She'd still get her answer.

'Fine. I'll be a minute.' Elena applauded as Ruth got slowly to her feet. 'God, you know how to get your way, don't you?'

'Yes, it is very easy. Be rich. Now hurry up.'

3

When Ruth followed Elena out of the house and down the front path, shoving the recycling bin out of the way, she half expected one of those low black limousines you see patrolling in circles round Selfridges to pull up, but no. Elena drove herself. She pressed a button on her key fob and the lights of a dark-red Porsche parked on the double yellows right outside the house blinked in welcome. And Elena drove well too, singing along to Queen but handling the car with a sort of careless, competent grace. It wasn't until they'd crossed the river and were working through the city that Ruth even noticed the grey saloon car following them. Elena noticed her clocking it in the rear-view mirror.

'Security,' she said with a short sigh. 'Sometimes I like to run from them in the streets, it keeps it interesting for us. But today I am very good.'

'What do you do, Elena?' Ruth asked.

She flashed a sideways grin. 'You don't ask what my husband does? Most people, they see me and say "and *what* does *your* husband do?"'

Fair point. Ruth didn't answer at once. She would have asked that question too, but the way Elena drove had made her think twice about it.

'I tell you *both* things,' Elena said, slowing for a red light and stretching out her fingers on the leather steering wheel. 'My husband is a businessman. Like an accountant. Me, I make things happen. Deals. Introductions. I help. I am like a management consultant. He is Arthur Andersen, I am McKinsey.'

'And this job you are offering me?'

'Appointments, parties, tickets, errands, charities! *Emails*. Who to give money to, who to ignore. Boring shit I don't want to do myself. If I could make you do pilates for me, that too.'

And people got paid five grand a month for that? Money worked differently in London though, a lot of the numbers didn't make any sense to someone like her. She'd learnt that idea at the wealth management place already. Learnt not to make faces about what the other girls thought was a 'total bargain'. Learnt not to choke on her tea when she saw the invoices come in for the bottled water and fruit baskets.

On the Bayswater Road Elena indicated left, turning onto a private street. There was an actual guard booth right on the road. The bollards dropped into the tarmac as Elena turned in. Ruth noticed a pair of policemen, semi-automatic rifles across their chests.

'The Israeli Embassy is on this street,' Elena said. 'And others. Romania, I think. And William and Katherine next door. Very safe.'

Guns didn't make Ruth feel safe. She looked out of the window. The road was lined with perhaps a dozen stuccoed mansions, each in its own plot. Tall windows, doorways with porticos on classical columns. Plane trees. Fairy land. Money land. Elena pulled up and as Ruth stepped out of the car even the sunlight felt more buttery than it had in south-east London. And it was quiet. She could hear birdsong.

Elena slammed her car door and dropped the keys into her handbag. The bag was Chanel. The keyring had a Tiffany fob. Pavement, low wall with iron railings but no gate, a gravel driveway edged with huge plant pots with squared-off chunks of hedge in them. A brick path leading from pavement to front steps. More gates either side of the house connecting the structure to the walls that marked the edges of the property. A dozen shallow stone steps to a porch. A man in a dark suit stood in the shade of the portico. He didn't greet them as they approached, or open the door. He wore shades and an earpiece.

'All right?' Ruth said to him and Elena gave a little snort of amusement.

'Good afternoon, miss,' he said. Not looking at either of them.

Elena pushed open the door. Ruth felt a shock of wrongness then realised: if you have armed guards at the end of your street and a guy standing on your front steps, you don't need to scrabble in your bag for a latch key. You don't lock your doors. OK.

The floor in the hallway was black-and-white marble tiles. Hell. Ruth hesitated. Had to take a deep breath before stepping forward. She couldn't look at tiles like these without seeing the aftermath of the explosion, or worse, the grenade coming to rest at the girl's feet. She could still feel the weight of it in her hand. Head up, Ruth. The walls were blistering white, with panelling picked out in black and punctuated with huge modern art canvases. Ruth's visits to the Tate meant she could recognise the Hirst and the Basquiat. The place was huge and everything shone like it had just been polished by unicorns. Ruth didn't think she'd ever seen a house this clean.

'Would I have to run the house?'

Elena shook her head, dropped her bag on the hall table.

'No. I saw your home. Anyway, I have Masha, she is cook and housekeeper, and she runs the staff. You don't work for the house. Just me.'

Then she stopped suddenly. Ruth, craning her neck to watch the staircase ascending towards a skylight, high above them, almost walked into her.

'It will not be boring, Ruth. You want to be a businesswoman for a career?'

What? Where she grew up people thought they were really lucky to get a job; no one dreamt of having a *career*. Careers were for rich people and southerners.

'Maybe. I'd like to help people.'

Elena rolled her eyes then pushed open a door. Ruth squinted in the rush of sunlight. A narrow room with vast windows leading to a terrace. Scattered sofas and low tables.

'Garden room. Downstairs is the family kitchen.'

There was a staircase behind them. Elena jogged down it and Ruth followed. Lower ground floor. They were deposited into a huge kitchen, its back wall like an old-fashioned orangery with double doors out to the garden in the middle. A patio with a path, then more gravel, then lawns and hedgerows beyond. The room was a sort of T shape, with an oak table in the cross bar which must have been twelve feet long. A set of window seats in pale green ran along the glass wall.

'Sweet. But no one comes to London to help other people, they come here to help themselves. Still. You want to help people? Get rich. I can teach you many things,' Elena said over her shoulder. 'How to deal with people.'

She pointed at a door on the right of the kitchen proper. 'Your office. Next to head of security. Opposite, housekeeper's office. Come this way.'

Behind the housekeeper's office a corridor opened out into an area like the lobby of a smart hostel. Another kitchen set-up, settees. Two round tables with Ikea dining chairs.

'Masha and head of security live here too,' Elena said. 'This area is for you and them. And for the breaks for the morning daily people.' She waved at a door in the far corner. 'To basement. Storage. Yuri and me have the real basement. Gym, cinema and garage, but it has a different staircase. Other side of kitchen.'

She strode on, passing one, two doors to her right, and pushing a third open.

'This is your room.'

She stood aside so Ruth could go in first. The room was simple. A double bed, a chest of drawers and a wardrobe, a sofa and a pair of easy chairs facing a TV. An empty bookshelf, a brightly coloured print above the TV. It was twice the size of Ruth's room in Brockley. She felt almost hungry looking at it. Wolf-ish.

'For answering emails?'

'For doing what I want without irritating me with little questions.'

'And what makes you think I won't ask irritating questions?'

Elena came in and sat on the bed, her hands tucked under her thighs.

'I feel it. I saw it. You saved my girl. Your employers say you are diligent. Smart. After the café, Yuri and me got many new people. I thought, that girl who threw away the grenade – that's who I want. So I came and got you.'

Elena got up again, wandered over to the window and peered out.

'For weeks and weeks after it happened, I couldn't leave the house. Now I start work again. So I need a new person.'

Ruth didn't answer. She had to say something soon, before this went too far.

'Come up to the library,' Elena strode off again. 'I have contract for you.'

Jesus, she worked fast. Elena had it all planned out. Ruth hovered in the doorway. She'd say no. The whole thing was too mad, too fast. Don't be impulsive, Ruth. Think it through. If something looks too good to be true, it probably is. She took one last look at the room though. Windows. Guess that's what made this the lower ground floor. They'd dug out a light well. The window had bars on it. Very safe. And the quality of it. You could tell that mattress wasn't lumpy and stained, the sheets weren't charity shop buys faded with a million washes. No.

Upstairs again, through the garden room. Elena was still moving fast, turning through the lobby into a drawing room which looked over the front of the house, then shoving open the doors at the back, which led into a library. It was like stepping between movie sets. The modernist palace was replaced by a country house set, something out of Harry Potter. A double-height room lined with books, the shelving broken up occasionally with oil paintings of pale women in flowing dresses, and furniture made of dark wood and leather.

'This is where I work,' Elena said, twirling round, her hands high. 'Here or in my bedroom.'

The library was big enough for the grand piano to be one of the last things Ruth noticed. Its lid was covered with photographs of family groups – some black and white, lots in colour, studio portraits and snaps in mismatched silver frames. Ruth drifted towards them. Family photos always seemed to attract her.

Then she saw it, in the middle: the two dark-haired girls, Katerina and Natasha, with another woman. The woman was turned away, her red hair covering most of her face, and the top of her head cut off by the frame. They seemed to be on a boat or on a beach; the air behind their heads was the pristine blue of meeting sky and sea. The girls were grinning wildly. Ruth reached out to touch it, then sensed Elena at her elbow. She felt awkward, off balance.

'The girls look happy.'

'Everyone is happy in photographs.'

'Who is that with them?'

'Pfft. The holiday nanny. The contract is on the table.' Elena pointed to a neat pile of papers on a low coffee table between leather settees in front of the fireplace. 'Go read it.'

'Elena, I need to tell you something.'

Before she could say anything else, she heard the click of a door, and turned to see a man, youngish, dark hair and suit, emerging from an entrance at the back of the library.

He had an earpiece, Ruth noticed, like the man on the step, but no shades. Too young to be Elena's husband, surely. And he didn't look like an accountant. He nodded to them and walked past them towards the dining room.

'Michael, meet my new PA!' Elena said, and he stopped and turned round. 'She's living here. Ruth, this is Michael Fitzsimmons. Our head of security.'

Michael Fitzsimmons glanced at Ruth, half-glanced really, then frowned at Elena.

'Elena, you can't just hire people off the streets. We need to get her checked out.'

'I got her checked out,' Elena said, in a sing-song voice.

'With whom?'

'Michael, I can pick up a phone. I will not tell you what number I dial every time. She checks out. Her references are good.'

Ruth had a sense Elena was enjoying this, the irritation of Michael Fitzsimmons.

'How can I protect you if you do this, Elena?'

Elena put her hands on her hips. 'No one has thrown a grenade at me since we hired you, Michael. You're doing a fine job. Very well done.'

She reached her hands out in front of her offering a flutter of ironic applause.

'There is an agency.'

It was like she was a pot plant or something. Furniture. Ruth felt her temper rise. She sat down on the sofa and pulled the contract over.

'But Michael, Elena says agencies are irritating,' she said, starting to read. She didn't need to look up to know she had caught his attention. Elena crowed.

'See! Yes! I think they are very, *very* irritating. My good friend Ruth is correct.'

'Where are you from?' Michael said. Ruth gritted her teeth. Her vowels slipped a bit if she was angry.

'Middlesbrough.'

She studied him over the top of her contract. Square jaw, tall, clean shaven. He was glossy too, not like Elena, but like a well-fed dog. Like a Labrador, something like that. Like grass-fed beef.

'How did you get here?' he asked. The patronising bastard.

'A bus. Then Elena drove me from Brockley in her Porsche.'

She returned to the contract. Forty hours a week, but out-of-hours calls to be expected. One free day a week, flexible and by prior arrangement. A non-disclosure agreement. She caught a reference to the ten grand severance payment. Mostly though she could just feel him looking at her.

'Very well. If you give me your driving licence, I can do my own checks now.'

Ruth lifted her eyes from the small print. He was actually holding his hand out to her as if she was just going to reach into her back pocket and get her wallet out. Yes sir, no sir.

'I haven't agreed to take the job yet.' He stared at her, a much longer, more assessing look this time. 'And I don't drive.'

Elena plumped down on the sofa next to Ruth, her arm along the back, and extended her long legs out, crossing her ankles on the coffee table and giving a rich throaty laugh.

'Bye bye, Michael! Go secure something!'

The irritated stare and outstretched hand turned into an amused shrug, a shake of the head.

'As you wish, Elena.'

He managed to make it charming. They watched him leave, the door from the library to the corridor clicking shut behind him, and there was a moment of silence as they both stared into the space he'd left behind him. He was like the waiter in the café. Giving off that 'we both know you don't belong here, so let's not have any trouble' vibe. It wasn't up to him to say where she belonged.

Elena swung her legs off the table again, leaning forward in the same movement and flicking open a low wooden box which sat next to the contract. Ruth had thought it had cigars in it, but no. A pair of Montblanc fountain pens.

'But you will take the job?' Elena said. 'I need you.' Ruth stared at the pens. 'I want someone with . . .' she paused. 'Someone with strong bones. Polite, but not always so "sorry sorry sorry". You have strong bones.'

Maybe she was better qualified for this job than she thought. Why not? This woman said she needed her and apparently no one else did. Not any more. Ruth thought of the money, the room. Like big golden apples ready to fall in her lap.

'If you buy me clothes, do I get to keep them?'

Elena nodded as if she thought this was a sensible question, then picked up the contract and leafed through it. She pointed to a paragraph.

'Only if you stay at least three months from the purchase date. We must keep the receipts.'

She stared for a moment at the array of photos on top of the piano, the crisp glint of the Mediterranean sky, and felt a pulse of longing under her ribs. Another life. Another fresh start.

'Fine. You got me.'

Elena cheered and clapped her hands together, then handed Ruth the pen.

4

Elena texted Ruth the next day saying she was sending a car on Wednesday morning. Three days from meeting her to moving in. When Ruth hauled her suitcase down the front path at the appointed time, she found Michael waiting for her, leaning against a gleaming Prius.

'Morning,' he said without smiling and hefted all her worldly goods into the boot with no visible effort.

She nodded, then slid into the front seat, waiting for him to get into the driver's side before she said anything. He started the car by pressing his thumb to the steering wheel and it purred quietly into life.

'Fetched by the head of security? I'm honoured.'

'Elena's idea,' he replied, turning out of the street onto one of the larger roads winding towards New Cross. 'She thought it would give us a chance to get to know each other.'

'Are you sure she isn't punishing you for something?'

He laughed, a short bark.

The car smelt new. Perhaps that was how the world was going to smell from now on: of paint and high-end cleaning products. She thought about her sad belongings in the suitcase. Some clothes, a few books, a handful of souvenirs. She fiddled with the seat belt, trying to get comfortable.

'Did you say goodbye to your flatmates?' he asked.

'Yes. We don't know each other that well. Once they knew rent would be paid until the end of the month they just wished me luck. They won't have trouble filling the room.'

She felt him watching her, a curious interrogative stare. It felt vaguely uncomfortable.

'So have you checked me out then? I'll quiz you. What's my blood type?'

He was watching the road again.

'O neg. Very dull.'

'Soz, man.'

He drove calmly. No aggression, no sighs of frustration at the buses, slowing to allow hungover students staggering across New Cross Road to reach Goldsmiths in safety.

'Rest of it was interesting though. Ruth Miller, born 27th January 1996. Father unknown, mother struggled with alcohol addiction. Seven foster homes, four care homes. Managed to get five GCSEs, then two A-levels second time round. A two-year course in Business and Administration at Middlesbrough College. Likes include reading and cinema. Done waitressing and data entry. Got a job at a local solicitors' office, then six months ago, moves to London to temp. Attracted by the bright lights were you?'

What was that, less than a hundred words? Her whole life in a paragraph. He had his facts straight though. She wanted to tell him they bought her a cake to wish her luck and say goodbye at the solicitors. She still had one of the candles and the card they'd all signed in her suitcase. Leaving that job had been another daft decision made in a moment. She'd been persuaded to sign up for an adventure, then when the adventure fell flat she was too proud not to follow through. Like this. Picking up the contract to annoy Michael. Signing the contract because she wanted to feel the weight of the pen in her hand. Action brings good fortune. Act in haste, repent at leisure. Jesus. Sometimes her head was just a bran barrel of stupid phrases like that.

'There are bright lights in Scarborough, Michael. Illuminations, every year. We went on the bus from the home one Christmas as a treat. What about you then? Since I don't have access to your file.'

Roadworks in Bermondsey. For the first time Ruth noticed he wasn't using GPS. He seemed to know the back routes and rat runs like a cabbie.

'Guess.'

'Fine.' She twisted in her seat. Studied his hands, the shape of his muscles under his well-cut suit, the line of the jaw, the texture and colour of his skin.

'Military, I think. Officer not a grunt. Not infantry. Bomb disposal or something like that.'

His hands tightened on the wheel. 'Close enough.'

'Lots of guys in the army where I come from. And I'm not done yet.'

'Go on.'

'Wait, I like this bit.' They were crossing Tower Bridge. Crowds filled the pavements and over their heads Ruth could see the Tower of London itself, while skyscrapers reared up beyond the buildings on the edge of the City. Black cabs and red buses occasionally blocked out the view of the river, the swoop of the bridge's painted ironwork. It was like the opening of a movie. She wondered if the feeling of being a tourist in this city ever wore off. He was watching her watching. Let him. 'OK. Home counties. Nice school. Small private one, or a grammar. Nice girlfriends but you never got round to marrying any of them, which makes your mum sad.'

He smiled. 'Surrey. And I'm telling Elena she hired a witch.'

'Yeah, you want next week's lottery numbers?'

Her voice sounded suddenly tired. He didn't reply, and she stared out of the window. Embankment. Westminster. Big Ben shrouded in plastic sheeting.

'You haven't told me how I came to be working for the Shilkovs yet,' he said finally, just as Ruth was twisting in her seat to look at the green and gold awnings of Harrods.

'No idea. Money probably.'

He didn't reply. Money. A simple word for a lot of weird stuff, Ruth thought, examining her hands, folded on her lap. Status, value. What is a person worth? At the wealth management company they had tables for it so they could advise their clients on life insurance. High Net Worth Individuals. Some of it was to do with if you had dependants or not. A couple of kids and the advised amount went shooting up. But if you had no family, you were allowed to live or die at no cost to anyone.

'So what's it like working for them?' Ruth asked eventually, not sure if she wanted to hear the answer.

'Interesting,' he said in that tone of voice that could mean anything.

They were approaching the house now.

'Let's get you settled in then,' Michael said. 'Today is admin. Tomorrow you start work.'

They went in through the back. The gate on the southern side of the house swung open as they approached and Michael drove through and crunched to a halt on the gravel outside the orangery-type doors of the family kitchen. Ruth got out and stood back, trying to get an idea of the place. Staircases of sand-coloured stone swept up either side of the kitchen to the terrace. So those central windows leading onto it must be from the sunroom. Above that were another two stories of windows, then slate grey roofs above, steeply pitched.

She jumped as Michael set the case down next to her. She pulled out the handle and tilted it forward.

'Elena and Yuri encourage the live-in staff – that's you, me and the housekeeper Masha – to use the front door,' he said, 'but deliveries normally come through one of the side gates and round the back. Hey, Sam! This is Ruth.'

Christ, she hadn't even noticed the man in a suit standing in a shadowed corner of the terrace. He raised his hand in greeting.

'How many guards are in the house?' Ruth asked.

Michael opened the door into the kitchen for her. 'Depends who is here and who isn't. And mostly no one *in* the house but me. Security sweeps of the house for bugs or anything like that are done twice a week but at random and by an outside firm. CCTV round the perimeter, nothing inside. As for guards, always someone out front and another out back. Three men on standby in the guard lodge at the bottom of the garden in case Elena or Andrei want to head out independently. I'm normally with Yuri. This is your office.'

He pushed open the door Elena had pointed out on Monday. Not bad. Desk, a screen, a landline. Filing cabinets in the two corners opposite the door. Ergonomic chair. A full lever arch folder in the centre of the desk and an iPad and phone next to it.

'So does Elena head out often? She said she likes ditching her follow car for sport sometimes.'

He shook his head. 'Far as I know, when she went to see you it was the first time she had left the house since the attack.'

'OK,' Ruth said faintly.

'Second thoughts?' Michael asked and she shook her head. 'Fine. I want to get the computer stuff set up now if that's all right with you, then I want to get back to Yuri's office.' He glanced at his watch. Nothing flashy.

'Where's that?'

'Oh, Yuri's office? Queensborough Terrace. Just the other side of the park. You can use the iPhone for personal calls, play Candy Crush on it if you like, but keep it with you. Once we've done this I'll leave you to read through the file. Your dresser is coming at three, and the stylist will be here at five.'

The what now? Play it cool.

'What are those?'

She pointed. There were chairs either side of the door and on each were stacked three cardboard cartons.

He grimaced. 'Oh, the misery boxes. They piled up while Elena didn't have a secretary. I hate to think what the email inbox is like.'

'Misery boxes?'

'Yeah. Look it's all in the file.' He glanced at his watch again.

'No need to be pissy about it, mate.'

That brought him up short. 'Sorry. I'm not always a dick, I promise.' She didn't reply. 'Jury's out on that?' He took an exaggerated breath, in and out. 'Fair enough. I'll get you set up.'

She offered up her fingerprint, tapped in a passcode which she swore wasn't her birthdate and by the time he left they were on friendly terms again.

Then she sat down and opened the file. A clean copy of her contract first, then her duties. Ruth went through the papers, trying to get the details to sink in. Bloody hell, there were enough of them. A helpful plan of the house too. Gym, cinema, bedrooms and offices. No need to leave at all.

Her title was Personal Assistant (Social and Charitable Enterprises), and her key job apparently was to go through the requests for Elena's time and money that flooded in every day. Elena, referred to in the contract as 'the Principal', was the only person Ruth answered to. No other member of the staff or household could give her instructions or commandeer her time without Elena's prior approval. Good. There were other luxury dogsbody duties – researching cultural events, whatever the hell that meant, gift buying and delivery. Running personal errands for the Principal. Ruth made a face, imagining herself picking up the dry cleaning.

At exactly twelve thirty someone knocked on the door and an unsmiling woman with steel curls and a grey dress came in with a sandwich and a bottle of water. She set them down on Ruth's desk.

'I am Masha. Housekeeper.' Ruth stood up to shake hands. Masha's skin was very smooth, her large eyes accented with layers of shadow. She could be a stylist in a high-end boutique. 'Your dresser is coming at three. Hair person at five.'

'Thanks for the sandwich,' Ruth said, receiving a tiny nod of acknowledgement before Masha turned and left the room. She sat back down, ate, and tried to read, the phrases 'your dresser' and 'hair person' bouncing round her head. The systems weren't too different to the ones at the wealth management place; diaries, contacts, email. She also had access to the visitor logs. She scrolled back through them. Members of the household just had their initials, while strangers got their full names logged and occasional extra details. Each day started with a rush of cleaning staff. Ruth clicked back to Monday. *E departure 1015. 1200 E returns with female guest (unknown).* Someone had added a note: *Ruth Miller hence RM.* Then this morning: *1000 MF & RM.*

She scrolled back further. No Es coming or going at all. A peppering of visitors for her though: *Jonathan Brooks for E. Refused. Cassandra de Montfort. Refused.* Yuri occasionally had visits from bankers and stockbrokers and he admitted them each time. He must work from home sometimes. Then she saw the entry for Saturday just gone: *Suzanne D'Arcy for E. Admitted.*

Strange.

She was going through her duty file a second time when she heard the back door open.

'Hiya! Is Ruth here?'

She opened her door. A thin, delicate girl – she looked about twelve – in a pink headscarf was coming in, dragging two huge suitcases behind her. Sam the security guy followed with two more.

'That's me.'

The girl looked her up and down and nodded. 'Classic size 12. Just as Elena said. Hello, babe! I'm Isme. Now let's go to your room and get cracking shall we?'

She seemed to know where she was going. Sam followed her with his cases, and Ruth trailed behind them with her battered case and a sense of profound fear.

5

The next morning when Ruth came into the library, a bundle of printouts in her arms, Elena was sitting on the leather sofa, arms resting on its back, legs crossed. The sun caught the highlights in her hair, glowed along her long legs, but her face was in shadow.

'Are you nervous?'

'Should I be?'

Elena snorted and patted the place next to her.

She was a bit, Ruth admitted to herself as she arranged the sheets in front of her. Ruth had been expecting to be kitted out in office suits and high heels, but Isme had just brought better versions of the stuff Ruth normally wore. All designer, all limited editions, but still mostly jeans, Converse and tops. A couple of cocktail dresses and high heels to go with them and she was sorted.

'Elena wants you to be yourself, babe!' Isme had said, nodding with approval as Ruth made a slow turn. 'Thing about this gear is that anyone who knows their stuff will see you're dressed like a freaking Saudi princess. Now knickers and bras. Then bags and wallets, and coats.'

Isme had had to wait a minute before Ruth was ready for that. She sat on the edge of the bed, breathing deeply, while Isme flicked her scarf over her shoulder and checked her watch. What had she done? If Elena turned out to be a monster could she get her room in Brockley back? It had been a fit of bravado, signing that damned contract, and now here she was. Uncharted territory.

She got a grip of herself. Life is uncharted. Get on with it, Ruth.

The clothes were all packed away in her room now, with lavender sachets and tissue paper, while Ruth's old stuff skulked in the darker corners of the wardrobe as if ashamed. The hair stylist liked her bob, but trimmed it and filled her bathroom with conditioners and styling products. Ruth hardly talked to her, she was so frazzled and raw from the attention.

'You look good,' Elena said.

Ruth bit her lip. She thought she looked good too. Laundered in someone else's money.

'Thanks for all this. I wanted to see you to thank you yesterday and ask you about . . .'

Elena waved her away. 'I was busy. Now I am working again I shall often be busy. You must think for yourself. Rule one. So what do the jackals and blood-suckers want from me now?'

Elena wasn't smiling this morning. Strong bones. Please and sorry and all that stuff was irritating. So get on with it, Ruthie. Business first.

The instructions in the folder had been clear enough. Its tone was thick with management speak, sections and sub-sections, but the basics were there. Go through the emails and written requests delivered from a PO box twice a week. Delete the obvious scams, assess the genuine personal appeals, grade the institutional requests, compile any threats with a copy for the head of security. Then present the pickings to Elena at 10 a.m. in the library and receive any further instructions from the Principal. Ruth had been at her desk late last night and since six this morning. She had got through about a third of the backlog that had built up since the attack, caught herself crying twice (sick kids) and found the email she had sent Elena after the attack among the rest. She'd deleted it.

'These are the hard copies of the requests that look genuine. Do I leave them with you?'

Elena pulled her phone out of her pocket and lent back into the sofa again.

'My God! I don't have time to read that crap. And even if I did, I don't want to read. Read me the crazy list. I see if I recognise any names.'

Some of the hate mail came from webmail accounts with meaningless return addresses. Some came from people who had taken the time to include their full names with their titles in brackets. Ruth had googled a couple of them and found Facebook pages filled with family events, births of grandchildren. Holidays marked *#blessed*. Some had obviously written Elena begging emails in the past and been refused, others had just spotted her photo in the newspaper and taken the time and trouble to find an email address for her, and share their belief that it was a great shame she and her children hadn't been murdered.

Elena yawned. 'I know one, two of those names. Give them to Brother Michael. He will flag them.'

'Why do you call him Brother Michael?' Ruth set the list to one side.

'Because he is like a monk. Like a warrior monk. Next.'

Ruth had her hand on the pile of printouts. It was an inch thick. Under it were those letters from the misery boxes that seemed legit.

'But I don't know how to decide on these individual ones, Elena. I mean, how much do you want to spend in a week? How do you choose? The file only says distribute funds as the Principal directs, and where to order prayer cards. What prayer cards?'

Elena's phone beeped. She looked at the screen and said something short in Russian under her breath. Not a happy word, Ruth was pretty sure of that. She started tapping out a reply as she answered.

'It is simple. So just do it. Rules are easy. Nothing over five thousand to any one person. Maximum for a week is twenty thousand. Choose the ones who you think will use the money well. Send it in cash. You tell them to pray for me. Prayer cards are in your office. Order more from Yuri's people if you run out.'

Ruth wondered if she was joking about the last bit, but Elena was still tapping away on her phone, chewing her lip. Then she locked the screen, shoved the phone into her back pocket and lent forward again. She stared at the table top for a second, as if coming to some decision, then looked up sharply. Back in the room.

'What about the thank-you letters for you – do you want to see them? Or a selection?'

Elena shook her head. 'No. Give them to Michael. All paper gets shredded and recycled.'

Had that been in the folder? Ruth thought of how many hours shredding all those letters would take. Elena must have seen the look because she laughed and patted Ruth's knee. 'Not by you! One of Masha's early birds will do it.' OK. 'Now, institutions! What do we have? I like art, animals. Some children. No addicts. Fuck them if they can't get a grip.'

OK. No addicts then. 'The National is planning an exhibition of Russian art from the nineteenth century . . .' Ruth began and Elena turned her eyes on her, wide and encouraging.

'Elena!' A male voice in the hall. '*Gdye ti?*'

'*Zdes*,' Elena yelled back, and the doors to the library from the hallway swung open. Two men walked into the room, one old, one young. The elder man was tall, his hair white and his skin deeply lined. In his sixties perhaps? The collar round his neck looked loose, but his long woollen coat fitted him perfectly across his shoulders. The other man looked like a photo from the older man's youth. The same height, same hairline, same eyes and narrow nose, but his skin was unmarked and his hair black.

The older man walked towards them, speaking in Russian, jabbing his finger at Elena. The younger man came in more quietly and shut the door behind him. Elena waited for a minute, maybe two, then when the older man drew breath held up her hand. Her palm towards him.

'*Podozhdi!*' Then she flattened her hand and turned to Ruth.

'Ruth, this is my husband Yuri. That over there is my stepson Andrei.'

Yuri glanced at her sideways, and his head twitched. Might have been annoyance or acknowledgement – Ruth couldn't tell – but he said nothing. Ruth felt Andrei's eyes flicker over her and he offered an unsmiling micro-nod too. Fine. She'd got used to people looking past her at her last job. Preferred them to the ones who looked too long.

Elena piled up the printouts and handed them back to Ruth.

'Sort out the individuals. We talk about exhibition later. I think the rest of this morning is red. My family wish to discuss my return to business.'

The library seemed tight and airless all of a sudden. Ruth held the papers and headed for the door to the hall without looking at either of the men. As soon as her back was turned, Elena opened up a stream of furious-sounding Russian and before Ruth had got into the hallway, the two male voices had joined in and were talking over her and each other. The door closed behind her with a quiet click, cutting off the sound inside entirely. Welcome to your new job.

Red time. Ruth's calendar synched with Elena's and each day had thick bands of scarlet running through it like arteries. Elena's work time. The document made it very clear: during those times Elena booked her own appointments and managed her own diary. She was not to be called, texted or spoken to, and if the Duchess of Cambridge herself turned up asking for a cup of tea she would be told to come back later.

Fair enough. Ruth took the printouts back to her office, grabbed her purse and headed for the front door. Coffee. A walk. Some air. She hadn't left the house since she arrived yesterday morning and she was thirsty for noise, movement. The house last night was too quiet to sleep in. Or her mind was too scrambled to allow sleep, even between those crisp clean sheets. She was painfully aware of the photograph on the piano, her need to know and the impossibility of finding the right moment. The right words. She needed to take a breath. That's what Pat Cunningham, her favourite foster mother, used to say when Ruth was too angry or upset to string her words together. Just take a breath, Ruth. OK. Press pause. Walking out of the house for a moment seemed like the best way of doing that, and overpriced coffee was the nearest available excuse. There was a Nespresso machine in the family kitchen and the staff kitchen of course. Live-in staff had access to both and any staff on duty were allowed to make use of them and take anything they wanted to eat from the burnished steel fridges in the staff kitchen area. Made a change from the locked cabinets of the group homes, or the passive-aggressive notes fastened to the Tupperware in her shared house.

She nodded to the security man on the front door. Twenty grand a week to give away. That was a freaky amount of power to have in her hands. Ruth felt as if a fairy godmother had just chucked a magic wand to her with a yawn and a shrug. She wondered what it would be like to get a begging email from someone she knew. She could be vicious – or gracious. A white knight or an avenging angel. What would the Cunninghams do with a grand? Take the kids on holiday? For respite and a few memories? Buy a better car? Or buy a rust bucket and blow the rest on one really good night? Decent shoes and a TK Maxx run for the whole family?

Ruth lifted her chin and felt the sun on her face. She could do this. Think for yourself. Elena wanted someone with strong bones. Fine. She could make these decisions better than any posh girl Elena's agency might send. Fuck's sake, if Ruth couldn't, who could? She could be good at it. She would be fair, decent. She had the power to make a difference to other people's lives when a week ago she was only just managing herself. Take the win, Ruth.

The Bayswater Road wasn't crowded. KFC and an estate agent, weirdly ugly office buildings. A bookshop. A waft of garlic from the Original Pizza Bar, of meat fat from the kebab shop. Then Caffè Nero. She turned in off the street. Suddenly sounds seemed louder, colours brighter. The hiss and flutter of the coffee machine, the smell of toasted bread and cheese. She wanted to tell people about her new magic powers. Wanted to ask the barista for her advice, the older woman in the sensible shoes in front of her in the queue. 'If you had twenty grand a week just to give to people . . .' Probably not appropriate. You're giddy, she said to herself. Take it easy. Order the coffee. Smile. 'You have a great day too.'

Back on the street again, she thought about walking further down the road towards Holland Park Station, but a sudden reluctance crawled up her spine. Too much new stuff already. The job, Elena, the house. Her head was pulsing with it. She thought of

Judith, one of her social workers, a massive woman who kept the younger kids in order by threatening to sit on them. It had been Judith who'd looked after her after she mucked up her A-levels the first time, her and Pat Cunningham; calmed her down, talked her through all the paperwork she needed for her re-sits.

'Love, you just tried to do too much new stuff at once! Then the pressure of . . .' She'd tailed off, patting Ruth's hand, then started again. 'Nobody's fit to be on their own at sixteen and handle everything you are going through. Go back to the Cunninghams, do your classes. Lean on what you know for a bit.'

The woman came from nowhere. One moment Ruth was heading back towards the house, lost in her own head and trying to chill, feeling all the feelings, next thing this woman was in front of her, blocking her way. Ruth stepped sideways to go round her, but she moved to block her path. She was in her forties. Anorak and grey hair plastered to her skull. Her sunken cheeks suggesting lost teeth.

'Can you help me?' she said. She was smiling at some point in the distance over Ruth's shoulder. Her hand was out. 'I just need a few pounds to get into a shelter tonight.'

Ruth opened her purse. Change from the fiver she'd used to buy her coffee. She fished it out from the stiff leather pocket and put it into the woman's hand. 'There you go.'

'That it?'

'All I've got, sorry.' Ruth felt a guilty prickle of annoyance.

'We could go to a cashpoint. You could get me more.'

Ruth let the warmth drop out of her voice.

'That's not going to happen.'

The woman was looking at the coins in her palm, but didn't move out of Ruth's way. Then she made a fist out of her fingers, and lifted her gaze. Her right pupil was cloudy, and Ruth felt a thrill of pity and disgust.

'Two quid? You've got to be taking the piss.'

The woman's face was flushed.

Sod this. Ruth began to walk past her but the woman shot out her hand, and grabbed her upper arm. She could feel the bony pressure of her fingers through the new designer jacket.

'I saw you come out of your house. You're one of those Russians. Bastards.'

Ruth turned to face her again.

'I'm from Middlesbrough, and if you don't let go of me right now, I'll break your fucking arm.'

At last the woman managed to focus on Ruth's face. She uncurled her fingers, let her hand drop to her side.

'They rape children, you know. That's how they make their money. Selling little kiddies to Arabs. And you'll go down with them, Middlesbrough.'

Ruth took a long slow breath. 'Walk away,' she said. 'Turn round, and walk away.'

The woman did, and Ruth watched long enough to be sure she was properly gone. She was wearing tracksuit bottoms and battered trainers, her ankles were bare, and Ruth noticed the purple bruising on the visible skin.

And there but for the grace of God go I, Ruth thought. I could have ended up like that without the right people turning up at the right time. The cheap high of cornershop vodka in the park, the boys and the men like Sid and his mates who liked to party with young girls. If the Cunninghams hadn't been able to take her in when she was fourteen for a couple of years and given her an idea of what stability, possibility looked like – if they hadn't been there to convince her she had brains and value as a human being – and if they hadn't taken her back when she messed up her A-levels . . . Too many of her friends from care had ended up in a bad place. Pregnancy, prison, fighting the social for custody, buckling under the weight of it. Self-medicating, grabbing any kind of escape when they could. Plenty of people had been through worse than Ruth had, crippled by the consequences of other people's decisions and then their own. She didn't kid herself it was because she'd been strong-willed or wise. She'd been lucky. Others hadn't been.

She realised. It was the new wallet. The jeans. What looks like kindness, a couple of quid, when it comes out of some ratty purse looks like a piss-take dug out from an Asprey wallet. Lesson learnt.

She turned back towards the house, and straight into Michael Fitzsimmons walking briskly along the pavement towards her.

'You OK?'

'Of course I am.'

But she said it too fiercely, all that stuff churning round in her head.

He was frowning at her, frowning down at her. She wondered if he bought his shirts just slightly too small to show off all that muscle. Maybe Isme bought them for him like that.

'She laid hands on you.'

'And yet, somehow, thank God, I seem to have survived.'

Ruth walked past him towards the crossing, and he followed.

'Did she say anything?'

'That the Russians rape children and sell them to Arabs.' She felt his reaction rather than saw it. 'What?'

'Nothing. Only that if she knows you work for the Shilkovs she might have been watching the house. I'll give her photo to the men on the gate.'

She sipped her overpriced coffee. The sugar made her teeth hurt.

'You took her photo? I thought you were rushing to my rescue.'

The lights turned and they crossed to the insistent panicked peeps.

'I had time to do both,' he replied, his voice as dry as sandpaper.

'They don't do they?' Ruth said as they reached the other side of the road. The traffic started flowing again behind them. 'I mean that's just bullshit, isn't it? Crazy woman spouting rubbish. Tell me. Now.'

She stopped and looked him straight in the eye, feeling the tension in her shoulders.

'It's bollocks,' he said firmly. 'Racist crackhead bullshit.'

Ruth studied his face. She didn't think he was lying, so what was making her spidey sense tingle? Something underneath what he was saying, something in the tone. Then she got it.

'You know. You know about the trial.' Her voice was dead but she could feel the nervous tremor through her body, like the vibrations of traffic. 'You had no right. No right at all.'

The coffee tasted like shit. Ruth flung the cup in a rubbish bin, half drunk, with all the other wasted things. He didn't speak, and she wasn't interested in anything he had to say anyway. So she walked ahead of him, through the gates and back towards the house.

6

Had he told the Shilkovs? What exactly did he know? Ruth returned to her office and sat staring blankly at the screen of her computer for twenty minutes, letting the memories wash over her. Even after all this time they never added up to a coherent picture. Just flashes of men's faces, her first police liaison officer. Everyone telling her how brave she was every five minutes. She didn't feel brave. She'd been angry, then terrified, then miserable, then triumphant, then terrified again.

Do something. Keep moving. Keep doing. She got up from her desk, picked up the papers in the printer and left the office to spark up the Nespresso machine in the kitchen. The coffee from the shop had been too sweet anyway, and this came in a china cup patterned with blue flowers. Then rather than going into her own office, she knocked on the door to Michael's. No reply. She pushed it open. It was just like hers, a functional cube with filing cabinets against the back wall. The ones in her room were a neon green. These an electric blue. One drawer, labelled 'Personnel'. She tugged at it. Locked, of course.

'Can I help you?'

For a big man he moved quietly. She took a stapled set of papers from under her arm.

'Michael. Just dropping off the crazy list in hard copy as per my instructions.' He didn't say anything, or offer to take it from her. 'Wanted to check my personal records too, to see what information about me you've illegally obtained.'

The corner of his mouth twitched in a smile. Then he came round the desk and towards the cabinet. 'If I may?'

She backed off, cradling her coffee, and he pulled a set of keys from his pocket, selected one and opened the cabinet. It was the sort of key you used on a five-year diary when you were a teenager. Not exactly high security. She watched as he pulled open the drawer and rummaged for a minute before pulling out a plain manila folder. The tab had her name on it. He dropped it on the table.

'Look for yourself, Ruth.'

She put down her cup and flicked it open. A reference from her last job warmly recommending her, an old one from the solicitor's office and her CV from the agency that had placed her with the wealth management company. Each of the points on it, her grades and qualifications, were neatly ticked off. As were her previous addresses.

'I spoke to the Cunninghams the day you signed that contract,' he said, 'while I was checking up on your previous addresses. They like you. Talked about how brave you were and that set me wondering.'

'And?'

He lent against the wall, crossed his arms. 'And I have my contacts, so I found someone willing to speak to me confidentially at Cleveland Police. He gave me the names of the defendants in the trial and the rest was googling the news reports.' Another helpful policeman. Ruth had never read the reports. She could imagine the sense of shock and shame that shot through the prose but it didn't convince her. Child grooming gang uncovered! Vulnerable young people victims of predators! Usual stuff. They had all sort of known what was going on, the journalists, the social workers, the police, the other taxi drivers, the bouncers, but they'd carefully avoided knowing for sure. Girls like Ruth, in cheap clothes and bad situations, were easy to overlook.

'I'm sorry if you feel I've invaded your privacy, Ruth.' He took the folder from her, returned it to the filing cabinet. 'But you're twenty-three and have no social media presence at all. That's a red flag. I understand why now.'

Social media was too much of a risk. Yes, she was promised anonymity when she testified, but some people knew who Female

J was. Or knew she was one of the females at any rate. Or guessed. Best way to stay safe was to stay off all that Facebook and Twitter stuff. She'd never thought of that, the day she walked into the police station and asked to speak to someone on the task force. How seven years later her life would still be constrained, defined by that one decision.

'Have you told Elena?' she asked Michael. 'Not that she'd care.'

'Yes.'

A burst of rage like a cold wave from her feet to the top of her head. She couldn't look at him. 'And what did she say?'

He lifted his hands. 'You're right. She made that snorting sound she makes when she's learnt something interesting, then said she couldn't give a shit. How did you know she wouldn't care?'

Ruth pulled at the hem of her shirt. Took a second. She'd just known. 'Because I don't think she had a rosy childhood either. There's a thing. It's not like a secret handshake or something, but if you go through that stuff, or the people around you do, you notice the signs other people miss.' Ruth swallowed and she wondered if she'd given something private away in the end after all.

She couldn't think of what else to say, so she turned away, but he stopped her.

'Ruth, there's something you should know. It's just hit the news. It was why I came out to find you.'

He picked up his iPad from the desktop, tapped at it, then pushed it towards her. She had to put down the coffee cup to pick it up. At first she couldn't take it in. Having him look at her, wondering what combination of pity and sympathy was plastered over his smooth square-jawed face made it hard to read. Finally what she was reading broke through.

'Is this legit?'

The article was brief. The Uprising, the social revolutionary group who had claimed responsibility for the attack in the café while Ruth was still fuddled with painkillers in the hospital, had published a manifesto.

'What the hell? I thought Counter Terrorism Command had decided they were full of shit.'

She clicked the link and the screen filled with text. It looked like a photo of a typed document – close spacing, the words running into and over each other. She scrolled down: images, photoshopped cartoonish meme things of men in suits hanging from lamp posts, buildings bursting into flames. Fists raised. She handed back the iPad like it was dirty.

While she was recovering in Brockley, the liaison officer had popped round to explain, slowly, that they were treating the initial Uprising claims with scepticism. The car had been found burnt out, the Halloween masks melted onto the metal, but the attackers had left no stray hair or usable fingerprints. Ruth's liaison officer said they'd probably been smuggled out of the country. It was an unusual sort of attack; the place, no suicide bombers, the total lack of useful evidence. Attacks by radical terrorists were rarely so neat. The papers tried to cobble together their philosophy of violent action against the privileged from fistfuls of tweets and postings. Someone on the news said the Uprising sounded like the Symbionese Liberation Army, the ones who had kidnapped Patty Hearst, so Ruth watched a bunch of YouTube documentaries about them. Not much of an army. A rich girl ranting at her parents. Interest in them had died down. Now this.

He closed the cover. 'The Uprising have included in the manifesto a few things that were kept out of the media, so that adds credibility to their claims of responsibility.'

'Things like what?'

'The masks, the number of grenades thrown. Calibre of weapons.'

'What do they want?'

'Justice for all apparently,' Michael said.

She saw the grenade spinning to a stop by her feet. 'Oh, justice was it? Lovely.'

'Just thought you should know.'

Mind your manners, Ruth. Be nice. You are in a nice world now. A clean, well-fed, polite world. She'd worked on it at the solicitors, got better with the constant smiling, the softened speech. Still, like her accent, sometimes these things slipped. Her mind was still echoing with the shimmering fall of glass and her palm itched.

'Yeah. Thanks.' Make an effort. 'You got contacts who can tell you any more?'

'That's all they can say this morning. There's no doubt this has caught the powers that be on the hop. If I find out more, I'll tell you.'

Ruth managed a smile and when she picked up the coffee cup her hand was steady. Justice? We all have our own versions of that, don't we.

Back in the office she tried to sink herself into the requests, trying to narrow them down, create some sort of system so she could con herself into thinking she was being fair, but she was sure she could sense him on the other side of the wall. Sense him knowing about the trial. God how she wished she could suck that knowledge out of his head. Once people knew about it, they treated you differently, especially the richer, more comfortable, more English types. You became like some Victorian waif in their eyes. They wanted to give you sugar and sympathy and a warm muffler. If you told them that that shit aside, you did OK, thanks, they just got even more impressed by your bravery and murmured about their charity contributions and how they hated the cuts to social care. Yeah. Hated that, loved how their stock portfolios were doing. Put it down, Ruth.

She made some phone calls to donations offices at the Tate and the V&A to introduce herself, worked on her system for the individual requests and after a couple of hours she thought she was making progress. The flare of memories the mention of the trial had brought up sunk back into the usual background hum.

Then her concentration was broken up by Elena's laughter outside in the kitchen, the thumps of bags being set down and the high sharp music of Russian spoken at speed. Ruth lifted her head just as the door opened and Elena peered round. She was beaming.

'Stop what you are doing. I am making dumplings. Proper dumplings.'

Ruth heard Masha saying something in Russian from the kitchen. Elena turned and shouted back at her then swung her gaze back to Ruth, a manic glee in her eye.

'Come. You can tell me about art exhibitions and laugh at me when I drop the flour.'

Ruth closed down her computer.

Ruth's job was to watch, and occasionally pass Elena things as the pristine kitchen disappeared under a dust of flour. Masha, who stared at Ruth with unsmiling curiosity for a minute, then shrugged and acted like she wasn't there, though was allowed to make up the fillings. That led to a series of debates in Russian which made Ruth think of a mother and daughter battling over the best way to do the Sunday roast. Masha seemed able to argue her corner.

In between, Elena interrogated Ruth about the art exhibition. This seemed to be how she took in information. Fighting with her housekeeper and covered in flour, she could still take in everything Ruth said, recall it and react to it in detail. She asked about the artists who would be featured, the offers of private views and curated talks, hospitality packages she'd be gifted for her support. Her mind sparked with the information while she worked the pastry on the granite work surface.

'They said they wanted to talk to you personally about the other sponsors,' Ruth said. 'They don't want to discuss that with me. Reasons of confidentiality, they said.'

'No.' Elena pushed at the dun-coloured pasty with her thumbs. 'Tell them if they don't talk to you, you will end negotiations. They will try and get round you. I will get a call from someone who has been asked by someone to make sure I am informed about your obstructive attitude. I will tell them you have my authority in little short words they can understand. The person who calls me will be embarrassed and pass on the message in even shorter words. They will then call you back and tell you everything.'

Ruth sipped her ice water. That sounded like it might feel pretty satisfying. 'Why do you need to know about the other sponsors?'

Elena blew a stray frond of hair out of her eyes. 'It is like sex.' Ruth almost choked and Elena grinned at her. 'I fuck you, I'm fucking everyone else you have fucked. Some bastard has syphilis, I could catch it too. Also, they are being a little tight with the presents and goodies. That means they have hopes of many other sponsors. It is Russian art, so maybe other Russians. And if I am trying to give a nice thing to someone I want to work with, it needs to be an exclusive, special thing. I say, "Come to the art exhibition gala with me, Sir Toby – I am a sponsor and I have exclusive tickets." If three others have said the same thing to him already, Sir Toby will not think it's special.'

'Who is Sir Toby?'

She shrugged and snapped her fingers until Masha handed her the bowl of fillings. Meat and something green. A lot of pepper.

'Businessmen, rich men, men with titles. They are all Sir Toby.'

'Are they married, these Sir Tobys?' Ruth asked, turning something over in her head.

'Yes. Half have wives younger than their daughters. Half have wives who scare them. Why?'

She was pulling out handfuls of the mix, rolling and shaping them in her fingers then placing them on the dough. Cutting and shaping.

'There's a Dior exhibition at the end of the year at the V&A. Maybe sponsoring that would be better for your purposes. A chance for the Sir Tobys to impress their women.'

Elena nodded. Ruth had been hoping to be praised for her brilliance, but instead the remark was evaluated coolly.

'Find out. I need a few things a year. One or two huge. Find me London's answer to the Met Ball. Where the real money is. And then find me the people, invitations even money can't buy. Watch what I do. Be clever.'

Be clever. Hell of a job description. What did the rich want? Same thing as everyone else. To be special. Exclusive this, limited edition that. OK, Ruth could work with that.

Voices in the hall, and Yuri appeared, with Andrei behind him. He looked round the kitchen door and began to laugh at the mess then approached his wife to be kissed, trying to hold himself back to avoid the flour at the same time. No shouting voices this afternoon then. Ruth slid off her stool, ready to make herself scarce, but it was Yuri who noticed her move and shook his head.

'Ruth! No! This lunch is in your honour, my dear.' His English was faultless, with only the vaguest trace of an accent. 'My wife tells me I acted towards the woman who saved my family with disrespect this morning.' He put his hand to his chest and bowed towards her. 'I apologise. As does my son.'

They all looked at Andrei. He smiled, and looked at once older and more handsome.

'Most sincerely, Ruth.'

No trace of a Russian accent in his voice. Pure upper-class English.

'Ha!' Elena said, clapping her hands together and sending up another cloud. 'She thinks you sound like Sir Toby.' Andrei shook his head, but appeared to understand the reference. 'Now did you find it?'

Yuri placed his briefcase on the table. 'It was hard to find, but for you, my love . . .' He snapped open the case and lifted the lid. Elena squealed. It was full of champagne bottles, but they looked cheap and the labels were in Cyrillic rather than French.

Elena was dancing now, swinging in circles, twisting her hips.

'Soviet champagne!' She sang the words. 'It is sweet as sugar and the corks are plastic and it is the only thing to drink with dumplings.' Then she grabbed Ruth's hands in her own. 'Welcome to Russia, Ruth!'

7

Lunch lasted a long time. There were toasts with the sweet champagne, and though Michael was summoned from his office to join them, Ruth noticed he only let the wine wet his lips before he set down his glass again. Yuri and Elena sang something in Russian, which made tears well up in her eyes, and Ruth learnt her first Russian words, *na zdorov'ye*, which meant 'cheers' – though the way Yuri and Yelena laughed, she didn't think she'd got the pronunciation quite right. Andrei grew flushed, and loosened his tie while Elena explained that the secret to getting the pastry right was using mayonnaise in the mix. Masha, who was trying to tidy the kitchen again, made some noise under her breath at that, and Elena span round with a stream of Russian. A long and passionate debate ensued until Masha threw up her hands and Elena glowed with childlike triumph.

Yuri asked polite questions about Ruth's last job and what Middlesbrough was like in fastidious English. Twice Ruth looked up and found Michael watching her. The first time he looked away, the second time, while Yuri was still laughing at something she had said about the amusement arcades in Redcar, he raised his glass to her and she felt a small current of electricity through her palms. Maybe she'd be all right here after all. Telling Yuri and Elena about where she came up was easy somehow. Not like at her last job or when she was chatting with her housemates. Probably it was them being Russian; she didn't feel like everything she said was being examined for signs she didn't belong in London, in Brockley, in a house of young professionals – even if they were all just as broke as her.

At last Michael looked at his watch and said something to Yuri. Of course he spoke Russian. Yuri nodded and stood up, then bent over his wife, hands on her shoulders, and kissed her forehead. She leant back and squeezed his hand with her own. Andrei started to stand up too, and stumbled slightly. Yuri said something to him, and Andrei flushed a deep angry red, then left the room without looking at Ruth again.

Yuri did not watch him go.

'Thank you for your company today, Ruth,' he said. 'I am glad to welcome you to our home.'

Ruth thanked him, and with a final squeeze of his wife's shoulder he left them, with Michael following behind. Elena fanned her face with her hand.

'Ach, I am drunk. At least I know it. Poor Andrei did not inherit his father's head for drink. Some English got into his blood at school perhaps.'

'What happened to his mother?' Ruth asked. Elena yawned, then drained the rest of the champagne in her glass.

'She died. Very sad. Yuri was a Party man, they had their baby just as Russia was . . .' she gestured with her hands – an explosion, a collapse, structures lifted into the air and crashing into earth in a flutter of her long fingers. 'But Yuri is a clever man. He knew what to do. She got sad and sick and died.'

Ruth frowned. 'People died of grief when the Soviet empire collapsed?'

Elena half shrugged. 'It is . . . people believed in something. Thought they had a place in the world. Then with perestroika, whole towns collapsed. The West said look: here is freedom and capitalism instead. For most people that meant no money, no hope, no help. Some died. Grief. Drink.'

Pat Cunningham talked about the eighties in the north-east like that. Ruth thought she'd seen things improve a bit in Middlesbrough, though, since she was a kid.

'Is it better in Russia now?'

Elena waved the question away. 'It is normal now. I was Yuri's mistress, and I was clever like him, so he married me. Perhaps it is not a surprise Andrei and I are not good friends even after all these years. We sent him to school here. He is now a proper English man. Firm handshake and all twisted inside.'

She stood up leaning heavily on the side of the table to force herself upright. 'I am going to sleep. There is a party tonight.'

Ruth snapped to attention.

'Your hair and make-up woman is coming at half past five.'

Elena yawned.

'Good. Send her up when she comes. Tell her she will have to knock very loudly.'

She began to sashay sleepily from the room and Masha started to gather up the plates.

'Elena?' She turned. 'Thank you.'

'*Nichevo* – it is nothing. You are helping me.' And she was gone.

Masha clicked on the dishwasher, took a final look around the kitchen, then went into her office and closed the door. Ruth waited in the kitchen, listening to the hum of electronics for a moment. Deserted again.

Two hours later Ruth was back in the library. One of the paragraphs in her contract stipulated that before any social occasion, Ruth would run through the guest list with the Principal and supply any general biographical information as required. Two hours hadn't really been enough, but she'd found most of the information in the contacts database. The library was empty when she came in, and the curtains had been drawn, leaving it shadowed. The folder tucked under her arm, she went over to the piano and the ranks of photographs, picked up the one of the two girls and the woman with the top of her head cut off against a bright blue sea and sky.

'My sisters.'

She almost dropped the photograph. The library was not empty after all. Andrei was slouched in one of the deep leather armchairs in the corner of the room, watching her. A copy of the *Economist* lay across his chest, a heavy-cut glass tumbler sat on the table at his elbow, and his eyes looked weary and red.

'But you know that. You saved them, didn't you?' The slur in his words might have been drunkenness or sleep, Ruth couldn't tell. She swallowed.

'I suppose so. Who is the woman with them? It's not Elena.'

He hauled himself upright. 'Who?'

Ruth walked over with the picture in her hand and showed it to him. She could smell the champagne and whisky soured on his breath.

'Megan.' He downed the final dregs in his glass. 'She looked after the girls during the school holidays, I mean it's not as if Elena was ever going to do that. Just a nanny.'

He said it bitterly, then yawned and didn't bother covering his mouth, treating her to a view of his slightly-too-perfect teeth.

'Where was it taken?'

'Croatia, last year on our yacht. I say yacht, it's more like a floating hotel.' He managed to sound boastful and sneering at the same time.

He grabbed the edge of the photo, jerking it and Ruth towards him, and then looked up at her, a half-smile creeping onto his face.

'You're not bad looking. Do you like clubs? I can get you into all the best ones. VIPs, celebs, the whole nine yards.'

Ruth kept her voice neutral. 'It's not my thing.'

'Oh go on. We could have some fun! There are always a dozen people in Tape who'll buy me a table and a few bottles of Cristal.'

'Can't you buy your own?' Ruth asked. His face crumpled.

'No. I'm the poorest person in this house. Michael earns more than I do. I have to ask for everything.'

Ruth was not feeling sympathetic. 'Tragic,' she said and he scowled.

'You have no idea what it's like,' his face creased into another sneer. 'God, I hope you're not one of those girls who knits. A crafty type, I mean . . .'

Before he could offer his thoughts, the door at the other end of the room opened and Elena came in. Andrei let go of the photo entirely and cleared his throat. He's frightened of her, Ruth thought as she straightened up. Good.

'What are you doing?' Elena's voice was irritated.

'Ruth was asking about that nanny we had for the girls, last summer.'

Ruth could hear the children's rhyme in her head.

Tell-tale tit, your tongue will be split
and all the doggies in the yard
will have a little bit.

Elena walked towards them. She was wearing a long, closely cut dress in sapphire blue, pearls at her throat and ropes of them looped round her wrists to match. Over her shoulders was a white shawl and her hair was half up, half down. A Botticelli dressed for the Café Royal.

'Oh her. And what happened to her, Andrei?'

He shifted uncomfortably. 'Ran away. Packed her things and went off.'

Elena smiled at him. 'That's it! No notice! Nothing! I think a man, or another job. The agency sent another girl, but Natasha and Katerina bullied her. Why are you asking again, Ruth?'

'Andrei saw me looking at the picture,' Ruth replied, walking back to replace it carefully on the piano. 'I wondered where it was. I've never been out of England.'

Elena looked disgusted. 'Korčula. A very beautiful island. But you don't have a passport? You will need a passport working for me.'

Ruth took the file out from under her arm. 'Of course, I should have thought. I'll sort it out. Shall I read you the guest list for this evening? You look stunning by the way.'

Elena did a neat little turn. 'Michael did the checks on you. He should have noticed you had no passport and handled it.'

Then the smile again. 'I know, I am having a good day. I should have dumplings and champagne all the time. Yes, read. I hope you are not going to run off like that girl, Ruth. My children liked her. She was good at her job. Not boring. Perhaps Andrei bothered her. He likes watching pretty girls, don't you, Andrei?'

'She wasn't my type,' Andrei mumbled, then puffed like an old man as he got out of his chair. 'I'll take a cab to the party.' The two women watched him as he left the room, the wrinkled back of his jacket looking pathetic somehow.

'So do you think it was a man or a job?' Ruth said when the door closed behind him. 'Why the girl left, I mean.'

'I think it was a man. Nobody would pay her better than me.' Elena was examining her nails. A neat French polish.

'You didn't think anything had happened to her?'

Elena raised one manicured eyebrow. 'Why? You don't pack your bag before you fall into water or get kidnapped, do you? Now, read the guest list.'

No, you don't. Ruth went through the list, supplying extra details – children, business interests, languages spoken – when Elena asked for them.

'And my guests?'

Ruth repeated the names that had a double asterisk on the list from the organisers, pretty sure she was messing up some of the pronunciations. Ralph is said *Rafe*, Cholmondeley is pronounced *Chumlee*. Another set of posh shibboleths, a code; like what wine to order and what to call the toilet. When she finished she found Elena was staring at her.

'What? Did I say the names wrong?'

'How should I know? But you didn't look at the list.'

'I remember things like that – names and bits of information. Funny brain.'

Elena nodded. 'Funny brain, is it? Good.' Then she looked at the thin watch on her wrist, half hidden among the pearls.

'Now go and dress. You shall come with me, tonight.'

Ruth was startled. She'd been expecting to spend the evening in her room, the TV burbling with some gameshow while she let herself think through the events of the day and cried a bit. Deal with stuff. Elena made a shooing gesture.

'Go! You have twenty minutes.'

8

The party was near Baker Street, a huge former church bathed in pink and blue lights. Ruth followed in Elena's wake up the shallow stone steps. Cameras flashed either side of them, and Ruth recognised the man in a tuxedo three steps ahead, turning with a smile into the fusillade of light. She rattled through the guest list in her head; yes, the actor, another 'next Bond' candidate.

The entrance was flanked by huge banners with the name of the charity, Restart, emblazoned on them. They fluttered tightly in the London breeze, lit by shifting coloured spotlights. A greeter, in a neat black suit with her hair scraped back, waited for them just inside the double-height doors. Ruth resisted the impulse to smooth back her own hair, pluck at the dress where it clung to her hips. Don't fidget. Someone was wearing too much perfume. It was like having a bouquet thrust down her throat.

'Ms Shilkov, so glad you could join us. Hi, Ruth. You are most welcome.'

The woman had a clipboard in front of her, and Ruth glimpsed columns of names and photographs. They knew what they were doing here. Memorise your guest list and greet everyone personally. Make them feel special before you ask them to open their wallets. They were efficient too; she'd only called and said she'd be accompanying 'Ms Shilkov' from the car on the way there.

'Is Yuri already here?' Elena asked.

The greeter shook her head. Not a hair moved.

'No, Ms Shilkov. We had a call saying he regretted he would not be able to attend after all. He asked me to remind you that you have enough art too, before the silent auction.'

Elena laughed. 'I shall ignore that, as it is a good cause.'

Ruth felt an obscure stab of disappointment, and for a moment couldn't understand why. Then she realised she'd been expecting Michael to be here too, and some part of her had wanted him to see her like this, in the dress and high heels with her make-up done, even if she'd had to finish that in the back of the car.

Elena put her arm through Ruth's.

'Ruth, we are going to make an entrance. We shall walk into the ballroom, stand and look around for three seconds, then I shall go and speak to people.'

'What shall I do?' She hadn't thought of that until now.

'You? Look. Learn. See how things are done. Go and have fun. Everyone will see us come in together, so many people will come and speak to you. Let them chat you up. Be judged. Judge them. That is what you are here for. Be seen. Then they will bother me less, and bother you instead.'

Elena patted her arm gently with her fingers. Almost a caress.

'You can tell me about any interesting ones tomorrow.'

She said it quietly, leaning close to Ruth's face as they crossed the threshold into the ballroom.

'OK.'

Elena came to a halt ten feet into the room, put her head back and laughed as if Ruth had said something very funny, then unlinked arms, squeezed her shoulder and gave her a fond smile before walking off towards a group of men in dinner jackets, her hands out towards them.

Ruth watched her go, and watched the men straighten and grin, congratulating themselves on her approach.

The room was vast. White walls, draped with more banners and washed upwards with blue light, punctuated with swirling pinwheels of white which occasionally resolved into words. *#Hope. #Future. #Restart.* The noise, a wall of loud voices, laughter and the thud of music, hit her like a blast of hot air and Ruth felt the sweat gathering under her hair in the nape of her neck.

'Champagne, miss?'

A waiter, his white tails spattered by the shifting coloured lights, offered her a tray of glasses. She took one, thanked him, and retreated towards the side of the room. It was edged with cabaret tables, just the right height for standing drinkers, each with a fat centrepiece of blue and white lilies. Weird, fleshy blooms. Deeper into the alcoves – this *was* an old church – Ruth glimpsed gaming tables, the booth for a silent auction, a man carving wafer thin slices of meat from a leg of ham on a stand, and another standing, hands behind his back, behind a bank of ice dotted with shucked oysters, each one topped with a little heap of caviar.

Andrei walked past her and nodded. So he had made it then. He had his hands in his pockets. Next to him was another man his own age in evening dress with a narrow face and slicked back dark hair. Peter Baxter, Ruth assumed. Andrei's plus one this evening. Elena had moved on from the men in black tie and was talking intently with someone in a corner at the far end of the room. A dark-skinned woman in green.

'Hi!'

Ruth turned towards the voice and found herself looking into the flushed face of a man in his forties. He was quite bald and between that and the heat he looked like a snooker ball with a thin-lipped mouth glued on. He had his hand out. Ruth shook it.

'I'm Greg Townsend. Townsend Industrial. You work with the Shilkovs? So great to see Elena out again! How many MPs did she buy tickets for here tonight?' Seven, Ruth thought, but she didn't say anything. 'Right. Well. Might I bend your ear for a moment?'

He looked like he wasn't going to wait for an answer then frowned. 'You do speak English, don't you?'

'Just about,' she said and he looked pleased.

'Fantastic. Look, I've heard a very quiet whisper that Elena's been talking to Glenville Solutions – it's not about these private partnerships with GCHQ the government is talking about, is it? Are she and Yuri lobbying for them? If they are, I—'

Ruth interrupted. 'I'm sorry, but I just work on Elena's social and charitable activities. I have absolutely no idea what you are talking about. I know nothing about her business affairs.'

He flushed and let out a dry, mirthless laugh. 'Really? What's the difference? Elena's charitable work is *all* business. Everyone knows that.' He seemed to struggle to get a grip on himself. 'Of course security in this country needs modernising. These bloody anarchists need stopping and the current crop in the Office seem to have no idea how to fight them. But Elena shouldn't get involved. What is she up to?'

He waited for a response again, and when Ruth turned from him, he put his hand on her wrist and tugged it.

'I asked you a question.'

She stared at his hand until he flinched it away and looked at him as he ran it through his thinning hair.

'That doesn't give you the right to an answer.'

'God, you're just like her.' From his tone Ruth guessed that wasn't a good thing.

He struggled to pull his wallet from his back pocket, pulled out his card and set it on the table next to her glass.

'Just tell her what I said.'

Then he headed for the doors back into the lobby. Once she was sure he was gone, she picked up the card and put it in her clutch. Nothing in the file told her how to behave with these people. She'd watched the other girls at the wealth management place deal with senior partners, clients. All the admin staff like her were women under thirty. All the senior managers were men. The two female account executives looked tired and handled the business of wealthy divorcees. Everyone was white. The admin staff were nice, friendly enough to Ruth the whole time she'd worked there, but they all seemed to be called Poppy and Jemima, and acted with their clients and bosses as if they were flirting at a cocktail party. Lots of big smiles and plenty of eye contact. Ruth's sharp black bob was said to be very chic, but they all wore their hair very long and flicked it over their shoulders when they were talking to their bosses. Ruth looked around the crowd, seeing if there were any Jemimas and Poppys in the room. Not many. Some girls, but mostly the women were older, jewels and long dresses, hair in thick curls. Ruth sipped her champagne again – it tasted of apples and toast – and lent on the table, her chin in her hand, just trying to take in the crowd, the sounds of braying laughter, the thud of the music. She was in the thick of how the rich lived now.

Greg Townsend was the first of a dozen people who approached her; the rest were all more unctuous and less prickly than he had been. One after another they made their way to Ruth and talked of exciting investment opportunities or touched base about donations to think tanks. Ruth listened, explained she just worked on the charitable side of Elena's business life, stayed cool and polite.

They pressed their cards, thick and deeply embossed, into her hand. 'If you could just mention we spoke . . .'

The last one was more interesting. She thought she recognised him, a craggy-faced man with thick hair. He gave her his name in a tone that suggested she should know who he was, and didn't offer a card or a sales pitch. Oh yes. Justin Tuchman. Academic. Ran a think tank. Elena had paid for his ticket too. 'I won't interrupt Elena, but tell her it's been a useful evening and the report is ready for release if she just gives me the word.'

'I'm her social and charitable PA,' Ruth said again. 'What report do you mean?'

He looked at her with mild surprise. 'Just tell her the Kellinghall Foundation report then. She'll understand.'

Ruth nodded, and he gave her a slight bow and moved away without saying anything else. The music stopped then, and all the voices seemed suddenly louder. Glasses chinked, and an MC invited applause for the inspirational CEO of Restart.

She turned out to be a striking Asian woman in a red evening gown. She gave a speech, thanking them all for their efforts to rehabilitate the victims of trafficking and welcoming to the stage a few of their success stories. Ruth's hand tightened round her glass as a dozen young women, two in nurses' uniforms, were paraded out to be applauded, then they shuffled off again and the silent auction began. Two middle-aged women, heavily jewelled collars around their necks, posed for a selfie with one of the nurses at the edge of the stage, their smiles wide and white, hers tight. The penlights read *#Empowerment*. Elena was talking to the dark-skinned woman again.

'Ruth?' The greeter with the slicked back hair put her hand on Ruth's arm. 'Can I just borrow you one moment?'

She nodded. 'Who is that woman with Elena?'

The greeter looked. 'Oh that's Suzanne D'Arcy.'

Well.

'She wasn't on the guest list,' said Ruth.

The greeter looked at her clipboard. 'Late addition. She only got back to this country a few days ago and said she was coming yesterday, just after Ms Shilkov actually. Now if I might . . .'

Ruth allowed herself to be guided out of the ballroom and back into the lobby. She realised she'd never made it further than fifteen feet in through the doors.

The relative quiet of the lobby made Ruth's head fizz. It had a backstage feel. Two more greeters, without their stuck smiles, were leaning against the reception desk and chatting. Waiting staff were exchanging jokes on their way in or out of the ballroom, shoulders slumping and steps slowing as they escaped, backs straightening, game face on as they went in.

'Sorry, what's your name?' Ruth asked as the fizzing in her ears subsided.

'Me? Anna,' the greeter said, surprised. She was short and as her voice dropped to a confidential whisper again, Ruth had to lean forward to hear her.

'So sorry to pull you out, only we've had a little incident with Ms Shilkov's stepson. I thought, perhaps you . . .?'

She blinked rapidly.

'What happened?'

Anna's shoulders dropped with relief.

'If you would just follow me . . .' She set off through another set of doors and Ruth followed her. The carpet became cheaper, and the dulled sounds of the party were replaced with the clatter of the kitchens and shouted orders. A man at the far end of the corridor was checking the trays of canapés being carried out in a fresh wave, nodding sharply at each one.

'In here.'

Anna ushered Ruth into some sort of storage room. Cabaret tables, without their tight cloths and bouquets, were stacked awkwardly along one wall and looked cheap under the fluorescent lights. There were no windows and it felt like an interrogation room. Andrei was sitting in a gold-and-velvet stackable chair, one of a few lined up against the opposite wall. Two waiters, big but looking awkward and confused, stood either side of him. Against the back wall one of the women who had been on stage was stood, one arm across her chest. A tall woman, strong lean arms and legs, dark-skinned. She was speaking to another of the greeters as Ruth and Anna entered, and though her eyes flicked over them, she didn't stop.

'It's bad enough you have us up there like fucking circus freaks for them, then he thinks he gets to put his hand up my skirt? Fuck him. You told me, *you* told me someone touches you, you call the police. Now I call the police.'

Ruth couldn't place her accent. French maybe.

'But Brittany, I'm sure if we can all just calm down . . .'

Andrei looked up, his eyes bleary and Ruth noticed a red mark across his cheek.

'She assaulted me. *I'm* going to fucking sue *her*.'

She got out her phone and texted Michael. *Andrei needs a lift home from the party and a guardian. Quietly and now.*

'You're lucky she didn't break your arm,' Ruth said as she slipped the phone back into her clutch bag. She felt much more at home all of a sudden. Fights, bad lighting, snarling drunks. This made more sense to her than the Sir Tobys at the party. She ignored the other greeter and put her hand out.

'Hi, Brittany. I'm Ruth. I work for Andrei's stepmother.'

Brittany hesitated, but Ruth kept her hand out. Brittany took it.

'What did he do?'

Brittany sighed and lent her head back against the wall. 'I went to the toilet and he was in the corridor when I came out, with his friend. They wouldn't get out of my way. He asked me if I still remembered some tricks from my old job. And his friend said they'd pay extra if I kept the uniform on.' She span round to her greeter again. 'I told you this would happen! Up on that stage, looking down on these bastards. You think I don't know them? These men?'

The greeter looked teary.

'But it tells such a great story. The hashtag is trending—'

'Fuck your hashtag!' Brittany said, each word flung like a rock, and the greeter looked suddenly tearful. She didn't have strong bones.

'Then what happened?' Ruth said calmly, still only looking at Brittany.

'I told them to go away, pushed past them and that asshole got behind me and put his hand up my skirt. So I hit him. Next thing I know I'm being bundled in here and they are fetching *him* ice.'

The greeter murmured. 'The Shilkovs donated over a hundred thousand pounds to the charity last year.'

That woman, Ruth thought glancing sideways at her, is an idiot.

Brittany blinked rapidly, staring up at the ceiling and her voice shook. 'So what? What? You are telling me I should be pleased my *price* has gone up?'

Enough of this. Ruth turned to her own greeter.

'Anna, could you and your friends take Andrei somewhere else please? Someone is coming to pick him up. Brittany, I'd like to stay with you for a minute if that's OK?'

A reluctant nod.

All of them but Andrei looked glad enough to be leaving. Between the four of them, the waiters and the greeters, they cajoled Andrei out of his chair and out of the room. The door closed. Ruth sat down, and after a minute Brittany sat next to her. Ruth took her phone out again. A message from Michael. *On the way.* She span her phone between her fingers, feeling the brushed steel and glass in her hands. Finally Brittany sighed deeply, then spoke.

'Are you going to offer to buy me off then?'

Ruth twisted round and grinned.

'Oh yeah, totally. Just wanted to give you a second. I'm sorry he did that. I'm beginning to think he might be a bit of a shit.'

Brittany was staring at the stacks of tables. They looked like broken limbs.

'I studied really hard to get my nursing qualification. Really hard. And I'm good at it too. But just *one* man like that can still make me feel cheap. I'll always be meat to them.'

'It'll get better.'

Brittany forced the heels of her hands into her eyes, and growled.

'Really? You think men like him will change?'

Ruth shook her head. 'No. I just mean they won't be able to make you feel like shit any more. Takes time.'

Brittany was looking sideways at her. Wondering if she was being patronised, or if Ruth had a clue. She must have decided it was the latter.

'I hope so. How long have you been working for them?'

Ruth turned over her phone again, like a card sharp shuffling a pack. 'It's Elena, his stepmother, I work for really. Today is my first day.'

Then Brittany started laughing.

They settled on five grand. Ruth got the cash from Anna and put in an I.O.U. in the kitty in Elena's name. By the time she had put the money in Brittany's hands, she had received a text message from Michael saying Andrei had been returned home. Back in the ballroom, the party was still in full swing, but Ruth's shoes were pinching and rather than dive back into the noise, now being coordinated by a celebrity DJ on the stage, she left a message with the greeters to say she was going home and stepped out into the evening air. The paparazzi had been moved off the steps, but on the other side of the road a small nest of men in thick anoraks with cameras around their necks still waited. They looked up at her hopefully then let their cameras fall to their sides again. She breathed deeply. The air was warm and drifted with cherry blossom. She had done well, her clutch stuffed with business cards, and though the champagne had left an acid taste in her mouth, she had enjoyed it. Different to the cava they'd had at her leaving do at the solicitor's office. Then she thought of the excitement she had felt handing in her notice, the fear that had followed, and a sudden weary grief flooded through her bones. A cab, then bed.

A movement, a flare of light in the darkness at the edge of the building and she turned round in time to see a woman, her sharp-angled face lit by a match flame as she held it to her cigarette. She was wearing a man's tuxedo, but cut to show off the long lines of her body and with no tie, just a high snow-white collar, accented with the shifting pulse of large opal studs.

'You handled that very well,' the woman said and then blew out a steady stream of smoke into the air. 'I'm impressed. How do you know she won't come back for more though?'

'She won't.' Ruth didn't ask what the woman knew or how she knew it.

The woman lifted her cigarette to her lips. It was very thin, and the paper was black. She looked like a forties film star. She put out her hand and Ruth shook it.

'My name is Jane Lucas. How do you know she won't?'

'Instinct. But if she does, I recorded the whole conversation including the deal on my iPhone. It's not like Andrei's in the running for Archbishop of Canterbury, so can't see the press will be interested. Police could have her on a blackmail charge if she tries anything.'

'The girl didn't notice you were recording?'

Ruth just shook her head.

'Do you think she'll sue the charity?'

Ruth put her hand to the back of her neck, rubbed it. God, she was tired.

'No. I think she'd be well within her rights, but pissed off as she is with them now, she's grateful to them really.'

Jane Lucas smiled. Red lipstick and pale skin. 'I'm glad. I'd hate to think the money I was giving these people was just going to lawyers.' Ruth realised she was holding out a card to her, it had just appeared between her fingers like she was a magician. She took it. Just the name, Jane Lucas, and a mobile number. Ruth had thought she was off duty. One last effort. This woman did not look like the sort she could just brush off.

'What do you do, Jane? Do you want me to talk to Elena about something?'

'Nooo,' she said it long, with a faint smile. 'That's just for you. If you ever want to know more about the Shilkovs, give me a call. Now, go get your cab, Ruth. You look tired.'

She flicked her cigarette end into the dark and went back into the party before Ruth could even reply. Weird. Another weird thing. She put the card into her clutch with the others and walked down the steps and across the gravel drive to the gates. A security guard was already hailing her a cab. She wondered why she had told the woman about recording Brittany. To show how capable she was? How useful? Perhaps she was just trying to show the woman she wasn't rattled by her first question. She gave the Shilkovs' address and sank back in the seat. Here I am, in my taxi, watching the lights flash by. Working for Elena. Elena who was impatient, didn't bother with please or thank you or sorry, but made dumplings and didn't patronise her, or overlook her. A good boss. *I think it was a man . . .*

She tried to think kind thoughts about people who move on, people who leave when they don't need you any more. It's just human nature. You just have to accept that, and it had to be easier to accept it, in these beautiful clothes, living in that beautiful house. She rubbed her hand across her forehead.

'Long night, love?' the cabbie asked.

'Yeah – work do,' she said and slipped off her heels. They would hurt more when she put them back on, but that pain was worth it for fifteen minutes of relief.

He snorted. 'My last work do was an egg on toast at the last proper café in Kings Cross.'

'I like egg on toast. Maybe I'll come to yours next time.'

'You're welcome, darling.' He flicked on his indicator, and nudged his way out into the stream of traffic on Bayswater Road. 'But it'll be smashed avocado on sourdough for twenty quid by Christmas and I'll be flogging myself to death in an Uber.'

9

Michael was waiting for her in the staff kitchen when she got back. No tie, shirtsleeves. If he was impressed by the outfit, he didn't show it and Ruth realised just at this moment she was too tired to care. He made her tea while she told him about the party and the Brittany incident. He took her phone and copied the recording onto his iPad. As she sipped, he listened to it on his headphones.

'Thanks, Ruth. You handled it well,' he said as it was done, sticking the headphones back into his pocket. 'You seem a lot older than twenty-three sometimes.'

She rolled her shoulders. 'I had to grow up fast. Which is more than you can say for Andrei.'

Michael nodded. 'I think he's beginning to realise he hasn't got his father's brains or his stepmother's instincts. Yuri gave him funds to invest, and he's made a hash of it so far.'

'He should take up knitting,' Ruth murmured then shook her head at Michael's confused expression. 'Nothing, ignore me. I'm knackered.'

He held her gaze for a long moment and Ruth felt her palms prickle again. He seemed to be on the point of saying something, then changed his mind and stood up.

'Good night, Ruth.'

'Good night, Michael.'

On Friday evening the girls came home for a weekend. Katerina and Natasha. Elena introduced her to them. Katerina, eleven, immediately hugged her, staring up into her face with huge blue eyes.

'You're the grenade girl! That is *so* cool!'

Natasha, who seemed more withdrawn, offered a handshake and a quiet thank you. For the rest of the weekend, all red in the diary, as Ruth made her way through the misery box backlog, they swooped round the house like swallows, clattering through the kitchen and chattering to Masha in Russian outside her office door, eating at the huge kitchen table or playing elaborate games in the back gardens. When they left on Sunday afternoon the house seemed even more empty than before.

The days began to settle into a pattern. On Monday Elena's diary was blocked out in red all day, so Ruth made phone calls, sorted requests and stuffed cash into envelopes for the deserving, or at least people she hoped were deserving. She began to work out the contacts database. On Tuesday at their morning meeting Elena gave her a list of a dozen or so names and told her to do something nice for them. Ruth looked at the names. Mostly men.

'What do you mean by something nice?'

Elena looked up at her, slightly impatient. Ruth could tell Elena wanted her out of the room again so she could concentrate on her phone. It was like the air was turning from blank to pink to red in front of her.

'Tickets, hampers, things which are cool and they will like. Read what they have been sent before. Make them feel special.'

'I take it these people don't get prayer cards?'

'Ha!' Elena didn't look up. 'No! *From the office of Elena Shilkov* cards. Next drawer down. Their prayers would do me no good. Now go away.'

Ruth found further guidance, thank God, in the paper files. Each of the names had a manilla folder in the cabinet behind her as well as an entry on the database. Each folder contained handwritten notes of gifts: what they were and when they were given. It gave her an idea of budget, but they seemed a bit dull and generic. She searched the internet for clues, and scrolling past their portraits – all in ties against bland backdrops and turned slightly sideways – found hints of their likes and dislikes and shopped accordingly.

Her only outings were to the pool in the Kensington Leisure Centre where she would go to swim most mornings while the house was still quiet – no one awake, it seemed, but the cleaning staff who appeared like ghosts as dawn broke, scattered through the house with plastic boxes full of rags and sprays, and left nothing but gleaming surfaces and a gentle citrus tang in the air behind them.

It took three trips before she realised one of the security team was following her to the pool each morning.

'I don't need a bodyguard to go for a swim,' she told Michael fiercely coming into his office with her hair still wet and a chlorine tightness to her skin.

He was staring at something on his laptop screen and typing, and without looking at it, pointed at a plate on the table.

'Wanna biscuit? Masha makes them for me. Apparently I remind her of a favourite nephew.'

'No, I don't *wanna* biscuit,' Ruth said. They looked good though. She was torn between being irritated and slightly jealous she didn't get morning treats from the housekeeper.

Michael hit return and the little swooshing noise from his computer indicated message sent. He turned and looked at her, taking in her wet hair and the scowl.

'Tough. It's not about you, Ruth. It's about security for the family.'

'What the hell do you think I can get up to at the swimming pool?'

He pushed himself back in his chair, tented his fingers together. Ruth realised he was playing, in his way, acting the patronising man rather than meaning it. At least she hoped that was what he was doing.

'If I thought you were up to something, I'd have blocked you living here in the first place.' Ruth resisted the temptation to remind him Elena had basically overruled any objection he might have. 'They are not watching you, they are watching for anyone else who might be watching you.'

'What?' Her question was muffled by biscuit. How had that happened? She seemed to have taken one and started eating it without thinking. Butter and sugar. Lord, they were good.

'You've seen the hate mail.'

Ruth dusted the crumbs off her top. 'I could just tell you, couldn't I? I mean if anyone bothered me.'

Not that she'd told him about Jane Lucas. But Jane hadn't bothered her as such – she'd just given Ruth her business card – so that didn't really count. She'd gone through the other people who had spoken to her with Elena, who had been vaguely interested in them and had made Ruth repeat everything Greg Townsend had said before dismissing him with a shrug. Though when Ruth had given her Tuchman's message that the Kellinghall Foundation report was ready, she had clapped her hands.

'Not good enough,' Michael said.

'It's going to have to be,' Ruth said. 'Fuck, I mean, I hardly leave this place. This is non-negotiable. I won't be followed. Can't be having it.'

A long silence as they stared each other down. Then he sighed.

'On the basis Elena would overrule me anyway, fine. No more following you to the pool. But if you are approached, tell me. Even if you can handle it we should be aware.'

Ruth grinned and took another biscuit.

'How long have you worked with the Shilkovs, Michael?'

If he noticed the turn, he didn't show it.

'I was hired the day after the attack. Elena was supposed to have a security detail with her. The sort of surveillance at a friendly distance like the one you have for your,' he saw her face, 'OK *had* for your swims. Unobtrusive, but close. It should have been them fending off hand grenades and making sure the girls were safe, not you. Yuri fired them all and one of his contacts recommended me to manage the agency security personnel he contracted at the same time.'

Of course Elena would have had security before the bomb. She didn't just become rich that day. It was like being in a hall of mirrors, this place. Things kept shifting, glimpses of the machinery of money and privilege, the interlocking gears of it spinning away under this smooth, elegant surface.

'So where were they? Her security team.'

'Good question. Arguing with a traffic warden outside the Wolseley, apparently.' The muscles round his jaw seemed to tighten. 'Anyway, they were sacked.'

'Seems a bit of a coincidence. Them happening to be out of the way just at that moment.'

She said it casually as the thought occurred to her, but his face changed. The shutters coming down.

'Counter Terrorism Command are still investigating the Uprising's claims of responsibility.' His voice became formal, his face blank. 'There's a lot of noise around their posts. People claiming to be working with them, others calling for them to be treated like ISIS. It's making mapping the network complex.'

Now hang on a minute. She swung forward in her chair.

'Wait. Is there any chance they targeted Elena?' He said nothing. 'Is there? Are they after oligarchs? Were they after Elena specifically? I thought … They didn't mention her in the manifesto.'

She'd read it. Big on outrage, telling her stuff she already knew about poverty and the unfair distribution of wealth. Then it turned into a lot of 'nationalise this, nationalise that' and 'workers on the board'. Community action groups. The end of advertising. Very hippie talk for men with semi-automatics. The air seemed to thicken between them. Then he stood up, passed by her chair, shut the door into the kitchen. He came close, one hand on the back of the chair and one on the arm leaning over her.

'What? What did you think? Did you see something you didn't tell the police, Ruth?'

Ruth felt a familiar rage shiver across her shoulders down her arms. She clenched her fists.

'*Back off*, man,' she hissed.

He sucked in his breath, just for a moment, then lifted his hands and stepped away. Ruth practiced her breathing. In for four seconds through the nose, out for four seconds through the mouth. Nice and steady. He waited. Ruth stared at the edge of his desk until she was ready.

'I don't know what I saw. Maybe a look, a nod or something between two of the men.' She could feel the fabric of the scarf in her hand again, the cool air of the café interior after the warm street. The smell of coffee and vanilla. 'I mean they had those stupid masks on, but yeah, maybe I saw a look before the man threw the grenade our way. But I don't know.' She touched her hand to her eyes, tucked a damp strand behind her ear. 'The police and the papers said it was random. I believed them.'

She turned to look at him. He was leaning against the wall, hands in his pockets and shoulders stooped. He looked almost human like that.

'Yeah. Maybe. But they drove past the Ritz and the Wolseley to attack the café, and they would have been more obvious targets for people out to punish the rich. And it seems like quite a coincidence, a woman with Elena's wealth and connections being there, and her team not with her. It bothers me. But they don't mention Russians in the manifesto. You'd think if they were targeting oligarchs, rather than the wealthy in general, they'd mention it.'

Ruth shook her head. 'Manifesto just goes on about English upper classes. You don't think there's something else going on, do you? Have you asked them?'

He laughed, a sarcastic bark. 'I have asked them. But they won't tell me. Look Ruth, if you find anything out from Elena—'

She held up her hand. 'No. I don't know anything, and I'm not gossiping with you.'

'I need to know.' He looked at her steadily.

'Then you are just going to have to ask them again.' She saw the struggle on his face. 'Look, maybe you're right, maybe she was targeted, but Elena's going out now. If she thought a bunch of crazies was after her, specifically, she'd stay in.'

He left his place by the wall and went to sit behind his desk again.

'No. As of the day she went to see you, she seems fine. Something's going on, and I don't like not knowing what it is.'

Her anger was just under the surface of her skin. Ready to reignite.

'Then you made a shit career choice working here, didn't you? I don't even know what they do! Not really.'

He flinched. 'Fine. Don't eat me. But you can trust me, Ruth. I don't want anyone to get hurt, including you.' She didn't reply, just hunched her shoulders and glowered at him.

He went back behind his desk again, opened one of the desk drawers and took out a bundle of papers.

'Elena thinks the sun shines out of your behind, especially after you sorted out Andrei.'

Elena had bought her a handbag as a thank you. A Chanel one, like her own but in a dark wine colour, because apparently Chanel are the best made. 'Bugger t' Birkin,' Ruth had said in a thick Yorkshire accent and Elena had laughed so hard she ending up in a sneezing fit. Michael pushed the bundle of papers towards Ruth.

'For your passport. You have an appointment at the office in Victoria for a fast-track application, Thursday at ten. Take these, just hard copies, and use Elena's credit card for the fee. Her diary is red that morning. I checked.'

It was a dismissal. Ruth took the papers and stood up, awkward with her bag still full of damp swimming kit and her jeans clinging to her thighs and waist where she hadn't dried herself off properly. When she had her hand on the door, he spoke again.

'Ruth . . .' she turned back. 'You have to be careful. Anything bothers you, tell me. I'll look after you.'

He had a nice smile. People with nice smiles had been claiming they would look after Ruth since she was seven years old. They hadn't done a very good job.

'I'll be fine, thanks.'

*　　*　　*

The next day a new misery box came. She worked through and found the last thing in it, an A4 envelope, thickly stuffed, was addressed to her, Ruth Miller, not Elena. The box was X-rayed before it was delivered, so Ruth wasn't afraid of what might be in it. Only it was odd to see her name. Perhaps a relations manager from one of the galleries had written the wrong name by accident.

She opened the envelope and pulled out a thick sheaf of printed pages. There was a long URL at the top of each one – printed from the internet then. One page on the top, handwritten. Block capitals. *THIS IS WHO YOU WORK FOR.* No signature, no return address. She flicked through the stack, expecting longer versions of the screeds of conspiracy theories and hate memes she saw on email, but no, as she looked through the pages she realised that all the articles were from proper news outlets. The *Washington Post*, *The Times*, the *Observer*, *Buzzfeed*. The last one was the longest, dozens of pages detailing the suspicious deaths of various Russians in London, and of some of the British people who worked with them. A helicopter crash, a couple of suicides. Another sheaf of articles worked itself up into a froth of self-righteous indignation about the use of shell companies to move money anonymously and tax-free around the world.

She read it all, then picked up the whole lot, including the envelope, and knocked on Michael's door. He was in his shirtsleeves, working at the computer, and looked up at her with friendly curiosity.

'This was in the misery box.'

He took it from her, examined the envelope and handwritten sheet with care and then flicked through the rest.

'You were asking what the Shilkovs did,' he said at last. 'Someone answered your prayers.' Then he added impatiently, 'If you're uncomfortable working for Elena you should get out. So talk to me, or leave. I don't know what you want from me, bringing this, landing it on my desk.'

He sounded raw somehow. As if the smooth grass-fed Labrador had suddenly growled like a street mutt.

She put her head on one side, watching him. A flush above his collar. 'You're head of security. I'm supposed to bring you weird shit. It's in the binder of instructions you gave me on day one. And if you read it, you'll see the people who end up dead are the ones who talk or try and leave, so you better think of something else.'

10

Going to the passport office felt like a grand excursion. Ruth was discovering that with enough money you can move through a city, even a city like London, without friction. Someone was always opening the next door, the car was just pulling up, the food was prepared, the table waiting. It even worked when you brushed up against the government.

Ruth had spent many hours in stale-smelling offices, sitting on chairs in corridors when her legs weren't long enough to touch the floor, waiting for a social worker to emerge from a conference room, then as a teenager slowly filling in forms to apply for maintenance payments, victim support funds. Now, with the papers Michael had given her and Elena's credit card, she was waved past the shuffling queues, greeted with a handshake and smiles and ushered into a private office with a pot plant in the corner. Once her photograph was taken, and the final form signed, her brand-new passport was pressed into her hand still smelling of warm ink.

'Before you go,' the man, a striped shirt, spectacles and a pink face, said, 'my colleague would like a word.'

Ruth agreed graciously, unthinkingly, getting used to this lady of London act, but instead of just another office, another pot plant, another fee or another signature, striped shirt led her to the end of the corridor and out into the stairwell. The carpets disappeared and it was concrete and linoleum. This was more like she remembered.

They climbed. Right to the top, then rather than leading her down another corridor, the man pressed the bar on the fire escape door and opened it, standing aside to let Ruth out into the grey air of the London morning. The roof. She looked at him, confused, and he gave her an encouraging nod. She stepped through, her boots scrunching on a thin layer of gravel and the door shut behind her. Was this a joke? She span round and struck it with her fist.

'Hey!'

'Calm down, Ruth.'

Ruth looked behind her. A tall slim figure was leaning against the parapet and looking out over the city, blowing clouds of smoke from her cigarette. The woman from outside the Restart party.

'Jane?'

'Hi.' She turned round so she was facing Ruth, her back to the skyline. 'I'm disappointed you didn't call me. And it's difficult to get you alone, so I thought I'd take this chance for another chat.'

Ruth walked towards her across the gravel. She didn't like heights. She didn't have the impulse to throw herself off high buildings or anything like that, they just made her stomach lurch and she felt suddenly clumsy and vulnerable.

'Do you work in the passport office? Was that man your colleague?'

'Sort of.'

Ruth felt the wheels of her brain turn slowly.

'Are you government, then? A spy?'

Jane laughed, a throaty, smoker's laugh. 'I think I'll go with "sort of"' again. I mostly work in an office.'

Jane was wearing a long Burberry mac, the belt undone, over a dark trouser suit and a silk blouse the same colour as the London sky. She was wearing opals again, this time as earrings under her thickly layered short hair. Her make-up was different too. Executive rather than forties vamp today.

'What do you want with me?'

She smiled. 'I trade in information. Want to swap? Tell me what Elena and Yuri are up to, and I'll tell you who you are working for.'

'Did you send me that shit about Russians and people working for them getting killed?'

'Interesting reading, don't you think?'

Ruth stuck her hands into her pockets. 'No,' she lied. 'All stuff I could have got off Google. I don't know what they are up to and I don't care. I just arrange sponsorships, dish out charity cash.'

Ruth saw a flicker of disgust on the older woman's face, just there for a moment, then gone. 'Oh I don't know. You had an animated chat with Greg Townsend the night we met.'

'He was animated, I wasn't.'

Jane dropped her cigarette and ground it out. 'And it's not just charity, is it? I mean an MP earns almost eighty thousand a year, plus all those generous expenses, and Cabinet ministers get almost double that, but you are sending some of them very nice care parcels.' She thrust her hands into her coat pockets. 'I'm sure you know more than you think, my dear. You are in the house after all. I'm certain you could learn a lot just by keeping your eyes and ears open. Have a chat to Andrei for example. Ask about who he met in Korčula last summer. I know Milos was there. But I don't know who else they had for drinks on that monstrous yacht.'

Ruth had been interested in only one person from that holiday and she already had her answers. She was moving on.

'Why would I tell you, even if I knew?'

Jane smiled. 'It's your duty as a British citizen. Your government is asking you for help. I also want to know why Elena, after hiding in her house for three months, suddenly hired a girl like you and started running about in the world again. What is she up to? What is she cooking up with Milos and Suzanne?'

A girl like you. Thanks. Ruth shook her head. She turned round and walked back towards the door to the stairs. There was a keypad on the right. Jane didn't move.

'I want to go now. Open the door.'

Jane followed her across the gravel, but she didn't punch in a code.

'It's important, Ruth. The Shilkovs are dangerous people. They've nearly got you killed once already. I'm just trying to help you understand what's going on.'

Ruth stared at the door. 'Let. Me. Go. Home.'

Jane brushed a speck from her lapel. 'Home already, is it? What do you think the Shilkovs will do when they realise you've been lying to them? That you tricked your way into that house?' How did she know about that? Ruth felt her blood chill and thicken in her veins. 'Sly little thing, aren't you?' Jane sighed theatrically.

Ruth moved fast, grabbing for the lapels of Jane's coat, but Jane was quick too, blocking the move, catching Ruth's right wrist and twisting it up behind her back. Ruth was bent over towards the gravel. She cried out and Jane shoved her away.

'You do have a temper, don't you?'

Ruth staggered, straightened up, felt her eyes getting hot. Her wrist ached and this woman made her feel like a kid again. A lonely angry kid.

'Just leave me alone!' Like saying that ever worked.

Jane lit another cigarette. 'Such a shame I can't appeal to your better nature. But you are interesting. I wonder what else I could find out about you if I tried? Worth thinking about. I'll be in touch.'

She punched in the number. The lock buzzed. Ruth pulled the door open and flew down the stairs, the rubber soles of her limited edition Converse squeaking on the turns. Stupid. Stupid. Stupid.

She was rattled as hell on the way back to the house. No banter with the driver and fighting the impulse to chew her nails off. Why did this woman need to know about Korčula? What could she find out about Ruth? Nothing. Nothing important. Impossible. And what good would it do Jane Lucas to rat her out to the Shilkovs? Should she report this Jane Lucas thing to Michael? No. That thing Lucas had said about Ruth lying, tricking her way into the house . . . If in doubt, do nowt. Fuck.

As they pulled up, the front door opened and a woman in a sage green suit walked down the steps. She cast a vague glance in Ruth's direction as she went and Ruth felt a twinge of recognition. Suzanne D'Arcy.

'Ruth?' The driver had opened her door and was waiting for her to get out.

'Sorry, Jay,' she said and clambered out. 'See you later.'

He nodded and she went up the steps and into the house. One out, one in. Could Suzanne D'Arcy be from Yuri's office? They handled a lot of stuff for Elena, from office supplies to bills, but the people who worked there usually had bulging briefcases with them and a harried look.

Ruth headed for her office, took her brand-new passport out of the bag and stared at it. When the door was flung open, she jumped.

'Got it?' Elena was glowing. Ruth showed her the passport and Elena swung her hips and twirled. It made Ruth laugh.

'Why are you so excited about my passport?'

Elena stopped dancing, her hands still held out, flexing her wrists. 'Because I am very happy. Because something fucked is finally going to be un-fucked and I need you to go on an errand for me. To Paris. You get a night in Paris. You go Monday morning.'

II

She'd never flown before, and it wasn't that she was scared, it was just she was aware that she would be having a new experience. She studied the plane from the walkway. It was very clean. That was good. Or did it mean it was new? Mike Cunningham had always said it was new cars that went wrong the most.

'Miss?'

Ruth handed over her boarding pass and the steward's smile lurched upwards in wattage when she saw 'first class'. Ruth was ushered into the second row of seats. First class on a hop to Paris might cost more than a month's rent, but on the small workhorse planes that went back and forth a dozen times a day across the channel, all that translated into was a bit more legroom and the hostile glances of all the economy class passengers who staggered past you, harried and resentful, into the narrower seats behind the curtain.

Ruth settled into her window seat, put her attaché case and Chanel bag under the seat in front of her and stared out at the runway. Isme had visited again in preparation for this trip with a couple of executive suits, and so Ruth was in a hounds-tooth jacket and pencil skirt, both Elie Tahari, and high heels, Manolo Blahnik. Ruth had decided not to look up what they cost this time. Last time she'd felt sick at herself and excited at the same time and hadn't liked it. Elena said the Parisians were too snobbish for jeans, even designer ones. She needed to project a bit more authority for this errand. An errand. To Paris. She would be staying overnight at the Ritz on the Place Vendôme. This was apparently important for her authority too.

The last time she got sent on an errand at her old job it was to get copier paper from Ryman's. The thought made her snort to herself.

'Something funny?'

Ruth turned away from the window and was treated to the sight of Michael Fitzsimmons reaching up to put his briefcase in the overhead locker. His shirt pulled up as he stretched, exposing a square of tanned skin above his belt. She refocused.

'Michael?'

He sat down in the seat next to her, straightened his tie.

'Yes, I'm coming to guard you personally.'

Ruth tried not to feel pleased. When she'd learnt what the errand was, her mouth had gone dry and her hands sweaty, which is a weird way for your body to react, but there you go.

'But your job is to guard the family, not me.' He gave her a sideways look. 'Oh. You're guarding the money.'

'I am. Guarding you is an optional extra.'

Ruth grinned. Michael sounded almost relaxed. Was it not being in the house? Even the way he sat in the seat seemed easier.

'What's in the briefcase?' he asked, glancing down at it.

'It's an attaché case, actually.' He waited. She didn't know what was in it. Elena just gave it to her and told her to keep it with her. She'd tried to open it in the car to the airport and found it was locked, but she wasn't going to tell him that.

'Why didn't you come to the airport in the car with me?' she said, changing the subject.

He shrugged, in a 'don't tell me then' way. 'Errands. And anyway, you left *way* too early.'

He plucked the flight magazine out of the pocket and started to flick through it. Two hours before flight time for international flights. That's what her e-ticket had said and she wasn't going to mess up her first trip abroad by playing it cool.

'Do you have to walk three steps behind me at all times? Will you carry my bags?'

'No and no. Don't push your luck, kiddo. Maybe Elena is just worried you'll go clubbing in her new jewels and gamble them away at the roulette table.'

Ruth laughed. 'Well that was plan A, obviously.'

'Tough. We run our errands and then a nice quiet dinner at the very safe, very expensive, very dull hotel.'

'No roulette at all?'

'Sometimes an elderly man plays piano in the dining room. Content yourself with that.'

'Would you like champagne, Ms Miller, Mr Fitzsimmons?'

OK, even in these small planes first class had its perks. Not that she was going to drink it, but it was nice to be asked.

'Just water, please.'

'Same for me,' Michael added. He went back to the magazine, and Ruth looked out of the window again. Trying to pretend she wasn't aware of him sharing the armrest between them. Of how she could feel the movement of the muscles in his forearm through the expensive fabric of their business suits.

Landing. Car service into the city. Place Vendôme. Narnia-like lamp posts and a bloody great column. The hotel, wrought iron gates and red carpet on the steps from the street. People who got their shoes dirty didn't stay here. Tapestries on the walls and marble floors. 'Superior' rooms on the fourth floor with marble bathrooms. Then car service to the Palais Royal. A short trip. For all that Michael had said he wasn't going to walk three paces behind her like a proper bodyguard, Ruth felt his increased awareness as soon as they got out of the car.

He still looked relaxed, but he didn't address any remarks to her and she could feel him scanning the crowds of tourists as they turned into the classical arcade. Ruth's heels seemed to make a lot of noise. She felt more conspicuous, not less, in her trench coat and shades among the neon crowds, Japanese and American, dressed in brightly coloured rain jackets against the sudden occasional showers, breathing on the shop windows and taking endless selfies or narrating their live streams. It took all Ruth's concentration not to hold her bag against her, cradle the attaché case across her chest. Michael had given her a briefing in London as soon as he'd been told about this trip. Now, walking through a crowd with half a million euros in her handbag, she was trying hard to do each thing he had taught her. Be aware of who is around you, but don't look. Know where your bag is, the attaché case, but don't clutch. If a pickpocket spots a well-dressed woman clutching her bag and scanning the crowd, he knows she has something worth stealing. If you get lost, or confused about where you should go, do not stop, do not hesitate or look around. Just walk into the nearest high-end shop like you mean it and check your Google Maps in there.

Ruth was glad he had come now. She felt slightly less like a tempting snack on the criminal buffet. Her first hour in Paris. She couldn't take much in, just the flashes of garden beyond the colonnade they were walking down, clipped trees in regimented rows, the pale gravel dazzling in the sunlight, patches of grass, fountain. The contrast made the pavement seem even thicker with shadows, and faces harder to see.

Michael touched her arm, nodded to the shop they were just passing. She recognised the name with a thud, couldn't believe she almost walked past it thinking about the tourists, the money, the intimidating architecture. She turned and pushed open the door.

The shop itself was dark. Even when she took off her shades it took a moment for her eyes to adjust. Dark stained-wood floors with one lovely but ancient looking Turkish rug in red and blue in the centre. Two discreet display cabinets, also dark stained wood. The one on the right of the room contained a single necklace. A waterfall of light. On the left another, a choker of rubies and opals. Opals. Jane Lucas.

Ruth hadn't heard from her in the days since she'd got her passport and was beginning to hope the woman had gone away, found someone who actually wanted to snoop for her.

Michael closed the door behind them and the old-fashioned shop bell rang quietly. At the far end of the room was a high counter, totally bare, a woman standing behind it. Mid-thirties, her hair caught up and twisted into a smooth chignon. She looked as carefully burnished as the cabinets.

'Mademoiselle Miller?'

Ruth nodded.

'I am Madeleine Fourget. I am so delighted to meet you.' She came out from behind the counter and put out her hand. Ruth shook it. No pressure in the fingers. It was like shaking hands with a silk scarf. She nodded to Michael. 'Mr Fitzsimmons.' She walked past them and locked the door through which they had come, turning the sign to closed. 'Do follow me.'

The second chamber was as sparsely furnished as the storefront. Three chairs round a dark wooden table. More richly patterned and artfully faded rugs. An ancient-looking dining table with half a dozen chairs set around it. Three glasses. Champagne in the ice bucket. In front of one chair were two flat boxes in dark navy, *Madeleine Fourget* stamped in flowing silver script on the lids. Ruth handed over her coat and sat down. Madeleine hung it up, then poured the champagne. Michael crossed his legs and sat back in his chair, and Madeleine lifted the lids from the two cases.

Ruth wished she still had her shades on. Inside the first box was a choker with a broad cascading collar. Emeralds and diamonds, set in silver. The emeralds were cut into leaf shapes, creating twists of priceless foliage. The diamonds became flowers, delicate and thin petals, like jasmine, among the green. Ruth didn't dare breathe on it. In the second box were a pair of long cuffs, made to match.

'These are stunning,' she said.

'Yes,' Madeleine said simply. 'Madame Shilkov has perfect taste. Almost impossible to do in the timeframe. But we managed it.'

Ruth blinked, got out her phone and took a photo, swooshing it off to Elena. They sipped their champagne for four, five, six seconds. Her phone dinged.

The message was one word: *Yum.*

Ruth opened her bag, removed the narrow bricks of notes and placed them in front of Madeleine. She took them with a polite smile and disappeared out of another door, returning with a neat cardboard folder in the same colour and design as the boxes.

'Here is the paperwork and your receipt. I would recommend that for security you keep the jewels on your person or in the hotel safe at all times.'

As she spoke, Ruth's phone buzzed again. A follow-up. She looked. *Go with Madeleine. Take briefcase.* It's an attaché case, Ruth thought.

'Now if you will come with me, Miss Miller. Mr Fitzsimmons, if you will excuse us for a moment.'

Michael looked wary, but only nodded. He was guarding the jewels after all. Ruth stood up and picked up the attaché case. Madeleine led her out of another door and upstairs. The expensive emptiness of the front rooms disappeared. The walls were roughly plastered, the stairs painted white with a dull grey carpet running up the middle. They ended in a landing. Two open doors through which Ruth glimpsed what looked like a busy office – filing cabinets, a pair of computers crammed onto a partner desk. An electric kettle on a shelf above a mini-fridge. Through the other she glimpsed a light room where two middle-aged men in shirtsleeves seemed to be arguing about a series of designs pinned up to a corkboard. Sounds of voices and the dull buzz of machinery. Lathes and polishers and the air smelt of metal. A closed door.

'I do not like Ms Shilkov using my offices like this,' Madeleine said sharply as she reached the top of the stairs. She turned round to make sure Ruth got the full sneer. Like what? Ruth wanted to ask. But she wasn't going to confess to this woman she had no idea what was going on. 'This is my place of business. I do not want to pollute it.'

Ruth felt her temper rise under her beautifully cut jacket.

'Given Ms Shilkov is a loyal customer, with a great deal of influence among the tiny, tiny group of people who can afford your work, I am sure you are happy to do her this small favour,' Ruth said.

She said it clearly, with punch, as if each word began with a capital letter. Then she waited. Madeleine blinked and, turning away, took two steps forward before she realised Ruth was no longer following her. Just waiting halfway up the stairs. One of the middle-aged men put his head out into the corridor. Madeleine wet her lips.

'We are of course delighted to be of use to Madame Shilkov. My English. I said the wrong words perhaps.'

She even managed a small smile. Ruth was sure English was not Madeleine's problem. Still, to wring a smile from a high-class French woman seemed, in Ruth's brief experience, to be no small thing. She hadn't smiled at half a million euros after all.

So Ruth waited until Madeleine looked very uncomfortable, then gave a swift formal smile of her own and followed her up the last stairs. I'm good at this, she thought. I know how to do this. Is that a skill you can put on your CV? Make people nervous, afraid? Stun them with money and a hard-bitch attitude? Whatever works.

Madeleine opened the door and stood aside to let Ruth enter, then shut it behind her.

Ruth found herself in a small, ratty-looking office with two men seated at a trestle table. They had takeout coffee containers placed in front of them. They were both pale-skinned and square-faced. Dark T-shirts, ordinary-looking fleece jackets. Football fans or ex-squaddies. If you spotted them in the pub, you'd decide to go and do your drinking elsewhere. One had his head shaved, the other had thick hair, darkly curled. He looked younger, but they had similar dark eyes. Brothers maybe. They looked at her, then away. Ruth's phone buzzed again. She looked at the screen. *Give them the case.*

Elena playing games. Why?

She almost dropped the case. Then she put it on top of the table and slid it across to them.

The one with the thick hair took a key from his pocket and unlocked it, lifted the lid.

'What's in it?' Ruth said. Not even knowing why she did.

He ignored her, but lifted out a bundle. Whatever it was – solid, six inches high, rectangular, – was wrapped in the blue Alexander

McQueen scarf from the day of the bombing. Ruth bit her lip. She hadn't seen it since she'd taken it to the dry cleaners, still covered in her blood.

He tore it away like a kid unwrapping a Christmas present. A block of notes, wrapped into a solid mass with cellophane. Then he pulled something from his pocket. A flick-knife. He snapped it open and split the package, then pushed one paper-bound brick to his companion. The bald guy opened it and ran a pen from his pocket over the top note, then the next, and the next, and said something in a language Ruth didn't recognise.

'Peace,' flick knife said, lifting his head to look at Ruth. 'It contains peace.' His companion continued running his pen over the notes, then started transferring the blocks of notes into a duffle bag on the floor. He pushed the attaché case back towards her. She closed it, took the key out of the lock and put it in her own pocket. 'You are staying where?'

'The Ritz.'

'Name?'

'Ruth Miller.'

'Good. An envelope will be left at the front desk for you in the morning.'

'Cool. Can I have that?' He followed her pointed finger to the scarf and shrugged.

'Take it.'

She reached across and grabbed it, and folded it into her handbag while he turned to his brother and said something in a language that sounded like Russian, but not quite. She repeated it in her head like a fraction of melody. Then he seemed to notice Ruth was still there. 'Go now. Goodbye.'

OK then. Do this. Do that. Go here. She felt like one of those robots programmed to sweep floors. A dumb little moving and carrying thing. Ah, come on, she said to herself. All this money, to take a few commands without all the please and thank you and sorry you'd get from the English. Don't get so up yourself, Ruth. So she walked out into the corridor again and found Madeleine was waiting for her.

The French woman had regained her sangfroid. She was two inches shorter than Ruth and still managed to look down her nose at her. She put another jewel box into Ruth's hands. A little one.

'Ms Shilkov says thank you. This is for you.'

Without giving her time to open it, Madeleine led her back to the second room where Michael was finishing his champagne. He examined Ruth's face.

'Everything, OK, Ruth?' he asked as he helped her on with her coat.

She showed him the box.

'Thank you from Elena.'

He seemed to accept it and stood up. 'Shall we get back to the hotel then?'

Ruth put the box in her coat pocket, opened the attaché case, and loaded the jewel boxes with the collar and cuffs into it with reverence. Perhaps Michael was taking her slightly shaken state as the normal reaction of a girl from Middlesbrough to this heft of diamonds. At least, she hoped he was. She closed the case, locked it with the newly acquired key.

'I'm ready.'

Madame Fourget did not offer to shake hands as they left.

12

And the rest of the day was their own. Paris in the early summer. The car took them back to the hotel and after Michael had watched the attaché case being secured in the hotel safe he suggested lunch. Ruth accepted with relief and half an hour after leaving the jewellers she found herself sitting at a friendly, touristy place on Montmartre. Red-checked table cloths and wine that came in a glass jug called a *pichet*. Ruth felt seized by relief. Her shoulders dropped as they sat at one of the pavement tables, the breeze teasing at strands of her hair. She felt free here. Wasn't that a song? A touch giddy. Michael charmed the waiters, his French a bit awkward but enough to gain their approval, and helped her with the menu, warning her off the steak tartar and recommending the creme brûlée for dessert. It was delicious. She ate, savoured, and opened her eyes to realise she was looking at him.

'Good?'

'You think I'm a fucking hick, don't you?'

He shook his head. 'Sorry. If I'm being patronising, I don't mean to be. But I know you've never been out of the country and I don't know much about fine dining in Middlesbrough.'

She patted the corner of her mouth primly with her napkin. 'Oh, we're very sophisticated. We have an Indian *and* a Chinese.' He grinned. 'No, it's all right. There are rich people in the north too and they have to eat somewhere. Of course McDonald's and Pizza Express were as fancy as it got when I was coming up, but when I worked at the solicitors the senior secretary, Sunny, used to take me out to nicer places with her. Made sure I didn't look like I was going to wee myself at the sight of two forks. Mind my manners a bit. Made me read the paper every day and talk to her about it too. Read more non-fiction and stuff. Before then I was all about the novels.'

'Sounds like a one-woman finishing school.'

'Yeah. She was. She even tried to work on my accent. Then I come to London and found all the posh kids trying to sound like they grew up on the estate down the road. After all that time I spent learning butter had Ts in it too.'

'I don't do that.'

'Yeah, but you're not a kid.'

'Ouch.'

After lunch he asked what she wanted to do and when she said she wanted something more interesting than the Eiffel Tower, and less touristy than the Louvre, he took her to Sainte-Chapelle. Didn't look much from the street, but once she got through the courtyard and into the church itself Ruth found herself awash in the light from a thousand thin panels of stained glass. It was like being inside one of Madeleine's creations.

When they got outside again Michael glanced at his phone and frowned.

'What is it?'

'Nothing. I have an errand before dinner. Can you get back to the hotel by yourself? It's about half an hour's walk.'

She nodded. Then he lent towards her, his hand on her arm, and kissed her cheek. His aftershave smelt of sandalwood.

'I'll pick you up at your room at eight.'

Then he was gone. Or at least he started walking away, leaving her at the edge of the flower market. Then he turned back and lifted his hand to her in farewell before he turned the corner.

Ruth took a breath. Lots going on and her blood was fizzing dangerously. He was hot. No one could deny that. And he seemed good at his job. He asked questions, but not too many and so far no mansplaining, no sexist or racist jokes. He listened. Seemed to really enjoy watching her at the restaurant. Took pleasure in her pleasure. She bit her lip. That was a dangerous line of thinking, but he seemed freer, more natural out of London. Come on, Ruth. Get a grip. Concentrate on the job. Do the job. Don't get distracted by some bloke with a nice smile and decent personal hygiene. She was not going to make doe eyes at Michael. Tonight would be a business dinner. And why was he in her thoughts anyway? Not like she didn't have other things to think about. The men in Madeleine's attic. Had she done something illegal? Should she text Elena? Ask what the hell that was about? Was this the sort of thing Jane Lucas wanted to know? Of course it was. That woman made her flesh creep.

Perhaps it was a test. Elena was testing her. Could she just do as she was told and be discreet? Screw Lucas. She thrust her hands into her pockets and scowled at the pavement. Her hand closed round the box Madeleine had given her. Damn, she'd totally forgotten about it.

She took it out and snapped it open. A pair of earrings, little diamond clusters. There was a scrap of card folded into the lid. Ruth pulled it out and opened it out. *No need to keep the receipt for these!* Elena's handwriting. Ruth was surprised into a laugh. Elena had sent the card to Paris so it could be put in the box, so Ruth would find it when she collected the collar and cuffs, had handed over the briefcase, and got her reward. Just like she'd sent those strange blokes the key to the attaché case somehow. Jesus, it was like a scavenger hunt or something. She closed the case and put it back in her pocket. Got out her phone. *Thank you.* A second later she got her answer in all emojis. Smiling angel; champagne glasses clinking; rainbow. Ruth grinned. Lifted her head.

She was in Paris. The air was mild and she had diamonds in her pocket and a five-star hotel room waiting for her across the river. She was even managing in high heels. Sod Jane Lucas, strange men in attics. Don't think so much, Ruthie. It'll give you lines. So she walked, meandered. Looked at the remains of Notre Dame. Wished it well. Crossed the river and walked along it past the funny shops run out of green boxes bolted along the walls, then through the Jardin des Tuileries. Statues and fountains. Managed to order a coffee at the pavilion and just sit and absorb the whole … Frenchness of it. Then she went home to change for dinner.

★   ★   ★

The man playing the piano wasn't that old, but the tunes he played were. She and Michael were the youngest people in the room by twenty years at least. He'd texted to say he'd be ten minutes late to pick her up, and when he did his hair was still wet from the shower, the muscles of his face tense, and he hardly looked at her. That got under her skin, because she'd taken care getting ready, all the time trying to pretend to herself she hadn't. But after the first cocktail in the bar, where they'd ordered their food before being led through into the dining room, he'd done a proper double take at the dress and how it fitted. That pleased her.

'So what is your job exactly?' she said, the idea of this being a business dinner still fluttering, valiantly, in her mind and victory – *made you look, made you stare* – loosening her tongue.

'You know what it is. Head of security,' he said.

'That's your title. I don't know what you *do* though. Other than arrange for me to get a passport and check I didn't lie about my GCSEs.'

Not that that was all he had found out, but they weren't going to chat about the trial here. It was done. In the past. Less said the better. Still the memories fluttered under her skin, of the rooms she waited in in court, cheap chairs, grey and windowless, smelling of old coffee and depression. Then the sight of the men in the dock, staring at her. The thick weight of hatred in their eyes. She blinked and looked around the room she was in now. This minute. The high windows, chandeliers, starched linen. She ran her fingernail over the cloth, feeling the thread count.

'Mostly I run the team that does the close protection work on the family. So a lot of admin. Creating rotas.'

He had a good half-smile. Wry. 'But when you're with Yuri, where do you go? I mean, do you have snipers on the roof of his office?'

He snorted then choked when the bubbles went up his nose.

'Think the Met would disapprove of that! No. I have an office in his building too and a couple of freelance researchers that work with me through his company. I look for weak points. I also do checks on the people the Shilkovs work with. Sometimes that involves getting delicate information out of people who don't like to talk.'

'What, you vet his clients?'

His mouth got tight and he shook his head.

'No. Yuri does that, I vet the people his clients do business *with* in the UK. Why are you asking?'

The waiter arrived and set down their first course with a flourish like a magician performing at a children's party. A scallop with a curl of a pale green sauce around it. The top scattered with caviar and topped with a pansy, a yellow and black mouth.

'I've been working in the house for two weeks and I don't know what anyone really does. Yuri is an accountant and Elena makes deals. Do I eat this flower?'

Michael was watching her closely. 'It's optional.' Then as she lifted it aside, careful not to disarrange the caviar, he added, 'why do you need to know what they do?'

'I don't need to know. I just want to.' She cut into the scallop, the flesh yielded softly and she ate. Clean, salted with the little bursts of caviar on the roof of her mouth, the sauce smooth and tasting of fresh peas. He was still looking at her when she opened her eyes again. 'Christ, it's like lunch all over again. Don't stare at women eating, mate. It's creepy.'

He laughed and set to on his own plate.

'Sorry. You know what curiosity did to the cat.'

She wriggled her shoulders as if to shrug something off. 'I hate that phrase. People say it to keep you in your place. Make you feel small. I don't know what killed the cat, but it wasn't curiosity. It was what the cat found out.'

He took a second to think about that. 'Fair enough. What do *you* think the Shilkovs do? Didn't that packet of dross someone sent you help?'

'No. It was all about the guys who basically took over Soviet industry and all the mineral rights and their power struggles as Putin took over.' She caught him looking at her again. 'Michael, if you say I sound articulate, or well informed, I swear I'll flick pea sauce at you. It's possible to talk about world affairs sensibly in a northern accent, you know.'

'Sorry. Hell, I'm always apologising to you, aren't I?'

'It's all right. I like it actually. So I think Yuri moves money. Makes rich people richer. But you don't get that house, this life by colouring inside the lines, do you? And given where they come from, the times . . .' She trailed off, remembering the gesture Elena had made with her hands on her first day, of worlds collapsing, exploding into rainbows.

He turned his eyes on his food. 'I'm not sure there *were* any lines in Russia when they made their fortune.'

She thought of the hints and accusations of violence in those pages she'd been sent – protection rackets, blackmail, fraud, the lawlessness. It had flared, then rather than disappearing had retreated underground like the roots of some pernicious weed, still gathering strength but quietly and out of sight. 'Then there's an influence game going on too. All those Sir Tobys Elena likes to cultivate. I feel like she's playing chess, but I can't see the board. Don't know what the moves are. Just that she uses tickets, favours, cash to move some of the pieces.'

She trailed off again, wondering if she'd said too much, not sure if she'd made herself look like an idiot or a security risk. She was showing off. Pipe down, lass. She blamed the cocktail and flushed, taking another bite of the scallop.

'If it worries you, Ruth, get out. You're a smart girl. You could get another job.' He didn't sound angry, or patronising. She loaded her fork again, not bothering to reply at once.

Strange. Three bites into this meal, and it was no longer a revelation. Just another thing to eat. She thought of the men in the upstairs room at Madeleine's atelier again. They had set all her alarm bells jangling. Did it worry her? Elena's elaborate way of setting the meeting up. Why had she wrapped the money in that scarf? And the shiver of violence they gave off. She didn't think she was wrong about that. Yup, she was kinda worried, yeah. Also kinda eating scallops in the Paris Ritz and wearing diamond earrings. Swings. Roundabouts.

'You can always tell me, you know, if something's bothering you.'

She bristled. Thanks, Dad.

'We've established I'm curious, not worried. Why don't *you* get another job?'

He gathered up his last forkful of food. 'It pays well. The research makes it interesting. There's nothing specific you can tell me about these Sir Tobys, is there?' The piano player moved from one fifties jazz classic to another. Ruth looked round at her fellow diners. The stiff, painted faces of the women, the grey-haired men, the silence.

'I'm not interested in gossiping about Elena's business.' She waited for him to point out she just had been but, bless him, he didn't.

Michael dropped his napkin on the table. 'Look, shall we get out of here? This isn't the real Paris. Let me take you somewhere more . . . or at least less . . .'

Ruth looked around her, the ancient diners and the massive pillars, the now-she-thought-about-it-quite-depressed-looking piano player.

'God, yes. I thought you'd never ask.'

13

She woke up the next morning in the half-light of dawn with a lurch and in a tangle of sheets, then shut her eyes, trying to sort out the jangle of memories from the night before. Oh hell. The lights of the Champs-Élysées. Drinks at a pavement café and then Algerian food in a brick-arch basement. The waiters wore jeans, she and Michael drank beer and the music was a scratch band of musicians taking requests from regulars in the crowd. He made her laugh, telling stories from his days in the army, she told him about running wild as a teenager in Middlesbrough and they'd chinked bottles to their war stories. Both stuck to the funny ones. Then a late-night jazz place where they danced. Michael could dance. And they walked back to the hotel and oh hell indeed . . .

She opened her eyes. Michael was on his side, turned away from her and the sight of his skin, the muscles of his shoulders, the slope of his waist released another flood of memories. Or not quite memories but sensations. The feel of his hands on her body, the taste of his skin. Somehow all caught up with the dancing in the club, the moment she bought condoms from the cheery bathroom attendant. The bizarre uncomfortable giggling feeling of sitting in the cubicle with her knickers round her ankles looking up the French for condoms on her phone, still not knowing she was going to sleep with him, nothing having been said but that sense of it coming, then of it actually happening. God, in the lift, that first kiss, the hunger of it and the relief. The break in the tension that had been rising and rising as they danced, flirted, talked nonsense about the strangers around them. She felt a little shudder of it in her shoulder blades. What made some men better in bed than others? Balance. Give and take. Reading her movements and pleasures, signalling his own moves. Confidence without being arrogant. Attentive without being needy. No wonder he was a good dancer. She bit her lip and allowed herself to savour the glory of it just a little longer.

Why did there have to be mornings? If God were just, were kind, she'd just be transported to her room and last night would be confined to a bubble, a neat perfect bubble. But now they would have to have a conversation.

Ruth had slept with two people since she arrived in London. One was a friend of one of her housemates, who had been fun, and fun in bed too, but when she'd been out on an actual date with him he'd spent the whole time talking about his job, his ambitions, his political opinions. She'd slept with him that night to avoid talking about why she didn't want a relationship with him and given him the whole 'I'm not really up for dating' talk in the morning. He'd taken it fine. Sent flowers when she was in hospital. The other was a work colleague and one of those impulsive lonely-and-don't-want-to-go-home hook-ups you can talk yourself into at the time, but which leave a bitter sort of aftertaste. She'd scarpered before he woke up the next day and they'd carefully avoided each other afterwards. He'd signed her get well card.

No chance of avoiding Michael. Ruth stared up at the ceiling. What did she want? More of last night. Yes, please. But what were they going to do? Walk back into the Kensington house hand in hand? Was it a sacking offence? Perhaps one of them could stop working for the Shilkovs? He'd been with them longer, but she didn't want to give up everything and go back to the agency on the basis of one night.

'Morning.' He turned over and lifted himself up on his elbow, then lent forward and kissed her. She tried not to breathe out. He smiled. Eye contact.

Could be worse. He wasn't avoiding her yet or giving her the guilty side-eye.

'Do you think we can keep our hands off each other in London?' he asked.

It was like she'd said all that last stuff in her head out loud.

She sat up, gathering the sheet round her and looking about for her clothes. Good, most of them on the floor next to her.

'Maybe. You're way more uptight in London.'

He laughed and put out his hand so it lay over the sheet across her thigh, stroking it and moving the cotton against her skin.

'We're not in London yet . . .'

She put her hand to his face and decided not to care if her mouth tasted of last night's beer, or if her hair was a mess. She could feel the rough texture of his unshaved cheek on her palm. Then she lent in and kissed him, let her hand follow the line of his neck, the hollow of his collar bone. Broke off, looked him in the eye.

'No, no we are not.'

They ordered breakfast in bed, ate it and then Michael grabbed his watch off the bedside table and looked at it.

'Oh, don't do that,' she said, scooping the last flake of her croissant off her plate with a moistened fingertip.

He shrugged and swung his legs out of bed. 'Sorry. Have to.'

A deep sigh. She looked at his back, put her plate on the bedside table. Bedside tables never seemed big enough. Not even in the Ritz.

'What was in the attaché case, Ruth?'

Ruth was careful not to dislodge the coffee cup. 'I don't know what you mean.'

He still had his back to her. 'Madeleine took you out of the room. When you came back the briefcase was lighter. I could tell by the way you were carrying it. What was in it and who did you give it to?'

So there was going to be a shit conversation this morning after all. And of all those bitter and awkward ones she'd been expecting, she hadn't thought of this one. 'I got a message from Elena. I did what she told me. I guess if she wanted you to know, she'd have told you herself. Are you pissed off she didn't trust you?'

He picked up his dressing gown from the floor and pulled it on. Stood up. 'So you aren't going to tell me?'

She felt a bubble of resentment rise up through her blood. 'Where did you go yesterday? After Sainte-Chapelle?'

'I was buying perfume for my mother. It's a tradition. I get it for her whenever I'm in Paris. I'd forgotten till the reminder went off on my phone. It made me feel bad.'

Family traditions for Paris trips. What sort of smug life do you have to lead to have those? And anyway, it was the buzz of a message, not a reminder.

'The attaché case, Ruth. It's important.'

'I've told you. It stays between me and her. Nothing dodgier than the bundles of cash we handed over to Madeleine. I don't understand what the fuck is going on anyway, so I don't know why everyone keeps asking me.' Shit. Too much detail. Keep talking. 'Is that why you slept with me? Get me loved up and ask?'

'Don't be stupid. Of course not.'

'Stupid, am I? Cheers.' Yes, be angry. That was easier. 'I don't work for you, Michael. You want to know about Elena's shit, ask Elena.'

He stared at her, and she stared back. All the fun of the morning evaporated out of the air, then he shook his head and headed for the bathroom. Ruth heard the shower go.

It was bullshit, that line about his mother and the perfume. She slid out of bed and dressed quickly, checked her bag. Key card still there. Good. She pulled out her phone and looked at it. She had time to shower and pack. Mess up the bed in her own room, so the maid didn't mark her down as a tart, though God knows why that should matter. She would steal the chocolate from the pillow at least. She bent down and put her shoes on, high heels again, but these hadn't pinched even with all the dancing. Then she paused. Michael's briefcase and overnight bag. Like something a doctor in *Call the Midwife* would carry, unzipped and sagging open. And lying on top of a balled-up pair of socks, a Filofax. The shower was still running. She shifted onto the chair, her back to the bathroom door, and picked it up. Opened it. Diary pages with lists of names. Mostly the security team. A few words in what she thought might be Cyrillic, though it didn't look like the printed version.

Then a tatty list of contact pages, some numbers. Then she flipped through to the back; there was a pocket where people would usually stuff business receipts. Michael didn't have receipts. But there was something there. She twitched it out. A photograph of a man. He was caught full length, mid-stride as he crossed a busy-looking street, turned towards the camera to check for traffic. Ruth did not recognise him.

'What are you doing?'

Shit. She hadn't heard the shower turn off. She dropped the Filofax into the open case and twisted round.

'Looking for your pretend bloody perfume.'

He had a towel round his waist now. He looked like a model in an aftershave ad. Only angry. The guys in the aftershave ads never looked angry.

He plucked his suit jacket off the back of the other chair. Under it, hanging off the back, was a gift bag, its handles tied together in ribbons.

Ruth flinched. 'Fine. Lucky Mum.'

She bent back down and put on her other shoe.

'I'm going back to my room to shower. I'll see you downstairs in half an hour.'

She stood up and he took a step towards her, slightly but not completely putting himself between her and the door.

'OK Ruth. But I need you to listen. I didn't sleep with you to ask about the attaché case. If that had been the idea, I wouldn't have waited till this morning to ask.'

And he wouldn't have turned his back to her before he asked either. For a second she wanted to tell him. About Jane Lucas, about the men upstairs and that strange twisted grin on the second one's face when he saw what was in the briefcase. The money. The scarf. Why that scarf? Then Michael ruined it all.

'I like you, Ruth. Get out of the house. Just get a different job.'

Change the bloody record. She picked up her handbag. 'You'd like that, wouldn't you? Elena's found me, someone she can trust, and you don't want that. You never wanted me to take this job in the first place, and now you think you can flutter your eyelashes and get me to leave? No way. Elena is the best stroke of luck I've had since I was fourteen years old and got landed with my first ever not-psycho foster family.'

'That's not . . .'

'Get out of my way.'

He stood aside, hands up. She went out into the corridor and back to her own room. She stripped and went straight into the shower, her heart still pounding. Sod him and his warnings. Ruth wasn't some china doll, she'd come up rough. It was how she knew to be careful round men like the attic guys, keep her mouth shut.

And she didn't want to leave Elena. It wasn't the stuff so much, the clothes and the caviar, but she was seen now. No one looked at her like she was going to steal the milk jug when she wore these clothes. Men and women with thick business cards and clipped accents were grateful for her time when they rang her on the phone, they hurried to get her the information she wanted, responded to her emails in minutes. Yeah, but that was just the Shilkov name. No, it was more than that. Her funny brain was being put to use and she could handle herself, in the backroom of a charity gig or in a high-end jewellers. And that felt almost as good as the contours of Michael's muscles beneath the snow-white immaculately ironed thousand-count sheets of the Ritz.

Michael was waiting for her in the foyer and stood up as she approached. The attaché case, now swollen with Madeleine's collection, was at his feet. All formal politeness. Fine.

'The car is waiting.'

'Good,' Ruth said. 'I'll be one minute.'

'The bills are paid.'

She ignored him and went to the desk, handed over her key card to a man with sleek black hair and a long nose. A very French nose, Ruth decided. Now she was an international traveller she could tell these things. 'Ruth Miller. I was expecting a message?'

The man nodded, then reached into a set of pigeon holes behind him.

'Yes, madame. Here you are.'

Just an envelope, with the Ritz logo and with her name on it. She turned round. Yes, there was a writing desk in the foyer. Whoever had left this for her had obviously written it here. Then she opened the envelope. A folded sheet of hotel stationery with *GIVE THIS TO ELENA SHILKOV* written on it in uneven block capitals, and another envelope inside. Stiff, like one of those envelopes digital printers send you with your hard-copy snapshots.

She put it in her handbag and handed the original envelope and note back to the receptionist.

'Could you get rid of these for me?'

He took them with a nod.

'Cheers, love.'

That got a micro-smile at least. Then she turned back to look for Michael. She had half expected to find him at her shoulder, but no, he was standing across the room staring at one of the TVs dotted around the edge of the foyer for the convenience of guests who couldn't be bothered to pick up one of the complimentary newspapers. But it was his reflection she saw first. The fine lines of his jaw sharper, the set of his shoulders tight. Then she looked at the screen. A jumble of emergency vehicles and old-fashioned greenhouses like they have at Kew, a French news anchor talking silently while her words appeared in yellow below her.

'What's that on the news?' The receptionist looked up from his terminal and watched for a second or two.

'A murder. A man found dead on the edge of Bois de Boulogne.' He hissed a little. 'A mugging, they say. An Englishman. Bad for business.'

Among the scrolling French she saw a name, James Tranter, and as the receptionist spoke the screen filled with the man's passport photograph. It was the same man Ruth had just seen in the photograph in Michael's Filofax.

'A mugging?' she asked, her voice cracking a little.

'In the daylight too,' the receptionist replied with a shrug. 'Yesterday afternoon.' He added something else in French she didn't understand, but she got the idea. A familiar 'world is going to hell' mumble.

Ruth forgot to thank him. She walked towards Michael, the envelope in her bag, the photograph in his. She felt them like radioactive bricks. As if they were letting off some sort of silent death beam right this very second that would eat their flesh away. She had to tell Michael. She couldn't tell him. She had to get away. She wanted to stay. She had to warn Elena. Warn her of what? She kept moving, thinking of the message he got, how unsettled he was when he picked her up for dinner. Had Elena sent him on a scavenger hunt too? She should never have looked in the sodding Filofax. Bloody curiosity. Just keep your mouth shut, Ruth. See no evil, hear no evil, speak no evil.

'Michael?'

He looked at her and for a moment his face was fierce and blank. Then he smiled. A full smile which made the edges of his eyes crinkle, but which stank of fake like a Louis Vuitton bag for a fiver in the station market. The desire to trust evaporated again.

'Let's go,' he said and she walked out in front of him to the waiting car.

14

It was still early afternoon when they got back to the house and the place was silent. Ruth unpacked in her room and checked Elena's schedule. All red until tomorrow morning. She unloaded her dirty clothes into the wash basket in her bathroom. While she worked tomorrow morning the basket would be emptied and the clothes returned, ironed and folded, to the right drawers before she started thinking about lunch.

Elena came bouncing into the office an hour later. Her jeans were tight, her blouse a sapphire blue flouncy number that made her look like a nineteenth-century fencing master. On her feet she wore bunny slippers with pink noses and attentive ears. Ruth pushed away her suspicions. She was being ridiculous. She was wrong about something. Everything. All her dark imaginings dissolved when confronted with Elena, that energy she brought into the room, her ridiculous slippers. So Michael had disappeared off in a hurry. Well, he did get the perfume, didn't he? The text noise was probably because the reminder he mentioned was actually a text from his mum. He'd been in a crappy mood in the morning because she wouldn't tell him what was in the attaché case. Probably hadn't even seen what was on the TV. Could she absolutely be sure that the man she'd seen in the photograph from Michael's Filofax was the man on the news? The voice in her head took on the familiar timbre of a barrister doing his cross-examination.

Elena dragged a chair out from behind the door and sat on it sideways. Ruth checked the diary.

'Yes, it is red! But I want to hear about Paris. I think you must have spanked Madeleine. Stupid woman sent me orchids this morning. The library smells like a funeral home.'

'She wasn't pleased you'd arranged that other meeting. Who were those men, Elena?'

She made a tusking noise and waved her hand in the air. 'Old friends. Sort of friends. Business. Did you tell Michael about them?'

Ruth shook her head and found Elena was looking at her with fond curiosity.

'Good. I thought you would not. You are shut up like a shell. I like that.'

'He noticed the attaché case was empty when I came down-stairs again though.'

She nodded slowly.

'Yes. He is good at his job. But I cannot read him. He is too English for me.'

'They left this at the hotel for me to give you.' She reached into her handbag and pulled out the envelope, handed it to her.

Elena grabbed it and opened it. Ruth couldn't see what it contained.

'Good.' She pulled out her phone and tapped a message, then turned her back to Ruth. She heard the fake shutter of the camera phone. She turned back, folding the envelope shut and stuck it and the phone in her back pocket. Then she swung round and put her elbows on the table.

'Now tell me the rest. You were in Paris twenty-four hours. You were at Madeleine's for forty minutes.' Ruth felt her face grow hot and Elena laughed.

'Oh, Ruth! With Michael? Was he good?'

Ruth hunched her shoulders and glanced sideways towards Michael's office. Elena rolled her eyes.

'Oh, he is out with Yuri.' Silence. 'Pah, you are not going to tell me. Very well. You are shell like a . . .'

'A clam?'

Elena clapped her hands. 'Exactly!'

The barrister in Ruth's head raised his eyebrows. OK. She'd been thinking nonsense. Yes, Elena grew up in a grey economy, maybe knew some shady people coming up, but so did Ruth. She couldn't be certain about anything she'd seen in Paris, and even what she thought she'd seen or heard didn't really add up. Pieces didn't fit.

Elena's phone buzzed and she pulled it out. Looked. Shimmied from side to side.

'Aha! This person might get earring too.' She tapped out a message. 'Put on your coat, Ruth. We are going for a drive.' Seeing the look of confusion on Ruth's face, she went on: 'I want to talk to you about the Sir Toby gifts. You have done well. I am getting nicer thank yous. But there will be more and bigger ones soon.'

'Such as?'

'I have to go. We'll talk in the car! Come on.'

Ruth got up, slightly dazed, picked her bag and her coat up from the back of the door and followed as Elena trotted upstairs. In the lobby Elena opened a door to the right of the entrance, kicked off the bunny slippers and stepped into a pair of high-heeled crocodile-skin ankle boots. She bent to zip them up, then pushed open the front door. It all seemed to happen in one movement. Ruth followed.

'So – some Sir Tobys, the interesting Sir Tobys, they get more than a hamper. Yuri's firm offers them a little tip or advice.'

The Porsche was parked on the street between a van belonging to a company that made ice sculptures and another belonging to the landscape gardeners. Both were green and gold. Elena clicked her fob and her car beeped softly in greeting.

'So you need to help arrange that with Yuri's people and the Sir Toby or his people. Sometimes they need to set up a company. You and Yuri's people will tell them how.'

She got into the driver's seat, and Ruth got in beside her, put her handbag at her feet.

'But I don't *know* how . . .'

Elena started the car. 'You will learn. It's very easy in this country.' She checked the rear-view mirror. Behind them the gate to the rear garage opened and one of the grey saloons of the security team emerged. 'Shit. I do not want company today.'

She drove to the end of the private road and the bollards eased down.

'Can't you just tell them that?'

Elena grinned. Wickedly. 'Yes. But this is more fun.'

First she waited, indicating left for what seemed like forever, then stamped on the accelerator and swung the wheel right, taking them almost under the wheels of a terrified-looking bus driver and making the cab driver coming up behind them on the Bayswater Road lean on his brakes and his horn.

'Jesus!' Ruth was thrown against the seat belt.

Elena swung left now, past a no entry sign, changing gears and whipping past parked cars before going right again through what looked like a dead end and then another left into a parallel street.

'So Sir Toby sets up a company and one of Yuri's companies lends his company some money. One of Yuri's people gives him a sensible piece of investment advice. Buy these shares. Sir Toby buys.'

The Porsche darted across a main road like a rat dodging between bins.

'Elena! Watch the bloody road.'

'But I'm explaining!' She changed gear and accelerated up a ramp way. A narrow dual carriageway. Very narrow. She weaved in and out of the traffic.

'In a week, two weeks, the share price goes up.' She made a take-off gesture with her hand. Ruth closed her eyes. 'Then Sir Toby sells. His company pays back Yuri's company. All very neat and . . .' She paused long enough to blow her horn at someone in her way. Ruth opened her eyes again in time to find they were coming off the dual carriageway and into ordinary London streets. Elena slowed down and started peering at the street names. '. . . Everyone is happy. Here it is.'

She parallel parked and got out. 'Wait here, Ruth.'

Ruth said nothing as the door slammed. The street was narrow, a back ally really at this end. Steel shutters and air conditioner units bolted onto the walls. A board of business names. A repair shop, a printers, a brewers. Ruth watched Elena ring a doorbell, say something into the intercom, then disappear into the building.

Her heartbeat began to slow down. She got out her phone and checked where they were. Penfold Place off the Edgware Road. Whatever. All that stuff about companies and things couldn't be legal. Colouring outside the lines again.

Five minutes. Ten. Then Elena reappeared from the building and got into the car. Ruth just had time to register that her mood had turned dark before Elena reached past her.

'What the fuck is that?' Elena said.

The scarf. Ruth's handbag had fallen over and tipped it out into the well. Suddenly Elena had it in her fist, shoving it in Ruth's face, grabbing Ruth's shoulder hard with her free hand. 'What are you doing with this, Ruth? You think I want to see this?'

Ruth shoved her hard.

'I saw it, so I asked for it! *You* were just using it as wrapping paper.'

Elena pulled back her hand to slap her. Ruth blocked the blow with her forearm. They were eye to eye.

'Elena, you lay hands on me I won't just resign, I'll punch you in the face and then I'll fucking resign. Sod you and the ten grand. I wanted it because nicking it was how I met you, so back off.'

The rage left Elena's eyes, replaced by confusion. 'You *nicked* it? Nicking is stealing, yes?'

Oh hell.

'Yes.'

The anger had gone completely now. Disappeared as quickly as it had come. Elena dropped her hands into her lap and frowned. 'But, Ruth, you came into the café to give it back. If you stole it, why give it back?'

So there it was. Ruth sighed and bent down to pick up her handbag, and fished out the Asprey purse. It clicked stiffly open. She felt around in the back section, pulled out a thin postcard and handed it to Elena.

Me and the boss! See you in London, babe! it said on the back, and the rest of the space was filled in with Xs – hundreds of them, in lines and spirals. Typical of Megs that, not to bother with any actual news or facts or names, but then to spend twenty minutes making all those kisses into a sort of folk art.

Elena turned the card over and looked at the picture. The image was beginning to fade a little, it was cheaply printed in some tourist trap where you could turn your photo into a postcard. Megan grinning at the camera in selfie mode, her red hair mixing with Elena's blonde against a bright-blue Croatian sky.

'The holiday nanny,' Elena said wonderingly.

Ruth swallowed. 'Megan Talbot. She was my best friend. Since we were like twelve and we met in one of the care homes. At least, I thought she was my best friend. After she started doing nannying down here she rang me. Told me I should come down to London too. We were going to get a place together. I wasn't sure but, you know, she persuaded me, and I handed in my notice at the solicitor's office. She was doing a season nannying abroad to save up for a deposit for a place we could rent while I worked out my notice. That,' Ruth nodded at the card Elena was holding, 'was the last I heard from her.'

Oh damn. She was going to cry. She swiped at her eyes. Spoke fast.

'She stopped answering my texts, but I'd already handed in my notice, so I came anyway. Too proud to admit she'd dumped me. Then I saw you with the girls in the street.'

'Why not just speak to me?' Elena asked. Her voice was just curious now, no heat in it.

Ruth felt the edge of the seat belt with her thumb. 'You don't look like the sort of person people like me can just wander up to. I saw the scarf hanging loose ... It seemed like an easy way to introduce myself, so I took it. Followed you. Got blown up.'

Elena handed her back the card and stared out of the windscreen while Ruth put it back in the wallet. Then Elena started laughing.

'Karma's a *bitch*.'

'Yeah,' Ruth was surprised into a damp laugh herself. 'I tried to ask, but then you offered me the job and sort of told me anyway.'

Elena frowned. 'Sort of. Yes. But you must have had other questions.'

Ruth blew out a long breath. 'I did. So I broke into the personnel filing cabinet in Michael's office and read the report in her file. After the dumpling lunch.'

The details about Megan that Andrei and Elena had given her were the same as those in the file. Megan Talbot, temporary nanny, had left while the yacht was moored in the busy marina on the island of Korčula. She'd taken her passport and belongings with her, apart from a few things which had been in the laundry and a book she'd lent to one of the deckhands. A moonlight flit. Very Megs. She hadn't informed the employment agency, and her mobile had been switched off. The agency found out that she had never filled in the 'next of kin' box on her employment form. Reading that had hurt. A reprimand was issued to the admin assistant who had stamped the form complete.

So Megan had left. Just gone off into the blue leaving Ruth to come to London in the dark autumn as they had arranged, then wait, and wait. Maybe it had just been guilt, that invitation, Megan's elaborate plans to share a house, save money, travel. Her whoop of delight when Ruth said she'd handed in her notice at the solicitor's. Maybe she meant it at the time, but Megan was quicksilver. Why should Ruth be surprised? Everyone had told Ruth that Megan was unreliable – the Cunninghams, Judith the social worker, Sunny at the solicitor's office when Ruth had shared the London plan. Hadn't Megan let her down before? Going off with men. Men like Sid and his mates. God knows, there were plenty of them. Some bloke she met in the park. Disappearing for weeks at a time? Dumping school and Ruth and foster families and coming back laughing about it or not saying anything at all. And Ruth had defended her. Said she wasn't like that really, not any more. That she had grown up, worked really hard. Only quit two jobs, and that was because one boss was a creep and another a psycho who treated Megan as a personal slave. She had great references now. Ruth felt another twist of misery under her ribs. She must have sounded delusional. But she'd been sure. Mystery solved

– everyone else was right. She had thought of all those unanswered texts she'd sent and felt like a fool again.

Ruth didn't know which agency Megan had been working for, when to expect her back. She'd been frustrated, then annoyed, then hurt, then annoyed again. So she'd come, got the house-share and the job on her own and tried to get used to the idea Megan had maybe ghosted her completely this time. But then she'd seen Elena on the street, recognised her from the photo and stolen her scarf so she could follow her into the café and ask about the missing nanny. She had got the answer (bad) and a job (good).

She had believed though that she and Megan had a bond. Surely the trial had made it an unbreakable bond? Megan could have run away then too, but she didn't. In the weeks before the trial started they'd been together all the time, talking through all the shit that had happened. And afterwards Megan had seemed to be sorting herself out. In general. The nannying course, her first couple of jobs in London. She'd seemed more settled, more hopeful than she had for years. But no. She'd chucked it all away again chasing after some man on a holiday island. Thrown Ruth away too and left her to a long, lonely London winter. That had hurt, that realisation. That had really, really hurt.

'Am I fired?' she asked eventually. Elena was staring out of the windscreen.

'You are a thief and a liar, and you threatened to hit me,' Elena said in a sing-song, then went on in her ordinary voice. 'No, you are not fired. I like you.' She tossed Ruth the scarf. 'Keep it. I shall get used to it. And I am sorry your friend disappeared.' She put her hand on Ruth's knee. 'And sorry I went crazy too. Seeing the scarf it . . .' She mimed a gag, as if she were about to throw up or had been punched in the stomach. 'I thought it was gone. Then it came back. So boom in my head! But also I got news I didn't like. I was angry before I saw it. So I screamed at you.'

'I'm sorry the news was bad, Elena.'

'Yes. Family. They can be a big problem.'

'I wouldn't know,' Ruth said. 'Only family I had was Megan and she dumped me.'

Elena put her arm round her shoulders and Ruth allowed herself to be embraced. She relaxed her head onto Elena's shoulder.

'Ah Ruth, we are your family now, *dorogaya*. Let's go home.'

So they did. Ruth picked at the dinner Masha had laid out for her in the staff kitchen, then showered and collapsed into bed. But sleep didn't come. Her mind wandered through her hurt, dwelling on every time Megan had let her down, run off because 'stuff was getting to her'. She sat up in bed and breathed deeply. She had to let this shit go. Just forgive Megan and be glad she had landed this plush job. Maybe that was karma too?

And she was unburdened. She had told Elena the truth, so Jane Lucas could sod off. But what about Michael and the men in the attic? The back street and the photograph in Michael's Filofax. And why did that name, James Tranter, sound so familiar?

Could she just ask Michael? No need to mention she'd snooped in his Filofax – just say the name sounded familiar when she'd noticed him watching the report. But *why* did it sound familiar? That could get her into trouble. Then she realised, a sudden sick realisation, and she swore out loud. Closed her eyes. Breathed. The name was familiar because she'd seen it in Michael's personnel files. It had been there on one of the tabs, when she'd been looking for that brief, heartbreaking and utterly useless file on Megan. *Talbot*, then *Tranter*.

She got out of bed and curled up on one of the armchairs. Everything got worse. The dead man in Paris had been an employee of the Shilkovs. And he had been killed the day they were in Paris. While Michael was off buying perfume . . . But he *did* buy perfume! Her insides felt small and tight. What had the men said to each other in the room above Madeleine's? The last thing. 'Jal yeo imya', it had sounded like.

Ruth reached for her iPad and opened up Google translate, tried different spellings to see what it could offer. Was it Russian?

Maybe. Or Serbian. The first bit kept coming up nonsense. She tried again, working backwards as her fears began to harden. Come on, funny brain. Then she stared at her screen. Hit the little speaker button again and again until she was sure. That was it, coming out of the slightly tinny speakers in a clipped computer voice. *Pošalji joj ime. Pošalji joj ime. Pošalji joj ime.* Send her the name.

15

The next morning Elena arrived in Ruth's office just as she was getting ready to come upstairs to the library. Elena sat down in front of the desk and waved Ruth back to her seat.

'No meeting for us this morning! This afternoon two of Yuri's people are coming to talk to you. Three p.m.' She lifted three fingers as if Ruth was too slow to understand the words alone.

'OK. Look Elena, it's not illegal this stuff, is it? I'm not sure I'm comfortable . . .'

Elena waggled her hand. 'It's legal-ish. Comfortable. I do not pay you to be *comfortable*. Now I know you can deal with Madeleines,' she went on, 'I have another errand. The briefcase with the cuffs and collar. You have to take it to this address.'

Ruth blinked. 'But Elena, I thought they were for you.'

'No. A very important present.' She picked up a pen and snapped her fingers till Ruth shoved her notepad across the desk. Elena wrote out an address in Holland Park, complete with postcode. 'Order a car. The case is for Suzanne D'Arcy only. She will be there until half-past eleven.'

Ruth took out her phone and used the app to summon a driver from their service. Suzanne D'Arcy. The name on the visitor logs. The person who had been to see Elena the two days before she turned up in Brockley. The woman at the Restart party. The woman coming out of the Kensington house on the day she got her passport and Elena had announced she was sending Ruth to France. The woman Jane had asked her about. Ruth had googled her that same day. Her mother was Nigerian, her father an English oil executive with an old English name and a CV of public schools, Cambridge, management consulting. There had been a scandal a few years ago. A change in governments had led to some difficult questions being asked. He had issued a mea culpa and donated large sums of money to orphanages in West Africa. Not before he'd got his daughter an education much like his own though.

'Are you going to fuck Michael again?' Elena continued brightly. 'I don't mind as long as you don't distract him from saving me from grenades. And no crying. I hate crying.'

Ruth grinned in spite of herself. 'I don't know. He was different in Paris. Less uptight.'

'A not-uptight Michael Fitzsimmons?' She stared up at the ceiling with a tight frown. 'No. I cannot imagine it.'

She underlined the address then bounced up from her chair to the door.

'We do the charity shit later. The earrings look good on you. Come see me when you get back. Even if I am on red time.'

Her damned imagination. The barrister voice sounded just like the man who had cross-examined her at the trial. The slight sneer, the disappointment when she insisted yes, it had been that man. It had happened, yes she was absolutely unshakably sure. Surer of that than anything she'd seen with her own eyes over the last day or so. He'd implied she was a fantasist, a girl from a broken background crying out for attention. Her library records, all the Harry Potters a dozen times over, crime and romance novels, had been thrust under her nose. The school report she'd been so proud of where the English teacher had praised her imagination was now used as evidence against her. She'd fought then. Hell yeah, she fought and the barrister had cast a conspiratorial look at the jury and got stared down by the dozen men and women in the box. They'd been on Ruth's side from the start. They loathed the barrister, and his accent and his attitude, and they'd liked Ruth. Liked how she answered back. Stood up for herself. They only took twenty minutes to find every bastard in the dock guilty as sin. Which they were.

Last night she'd convinced herself she would resign. Leave the Shilkovs. This morning it seemed unnecessary. Daft. Legal-ish isn't *illegal*. Could she swear the personnel file she'd seen was for James Tranter? Was the guy in the photo really absolutely the man on the news? She'd only seen the image and the name for a second. Exactly how good was her Serbian? And working for Elena was certainly interesting. And it gave her a home. An image of the bars on the windows flashed through her mind. Very safe.

The car pulled up silently in front of a neat house with a wrought iron veranda strewn with wisteria and a chequerboard pathway. It looked modest in comparison with the Shilkovs' house. Ruth told the driver to wait, walked up the path and knocked. The door knocker was a lion's head, polished to a dull gleam. It stared at her; Ruth could swear it was ready to growl. Just as it began to get awkward, and she wondered if she should knock again, the door was opened by the slim woman from the party, her hair piled high on her head. She wore a loose silk kimono over a tight turquoise vest and leather trousers.

'Suzanne D'Arcy?'

'I am she.'

'I have something for you from Elena Shilkov.'

Suzanne nodded and opened the door, allowing Ruth inside. The hallway was relatively narrow, more black-and-white tiles on the floor, old furniture, a gold-framed landscape on the wall.

She closed the door and walked past Ruth into the interior. 'Come into the kitchen.'

The kitchen turned out to be a vast semi-glassed room, kitchen and signature dining area combined, as the estate agent's brochure would say. It had the same, clinically clean and lemon-tinged scent as Elena's house. Sterile. After the sweat and food stinks of the group homes and foster families, the takeaway and toast whiff of the shared house in Brockley, Ruth was living in a world that didn't smell of humanity at all. The realisation shook her slightly.

Suzanne leant on one side of a marble island. 'Well?'

Ruth pulled herself together and put the attaché case on the black quartz worktop. She opened it and removed the two boxes, then set the case back on the floor.

A flicker of a smile when Suzanne saw the name on the lid.

Suzanne lifted the lids and her smile broadened. 'These are one of a kind?'

Ruth nodded. 'Absolutely. We paid a premium to have the design drawings destroyed.'

Suzanne raised her eyebrows. 'You mean Elena did.'

Ruth had to acknowledge that.

'Where are you from, Ruth?'

'Middlesbrough.'

Suzanne lifted the collar out of the box and held it up so the light flooding into the room caught the glimmer of the stones. The emeralds somehow looked darker and more intense in natural light.

'Your parents didn't send you away to school to get rid of that accent?'

'I went to the local comp.'

She stared at the jewels, her head on one side.

'If your little friends there could see you now . . .'

Ruth turned to look out of the back window, shifted her weight to one hip. 'Oh, I don't know. A bunch of them do deliveries, I think. Deliveroo. That shit.'

Suzanne's eyes flicked up, then she lowered the collar back into its box. 'How charmingly eccentric Elena is.'

'Do you mean it's eccentric to hire someone like me?'

Suzanne offered a professional smile. 'Yes, she likes to mix things up occasionally. Put the establishment into a flutter.'

'And you?'

She picked up one of the cuffs and fitted it round her wrist. It seemed to glow. 'Sweetie, I don't need to do anything to get their little hearts pounding. A black woman with an old English name? I walk into a room and they act like a fox has strolled into the hen house for pre-prandials. I would imagine it amuses her to use you to stir them up too.'

Ruth almost smiled.

'But she does have perfect taste.'

'Madeleine said the same thing,' Ruth replied.

'So many of the Russian women are crass, but Elena manages to marry exuberance with a certain quirky individuality which means she rather carries it off. My style is safer as a rule. Modern classic, I like to think. My parents sent me to Cheltenham Ladies College. Lagos to the Cotswolds.'

'Oxford must have seemed a right melting pot after that,' she said.

Suzanne's eyes widened then she laughed. 'Oh, it did. So you did your homework? Explains why you didn't assume I was the home help when you opened the door. You'd be surprised how many people do.'

'That, and I saw you talking to Elena at the Restart gig. And coming out of the Kensington house last week.'

'My, how observant,' she murmured, staring at the jewels again.

'I heard you'd been out of the country for a while.'

'Yes, since just before that terrible attack in the café. Milos and I were visiting his properties in America.'

A man walked into the room, dressed in jeans a bit too tight for him and a long plaid shirt. He was older than Suzanne, fifty maybe, his hair fairly black and his fleshy face pitted with old acne scars. He was barefoot, and eating Häagen-Dazs ice cream straight out of the tub. He lifted his hand in greeting to Ruth with a quick grin, then whistled at the cuff round Suzanne's wrist.

'Nice.' He peered down at the box with the collar in it and put the spoon upside down in his mouth, removing it clean with a smack before digging into the tub. 'Very nice.'

'A gift from Elena Shilkov,' Suzanne said, and put her slim arm around his waist.

He looked at Ruth, his eyes bright, as if he was about to laugh. Ruth found she liked him. 'This is Ruth. She works for Elena. Ruth, this is Milos.'

'Cool. Want some ice cream, Ruth?' He held out the tub towards her. He had an accent, Eastern European?

'I'm all right thanks. Don't want to spoil my dinner.'

He snort-laughed. 'More for me. Tell Elena I like the gift.'

Suzanne looked at him, pouted slightly. 'Can't I keep them, Milos?'

He patted her on the behind, then returned to his ice cream. 'Sure.' Suzanne fit the second cuff onto her wrist. 'And tell Elena no more fuck-ups, OK?'

Less laughter in his eyes now. Ruth was sure Elena didn't fuck up, but she felt arguing with this guy would not be wise.

'Will do. Anything else?'

He looked at her for a long moment. 'Yeah. Tell Elena if she wants to move now, I need a name.' Then he lifted his hand in farewell and ambled out again, sucking on the spoon.

Suzanne turned her arm in the light so the cuffs cast green-and-white shadows across the room.

'Do you have any message for Elena?' Ruth asked her.

'No. You can find your own way out, can't you?'

Ruth picked up the attaché case and left Suzanne admiring the patterns of light her jewels cast across the polished floors.

16

The car wasn't outside. Ruth guessed Jay must have been driven off by traffic wardens and walked back towards the junction to flag him down, thinking of Suzanne. What has she done to deserve that sort of gift from Elena?

'Ms Miller?'

Ruth had reached the end of the street and almost walked straight into a man of about her own age in creative casuals, suede jacket, retro messenger bag, trimmed beard and smooth skin.

'Who are you?'

'Just a messenger.' He pulled a map from his bag. 'If you could just point out where we are? Jane says meet her at your local Caffè Nero at four tomorrow afternoon. Bring a magazine. Leave your phone at the office. Sit at a table by yourself and she'll join you. When you get back to the office today, there's an email from Jimmy Reeves. It's bollocks, but read every fourth word. Send your usual holding reply to confirm the meeting.'

He rattled all this out, head bent over the map. Ruth pointed randomly at a place in the middle. He folded the map away.

'Thanks so much,' and he was off with the right sort of cheery wave. Jay pulled up and she got into the back seat.

'Everything all right, Ruth?' he asked. He was Nigerian too, shaven head and huge glasses that gave him an owlish look. 'I had to go round the block. Traffic warden.'

Bet there was.

'That's fine.'

'Ruth, you want to watch boys like that. The ones who show you a map. Sometimes they use it to distract you and pick your pockets.'

Yes. Yes they did.

'Yeah, I'll watch out for that.'

'I mean – you know this. Who uses maps these days anyway?'

He pulled out onto the main road and turned towards Kensington.

The guard on the door to the house stopped her.

'Ms Miller? Mrs Shilkov is in the library.'

'Thank you.' Ruth didn't recognise this guy. 'Are you new?'

'No, miss. Just been on holiday. Tenerife. It was lovely. Name's Ben. Ex-police.' He said all of this looking forward, still scanning the street.

'Nice to meet you, Ben. And I'm Ruth, not Miss.'

She went in, deposited the empty case in her office, then went to the library and knocked.

'*Vkhodi!* Come in!' Elena said.

Ruth pushed the door open. Elena was sitting on the sofa with Yuri, their heads close together and a coffee tray between them. The cups were dirty and a stack of papers lay nearby.

Yuri looked up at her. He gave her a courtly nod and stood, gathered up the papers and left through the rear door. His study.

'I didn't mean to disturb you.'

Elena looked distracted. 'I told you to come, you came. Tell me what happened.' She didn't invite Ruth to sit down. 'All of it.'

Ruth recited the whole conversation. 'Who is Milos?' she asked when she had finished.

'Her better half,' Elena said and tapped her phone against her teeth. 'Nothing else?'

'A man asked me for directions. Jay, the driver, was afraid he was trying to pickpocket me, but I didn't get that vibe off him.'

'OK. Good. Thank you. Now go away.'

Nothing of the womanly intimacy of this morning then. Yuri was here. Did that mean Michael was in the house too?

'Shall I take the tray?'

'No.' Elena frowned. 'Do not fetch and carry. You are not my carrying stuff person. And you do not need to be best friends with all the staff. Don't lower yourself, Ruth.'

'I've been fetching and carrying for you for the last three days. What's the difference?'

That broke her out of whatever mood she was in. She laughed, a swift sharp jolt.

'Ha! Ruth will not be put in a box. We haven't squeezed the fight out of you yet, have we?' Ruth kept her expression neutral. 'Good. Good. Fine. Very clever. But you know there is a difference. Leave the fucking tray.'

Ruth nodded and left the room. She returned to her office. Was there a difference? Of course there was – it was like the suit, the designer jeans. A network of signals so the right people would recognise you, acknowledge your status, respect your authority. Ruth had never had either before and it felt good. Gave the world a sugar coating, made it pliant and sweet.

The door to Michael's office was shut. She didn't knock, but felt her skin prickle at the idea he was inside. Did he know she was in the house? Of course he did. She had been logged in, just like everyone else. She turned on the computer and tried to focus on the flood of begging emails, something to ground her.

She'd made a start before Elena turned up this morning, but there were still a hundred to go. She made herself open them in the order they arrived and deal with them in the usual way, sorting for further research, getting rid of the obvious scams. Then she saw the one from Jimmy Reeves. Her cursor hovered over it. No. She had to do them in order. Three to go, then two, then one.

Jane could sod off. She had nothing on Ruth now. She'd go to the coffee shop and tell her so to her face. Come back and warn Elena about the approach. Then, if it turned out James Tranter was an ex-employee of the Shilkovs, she'd just resign. Walk away. Get on with life. She'd got her answer about Megan, she'd seen what life was like in the land of money, but going through the emails had worked. She couldn't just float above the world in the Shilkov bubble. She had skills, she had value and she could carry some of that confidence away with her out of this house even if she had to leave Elena and Michael behind. It felt like a decision. Like the right decision. She reached the Jimmy email.

The request was well written. Jim was unable to work after early-onset arthritis and his wife was on a zero-hours contract working for a care provider for the local health authority. Her car was old and unsafe and they were afraid they wouldn't be able to get it through the next MOT. An everyday story of country folk. Two kids, one with special needs, both under ten. Jim doing the bulk of the childcare. At the ends of their tethers. Nothing strange about it at all. But if you read just every fourth word. 'I know the truth about the trial. And I can prove it.'

She read it once. Then again in case she'd been seeing things. No no no. She could feel a coldness in her gut radiating out over her whole body. Her scalp tightened. It was impossible. No one knew the truth, only her and Megan – that was the whole point.

And I can prove it. She was going to throw up. Yes, probably. If someone like Jane Lucas suspected the truth, she probably could prove it. Then what would happen? The scenarios unspooled. Ruth covered her eyes with her hands. It didn't help. No, not now. Not just at the moment she'd got a grip, made a plan. It all exploded into ash and horror around her.

She checked the shared calendar for the following afternoon. From three to seven was red, so she was officially allowed to organise her time as she wished. Which could include the trip to Caffè Nero.

She pressed reply and sent her usual holding answer with shaking fingers. 'Thank you for your message. We always research these requests carefully, so will be in touch when our checks are complete.' Usual holding reply, the man with the map said, meant a meeting could go ahead. So they knew what her usual reply was. She wondered if they had hacked the system, or if she had already answered a dozen requests from MI5. She'd probably sent them an envelope stuffed with cash and a prayer card. Bastards. One way to fill Her Majesty's coffers with some of the Russian money flying about London. When someone knocked on the door she jumped out of her seat. Then hit send.

Masha put her head round the door.

'Ruth! Misery package.'

Ruth got up and followed her out to the kitchen, her legs watery. The door to the rear of the house was open. A guard and a nervous-looking courier were standing on the threshold. She crossed, thanking Masha with a nod, took the package and signed for it. It was heavy.

She carried it back to her desk and opened it. A thick slab of unopened envelopes.

'Here.' Masha had followed her in. She set a plate and a mug on her desk. 'Sandwich. Coffee. If you work, you must eat. You forget to have lunch too often.'

'Thank you.'

'*Nichevo.*'

The box contained some handwritten appeals for money, but roughly half were usually thank-you notes. People asked for things by email, but when the cash and prayer cards arrived an electronic thank you wasn't enough. Ruth needed to calm down, stop thinking about the Lucas email, so she read them all, taking in the texture of the discount market notelets printed with forget-me-nots or sunflowers, the careful penmanship.

Each one conjured up a kitchen table in a small town, the cooking smells, the confusion of plastic toys underfoot, the mug of tea on a coaster, cooling as the writer, normally a woman, tried to convey just how much the bundle of cash from the Shilkov household meant. What they'd spend it on. The sudden blossoming of relief and hope on each page. Almost all of them included a promise to pray for Elena and her family, *I don't believe it myself* or *It's not my religion, but I shall*. She ate the sandwich, felt the wave of panic retreat a little.

Ruth remembered a thing she'd read in the newspaper about sin eaters. Medieval outcasts who would, for a generous fee, take on themselves the sins of the dead to allow them free passage into heaven. She remembered the monks paid to pray over the tombs of the powerful. What were Elena's sins, that she needed the assistance of all these prayers? What in modern London did she carry under her designer outfits, in her heart, that she still felt the need to be prayed for in a secular age, an irreligious, shameless city? Shame. What was Ruth ashamed of? Not much. Anger, fear, hurt. Those she felt, was feeling, but she was not ashamed. Not yet.

She hadn't handed any of the thank-you letters over to Michael for disposal. It just seemed wrong. That would make her ashamed, just trashing all these letters. She couldn't keep them, but they should be recorded in some way. She looked at the computer. Well, that's what it's for and maybe it will stop me thinking for a while. She started reading through the tutorial on how to create a database. It helped. By the time Yuri's people, an elderly man who had a soft voice and a woman of Elena's age who didn't, arrived punctually at three she could pay attention while they talked her through shell companies, haven accounts and how to communicate discreetly when needed. Her head was pounding by the time they left. Then she worked on the database some more, wrote some emails to sponsorship relationship managers, block-booked tickets for an event at the National Gallery and actually managed to sleep.

17

'Ruth?'

Midday. Her first list of 'bigger' favours from Elena in front of her. Appointment with Jane Lucas at the coffee shop ticking closer.

Michael was standing in the doorway. Jacket off, no tie. Folder under his arm. It felt like a shock to see him. They came back Tuesday morning – it was Thursday now and their paths had hardly crossed. She couldn't handle a conversation with him now about Paris, not with thoughts of Jane Lucas choking her. Professional. This is work time. She looked at him and then back to her screen.

'Hi. You need something?' She put the list of Sir Tobys in the top drawer of her desk.

He came in and sat down on the chair. 'Just wanted to show you this. They're all possible threats to Yuri and Elena. We make sure everyone in the household sees their faces once we have photos.'

All business then. He doesn't want to talk about Parisian hotel rooms or murder victims either. London Michael. Good. He put the folder on the table and they both leant forward. Despite herself Ruth could still feel her skin prickle at his closeness. He opened the folder. Inside was a photograph of a middle-aged woman wearing a fleece and grinning at the camera in friendly grandma mode. Ruth turned it towards herself so she could see it clearly. Left her fingers on the edge of the 10x8 printout. He didn't move back.

'Sally Jones. Fifty-two. Probably harmless, but she's been post-ing to a lot of conspiracy sites. Lots of talk about how someone should do something about foreigners taking over London. Works at the council office in Battersea.'

He shifted the photograph to the bottom of the stack. The next one was of a thickset man squeezed into a suit and tie. It looked as if the photo was taken at some sort of formal function he didn't want to be at.

'Did your mother like the perfume?' Damn. Wasn't supposed to mention Paris.

'I haven't given it to her yet. Steven Williamson. He is more of a concern. His own social media profile is light and pretty anodyne, but he spends a lot of time on conspiracy websites using a pseudonym and seems to have focused on Elena and Yuri as special subjects. He applied to be on their security team at one point and was shown the door. Looks like he took it very personally.'

'How do you get this stuff? About people's social media and things?'

He didn't look at her. 'Yuri has people.'

'So what might this guy do? Is he part of the Uprising?'

'Lots of people claim to be part of the Uprising, but that doesn't mean they are. We don't even know if they have a formal command structure, or if they're just relying on inspiring lone wolves to carry out attacks.'

Ruth was in the shop again watching the first man shoot into the ceiling, the others getting ready to throw the grenades. Yes, they were wolves. Not lone wolves though. She had come face to face with a well-organised pack. She realised he was looking at her. Giving her a moment.

'Go on.'

'If any of the crazies have serious intentions to harm, the first thing they'll do is start watching the house. We need to make sure we spot that. Warn them off. I've sent someone to get better pictures of this guy.'

'How do you warn them off? Baseball bat? Quiet word with their employers?'

His fingers brushed hers, unnecessarily, as he consigned Steven to the bottom of the pile.

'A letter from the lawyers. Very gangster.'

A few more faces. Ruth recognised some of the names from emails. She thought about the kids she used to be careful around in care. The ones who blustered and threatened were usually OK, just scared and angry like the rest of them. No, it was the quiet ones you had to watch.

He looked up and their eyes met. 'Look at the next picture, Ruth.'

She did. It was of one of the men from the upstairs room. The one with the hair.

'Who is this?' she said a bit too quickly.

'I don't know. I noticed him while we were waiting for the car outside the Palais Royal. He seemed to be taking an interest in you so I took a picture of him.' He had been quick. Ruth hadn't even noticed it happen. Her mind had been foggy with jewels and blocks of five-hundred-euro notes. She had to watch that. 'Do you know him?'

She stared at the picture for a second then shook her head. 'I can't tell you one way or the other, I'm afraid. Not a great picture, is it?'

Then she dared look up. He smiled at her, carefully.

'No. I'll try and get some more information together.'

For a long moment neither of them moved. He must know, or at least suspect this was one of the men she had met in Paris, but she had managed to phrase her answer so she didn't outright lie, even if she didn't give him the information he wanted. She sensed somehow, through her skin, that he had noticed.

Then she sat back. 'I have a heap of these emails to get through still. Do you need anything else?'

He closed the folder again and got up to leave. 'Not right now.'

Three forty-five. Her lunch was eaten. The box dealt with. A new flurry of emails had come in and she had spoken on the phone with Mappin & Webb about some Sir Toby commissions scheduled for the end of the day. A perfectly reasonable time to grab a breath of fresh air. She picked up her bag, leaving her phone half buried under the folders on her desk, and headed out of the house, nodding to the man on the door as she went.

She set off along the Bayswater Road. She'd spent so much time in the house the street still felt unfamiliar. A smattering of tourists, half looking flustered by the crowds, half blithely ignoring them and halting in the middle of the pavement to stare in at a window, or point towards the palace, oblivious to the tuts and sighs of the Londoners power-walking around them. The Chelsea tractors were beginning to surge along the streets. Cars designed for the country without a speck of mud on them, as housewives and nannies headed off to collect the kids from school.

Ruth hesitated outside Caffè Nero, then went in, got her black Americano and ignored the cakes. As instructed she found an empty table near the back and took out one of her hip art magazines. Looking for names. Connections. Deciding on the impossible-to-get tickets and items that Elena could feed to her Sir Tobys like pearls.

Five minutes later Jane sat down opposite her. Ruth almost told her she was waiting for a friend. It was not that Jane was disguised in any way, only her hair was unbrushed and she was wearing an anorak and a striped sweater over jeans. No make-up, which made her look older. She looked . . . average. She noticed the moment of confusion on Ruth's face and the corner of her mouth twitched. She juggled a plate and mug onto the table and put an overstuffed handbag on the floor.

'It is a superpower, you know, invisibility. The one most coveted by spies and yet enforced on middle-aged women. If I don't dress in my power suit, I can walk past trained agents and I don't even register.'

'Afternoon.'

She pulled a piece off her muffin and ate it. 'So? Had a think? Ready to cough up what I need?'

Ruth swirled the coffee in her cup, watching the bubbles clinging to the edge for dear life, then disappearing.

'I told Elena that I stole her scarf. That I tricked my way into the house. She forgave me.'

Jane looked pleased. 'Wonderful. That should build trust.'

She looked much less intimidating today. A last breath of hope.

'Maybe you won't do it. Maybe you'll stay quiet about the trial, even if I don't do what you say.'

Jane smiled as if they were just swapping small talk. 'I wouldn't want to test that hypothesis if I were you. If you won't help me, then I'll need to get you out. Elena will be disappointed that her experiment – hiring a plucky street kid – failed, and inevitably go to one of the agencies. Her top applicants will all be my people.'

'Then I could just leave! No harm no foul. Put your people in if that's what you want.'

She shook her head. 'No. No, I don't think so. Time is of the essence, dear. It would be much better to keep you in place. And I do have a vengeful streak, I'm afraid. If you won't cooperate, I'll turn you in. If you try and leave, I'll turn you in. Honestly, Ruth, did you really think an appeal to my better nature would help? Just shake hands and part as friends? No. That won't happen. I have you just where I want you.' She pushed her plate towards Ruth. 'Would you like some of this, it really is very good.'

Ruth started to stand up, but Jane grabbed hold of her arm.

'Sit down, you stupid girl and think. Do what I want and you can make of life whatever you will. Go against me and I *will* destroy you. It is that simple. I really can't believe you thought you'd get away with it. Now sit.'

She sat. Oh, if it had just been her own skin, she could have walked off now, maybe, but there was too much at stake. She found her voice turning wheedling, pathetic. She hated it and couldn't help it. 'Jane, if things get . . . what if Elena asks me to do things that are illegal, that are just wrong?'

'Oh, dear girl. You will do exactly what you are told.'

Bars on the windows. Guns at each end of the street.

Ruth inhaled and exhaled, one, two, three, four on each breath. It didn't help. She was held down, trapped under that decision she had made all those years ago. 'What do you want me to do?'

Jane pressed her hands together and beamed. 'Excellent. Now why were you at Milos's place?'

'Elena sent me to deliver jewellery to Suzanne D'Arcy.'

Jane sat back and raised her eyebrows. 'Really? How interesting. Expensive jewellery?'

'Yes, very,' Ruth said. The coffee machine fizzed and she jumped. Jane tilted her head on one side.

'How are your nerves, Ruth?'

'Fine, thank you, Jane. Who is Milos?'

She seemed to consider for a while before she decided to answer.

'Milos is, depending on who you ask, a respectable and modestly successful property developer from Serbia, or a former member of the All Stars – a group of jewel thieves.'

'Jewel thieves?'

'Yes. Lots of daring raids across Europe. Though the rumour is they've branched out into other specialist mercenary work. They are based in Paris for the most part, keep some of their low-ranking members there while the bosses come and go as they wish.'

'What sort of mercenary work?'

'You want details, do you? People who want to persuade their business partners to say, take a certain deal. Others who want their art collections stolen so they can claim on the insurance. Arson. Though they are said to be picky about who they work for, which is why we only have rumours.' Ruth looked down at the table. 'OK, Ruth. You'll tell me everything that has happened in the house since you arrived. And then we'll talk about next steps. Andrei dear, go out with Andrei. He was in Korčula. Get him to tell you who else was there.'

Ruth felt sulky. 'What? I just ask him, do I?'

'Build trust, but don't take too long about it. In the meantime I want to know what is going on in the house *now*, please. Who comes and goes. Do you know how to access the visitor logs?'

'Yes.'

'Excellent. Well done. Make a hard copy of them, please. And by that I mean write them down yourself, not just copy and paste and print. Their system will be able to tell if you've done that.'

Twenty minutes later Ruth left the café, the magazine under her arm. She felt she'd left a little of her soul behind.

18

Getting Andrei to ask her out to a club was too easy. He often came to the kitchen when he was in the house, chatting in Russian with Masha. He seemed far easier with her than he did with Elena. He was in the kitchen when she got back.

'Nice walk?' he said.

'Needed a break from the emails,' she said breezily and Masha sniffed in a way that almost sounded sympathetic. It only took a minute of chatting and asking the right questions to get an invitation to go out that night after dinner, if she wasn't needed. She wasn't.

Ruth returned to the endless inbox. Not much left. She opened messages automatically, trying to think how to get Andrei to say something that would get Jane Lucas off her back. Flattery. That worked, didn't it? She'd seen how it worked. Make big eyes, touch a man on his arm. Ask him to explain more to poor stupid airhead girl about how clever and important he was. But Ruth didn't have much practice at that. When she'd wanted to know what Michael's job was, she'd just asked. Not that she thought he'd told her the whole story, and he was too smart, too sharp-eyed to fall for the fluttering eyelashes act. Andrei though, as far as she should tell, went around in a bubble of his own self-pity and entitlement. What if he did tell her something terrible about how Elena and Yuri had made their money and what they did with it now? Ruth stopped opening emails and stared at the door.

Jane Lucas was supposed to be the authorities, the good guys. That was a sick joke. The authorities had been lying to Ruth since she was five years old. Of course you'll see your mum soon, we'll find you a safe place to stay. These people will look after you. Trust us.

Ruth wiped her eyes with the back of her hand. Too many bastards in the world. No wonder Megan had got into the habit of running when she had the chance. God, Ruth wanted to run now.

And in the house? Elena was funny and generous but Ruth was quite sure she was dangerous too. The rage in her eyes in the moment she saw the scarf. Michael? Michael 'trust me' Fitzsimmons? Smooth, charming when he wanted to be, but Ruth felt in her gut there was something off there too. Some false note that meant she wasn't going to tell him anything if she could avoid it. And that man killed in Paris while he was supposed to be getting perfume for his mother. Too many secrets, too many lies, too many dragons. She was trapped.

The club was behind an unremarkable door off Piccadilly. A square opening like a garage door with two bouncers and a velvet rope, and a long queue of young men and women, snaking back from the door down the street. They were talking, smoking, staring at their phones, ignoring the subtly spotlighted artwork in the windows behind them.

The car drew alongside the pavement and Andrei waited for the door to be opened for him. He got out then turned to offer Ruth his hand as she climbed out of the car.

'Bet they didn't have clubs like this in Middlesbrough,' Andrei said smugly.

Ruth replied with a half-smile. It was true that outside Haze the queues wound past shutters rusted in permanent closure rather than high-end boutiques, but other than that there wasn't much difference yet.

'Evening Mr Shilkov, evening miss,' one of the bouncers said, unhooking the velvet rope as he did. OK, long winter coats rather than bomber jackets on the bouncers. That was a change.

Andrei offered his arm and she took it, and they went into the empty garage area. A woman sat behind a high desk. Her hair was swept up like Audrey Hepburn's in *Breakfast at Tiffany's*, and she wore huge shades to match, but her lipstick was a fluorescent green.

'Andrei, lovely! Who is your plus one?'

'Ruth Miller. She works for Elena.'

Audrey lent over her desk and offered her hand to Ruth. They shook. 'Welcome to Bleeding Heart, darling Ruth. Such a pleasure.'

Given the dark glasses, Ruth couldn't tell if she was being looked through or past, or if she was under careful observation.

'Pleasure's mine, I hope,' she said. Audrey trilled with laughter, then waved them towards a staircase behind her.

'You're behind the rope, of course, dears.'

What rope? They were already behind the velvet one strung across the doorway.

Andrei nodded. He let go of Ruth's arm and began to descend the staircase, too narrow for them to walk down side by side. Ruth was pleased about that; she had felt like she was being led out into the set of *Strictly*, and this way she could hang on to the twisted balustrade.

Clumps of fairy lights bundled down the stairs and along the walls, old movie and stage posters lined the walls. She thought maybe this place would be more fun than Haze, maybe more like the place Michael had taken her to in Paris. The stairs turned at a sharp angle and suddenly they were emerging into a much bigger space. The music seemed to triple in volume. The floor, walls and ceiling were covered in a mosaic of mirror tiles, studded with gold and silver accents, and pearl-coloured pulsing bulbs.

It was packed and the ceilings were low and perspiring. A DJ in a booth, one headphone held to his ear. A bar of glass and steel with huge stands of white and blue flowers. An aquarium, or a film of one, across the back of the room. Coral, fishes, the occasional shark. At each end of the bar was a stuffed peacock wearing a top hat and above the split shelves of liquor behind the bar was a huge cartoon red heart with a dagger through it.

She paused on the bottom step trying to take it in. Andrei turned and took her wrist.

'This bit is just for the proles. Come on.'

Some proles, Ruth thought as she let herself be led through the crowd. Some were dancing, some were shouldering their way to the bar. It was hard in the crush to tell the difference. He led her to what seemed to be the back of the room, but the crush just got tighter. Jesus, it was a Thursday night. Didn't these people have jobs to go to?

'Ruth! Oh my God!'

She turned and lost Andrei's hand. It was the advertising account manager from Brockley who always seemed to have a cold. She looked bright-eyed tonight. A speck of white powder on her upper lip. She was holding a glass of melting ice and a pale fizzing drink. It had a straw and a peacock feather in it.

'Hey, Sandra.'

'What are you doing here? I mean I come here all the time, but I've never seen you here before.'

'Just with a friend,' she shouted back, trying to see where Andrei had gone. This was going to be a great report for Jane. Soz, I lost Andrei three minutes after getting to the club, but I'm pretty sure my old housemate is a cokehead.

'Is he going to peer at the celebs behind the rope?' Sandra had to lean so close to make herself heard over the assault of the music, Ruth could smell the sourness of her breath.

Then Andrei was back, looking annoyed.

'Come on, Ruth, or you'll get stuck out here with the wannabes.' Ruth let herself be dragged away. Sandra was watching them go, her mouth slightly open.

Another rope, sectioning off the crush from another part of the club. Another bouncer on each end of it. These greeted Andrei too, the rope was unhooked and Andrei put his hand on the small of Ruth's back to guide her through. Ruth was conscious of being watched; with envy and resentment by those on Sandra's side of the rope, and with lazy interest by those already here. Her celebrity spotting had never been much good, and if there were any really famous people here, she didn't recognise them. Standard beautiful people, but younger than the ones at the Restart party. A new soundscape. A waitress with glitter eye shadow and a plunging silver top greeted them and led them towards a booth just off the centre of the room. Andrei whispered something to her, and she returned while Ruth was still shuffling her way round the banquet with a bottle of champagne. The ice bucket was clear plastic. Of course, that way everyone else could see if you were drinking the good stuff. Anxiety of influence, Fear Of Missing Out. The table was very low, like a coffee table, and Ruth felt conscious of the cut of her dress as she leant forward to take her glass.

'I thought you were poor, Andrei.'

He shrugged. 'Oh, I have a tab *here*, like the tuck shop at school. It's ready cash they keep me short of. I'm twenty-nine years old, but they treat me like I'm still a teenager. Do you like it?'

She looked around again. The music was still too loud, but the lighting in this area was more forgiving, and though busy it was wasn't half as bad as the crush in the main bar. She noticed that the customers beyond the rope had two or three arches along the bar where they could look in.

'Are we the entertainment?'

'Or they are ours,' Andrei said. I'm through the looking glass, Ruth thought. The idea came lightly, then seemed to strike deep. She'd punched through to the other side, the world of Shilkovs and Sir Tobys, where paperwork was fast-tracked, where beautifully dressed men and women fell over themselves to be helpful, where banks who refused to issue cards, overdrafts, the benefit of the doubt to her as a kid getting by in Middlesbrough now came to see Yuri at home, obsequious as footmen in period dramas, offering helpful suggestions as to how he could wrap up his millions, the millions and billions of others, and keep them safe from the grasping hands of the undeserving not-rich-enough.

Make an effort Ruth. 'Thanks for taking me out. I haven't been anywhere like this before.'

He puffed out his chest. 'You have to have one of their pearl martinis before you go. They are absolute legend.'

'So what do you do for your father, Andrei?'

He sipped his champagne, looking past her into the shadows. 'Oh, I do a lot of client liaison. My dad doesn't like places like this, never has, but a lot of his clients do. So I show them a good time, until they've found their feet a bit.' His attention settled on her briefly. 'But of course, what I want to do is use my social connections to really get on the inside track of some larger projects of my own, and bring those opportunities to Dad. But Elena almost always finds a reason why he shouldn't invest.'

'You don't get involved in the work they're already doing? All the stuff Elena is seducing the Sir Tobys for?'

He became briefly animated. 'Most of them are just about stuffing through some really small banking regulations or loosening the paperwork around investments and things. Dad gets excited about it, but I'm more of a *vision* person. I want to see the broader landscape. Some of their stuff is interesting. Like Glenville Solutions, though I think we should be pushing to get our people on their board. Like me. So I'm interested in that one. And I was there when it started coming together in Korčula.'

He laughed as if he'd said something funny. Then lifted his hand.

'Peter!'

His plus one from the charity do in the church. He looked like a cruel version of Hugh Grant in the *Four Weddings* days, floppy haircut and high cheekbones, but a thuggish squareness to his jaw.

'Peter!' Andrei called again. His friend lifted his chin and slouched over. 'I'm taking Elena's new girl out. Want a drink?'

'Fuck off, I'm not drinking that shit tonight,' Peter said, flickering a scowl towards the champagne in the bucket. He signalled one of the hostesses. 'Get me a Royal Dragon, will you, and half a dozen glasses.'

Andrei looked unsettled. 'You celebrating?'

Ruth reckoned he had been for a while – there was something a bit loose about his movements. She picked up her champagne glass as his hand swept by it.

'I'm celebrating you, mate! Just had a text from Yuri asking me for dinner tomorrow. He and Elena want me to meet a few people.'

The hostess arrived and opened the bottle. Peter grabbed it from her before she could start to pour and waved her away without bothering to look up. Ruth looked at her. The flash of rage and contempt which flickered for an instant behind her smile. Andrei was frowning.

'You're coming to dinner? First I've heard of it.'

Peter shoved the shot glasses towards them. Ruth stared at the bottle. There were gold flakes floating in it.

'Thought you must have told them I'd been helping out.' Ruth looked at the bottle again. She'd read about this stuff. She couldn't drink it. The idea repulsed her.

'I did, but I didn't get the impression Elena was pleased about it.'

They both knocked back their shots, and Peter looked between her and her untouched glass. 'Have it, then.'

'It'll make me throw up.'

He took it and poured it down his own throat. One of the flecks of gold stuck to his lip, and he licked it away with a flick of his narrow tongue.

'You're wrong. Sunny days ahead.' He nodded towards the champagne. 'You back on the tab again?'

Andrei curled his lips. 'Yeah, you know. Expenses.'

'So did Elena say anything else?' Peter asked, almost casual.

He's frightened of Elena too, Ruth thought. He just hides it better than Andrei does. Andrei turned sulky. 'Nothing. I'm out of the loop. But you know . . .' Ruth felt rather than saw him nod in her direction, 'after the thing . . .'

Peter was pouring more shots for him and Andrei. 'We're golden, mate. Relax. Coincidence and my people are amazing. We're on the inside. Tomorrow we'll get to hear exactly what's going on and how we fit in.' Mate. She hated it when posh boys called each other 'mate'. Andrei still looked unsure. Peter clapped him on the shoulder. 'After what you did for them? Talk about commitment.'

Peter seemed to remember Ruth was still there. He looked at her, his head on one side, the bottle hovering over a clean glass. Classy.

'Sure you don't want one?'

In for a penny. 'Go on.'

Peter giggled. 'Aye oop, then.' He poured the shot and she took it and knocked it back while they watched. She felt the chill, petrol taste of it slither into her stomach. Now I'm fucked, she thought. I've eaten the fruits of fairy land and that never ends well.

19

Ruth learnt officially about the dinner party the next morning during her meeting with Elena. Ruth's ideas on the sorts of favours and gifts she could arrange for Elena to do had pleased her boss.

'You are thinking like a grown-up, Ruth. Very good.' She picked up a notepad from the table and scrawled down a list of names. 'These are your most important Sir Tobys now. The people I would like to put in my pocket. Find out what they need. Work out how I can get it for them.' She drew a box round the two names at the bottom. 'These men are just greedy. They want money, a chance to "invest" in mining rights in Russia and Ukraine, so talk to Yuri's people, but they also need just a little boost for their ego. A little thing to make them feel they are not really greasy pigs finding a place at the trough but grand and important.' She added stars to the other names. 'These men though – they *are* grand and important. A little vain, perhaps. Not as rich as they think they should be, but if you can find me something special for them, I would be very pleased. More diamond earrings pleased.'

She took the note. 'OK.'

'Do you have friends in London, Ruth?'

She almost missed the question.

'Haven't been here long enough to make many real friends. A few acquaintances. And the relationship managers keep asking me out for coffee and drinks. Why do you ask?'

She lay back on the sofa, her hands thrust into the pockets of her jeans. 'Go out tonight. We are having people for dinner, so the kitchen will be busy with caterers and all the flim-flam. Be gone by six, don't come back till ten.'

Ruth was confused. 'Shouldn't I brief you on the guests? Organise things? I thought I was your social secretary?'

She shrugged and stared over Ruth's head. 'I know all these people better than I know my own children. You organise big social, this is little. And private.'

'OK.' Ruth stood up. 'I'll get someone to buy me dinner.' She paused. 'Elena, can I ask you something?'

She had her phone out again and was tapping away. 'Sure.'

'Why do you ask people to pray for you?'

Elena put down the phone and lent back. 'Perhaps I know I am a terrible person who needs their prayers.'

Ruth frowned. 'I don't think it's that.'

She grinned broadly. 'OK. I will tell you the truth. God is an arse. His little miracles! If he was an honest accountant I would go to heaven in a Lamborghini. This money you send out – we have healed the sick, comforted the poor, educated the orphans and given succour to the weak. What has he done? Invented cancer!'

'So why do you ask people to pray to him for you then?'

'Because I shall go to hell. And fine. I shall go. Fuck him. But while I am here, I like the fact all these people are saying to him – oh God, Elena is so kind, Elena has helped me, Elena is a beautiful, beautiful saint. Oh God, please be nice to Elena.' She chuckled, a rich low sound low in her throat.

Ruth got it. 'You are irritating God.'

She nodded, making her blonde curls bounce. 'Yes. God and Jesus too. They have to listen to all those prayers. I like thinking of them trying not to show they are annoyed. Because they need the prayers like the Sir Tobys need the calls from Yuri's people.'

Ruth was going to ask something more, but Elena cut her off.

'Enough. Go.' Ruth got up and was heading towards the door. 'Ruth?' She turned round. 'I like the thank-you database. I shall read it before I go to sleep sometimes. Thank you.'

In the end Ruth called one of the relationship managers at the V&A and agreed to meet her at a drinks reception at the gallery. All day the feeling of pressure in the house seemed to increase.

An email came in from 'Jimmy'. 'What have you got?' Not much. She had a fistful of whispers, that was all. She knew that Peter and Andrei had got excited about tonight. She could tell Jane that. No. Better to wait as long as she could. Work out what was going on herself before she decided what to tell Jane. Elena had coloured her diary red, but Ruth could hear her through the office door, her voice sharp, talking to Masha in the kitchen, and when Ruth emerged to fetch a coffee just after lunch the cook's jaw was set in rigid lines. There was a seating plan on the table, the names written in Cyrillic, Elena's handwriting. Ruth saw it on her way to the machine. Guess who's coming to dinner? Peter Baxter for one. She put her cup under the spout, pressed the button, heard Masha's annoyed-under-her-breath grumbling even over the buzz of the machine. Who were these people that Elena knew better than her own children, and why did their coming make the house feel like thunder? The machine shuddered to a stop and Ruth walked quickly back to her office, scooped up her phone from the table top and stuck it in the top of her jeans. Then she returned to the kitchen, placing her cup next to the plan. A half-dozen names around a square. Masha looked up.

'Forgot the milk.'

Masha tutted. Ruth went to the fridge and fetched the heavy glass bottle from the door, took it back to the table. Masha had her back to her, chopping green herbs on the central island. Ruth pulled out her phone, studied it as if she'd just got a text, flicked on the camera and managed two, three snaps of the page.

'What are you doing?' Masha had turned round.

'Just checking on my arrangements for tonight,' Ruth replied. She put the phone back in her jeans. 'I'm going to the V&A. You need any help?'

'I have help. Get coffee on that paper, I shall put you in a pie for first course.'

Ruth poured the milk into her coffee. Carefully. She carried the bottle back to the fridge.

'Are they picky eaters?'

This normally sent Masha into a rant about the twitchy eating habits of the rich, though as far as Ruth could judge Elena and Yuri ate whatever was put in front of them with pleasure.

'They will eat what they are given.'

Ruth only nodded then carried her cup back to her office, leaving her door slightly open. She sat at her desk, picked up the phone and looked at the pictures she had just taken. All blurred. Shit. She looked at the door. Could she risk going out again? Maybe if she sent the pictures to Jane they'd be able to enhance them or something? She looked again at the photo. Didn't look likely.

She willed herself to stay in her seat. Listening. Masha would need to leave the kitchen at some point, wouldn't she? Ruth didn't dare trying to start work in case she missed something. She stared at her cooling coffee cup, counted the seconds under her breath.

The buzz of the service entrance door. Masha's footsteps then her voice.

'Yes, yes. Prepare in staff kitchen. Take flowers there. Hurry. Come with me.'

Ruth opened the door fully again, in time to see Masha showing in a pair of young women in green fleeces, almost invisible under high stems of foliage.

She had what, a minute maybe? She got out her phone and went to the kitchen. The paper was no longer on the table.

Ruth could hear Masha issuing sharp commands. She looked around the surfaces of the kitchen – the room had never seemed so large. There. On the soft seat under the window where Masha sat in the afternoons to go through her secret binders of recipes and lists. Ruth walked across and lifted the paper so the light fell clearly across it.

Footsteps. Another clear shot. One more. She looked up. Masha was right in front of her.

'Ruth?'

'I was on my way to the loo. Saw it on the floor.' She smiled brightly and held it out to Masha. 'Don't want the florists to march all over it.'

Masha took the page doubtfully. 'Thank you.'

Ruth shrugged, then headed to the lavender-and-lemon-scented toilet and sat on the seat. Heart thumping. Checked the phone. Yes, the names were clear this time.

She stood up ran the cold tap over her wrists, then retreated back to her office. This time she closed the door.

20

The reception at the V&A was beautifully done. A smooth and courteous security check. Champagne or elderflower presented as she passed through and her host, an extremely well-preserved woman named Gloria in her early fifties swooping down on her with a smile of welcome. Ruth had decided not to try her poor stock of London friends when she needed an excuse to be out this evening, instead making it a semi-professional night by accepting the chance to 'see how we do things at our more exclusive events'. They did things very well. They offered their sponsors the flowing champagne and caviar-based canapés as expected, but everything, from the glasses to the flower arrangements on the cocktail tables, was subtly themed around the designer the exhibition was to celebrate. The gift bag contained a booklet of free admissions, invitations to the gala dinner which would end the season, a limited-edition catalogue with 'Patron' embossed on the cover, and a limited-edition perfume. So you'd be able to smell the ultra-rich from across the room, if you knew the code. Ruth nodded and smiled her way through it, and found that in return for another ten thousand pounds Elena would be able to invite up to three guests to tour exhibitions like this with a curator, who would open the cases and let them handle the actual clothes being displayed. That could work on the wife of a Sir Toby, she thought.

She recognised one or two faces making small talk around the cabaret tables from the event in the church, and enjoyed the opera flash mob who appeared from the crowd to sing. Then doors to a second hall, a recreation of a New Orleans gambling saloon where the designer was supposed to have got their inspiration, were opened and the increasingly elevated guests were handed piles of gambling chips.

Ruth had to decide. Go in. Make friends. Place a bet. Or get out of here. Find a quiet bar where she could read a book until her anti-curfew of 10 p.m. She put down her glass and turned away, then felt a touch on her arm.

'Ruth? It is Ruth isn't it?'

A petite girl of her own age, huge blue eyes and masses of curled blonde hair. She made Ruth feel like a monster. She was familiar though. She heard a thumping beat in her ears and a clatter of applause.

'I'm Georgia! I met you at Bleeding Heart?'

'Georgia! Hi.' Ruth remembered her now, one of a crowd who took a round of shots from Peter as the evening ground on. She'd been wearing a shimmering mini-dress then, now she was wearing a knee-length skirt and a ruffled blouse. Reminded Ruth of one of Elena's 'and later I go fencing and pirating' outfits. 'I didn't expect to see anyone from Bleeding Heart here.'

Georgia shrugged. 'No. Not my thing. At all. But Mummy and Daddy were super keen I come and I dinged the BMW in a car park yesterday, so I'm being good daughter this evening. Mummy wants to introduce me to a surgeon. I hate surgeons. All psychos. Piss them off and they'd be all over you with a scalpel in your sleep. What are you doing here?'

'Checking out the hospitality for Elena.'

Georgia made a face. 'Urf. Elena scares me. Not that that takes much, delicate flower that I am. But she scares Dad and he grew up in south London, you know. Made his money in scrap and I've seen him make prime ministers shit themselves. Isn't it frightening, working for her?'

Ruth shook her head. 'She's been good to me. And it's an interesting way to make a living.'

Georgia said something under her breath. 'What was that?'

'Just a Russian proverb about life not being like walking through a field.'

'You speak Russian?'

Georgia shrugged again, looking around her. 'God, you and I are the only people here under a hundred. Yes. They offered it at GCSE and A-level at my school. So many Russian kids there already. Easy As for them and it impressed the hell out of my dad when I learnt it.'

Ruth decided to risk it.

'Can you read Cyrillic? Just I have this list of who Elena is wining and dining tonight, and I can't read it. Just want to make sure if there's anyone I should know something about.'

'Sure. As long as you promise to hang around for another half-hour and hit the tables with me.'

'Fair play.'

'You do say funny things. Show me then.'

Ruth took out her phone, found the best image and zoomed in.

Georgia scanned the list, her head tilted to one side, and moved around the image on the phone with an elegantly manicured finger.

'That's Yuri, that just says "me", so Elena I guess. Andrei is on the other side of the table, and that's funny – that's Peter Baxter! You know, Andrei's friend, from the club. Creepy shit. He dated my friend's sister once and was a moody, moody boy. Coked off his face half the time. Let's see, Noah Warrington, Milos, Marguerite . . .' She rattled off a couple of other names, both Sir Tobys. 'I wonder why Elena is having Peter to dinner. Are they doing an intervention? Andrei's been hitting the sauce pretty hard in the last few months. All very "woe is me" and tormented.'

Ruth bit her lip. 'Look, you won't say anything will you? It's supposed to be private and if I've just let the cat out of the bag . . .'

'Ha!' Georgia put her hand on Ruth's arm again. 'I once, having tea in the kitchen, said something about Andrei to my dad and he made me swear never to speak of the Shilkov business again. So I won't say anything. Now let's gamble.'

'I've never played roulette,' Ruth said, looking into the room beyond, the crowd slick with jewels.

'Oh, sweetie! I suppose you just had scratch cards and slot machines "oop north".'

'Dog racing too,' Ruth said dryly.

'Really!' Georgia linked her arm through hers. 'How glorious, you super girl. I just adore whippets. Come on, I'll show you how to lose a fortune at *vingt-et-un*.'

Ruth enjoyed herself for an hour at the tables. The money was play, and the prizes selections from the V&A gift shop, but Georgia's chatter and wide-eyed charm allowed Ruth to step out of herself, the clotted atmosphere of the house, her feelings about Michael, about Elena, Jane's threat and demands. The spike in her blood she felt as a dealer turned a card or span the wheel blotted them all out and she was simply alive and young in the world with a glass of champagne in one hand and a fistful of raffle tickets in the other.

Carefree. That's what Georgia was. Ruth had been born into a difficult home. Her mum had tried, but still her earliest memories were of casual, sudden violence. School was a place to keep your head down. Move quietly and have an eye on your exit routes. The group homes she'd been in all had dangerous spaces, and there were always spots on the way home where certain kids hung out which you approached warily and flew away from in relief. She'd liked the library, then her room at the Cunninghams, but there was always a lot of not-safe space in between until after the trial and college. Georgia, it seemed to Ruth, was the product of total security. She seemed confident that every comment she made would be received with warmth, that she would be welcome in any room she walked into. A life of fear was not just unknown to her, but somehow unimaginable. Ruth's phone buzzed. Michael.

Stay out. Will text you when coast is clear.

'Who was that?'

Ruth closed the screen, slipped the phone into her clutch. 'Michael, head of security.'

Georgia batted her eyelids. 'Oh, I've seen him around! Absolutely edible. Lucky girl, getting to work alongside him every day.' Ruth felt she was under close examination. She felt her slight smile begin to feel fixed and false. 'Oh well, don't tell, my sphinx of the north. Look, I'm going to ditch this place. I've done my daughterly duty. Do you fancy coming to the club? We can do shots and dance on the tables.'

Ruth nodded towards the roulette wheel. 'I've had all the excitement I can handle tonight.'

Georgia rolled her eyes, flashed a pearl white smile. 'Fair enooof, petal. See you at the next thing.'

Ruth went to retrieve her coat. As the check girl put it into her hands, she still couldn't quite believe she was allowed to put it on. The heaviness of the cloth, the slithering silk lining. How long did you have to live like this before it became ordinary? Longer than she had, it seemed.

She stepped out into the chill of the evening. Almost ten. She was knackered. Could she just ignore the text? Go home? She could take the back door into the kitchens, slip in unnoticed and curl up in the armchair in her room. Pretend to come back when Michael sent his 'coast clear' text. Fine. That *might* work. Michael. That wry smile. Another night with him could be a better way to get out of her own head than the roulette table.

She hailed a cab and got it to drop her at the end of the road. Nodded to the guards. Nodded to the just-back-from-Tenerife guy on duty at the front door, but headed round the side of the mansion. Keycode lock. She typed in the first three numbers. Then she wondered where in the house Michael would be. Would Tenerife tell Michael she had come back? Would the keycode send some notification to his phone? He might be angry she'd disobeyed him. She glanced at her phone again. Five minutes past ten, so she was obeying Elena's orders and no one else was allowed to tell her what to do. Oh sod it. Her feet hurt and these people where just driving her crazy. She punched in the last number and pushed open the gate. The path ran alongside the light well. She glanced down. The light was on in her room and someone was inside.

She stopped, then stepped out of her shoes and moved closer, looking down the steep angle and into the window, through the bars. Just the reading lamp lit, a patch of moving shadow. Then a figure moved into a small field of view. It was Michael. She felt sick. Maybe he was looking for her. No, you knock on a door and leave again if that's what you're doing. The softness in the air was turning into a gentle mizzle of rain. She could feel the damp chill of the walkway through her stocking feet. She stayed where she was. Breathing quietly. Watching.

Michael was holding something, staring at it, and as he came near the window she saw what it was. The photo she kept on her bedside table, a stupid shot of her, the Cunninghams, and Chris, their own son, crammed on the sofa one Christmas. They wore paper crowns and slightly dopey smiles. Michael was smiling, and as he did he stroked his thumb over the edge of Ruth's teenaged face.

Christ. He really does like me, Ruth thought. Like really – not just work friends with benefits or a fling, something much more than that. She felt a dizzy pleasure; a shot of adrenaline straight into the heart. Relief. Then a lurch as her evil voice, the voice of snark and bad news curled its lip and asked, 'So what the fuck is he doing searching your room?' Good point.

Michael's head turned sharply towards the door as if he'd heard something. Not her though, thank God. He disappeared from the corner of the room she could see and the light went out. What now? Ruth stepped back carefully into her shoes. She wanted to slip in unnoticed more than ever now. Think about what she had seen. There was nothing for Michael to find in her office or her room. Perhaps he'd sent her the message so he could go through her things. Perhaps it was something creepy, sexual, she thought, feeling the rain breaking over her skin. No. It didn't feel like that. Didn't feel good, but didn't feel like that. She could confront him. If he was pissed off at her for coming home before she'd got the all clear, she could be pissed off right back at him for going through her room. Air needed to be cleared. The atmosphere was so thick between them at the moment it felt as if she couldn't get oxygen into her lungs.

She straightened up and walked on slowly down the sloping path to the back of the house, her heels tapping quietly on the paving stones, then she turned the corner, ducking under the wrought iron and glass canopy which extended over the back path, then stopped.

On the terrace above, the doors to the sunroom burst open letting a tumble of light and sound into the back garden. Ruth stepped back instinctively into a patch of darkness between a decorative uplighter and the brick wall, and looked.

Elena, Yuri, Andrei, Milos and a tall spare man who cast a shadow like a spider were standing in the doorway, and just ahead of them on the terrace itself was Michael. He was pushing another man in front of him, his arm forced up his back. Peter Baxter. He was providing all the noise.

'For Christ's sake! Andrei, say something!' Michael kept him moving. 'It was a misunderstanding! I'm *sorry*, for God's sake!'

A car drew up from the garage as Michael forced Peter down the broad shallow steps from the terrace. Peter's faced passed from light to light on the steps; he looked drunk, angry, afraid. His tie half undone and his hair messed. A redness on his cheek and throat as if he'd been hit.

'Jesus! Let me go, you fucking arsehole. Andrei! You can't let them do this.'

The driver got out of the car and opened the back door. Michael bundled Peter into the back seat and closed the door on him. He said something to the driver, who stepped aside, and Michael got into the driver's seat himself. Ruth watched as Peter tried to open the door from the inside, then thumped his fists on the window, then twisted round to slap his palms on the privacy wall between him and Michael, then back to the window mouthing the same protests up at his hosts on the terrace. Ruth couldn't hear him any more, but she watched, forgetting to breathe herself; the panto-mime of rage and fear on his face in the half-light, the dull blows of his fists against the window. The car pulled quietly away. The Shilkovs and their guests watched it go, then turned back into the house.

21

Ruth stayed by the wall in the lightly falling rain, staring at the door onto the terrace as it closed. Didn't look like Peter's dinner had gone as he'd hoped. She remembered him licking the gold off his lips at the club with his narrow tongue and wondered what he had done to be carted off in disgrace. Turned up drunk and high perhaps, *fuck them if they can't get a grip.* Been crass. She could imagine him, over-confident and self-satisfied, saying something to piss Elena off, and she wouldn't look down her nose and try and ignore it. She'd slap him and throw him out of the house. That glint in the waitress's eye at the club. A moody boy. Time someone taught him a lesson. Ruth had been at plenty of parties where someone had needed to be wrestled out of the door. She didn't think it was that common a happening at dinner parties in houses like this though. But what did she know? She knew enough about Peter to have marked him down as a greasy little cokehead, so why had Elena invited him in the first place? She must have got his measure years ago. Then she saw Peter's face again. He had looked afraid. Not just angry and humiliated, but afraid.

Ruth stared at the raindrops beading the potted palms in the halos of the uplighter. Then her phone buzzed in her bag, startling her out of her funk. A text from Michael. *All clear*. He must have sent it from the car.

She pushed herself away from the wall and went in through the back door into the kitchen. It was immaculate, and the dishwasher sloshed quietly in the corner. The always-on LEDs sunk into the underside of the cupboards cast just enough light to allow the family to raid the fridge at night without risk of injury. They had the same ones in the staff kitchen. The weather was getting worse outside, handfuls of rain spattering against the windows. No sign of anyone else around.

She realised she was hungry. A girl can't live on canapés and champagne alone, fun though it was to try. There would be leftovers in the staff kitchen. She walked down the corridor, took a glass, ran filtered water into it and opened the fridge. Why had they had Peter to dinner? That spidery man in the doorway must be one of those other names on the list. Which one? She didn't know all the Sir Tobys' faces yet.

She remembered what Milos had said. *Tell Elena I need a name.* The usual cheese and meats, and plates of leftovers under wax eco-friendly versions of clingfilm. Elena and her household led a life of unashamed consumption, but they had their quirks. Strict recycling, glass bottles of filtered water, minimal plastic. Ruth took out a plate and lifted the covering. Salmon en croute, thick slices of it. The bowl next to it was full of tiny boiled potatoes flecked with pepper and shiny with truffle oil. I know what truffle oil smells like now, she thought. If they could see me now. She made up a plate and returned the remains to the fridge, then stepped out of her heels and ate at the counter, listening to the velvety silence, the subtle hum of the fridge. Tried to stop seeing Peter's face behind the passenger window.

Michael had been searching her room, Michael's face as he looked at her picture. Oh, what did it matter what he felt for her? He couldn't get rid of Jane Lucas for her. He was another tie, another complication, not a way out. No. People can be loving and affectionate one moment and gone the next. Like Megan. Like Mum.

The salmon was good, the potatoes earthy and light. She finished, put away the plate and started reading the copy of the *Evening Standard* that lay folded on the table by the settees. Lots more stuff on the Uprising. Four pages in the middle devoted to the latest findings. Someone had been combing the message boards for the earliest references, the growth of support for the

violent overthrow of the one per cent. The reporters had hauled
in a couple of psychologists to speculate wildly about the sort of
personality who might be behind the manifesto. Might be a
man, might be a woman. Might be the work of more than one
person, a forensic linguist said, as different paragraphs indicated different levels of education. Whoever they were, they
were angry. No shit. It was all online though. No pro or anti
marches in the street. But then that was what the manifesto said,
that the time for marches was past. It was time for action. Her
palm itched.

Still silence, just the hum of the machines. God, she'd experi-
enced the rage at first hand, but now it seemed she was insulated.
She glanced at her watch. Half eleven already. Bed.

'Ruth?'

It was Michael, hesitating in the corridor.

'Michael! Did you eat?' she said, then yawned and stood up.
'The salmon is good.'

He shook his head and started pulling off his tie. 'Not hungry.'

'You've got to eat, pet.'

He came in and sat on one of the stools at the other side of
the kitchen island. She fetched him a glass of water, put salmon
and potatoes on a plate, pulled a fork from the drawer, pushed
it all over to him. He had been staring at the sky-at-night
patterns of the granite island top, and when the plate entered
his field of vision he looked surprised, glanced up at her and
nodded, then picked up the fork and started to eat without
further comment. She watched him. He looked knackered.
Knackered and miserable. She wanted to ask where he had
taken Peter.

She refilled her own water glass.

'So how was it? Elena's dinner.'

He swallowed, cut a potato in two with his fork and poked at
it.

'I wasn't there. Closed doors, only Masha actually serving food.
But Andrei's friend, Peter, got into a fight somehow and I was
summoned to throw him out.'

'A fight? With Andrei?' Ruth sipped. Michael ate, finished chewing and swallowing before he replied, his lips shiny with truffle oil.

'I don't know. When I arrived he was slumped in his chair looking like he'd gone a couple of rounds with someone. No one else had a mark on them. He started shouting when he realised I was there to throw him out.'

Ruth watched him eat. He'd begun destroying the food now like he'd just run a marathon. 'How does that work? Do they have a panic button or something?'

'There's an app. Alert to my phone and radio if I'm wearing it. Have you met Peter?'

'Yeah. Couple of times. He was at the club last night. I thought he was a douche. Was he pissed?'

His jaw tightened when she mentioned the club, but somehow the plate of food had disappeared. She watched him scrape the last of the pastry flakes onto his fork and eat them. Remembered the croissant in bed in Paris.

'Yes, off his face I think, though the rest of them, Andrei included, looked pretty sober.'

It sounded true. Perhaps it was the tiredness in his voice that gave it the ring of truth. 'Why did you go to the club with Andrei?'

Ruth sipped her water. 'Just *curious*. But I didn't like it much. Preferred the places you took me in Paris.'

They smiled at each other, and Ruth felt it in her blood.

'Hope Peter didn't give you any trouble,' she said.

He broke eye contact. 'Nothing I couldn't handle. I drove him to Ladbroke Grove Tube, let him out there.'

'Not all the way home?'

He stared down at the empty plate for a long moment. 'Just obeying my instructions. The main thing was to get him out of the house.' He pulled himself together. 'What about you? Pleasant evening?'

'Delightful. A very sweet girl thought my accent was totally *smashing* and asked if I thought a million was enough to buy a decent little flat in Shoreditch or if she should hold out for more.

It's part of her leaving-home package, apparently. I told her my leaving-home package was sixty quid and a leaflet showing where the Jobcentre was, which she thought was *killingly* funny.'

Michael smiled into his water glass.

'Why don't they ever question it?' Ruth put her glass down on the top, moved it back and forth tracking the moisture across the black and silver streaks. 'I mean, she's not stupid. She must know that other people exist, don't have what she has just by being born. But she just accepts it. This is the way the world is and it turns out to be hers. Everyone else is just furniture.'

Michael rinsed his plate and put it into the machine. Well-brought-up young man.

'You joining the Uprising?'

She held up her hand so he could see the scar. 'Not my favourite people.'

He nodded. 'It's the divine right of the posh.' There was something rough in his voice. Like a bubble of a former life, a harder life, had broken into his speech and burst. 'Could you ever work for someone like her?'

Somehow he had come up close to her now, placed his hands on her hips. She put her hand round the back of his neck, her fingers brushing the short hairs on the back of his collar.

'I don't know. Probably not. I respect Elena. She came up hard and whatever she's got, however she got it, it wasn't handed to her.'

He lent in and kissed her, long and slow, and she yielded to it, felt the twitch of desire in her gut.

'Be careful, Ruth.'

She stepped away. 'You are king of the cryptic warning, aren't you, Michael? Can you tell me what I should be careful of exactly?'

'Can't you just trust me?'

There it was. He had stayed where she left him, his arms out, empty palms facing towards her, a gesture of appeal. He still looked tired, worried. It was rich considering she had seen him going through her room. She bent down and picked up her heels, dangling them from the fingers of her left hand, and put her hand to his cheek. The rough late-evening stubble. She spoke softly, kindly.

'No, of course I bloody can't. Trust has to be earnt. You don't just get to ask for it.'

Then she walked past him and back to her own room.

22

Ruth was at her desk the next morning at seven, but her first coffee had hardly gone cold before Masha knocked at her door and pushed it open.

'Ruth! Elena wants us now! Library.'

Masha watched Ruth as she got up and picked up her iPad. 'I had some of the salmon when I got in last night, Masha,' she said as she came round the desk. 'It was delicious.'

Masha took off her apron and hung it up next to the fridge as she passed.

'Yes. But it is boring to make. Rich English only eat salmon and chicken. The lords and ladies like pigeon. Pigeon is more fun.'

Masha's hair was styled into smooth curls, her lipstick red. 'Do you have children, Masha?'

'Two. Boys. In Russia.'

The beginning and end of small talk. Masha knocked on the library door and waited until they heard Elena's voice summoning them in. But she was not alone. She was sitting next to Yuri on the sofa. Andrei, his face crumpled like damp sheets out of the machine, was sitting in an armchair by the fire. Michael stood slightly behind him. And on the chesterfield opposite Yuri and Elena were two other men.

The older one had grey in his hair, but a wiry build and a bland suit and tie, like an executive chewing his pen in a stock photo. No – his eyes were harder than that, Ruth thought as he glanced at her. The other was younger, similar suit, similar tie and a notebook. Short hair and clean shaven. Police. She felt her stomach lurch.

Jane Lucas had worked out Ruth was holding out on her and turned her in after all. It was over. She should have stayed where she belonged, where she knew the territory, in Middlesbrough, listened to her friends. And now the world was falling apart. She heard the sound of shattering glass again. Was she shaking? Just say nothing. You know nothing, so say nothing.

'Sit down,' Yuri said, and Masha and Ruth took their places on the leather sofa opposite their employers. Edge of the sofa. Knees together.

The older stranger cast his eye over them without much apparent interest. Maybe they weren't here for Ruth after all. 'My name is Detective Inspector Brooks, and this is my colleague DS Matthews. You are Masha Polikova and Ruth Miller?'

They admitted to that. If they were here for Ruth, why was Masha important? A sudden, painful moment of hope.

DI Brooks wet his lips. 'I have some rather distressing news, I'm afraid. I've informed Mr and Mrs Shilkov, and of course Andrei here and Mr . . . err Fitzsimmons, but I understand you were both acquainted with the gentleman, so we thought we should tell you too.' He paused. This wasn't about her. OK. But what was it? He ran his hand through his hair. 'I'm very sorry to tell you that Mr Peter Baxter was found dead early this morning by the train tracks where they pass between the Westway and Bartle Road.'

Andrei, say something! Ruth blinked away the image of him beating his palms against the car window. She was going to be sick.

'Dead?' she said. 'Did you say *dead*?'

Brooks nodded again. 'I'm afraid so, Miss Miller.'

'Peter's *dead*?' Ruth said. Her brain felt slow and thick. 'What happened, how did he die?'

Brooks wrote something down. 'You knew him well, Miss Miller?'

'I met him at a club the other night with Andrei.' This couldn't be true. Ruth looked around at the others – Elena, Yuri, Andrei – but none of them looked back. 'Are you sure it's him?'

It's not him. They sent him home because he was pissed. That was all. Elena and Yuri were both watching the policemen, their faces suitably grave. Andrei stared at his hands, clasped white in his lap.

'There is no doubt about the identification,' Brooks said, glancing back up at her again. 'I understand he was a guest here last night, and was asked to leave sometime around 10 p.m. We are just trying to establish a timeline.' A tight smile. 'Ms Polikova, you were in charge of the catering last night, I understand?'

Masha looked down her nose at him slightly. 'I cooked with the hired people. I carried. I finished serving at nine. Left the guests with their coffees and brandies and those funny little chocolates. I dismissed staff. Michael logged them out. I cleared up and went to bed at ten. No one said anything to me about him. But he was drunk during the meal. Dropped his fork. Sauce on table cloth. But he was always a careless boy. May I go now, Mr Policeman? I have to make lunch.'

Ruth looked sideways at her perfectly calm, perfectly made up face. No sign of shock or distress. But Masha had been here for years, Peter was Andrei's best friend. Shouldn't she be trying to comfort Andrei? Ruth had seen the way they were together, chattering in Russian, affectionate, warm, but now Masha wasn't even looking at him. Was that having strong bones? Ruth could feel shock and distress closing her throat. She had hardly known Peter and didn't like what she had seen, but the fact that he, that face, his body, even his noxious personality had just been wiped out, dead at what, twenty-nine, was obscene. *It was a misunderstanding! I'm* sorry, *for God's sake!*

Brooks made a note, his brows flexing and unflexing. 'Certainly.'

Masha got up, turned round, making her skirts flare, and walked out of the library, closing the door behind her.

'Was it an accident? You said he was on the train tracks.'

Brooks turned his attention to Ruth. 'We don't know that yet, Miss Miller, and he was found on waste ground *by* the train tracks, but a train can strike a body and throw it some distance, I'm afraid. Did you see him last night?'

Her mouth went dry. What should she say? Be a clam? But the door codes probably logged her in and out. Ben on the door had seen her. The taxi had most likely logged her arrival time at the end of the street.

'I was out most of the evening at an event at the V&A,' she replied.

'That wasn't what I asked, Miss Miller.'

He was looking past her again. Was it the fact she was a girl that made her invisible? Or the accent? Or the fact she had shown some actual human feeling. 'I know and I prefer Ms Miller or Ruth, thanks.'

He waited. Time's up. What had the Shilkovs said? Whatever it was, Masha's story had fitted, and Brooks himself had said Peter was asked to leave.

'Yes, I did see him. Very briefly.' Elena looked up at her curiously, Michael stared at her. 'I saw Michael putting him into a car and driving off, a few minutes after ten. Peter looked pissed. He was shouting, but I couldn't quite hear what. Michael seemed to have him under control.'

'And what did you think about that?'

She wanted to ask why he cared what she thought of a sudden, but doubted that would help. 'I thought how embarrassed I'd be to get as pissed as that at a posh dinner.'

'And then?'

'I went into the house, had something to eat from the staff kitchen. Michael came in, and I got him some food too. We chatted, then I went to bed.'

'What time was that? When Mr Fitzsimmons returned to the house?'

'About half eleven. I was just thinking of heading to bed but stayed up a bit longer. Michael said Peter had been drunk and needed taking to the Tube.'

Brooks nodded, slowly. 'But you couldn't hear anything that Peter was saying as he was bundled into the car?'

Ruth pressed her knees together. 'You make it sound like Michael shoved him in the boot. He just put him in the back seat. I think Peter might have been shouting for Andrei.'

'And did Andrei respond?'

'I didn't see anyone else,' she said quickly. 'Just Michael driving Peter off. Was it an accident? Was he mugged? He wears— he wore a Rolex.'

Brooks grunted over his notebook. 'That's unclear at the moment, *Ms* Miller. But he left his watch at home, and he was still wearing his signet ring.'

'Could have been suicide,' the DS on the sofa chimed in. His voice was more cockney than his boss's. 'We shouldn't have been able to identify him yet, but his prints were in the system from an old drugs possession charge.'

Andrei let out a sort of gulping groan and everyone turned to look at him instead. Ruth noticed he had a glass on the table next to him already.

'Peter and my stepson were friends a long time,' Elena said gently. 'Has his family been informed?'

The DS looked at his notebook. 'Yes. His sister has identified his personal effects.' Ruth remembered how the signet ring on his little finger had caught the light in the club. 'Do you know the family, Ms Shilkov?'

She shook her head. 'I may have met them. School event perhaps. Years ago. You have your timeline. Are we done now?'

'Not quite,' Brooks said. 'Why did you invite him for dinner?'

Elena was about to speak, but Yuri put a hand on her thigh. 'My wife and I wanted to talk to him about his future. My wife was not convinced of his talents, but he had emailed me several times. I thought, perhaps I could help him. But he arrived drunk, drank more. Gentlemen, we should listen to our wives.'

They nodded, a sudden little club of married men admiring the intuition of the ladies. Lovely. The policemen got to their feet.

'Thank you, sir. If we have any further questions, if we need to speak to your other guests, we will be in touch.'

Yuri stood up too and reached out to shake their hands. 'If you wish to speak to us again, please contact my lawyers. Verniers Lee, Old Bailey. Ruth, my dear, would you be so kind as to see these gentlemen out?'

Ruth led them through the hall and opened the front door for them. The DS handed her his card. 'If you think of anything else Ruth, give us a bell.'

She looked at the card. Kensington Police Station. 'Will do.' Then she ushered them out onto the street and paused on the threshold long enough to see them stop on the pavement and look up at the mansion, the gardens, the guards. She shut the door.

The door to the dining room was open and she paused, looked in. The cleaning fairies had done their dawn work already of course. It looked exactly as it had the first day she had seen it. Pristine, not even the scent of liquor or food or blood in the air.

Ruth retreated to her office and found Michael waiting for her. No. Not now. He stood up as soon as she came in, as if he was her employee waiting to be bollocked by the boss. She shut the door.

'Did you kill him, Michael?'

'Of course I didn't.'

'*Of course I didn't*,' she repeated, mimicking his round vowels, the high-stepping plosives. 'Why "of course"? You're ex-military. You work security. You are trained to use violence when you're ordered to, aren't you? And we work for people who came up in Russia when it was kill or be killed. I don't know why you're acting like I just asked the bishop if he was taking bets on the two forty-five at Doncaster.'

He breathed deeply, like he was trying to control himself. She looked at his hands, thought of him killing Peter with them, then eating the supper she laid out in the staff kitchen, placing those long fingers on her hips for that kiss goodnight. She couldn't tell if it was fear or disgust that was making her heart hammer so hard.

'I drove him to Ladbroke Grove. I unlocked the doors. He got out and started swearing at me. I drove off. I had nothing to do with his death,' he said. 'You have to believe me, Ruth.'

Oh well, that's all right then. As he's asking nicely.

'You took him somewhere, against his will, and now he is dead. Tell yourself whatever you like, Michael.'

'For Christ's sake, you know I was here. I didn't have time.'

She didn't sit down, just started arranging the files on her table to occupy herself. Tapping papers into piles with no real idea of what she was doing. But focusing on the edges of the paper, the crisp printouts of misery and gratitude, made her feel better and gave her a reason not to look at him.

'How long does it take to kill someone? Give me a break! You could have killed him, stopped off at Greggs for a pasty and still have got back here by half eleven.'

'He was pissed. It was probably an accident. People like the Shilkovs don't care enough about people like Peter to kill him.'

It sounded true. Peter was nothing. Those people who had died in the dossier Jane had sent her were all important, rich, had deep dealings with the wrong people. Maybe he was right. Oh, please God let that be true.

'You really think so?'

He took a step forward, put his hands on the desk.

'Ruth, just leave. If you think that you're living with a pack of murderers, then just get out, for fuck's sake.'

Oh, for crying out loud. Not the answer she was looking for.

'I can't.'

'So tell me what you know! Paris, that attaché case. What are you and Elena cooking up?'

She felt the tears hot behind her eyes and slammed down the files hard enough on the desk to make him recoil.

'Why don't *you* leave? Why don't you tell me what happened to James Tranter?'

He took hold of her arm. 'How the hell do you know that name?'

Trust to anger. Let it speak for her.

'I saw you watching the report of his murder on the French news at the Ritz, so I looked him up on the computer when I got home. He's in the logs from before the attack. James Tranter, henceforth JT.'

Probably. Would he buy it?

They stared at each other. Ruth saw the appeal in his eyes. She wanted to believe he was a good man, but then she saw again the expression on his face when he got the message in Paris, the determination as he manoeuvred Peter into the car. She remembered the character witnesses at the trial who paraded into the witness box talking about the men she knew to be monsters. A family man, so good to his neighbours, loves his wife and children. You could order a meal in France, treat a woman well in bed and still be a killer.

Jekyll and Hyde isn't a fairy story. It's every fucking day.

'I have to get on with this, Michael.'

He nodded, turned on his heel and left. A new message pinged up Ruth's screen.

'Meet at twelve today. In my room. New project.'

23

Ruth had never even been upstairs in the house before. Nearly three weeks and she'd never got higher than the ground floor. Only when she put her foot on the first stair did she realise this was bizarre. Her world was the library, the kitchen, the office and the staff area. She felt as if she was trespassing by climbing the wide staircase. The stairs were marble with a black carpet running down the centre. On the first-floor landing, the floors were stripped wood with a huge Turkish rug in the middle. Bit like the one in Madeleine's showroom.

The paintings were different up here. Instead of the modern showpieces downstairs, the landing was decorated with religious art. Icons done in smoky colours of saints and Bible scenes, heavy with gold leaf. She could almost smell the incense coming off them. She turned round. On the half-landing by the window facing the street was a large painting done in an impressionistic style of a landscape, thickly green. An onion-domed church with two small priests in black walking towards it. It looked like it was there as a transition between the relentless Western modernism of the ground floor and the ancient Russian feel of the first. She knocked at the door at the back of the landing, heard Elena's call: *vkhodi*. She knew that meant 'come in' now. Her third Russian word. The first was cheers, the second *khorosho* which meant good, fine. Elena said it when she was done with one topic and wanted to move on to another. Now she had number three down. Then she had her three words of Serbian: *pošalji joj ime* – send her the name. And Milos had wanted a name too. Is that why he had come to dinner?

The door opened into Elena's private study. It looked big enough to be a luxurious listing for any estate agent all by itself. For some reason Ruth was expecting it to be decorated in all white, but the main colour turned out to be a deep green. The wallpaper looked like silk and was patterned with silver birds in flight, and twisting foliage. The furniture looked antique, sort of Edwardian. No religious pictures on the wall. Elena had an actual desk here, facing the window, which looked out over the rear gardens. Between it and the door Ruth had just come in through were a pair of sofas in green leather facing each other.

Elena was at the desk. She twisted round to watch Ruth looking.

'Nice?'

'Lovely,' Ruth replied. 'I wouldn't work anywhere else if I had this.'

Elena got up from her desk, tapped a message into her phone and crossed the room to throw herself onto one of the sofas.

'It is useful to work in the library. There I am near Yuri when he is home. But here is where I am during much red time.'

Ruth sat down. Elena was still watching her carefully.

'You want to ask about last night. Ask.'

Ruth put her papers on the table. 'OK. What happened?'

Elena yawned. 'Peter got drunk. He was stupid. We told him to leave. He didn't want to. Arsehole. Michael took him to Tube station. He tried to take a shortcut across the train tracks and got knocked down.' She twisted slightly in her seat to look out of the window. 'I am sad for his parents. But I was always sad for his parents. They are small people with a greedy arsehole for a son. At least he cannot stir any more shit for them with his drugs and stupid.'

Brutal. 'Small people? You mean not as wealthy as you?'

She snorted. 'No. Small. People who do ordinary things. Things in front of them. They are like sheep. Like my Natasha says *sheeple*.' Elena caught Ruth's frown. 'Pah! I know everyone is very special. I like sheep. Very cute. I still eat mutton.'

She should let it lie, but she couldn't. 'A lot of those sheep pray for you.'

Elena's face twisted with surprise. 'Nonsense! *They* are not sheeple. They thought, I need help. I shall find help. They found rich Russian who likes being prayed for. That is not sheeple behaviour. Enough. This is boring and we have work.'

'No, Elena. Not yet.'

Elena raised her eyebrows. Ruth ploughed on. 'How do you know Peter's death was an accident? The police couldn't say so this morning.'

Elena tapped something on her phone again and the message alert pinged on Ruth's.

'Read that.'

Ruth looked. Elena had forwarded her an email from the Shilkovs' law firm. In dry terms it stated that the police had been able to establish that Peter had stumbled onto the railway tracks between eleven and midnight and been hit by a passing train. The body had been clipped again by another train before it was spotted and the authorities alerted in the early hours. The police had already informed the coroner that they believed the death was due to misadventure.

'That was quick work,' Ruth said.

'It was an easy case,' Elena replied. She thrust her hands into her jeans pockets, leaving her phone, screen down, on the table.

'How is Andrei?'

The faintest flicker of disgust crossed Elena's face. 'He is very, very sad. But it gives him an excuse to drink in the daytime, so some little bit of him is happy.'

Ruth could feel the irritation in Elena beginning to build. The window for asking questions was closing.

'I met Peter,' she said. 'Why did you invite him for dinner?'

The irritation was replaced with the glimmer of a smile. 'You heard Yuri tell the policeman. He was a loser. Loser even when he was a little boy and he and Andrei would watch me by the pool. Nasty little boys. But Yuri loves his son, and we must help family. Andrei wanted us to introduce arsehole Peter to important people. We say OK. Bad idea.'

It sounded plausible. Reasonable. The Shilkovs had tried to do arsehole Peter a favour, and he'd screwed it up, made a fool of himself and then in his humiliation and drunkenness wandered in front of a train. Case closed. Kinda.

Ruth opened her notebook. 'I've got some ideas of things for your Sir Tobys. Judging from social media and profiles of them, the less important ones I think would react very well to these sorts of gifts and invitations.'

Elena took the list from her and scanned down it. Royal Box at Goodwood, Centre Court tickets, invitations to opening nights and aftershow parties. Some presents, lightly disguised as influencer offers of jewellery, clothes.

Elena nodded. 'Do I have to go to all this shit?'

Ruth shook her head. 'I don't think so. Unless you want to. The tickets arriving by courier in a nice gift basket will do it.'

'Fine good. Do all this. Now what of my real Sir Tobys? My big fish.'

Ruth drew in her breath. 'This gentleman,' she wrote down a name and pushed it across the table to Elena, 'has a Degas painting in his collection. He would be willing, for a generous arrangement with Yuri's people, to sell it to your Sir Toby at well under the market rate, and to make it clear he is doing so as a favour to you.'

Elena laughed to herself. 'This, Ruth. This is very clever. You are already half me. It was a shame you were not born in Russia, I think you would have been a great success.'

Ruth felt a prickling of her skin. She was proud. She had thought the plan too complicated, too expensive for Elena. But she had managed to do what Elena wanted: find the unfindable edge of leverage, of avarice in the smooth walls of Sir Toby.

Elena flicked the paper with her finger. 'And if it goes tits up, we can tell everyone we arranged the deal and that will be very embarrassing for Sir Toby. You bring me sticks and carrots. Good. What about him?' She pointed to another name on the list. Bakewell.

'Do you really need him? I've been through the files. He's politely declined every invitation. His campaign returned the money Yuri's company contributed at the last election.'

Elena's upper lip twitched. 'No mistress and his kids too young to be cokeheads. It would be nice if he kept his mouth shut, but fine. We can do without him.'

No mistress and his kids too young to be cokeheads, so when gifts didn't work, she must be ready to blackmail. Ruth's head felt oddly weak. Why should this be a surprise? All fun and games until someone loses an eye. Peter in front of a train. Private detectives – more of their people – going through the bins of the MP who kept refusing Elena's hospitality.

'OK. Now the new project. You remember the man from the Restart party?' Elena asked.

'What, Townsend?'

'Pfft! That loser. No. The other one.'

'The man with the Kellinghall Foundation report. Tuchman. Yes. What about him?'

'Clever funny brain! We are organising a little party for his report.' She began writing again. More names. She touched her phone alive and scrolled back and forth on the screen, adding more. 'And the Sir Tobys too. They are invited. Make sure they know if they like their presents they can show it by coming. A day symposium. Big dinner afterwards. At the Dorchester. We call it 'Growing Security Together'. One of Yuri's people will contact you about all the printing and banners and shit. Michael will do passes. Invite Bakewell too, why not.' Elena went through her papers and pulled up another sheet. The handwriting on it wasn't hers. Yuri's, but not in Cyrillic thank God. 'These are the speakers and the titles of their speeches. At the end of the day a highend dinner, and this man,' she circled a name, 'he speaks after dinner.'

Ruth took the pages. She was going to have to step up her game. Paying for opera tickets and haunting social media to find some businessman's art kinks was one thing. Organising something like this was different.

'And when do you want this to happen?'

'Today is 22nd. Make it happen week on Tuesday.'

Ruth blinked. 'You're kidding. The Dorchester will be booked, half these people probably won't be free. Why does it have to happen so fast?'

Elena smiled, but it was a dark smile. 'For me, they will be free. Speaker's fee is ten grand for the talks. For the after-dinner man, pay whatever they want. Journalists, professors, think-tank people go to all the sessions. Pay whatever needs to be paid. High end. Give the Dorchester the card. And it is not happening fast. It just looks like it is.'

'But why?'

'None of your business,' she replied cheerfully. 'Very useful English phrase. But think of cats. They creep very quietly. Then they pounce. I am pouncing on the Dorchester.'

Impossible. 'But Elena, this is going to cost a fucking fortune. We'll have to compensate the people who had the rooms booked.'

She rolled her eyes. 'Show me your credit card.'

Ruth frowned, but Elena just waited, so she slid it out of her phone case and set it on the coffee table in front of her boss. A little black rectangle with Ruth Miller and a long number printed in silver. Elena lent forward and tapped it with her fingernail.

'You walk into Boeing, put it on the table and say I'd like a 737, please Mr Boeing. They will ask you if you want a bow tied round it. Go to Tiffany. Let them sniff this card and they will throw out all the duchesses and lawyers buying keyrings and shut the whole shop for you.'

Ruth stared at it.

'I used it to buy a blueberry muffin on the way to Paris.'

Elena laughed. 'I know! You did not even go to the first class lounge where they give you that shit for free!'

Ruth picked it up again, carefully, and put it back in her phone case.

'Use it, Ruth. It is not a card, it is a sword. Use it like you mean it. Commit. Anything else? You have, I think, lots to do now.'

Understatement.

'Why did you pay for the jewels in cash? When you have a card like this?'

Elena threw herself backwards on the sofa.

'Cash is quiet. Also Madeleine is very proud. Paying her in cash makes her feel a little dirty. A little tainted by oligarch sleaze.' She said the word sleaze with relish. 'But she will not say no to so much money. And she wanted to make the piece. She knows it will irritate Harry Winston's designers.'

Ruth got up, looking at the pages, and made a bit unsteadily for the door. Elena made a hissing noise and called her back. She was staring at her phone.

'I have to meet someone here tomorrow morning. Quietly. And the girls are at home from this evening. Take them to Tower of London, please. I promised they could go.'

Ruth hesitated, Elena's voice grew sharp. 'What? You have plans?'

'No, I just thought the girls would be disappointed not to go with you.'

Elena waved her hand and the weather changed. She swung round to throw herself lengthways on the sofa, crossing her ankles. 'I am boring mother. You are cool girl who threw away the grenade. They will be very happy.'

24

The hotel manager did sort of freeze when she handed him the card that afternoon. Then he called in a dedicated relationship manager called Philip, who looked a bit as if he was going to throw up when she named the date, but didn't. What a pro. Of course the people who had booked the rooms would be compensated.

Then they got to work. It took most of the afternoon and Ruth's brain ached with thinking for herself. Whatever it takes. Use it like you mean it. High end. Rooms for the arrivals, rooms for the sessions, rooms for people to have tea and coffee in between. Crush Hall, the Gold and Silver Rooms, the Ballroom of course and yes, the Orangery. No, not some sad table with rows of cups and weak coffee out of a flask. Waiter service, savouries on the tables. Good barista-made espressos and lattes. Lunch would be table service again, à la carte. Yes, they could use the Bistro menu. Yes, the Shilkovs would cover wastage to ensure speedy service. Dinner would be four courses, vegetarian and vegan choices available all day.

The two men made notes with fountain pens in branded note-books. After two hours, the manager asked for a minute and after rattling away at his phone's calculator for a while wrote down the final figure and underlined it.

'Ball park, of course. I'll email you the breakdown and final figure once I've been through all this in more detail.'

Ruth glanced at it. How many streets round her first care home would that buy?

'That's fine.' She handed them the credit card and it was treated with proper reverence.

When she got back to Kensington she emailed all the speakers first, mentioning the fees and the first-class travel. The acceptances started arriving in her inbox before she got to the end of the list. At seven Michael came in, all efficiency.

'Yuri has told me. Have you got the lists?'

She hit the print button and the machine purred to life. He went and stood over it, plucking out each warm page and scanning it.

'When I saw the report about James Tranter on the news, I was just surprised, Ruth. I recognised his name too.'

'OK.'

'You've seen the report on Peter's death?'

'Yes.'

He hesitated for a second as if he was going to say something more, but didn't.

She got to bed at midnight.

Katerina and Natasha were waiting in the library with their mother when Ruth came in the next morning. Both girls were slightly overdressed for a visit to the Tower in the way tween girls can be. Katerina, the younger of the two at eleven, was in thick purple tights, ankle boots and a dark-green denim pinafore dress. Natasha, thirteen, was in cords and stripy shirt with a long gold chain round her neck. Hair long and straight, swept over their shoulders and held back with Alice bands.

Elena glanced up from her phone.

'Girls, you remember Ruth? She is taking you to the Tower. Say thank you again.'

Katerina said it brightly, grinning, head on one side. Natasha more softly.

'Oh, the grenade girl!' Ruth was startled by the new voice. A woman in an ivory business suit was sitting at the piano. 'That's what Katerina calls you, isn't it? How exciting to meet a real-life heroine.'

'You are not meeting her, Marguerite. She is going out.'

Marguerite. One of the guests at Peter's last dinner party was called Marguerite. It had to be this woman. She stood up and walked behind the sofa where Elena was sitting, lent her elbows on the back. She was roughly Elena's age, perhaps a little older. 'Yes, I know. We have to plan for next week. Still a bit of a thrill. What *were* you thinking?'

'That I was doing something very stupid,' Ruth answered and Marguerite laughed. It sounded genuine. 'Are you coming to the conference? I don't think I saw a Marguerite on the guest list.'

'I'm not coming, sweetie. Just tactical support.'

'Go away, Ruth,' Elena waved them out. 'Michael and Sam go with you.'

Ruth already had her jacket on. 'Cool.'

'Oh and give them lunch somewhere. They eat anything. If they are bad feed them out of bins.'

Katerina giggled and Natasha plucked at a loose thread on her top.

'Great,' Ruth said. 'I know a bin where you can get decent cold pizza if you're OK with fighting the rats off.'

The girls stared into her face, checking to see if she was serious. Ruth gave them the hard stare for one, two seconds, then winked. More giggling.

'Come on then.'

The girls got to their feet and kissed their mother. Katerina threw her arms round her mother's neck. Natasha was more reserved, leaning into Elena's proffered cheek. The girls waved goodbye to Marguerite.

Ruth had been up since five, putting a few hours in at the desk before coming to fetch the two girls. Elena had been right, the acceptances had tumbled in. Even Bakewell's people accepted on his behalf. Her fears and suspicions seemed ridiculous; Peter was killed in an accident. She adapted. With the girls here and Elena joking and the sunshine, the buzz of tension seemed to recede into the background.

In the car Katerina sat in the middle of the back seat and aimed a stream of chatter at Sam and Michael. Sam drove, and Michael chatted back to her. Friendly, laughing at her jokes and putting in all the necessary *I see*s and the occasional *No, really?* Katerina blossomed under his attention like one of those paper flowers you drop in water and watch unfurl. Ruth wondered where he got the skill from. Most men were much less patient with children and he'd told her he was an only child. Cousins maybe. A basic kindness. *Trust me.*

Ruth realised she was being watched too. Natasha had turned from the window and was observing her observing Michael and Katerina. Ruth realised she probably had a slightly fond smile on her face. Natasha looked briefly embarrassed at being caught staring and Ruth winked at her. Natasha smiled back. Yes, the exchange said, Katerina is a flirt and Michael is being nice to her.

'Why isn't Andrei coming with us?' Katerina said.

'I think he is too sad about his friend,' Michael replied smoothly.

'Oh! I'm glad it is just us anyway. He gets bored when Mum makes us do things together.'

'Andrei came to see me in the hospital every day,' Natasha said quietly.

'That was nice of him,' Ruth said.

'Yes. Dad did too but he was mostly yelling at people on his phone.'

She was looking pale, Ruth noticed, paler than when they had left the house. She glanced out of the window. Damn it. They were going down Piccadilly, past the café. It had reopened while Ruth was recovering in Brockley, bullet holes filled in, glass replaced, blood and splinters swept and mopped away. Katerina was chattering to Michael again. Ruth reached out behind Katerina and touched Natasha's hand.

'Natasha, can you remember when you did the Tudors? Do you like history?'

Her fingers were cold. 'I do a bit. Science is my best subject though.' She took a deep breath, fixed her eyes on Ruth, but her glance kept skittering off out of the window.

Ruth pulled out her phone. 'See what you can remember – look there's a quiz on my phone about Henry VIII's wives.'

It was a daft thing with animations on it, cartoon versions of the tyrant and his victims, but Natasha giggled at it.

Ruth couldn't help thinking Andrei was too selfish and self-absorbed to be much comfort to a frightened girl in hospital. Better than nothing though. Elena hadn't been able to leave the house once she'd been let out of the hospital herself. So Natasha must have been there with a brand-new security team, and visits from Andrei. She wondered if Natasha had been like Katerina before the attack, another carefree child. Carefree, not in care. Some words gather a casual cruelty around them.

They got out of the car near the visitor's entrance to the Tower and Natasha handed Ruth her phone back with a polite thank you. Then the girls checked nothing had fallen out of their bags, slid over the seats and clambered onto the pavement. One of the security team – Ruth had seen him on the door a few times – came and spoke to Michael while the girls snapped selfies and argued over which filters to use.

'All OK?' Ruth asked as other security guy moved away again.

Michael had changed again; not quite Paris relaxed, but he seemed easier than in the house. He patted the chest of his jacket.

'Got the tickets. Grant reports nothing suspicious going on apart from the prices in the gift shop.'

Ruth stared at the mass of the crowd flowing like water around the walls.

'Are we allowed to talk to you or are you in full ninja-focused-on-threat mode?'

He blinked, raised his eyebrows and replied in an offended voice. 'I'm always in full ninja mode, madam.' She smiled. 'No, Grant's going to do the real close protection. I can be a tourist with you guys.'

'You ever been here?'

'Once. School trip. I explained the history of the Crown Jewels to a very patient beefeater. You?'

She stuck her hands in her pocket.

'I wanted to when I got here, too expensive.'

'I think you'll enjoy it.'

*   *   *

She did. At first the girls darted around them like puppies, filming, taking pictures of walls, ravens, each other, then slowly they began to settle. Katerina danced attendance on Michael, explaining the Tudor dynasty to him and counting off the wives of Henry VIII, with some unlikely sounding elaborations and diversions, on her fingers.

Natasha stuck closer to Ruth, and once the initial excitement of the Tower was done, she listened to the Warders with polite attention and grew quiet.

'What are you doing in history this year?' Ruth asked.

'This year we are reading war poetry. It's very sad.' Ruth's attention was caught by Katerina again. A Georgia in the making. What happens to a serious ultra-rich girl like Natasha? Who does she become?

'Do you like school?'

A shrug. 'My teachers are nice. And some of the girls. Most of them are like Katerina though.'

'I saw a picture of you on holiday in Korčula last year. Looked fun.'

Her face brightened suddenly, a big grin splitting it. God, was I ever that young, Ruth thought. 'Yes, that was brilliant. We went swimming and Megs took us round the old city and we got our faces painted and fans with pictures of the buildings on them. Would you like to see them when we get home?'

'Yeah, that would be great.'

'She talked like you.'

Ruth wondered if Elena had told the girls she'd been friends with their old holiday nanny. Unlikely. 'Did she? Maybe she was from the north too.'

'Yes, she came from a town called Middlesbrough and she didn't have a mummy or daddy. She was really, really nice though.' Natasha's shoulders slumped slightly. 'Then she went off without saying goodbye.'

Without even saying goodbye to the kids? Megs had disappeared off in the past without saying goodbye to Ruth, but that was different. She wouldn't just disappear on kids in her care. They knew exactly how that felt.

Ruth rested her hand on Natasha's shoulder. 'I bet she sent you a postcard or something and it got lost. Foreign post can be crap.' She felt Natasha's wide-eyed stare. 'Sorry, rubbish! I said rubbish!'

Natasha giggled. 'Of *course* you did, Ruth.'

'Was she your nanny for long?'

Another shrug. 'No, just that holiday, but I really liked her. She taught us spy things.'

Ruth had to be careful not to stop walking. 'Spy things?'

'Yes, Mummy and Daddy were having loads of business meetings so we snuck about taking photos of them and writing down our observations and stuff.'

Ruth couldn't speak. What the actual fuck?

'We were reading Alex Rider books,' Natasha went on, 'so Megs said we could practice being spies too. It was really fun. Then she left and it was really boring. This other girl called Sandra came, but she just sat by the pool on the boat and texted her boyfriend so we didn't have any adventures after that.'

The Alex Rider books. Of course. Megan had liked them when they were both kids. She'd tried to nick one from the library once, and got caught. A lady saw her getting told off for it and bought her a copy, just like that. Every time Megs and Ruth were in town for a month afterwards they tried to find this new fairy godmother in the hope she'd buy them something else. They never managed to find her again. Megan would get how kids Natasha and Katerina's age would love the mix of mischief and play of being spies.

'She sounds nice.'

Natasha nodded. 'Yes. She was cool.'

Katerina came barrelling towards them. 'Can we go and see the jewels now?'

'Of course.'

A lost postcard. Alex Rider books. A spin on a holiday diary for a couple of lively kids. A new man, a chance to dash off on a new adventure. Nothing to see here. But still the world seemed to contract and darken around her.

*   *   *

The rest of the morning went smoothly. The girls were impressed by the crown and peppered the beefeater with questions. He handled the onslaught well while Michael and Ruth watched. Some of Katerina's enthusiasm seemed to rub off on Natasha and when Katerina spotted something else shiny in the far corner of the chamber, they scrambled off through the crowd together.

Michael and Ruth were standing hip to hip, watching them go. Michael's hand found hers. Their fingers intertwined in the narrow space between them, and she shifted her weight so their hands were pressed between their bodies for a moment. It set off a pleasing cascade of memories through her skin. She hoped Grant wasn't watching.

'Smart young ladies!' the beefeater said, mopping his brow with a linen handkerchief. 'A credit to you both.'

We look like a couple, Ruth thought. We look like a happy young couple with shiny, shiny children. Shit. How wrong people can be.

Michael only smiled at the old man. 'Thank you.'

They unwound their fingers and followed in the wake of the girls, not quite touching.

25

The girls wanted burgers for lunch, and at a nod from Michael, burgers were what they got. Michael sat with them while Grant kept an eye on exits and entrances. The girls seemed fascinated and delighted by the noisy clatter of the place, and with its American diner vibe with hipster stylings it didn't set any alarm bells off in their heads. Michael drew faces in the ketchup and stole their chips, which seemed to delight them both. Ruth bought them crown hairbands and gold pens in the gift shop and they both fell asleep in the car on the way home.

Their rooms were on the third floor. When they got back to the house, the calendar on Ruth's phone showed Elena as red. Katerina wanted to watch cartoons in the kitchen with Masha, but Natasha asked if Ruth wanted to see her room.

'Sure!'

They passed from Elena and Yuri's floor into the third storey. Masha lived up here, symbolic of her rule over the household perhaps, and the girls both had their own rooms with another room for whatever nanny was required over the school holidays.

'Did your nanny Megan stay here?' Ruth asked.

'No, she met us on the boat,' Natasha replied tugging her hand as they crossed the landing to her room. Good. The temptation to come up here and sit in the room and wonder would have been too strong.

It was a sweet room, very neat, with a plain pine desk and a narrow single bed with a yellow silk coverlet. The walls were covered with framed pictures from fairy tales and behind the door was a tall bookshelf packed with coloured spines and lined with small toys and souvenirs. Natasha sat Ruth on the bed, fetched a blue-and-white fan from the second shelf and passed it to her. Ruth unfolded it while Natasha got to her knees and pulled out a box from under the bed.

The fan was prettily hand-painted with the outlines of old buildings, boats and a craggy coastline, and *Korčula* was written across the bottom.

'It's lovely!' Ruth said and fanned herself.

'I know,' Natasha replied. She was taking things out of the box now, blankets and old games. 'Here!'

She held up an outsize leather notebook and waved it above her head. A couple of Polaroid photos fell out of the back. Ruth had an image of blue water, the slightly sepia-coloured wood of a deck.

'Oops!' Natasha gathered them up and then bounced onto the bed next to Ruth. She seemed much more cheerful now they were back home. Relieved. Ruth wondered if being out in the city had bothered her more than she had said.

'It's our spy journal. Megs got us to make up stories about the people, because it was quite a boring holiday otherwise. Just motoring around and people coming to our boat to talk and talk. I prefer skiing. I like skiing. Making up stories is fun though. And so was being sneaky.'

Ruth opened the notebook on her lap. The first page was filled with a drawing of a rainbow over a castle. Ruth used to draw things like that herself, but always got frustrated when what she saw in her head refused to appear on the page.

'Not that. That's just silly. I did it when I was very young. Like a year ago.' Natasha turned the page to a scrap of a diary in a round and careful hand. *Arrived in Korčula. Had sandwiches and Coke. Katerina and my room has a porthole, but Megan's doesn't. She says she doesn't mind because she won't be there much anyway. Megan has red hair and says 'tuthbrush'. Her swimming costume has stripes on it and has a skirt attached to it.*

'We were supposed to write a diary for school, but it was boring, so Megan said we could do this spy journal instead. We gave all the people who came to the boat spy names and wrote down what they were doing and saying and took photos.'

Ruth flicked through the pages. The writing was smaller and full of numbers.

'What are those?'

'Oh just times and things. Sometimes we made notes in Cyrillic too.'

Under the notes was a story about how their parents were actually the King and Queen of Albania. One man was plotting to return them to the throne and another was trying to poison their tea, but a princess spotted the ruse and knocked over the cup. On another page was a description of the throne room on the boat.

'And Megan bought us a Polaroid camera to take the pictures because phones are very insecure, you know.'

'I see.'

'Yes,' Natasha nodded seriously. 'Katerina and I showed it to our teacher at school when we got home and she said it was very imaginative and more fun than normal holiday diaries. We got As.'

Ruth couldn't help it. She turned past a thick wedge of blank pages to the folder with the Polaroids and started looking through them. There weren't many of them. The spidery man. Milos. Suzanne. Another woman with her back to the camera. Marguerite.

'Was Marguerite there? The woman your mum was with today?'

'Yes. Lots of times. We called her Princess Perfect.'

'What's her second name?'

No answer, just a shrug.

Ruth stopped dead at a picture of Megan sticking her tongue out. She looked beautiful.

'Then Andrei saw Megan with the camera and got very cross. Maybe he shouted at Megan about it, because the next day Megan wasn't there any more. We carried on with the diary, but it wasn't as much fun.'

Andrei saw the camera. Andrei got cross. Megan disappeared. Oh Jesus. Ruth tucked the photos back into the folder and handed the diary back to Natasha.

'It's really cool, Natasha,' she said when she could trust her voice. 'Thanks for showing me.' The little girl returned it to the box under the games and blankets. 'If Andrei was cross about the Polaroid though, wasn't he cross about the spy diary?'

Natasha rolled her eyes and sighed. 'We didn't tell Andrei about the *diary*! Or the photos we'd already taken. Mummy might have thrown that away and then we'd have had to do a whole boring holiday diary for school and that would have been a complete and absolute disaster!'

Ruth nodded. Her mind was going too fast. She needed a minute. A day. A month to pull it all apart. 'Fair enough. Shall we go downstairs and see what Katerina is up to? Perhaps Masha is cooking.'

'Cool!'

One of Natasha's hair scrunchies was on the dressing table. Ruth scooped it up and put it in her pocket.

The girls were driven back to school that evening and Ruth received fierce hugs from both of them. The next day, Ruth got back to work on the conference, and Michael was out – a rare day off, visiting his family. Ruth was sitting alone in the staff area in the basement when he came back. He was dressed like a Sunday supplement ad, cords and open-neck checked shirt undone over a T-shirt, a leather bag over his shoulder. She could smell the country air on him.

'Hey,' she said, then turned back to her book.

He put the bag down and opened the fridge. 'Have you eaten yet?'

'Why? Did you shoot something delicious in the countryside?'

He closed the fridge door. 'My parents aren't in the shooting set. Roast dinners and country walks, not horses and ancestral homes.'

Ruth put her book down on her lap and stretched along the sofa. 'It's confusing, you know. All these different sorts of posh. I thought it was just one great mass of them. Now I've got to sort out landed gentry versus oligarchs, and Sir Tobys versus privileged chancers.'

He flicked on the kettle. 'The young girl's guide to the super-wealthy. You should write that.'

He got a foil-wrapped package out of his bag and grabbed plates. Ruth lifted herself up on her elbow so she could see over the top of the sofa and watch what he was doing. Great doorstep sandwiches.

'Mum's roast beef,' he said, dividing them between the plates. 'I hope you like horseradish.'

He reached into the fridge again and took out a couple of cans of beer. Their labels were crazy street art confections – skulls and rockets. Ruth had a sudden pang of longing for Newcastle Brown. A flash of memory of leaning up on a slightly sticky bar trying to look older than she was and ordering it. A smirking Megan at her elbow. Bottles of dog. Paying for them with stacks of twenty pence pieces she and Megan had jimmied out of the dodgy payphone on the high street. Megan. An image of her instead of Peter being bundled into a car, beating her palms on the window. What do you do with thoughts like these?

Michael set the plates on the table, opened the cans. Pushed one and the plate towards her. She couldn't eat. She had to eat. She had to stop thinking about Megan. She couldn't stop. Maybe they'd sacked her and didn't want to say. Maybe she'd run off because Andrei frightened her. No. He wouldn't scare Megan. But he might piss her off enough so she'd just bail. Grab her bag and walk off into the night.

'Drinking on the job?'

He was resting his elbows on his knees, leaning forward so the plate would catch the crumbs. 'Not on duty yet.'

Ruth swung herself upright and started in on the sandwich.

They didn't talk about the conference or the family, attaché cases, James Tranter or Peter. Ruth needed this. A moment to remind her what normal could feel like. Just swapping words with another human being, the hoppy tang of the beer, the pleasant burn of the horseradish. It wasn't dinner at the Ritz or dancing in Paris, but there was a sort of comfort to it. She asked more about his family, his school and he asked her about finding her place in Brockley, what the wealth management company was like. She answered him, and felt sorry for him. He was being sensitive – not asking about her family, her school. Nothing that reminded her of the trial, but it was still there hovering in the background. The memories were toxic, and now Jane's threat was twisting them into something even more painful. Put it down. Ignore what hurts. Push on to the next thing. Concentrate on the shape of his smile. It could work for a little while. When they threw their cans in the recycling, put their plates in the dishwasher, it seemed both easy and right to take his hand and follow him to his room.

26

Ruth was up at the crack of dawn to continue her pursuit of all the speakers Elena wanted for her 'little party' at the Dorchester. Ruth had made good progress already, using the name Shilkov when necessary to get past secretaries and PAs, and it was amazing how quickly diaries opened up when she mentioned the speaker's fee. Still, there was a shedload more to do. Just breathe, Ruthie. You got this.

Then some of Yuri's people rang to talk about timetables, and sort out the printing of brochures and information packs. Ruth had to check the names were all spelt right, coordinate the timings of the sessions with the hotel, arrange first-class travel, cars – the list went on and on. Peter was drunk and had an accident. Megan ran away. She repeated it like a mantra. Trying to burn it into her brain.

Yuri's people bombarded her with calls and emails all afternoon but by 4 p.m. they had sent over a PDF of the proposed brochure. The logo of the American security firm, Glenville Solutions, was featured discreetly on a couple of pages, along with a number of other companies Ruth had never heard off. All bland, mean-nothing names. The main logo on the cover was that of the Kellinghall Foundation. Tuchman's think tank. The logo was a sort of Georgian townhouse front door. Pillars and a fanlight. Very English. The name Shilkov appeared exactly nowhere. The talks all sounded deeply dull. The report itself was called *Security Priorities in a Globalised Age*. The rest looked at first glance like variations on a theme. *Nation States and Social Justice. Private and Public Partnerships: Security and Data Co-operation*. Why was Elena blowing so much money on lecturing a bunch of MPs about this?

Ruth continued through her list of attendees and discovered some were journalists or opinion writers. She started to put together orders for the gift bags for the non-speakers, a grab bag of expensive bon-bons, more tickets, things she could mention casually to anyone who seemed reluctant to change their plans and attend. She gathered photographs for the greeters, and in the case of the titled, included notes on how they were to be addressed. Two former home secretaries and some Americans who had been on the National Security Council.

She'd give the list to Jane, and the list of the Sir Tobys and the fees they had received. Maybe keep the Yuri's favours list in her back pocket for now. She'd give the same account to Jane of Peter's removal from the party as she had given the police. All these mechanical tasks, fiddly, easy to fuck up. She had to keep checking and re-checking as she swapped between browser windows, copied and pasted biographies and travel details and like a pulse, every other second she saw Peter's face in her mind's eye, or the twist of Jane Lucas's mouth. *I will destroy you.* She replied to an email from the relationship manager at the Dorchester about the savouries to be supplied at the afternoon coffee break and wondered what going to prison would be like. Changed the car pick-up time for a Cambridge academic who didn't like trains as she wondered whether she'd even make it to prison if Jane followed through on her threat. They would want to be revenged. They, those blank-staring men, they would demand it bloody and immediate and this time no one would defend her.

At sixteen minutes past five, it suddenly got too much. She got up, left the office and went to her bedroom on the lower floor. She shut the door, sat on the bed and burst into tears. It was pathetic, pathetic to cry but she couldn't help it.

'Megs. What have we done?'

Then she washed her face and went back upstairs, back to the desk, back to the emails. One foot in front of the other.

Michael came in during the evening asking for the updated list of attendees for his security checks. She got up to fetch them from the printer and he must have seen something in the way she moved, because he put them on the desk and then put his arms around her. She froze, but he didn't let go. Perhaps he was like her, not aware of what was going on in the house, not really. Maybe he was trapped here too in some way, but how could he be? A mother who likes perfume from Paris, an army officer, he would never need to face the compromises that had ended up miring her here, stuck by Jane Lucas. Held in place, in this terrifying wonderland by something she did seven years ago. Held in fear, by fear. Michael knew who he was working for though. God, maybe he liked it. Complicit in it all but somehow maintaining deniability. Holding himself at a distance from the dirty work. Whatever was keeping him here, it wasn't fear. She needed a second of release though. A moment out of her own mind.

She let herself relax into his arms and he kissed her, hard. A desperate hunger in it. But still, the longer she was with him the more she thought there was something off in his posh boy scout act. Something in the way he touched her, the edge to his voice when he was angry or frustrated. His face when the shutters came down. Shit, having grown up how she did, having seen what she had seen of what people could do to each other could she really convince herself that his good teeth and good breeding meant he wasn't the sort of person to kill on order? She pushed him away, handed him the printouts again and ignored the injury in his eyes as he turned and left her office, closing the door behind him.

27

Wednesday morning. The conference was less than a week away. Elena wasn't much in evidence. She cancelled their usual morning meet, but sent a list of names – new people to invite.

Some were delighted. Others needed to be cajoled. Ruth was glad she'd put together the goodie bags. Classes were cancelled, meetings rearranged. As Ruth worked, news alerts pinged up on her screen, and mostly she ignored them – she seemed to get American ones most of the time. Then she saw a familiar name and clicked on it. It was the Sir Toby who was coming to the conference, but who had been turning down gifts and favours from Elena for years. He wasn't even a Sir. Just plain John Bakewell, MP. The article was about him fighting for prison reform. She clicked on the video while listening to a university's hold music on the telephone. John Bakewell was on a panel, delivering a dressing down to some smooth-haired woman who had called him a communist. He spoke pithily, but with passion. He was all for private enterprise, of course he was, but there were some things the government should run itself and prisons were one of those. 'These places need to be answerable to the people, not to shareholders.'

'Yes?'

The voice on the phone startled her. She closed the screen, refocused on her notes. 'Is that Dr Greenleaf?'

'Speaking.'

'Ruth Miller here, I'm calling from Elena Shilkov's office about the session next week. We wanted to make sure you had received the advance copy of the report.'

The voice on the other end of the line sighed deeply. 'Yes,

I've got it and yes, I think I can make it work. Any journalists coming?'

Ruth rattled off a few names.

Dr Greenleaf made a noise somewhere between contentment and contempt. 'They are more what I'd refer to as columnists than journalists, my dear. Friendly to reforms of the cyber security set-up in this country anyway. Can't I send a junior lecturer to read out my speech? It's not as if anyone will be listening.'

He sounded broken. 'We want you to read it in person, Dr Greenleaf. And there will be a question-and-answer session after each speech.'

'Fine, fine. The Shilkovs fund my chair here and three junior lectureships. I'll play nicely.'

'John Bakewell is coming. Perhaps he'll have an interesting question for you,' Ruth blurted.

An intake of breath at the other end of the line. 'Ha! Living dangerously. Perhaps he will. Normally has plenty to say about private money in government. Though even if he does, much good it will do.' A pause, then he became all business again. 'Apologies, dear girl. I've had a grim morning and now I'm taking it out on you. Please tell the organisers I'm delighted to come and read my speech, you have my email for the travel arrangements? Good. I'll invoice you by return.'

Then he hung up. Ruth watched the clip again.

The house wasn't empty until three. Elena swung in to tell her she was going to a meeting near Westminster then going to bid at Christie's on behalf of one of Yuri's clients.

'Perhaps I shall pick up a present for you too!'

'Don't get me anything that will break if I drop it,' Ruth replied. 'I can't be trusted with fragile things. Clumsy.'

Elena laughed and swirled back out. Michael's office was empty which meant Yuri would be out too. Then Masha said she was going shopping.

Ruth sat staring at her screen for twenty minutes, willing herself to get up and go, somehow finding it impossible to move. It needs to be done, so get it done. She said it to herself half a dozen times, but somehow she couldn't stand up.

Then she was at the door. The silence of this house. Even when the family and the staff were there somehow the walls ate sound. Thick doors, thick carpets. No whisper of traffic through the double-glazed windows, no birdsong from the garden. When Ruth did step outside the house the cacophony of the world was becoming more and more of a shock.

She climbed the stairs, didn't pause on the main landing, headed on up to the girls' rooms and opened the door to Natasha's. Even this space seemed strangely dead without the little girl in it. She put the scrunchie back on the top of the chest of drawers and left the door open, then knelt on the carpet at the foot of the bed, pulled out the storage drawer and took the journal out from under the pile of blankets and games. It was so bulky. How many pages were written on? A dozen, two dozen. She set it on the desk where the light from the garden fell on it, took out her phone and began to take photographs, a double page at a time. Then she laid out the Polaroids and photographed them too. Forever in measurable time. The silence seemed to thicken around her until she could hear the flow of her own blood. As she gathered the pictures into the back of the book her hands were shaking. Then she found she was just holding the one of Megan, staring at it.

Megan liked spy books. Megan was the sort of person who *would* think up a fun variation on a boring what-I-did-on-my-holidays journal. Megan was the sort of generous – impulsive, daft – girl to buy a Polaroid with her nannying wages for a kid who had a five-grand laptop and wore Chanel tights. But. It was a coincidence, wasn't it, that she decided to do those things just when the Shilkovs were using their boat to run this series of meetings Jane was so interested in. She thought of a line in some police procedural they'd watched in the common room at the home. About not believing in coincidences. But why would Megan . . .

Fuck. Now is not the time to crap on. Move. Move, Ruth. She put the phone in her pocket and the Polaroid back in the journal with the others. The journal in the storage box. The box back under the bed. Then she left the room, closed the door behind her and trotted back towards the first landing. She was already starting down the main staircase when the door to Andrei's room opened.

'Ruth?'

She twisted round. Andrei was standing in the doorway, frowning. He looked like shit. His face hollowed and grey, sweatpants and a dull-purple T-shirt.

'Hey.'

'What were you doing upstairs?'

'I found one of Natasha's hair things in my bag. Thought I'd put it back in her room before I forgot about it.'

His face creased. 'You were up there for ages.'

She smiled. Bland, just a touch of wry. 'I started looking at the pictures on her wall. Fairy tales. They're lovely. Wish I'd had stuff like that.' Distract him. 'Are you OK, Andrei? You look rough.'

He ran his hands through his hair, his shoulders slumped. 'Like you care. No one does.'

Ruth sighed, then sat on the top step with her back to the wall, facing him, and folded her arms.

'I asked, didn't I?'

He came out uncertainly. Bare feet. And sat down on the step next to her.

'It's Peter's funeral tomorrow afternoon. I don't want to go. His parents and sister will be there. Dad said I should go to show respect. Elena doesn't care one way or the other. She doesn't think Peter's family are important enough.' He looked sideways at her. 'Will you come with me?'

I'd rather scoop my eyes out with a spoon, Ruth thought. 'I'm really busy with the conference coming up.' She took out her phone. 'What time?'

'Three fifteen. It's at Putney Crematorium. I've booked the car. And Michael wants Ben and Sam to come.'

She had a meeting with Elena in the morning, if it didn't get cancelled again, and a backlog of misery mail and envelopes to stuff as well as a hundred things to do for the conference, but Jane Lucas had told her to get close to Andrei. And who needed sleep?

She'd only ever been to one funeral, when she was eleven years old. Her mother's. Her memory of it was fuzzy, people mussing her hair, a couple of stringy men giving her warm pound coins from their jeans pockets. One bloke gave her a fiver and she had thought for a year that meant he was her dad. She'd only cried about it once, three years later on Pat Cunningham's shoulder. The memories had got easier to bear after that though.

'Please come, Ruth. I don't want to go by myself.'

Deep breath.

'Sure, I can come with you.'

His face split into a relieved grin and for a second he was attractive, in a little-boy-lost sort of way. Then Ruth remembered Brittany and the flicker of sympathy was doused.

'The car is booked for two fifteen,' he said and stood up. Put out his hand to help her to her feet. 'Thank you.'

Elena said she didn't care if Ruth went to the funeral or not when they met the next morning, then grilled her for twenty minutes about the arrangements for the conference in detail, super-fast.

When she snapped her fingers under Ruth's nose as she searched through her papers for the name of the firm that were providing the engineers for the AV system, the Dorchester's preferred suppliers, Ruth lost it.

'Fuck it Elena, if you don't want me to go to the funeral, just say so!'

It came out without her thinking. It took a second before she dared look up. Elena was staring at her. Ruth couldn't decide whether to apologise or not. Not.

'Why do you want to go?' Elena asked, her stare still fixed and hard. 'You think maybe you'll fuck Andrei as well as Michael? Perhaps you can earn more than I pay you on your back.'

Ruth looked straight back at her. 'He keeps banging on about how poor he is, so that would be dumb. And I'm not a whore, so if I do fuck him, it will be for free.' The corner of Elena's mouth twitched and Ruth continued, her voice a bit softer. 'But I don't like sad angry drunks, so not much chance of that.'

Elena had a long cashmere cardigan on today. She stuck her hands in her pockets and wrapped it round her.

'Your dad was a drunk?' she asked.

Ruth shook her head, returned to sorting through the papers. 'Never met my dad. It was my mum.' She found the piece of paper. 'She tried her best, but not always. There. West One Engineering. References supplied and the two staff who will be on site have been security checked by Michael.'

Elena stretched. 'You are right. I do not care. The Dorchester say they are good, they will be good. You are young. I was afraid maybe Andrei looks romantic to you.'

Ruth shook her head, put the papers back in order.

'What? Poor little rich boy? No. I felt sorry for him. He asked. I said yes.'

They were in Elena's rooms again today. 'How did the auction go yesterday?'

She shrugged. 'Good. I bought a Picasso.'

Ruth looked around. 'A Picasso? Can I see it?'

Then Elena laughed and swung herself off the sofa and to her feet. 'No. I didn't see it. Only photos and certificates. It is in a freeport in Switzerland. From there it goes onto the yacht of a very rich man who gets seasick. The yacht is a money ark. Full of beautiful things in clever boxes to keep them safe.'

Ruth understood. 'This is about money.'

'Always.' Elena was staring out of the window. 'If the picture is never imported anywhere, no tax to pay. Yuri helped write the laws across Europe. Clever little lines, buried in sub-section this and that. Like truffles. So while the pictures stay on a boat they can even come up the Thames so the ones who like to look occasionally can have a little visit. Prettier to look at than gold bars.' Then she turned round. Switched on again. 'But I got you a present you can't hurt by dropping. Don't fuck up my party next week and you shall have it.'

'And you're OK if I go to the funeral?'

She shrugged. 'Go if you want. But learn to say 'no' more. You have this thing in you. Even if you are a clam. You want to help people. It is dangerous, *dorogaya*.'

28

They didn't speak on the way to Putney Crematorium. Ruth had found Isme had included a reasonably sober black dress in her wardrobe. She tied her hair back and kept the make-up light. Michael insisted on sending a second car and another two of the security team. When Ruth asked why they got so much more security this time rather than when the girls went out, he told her people might expect the Shilkovs to send someone to the funeral. She should keep her eyes open. On the way she assumed that Peter's family and friends would create a crowd big enough to give her and the security detail a bit of cover. When the car drew up and she stepped out, she realised she was wrong.

Peter was mourned by few, it seemed. She and Andrei stood awkwardly in the almost empty car park behind the chapel. Ruth studied her phone and Andrei smoked. His hand, as he lit his fag with a gold Zippo, shook. They were early. Ruth spoke to a harried woman in a beige cardigan who confirmed that, yes, this was where the Baxter service was to take place. The previous funeral was just finishing off. Ruth listened to the thin singing drifting out of the chapel and prayed – well not *prayed* prayed – hoped to heaven that they wouldn't have to sing.

'Starts at three forty-five not three fifteen,' she said. Andrei nodded, but didn't apologise for getting the time wrong. 'Fancy a walk?'

He let her lead him between the graves and monuments towards the wall where the chapel was divided from the park beyond. From here they could watch people arrive without feeling like they were the reception committee. A car drew in and two sharp-suited men got out. The beep of the alarm setting seemed to echo out over the whole graveyard.

'That's Yannis and Jacob. They own the Revolution Club in Mayfair. Surprised they bothered to turn up.' Andrei said.

'Revolution Club?'

'Yeah, it's themed with busts of Stalin and Lenin and things. It's cool.'

Sounded twisted to Ruth, but there you go. A taxi arrived and a couple in their twenties emerged. The man, a bit thick at the waist and his hair already thinning, fumbled with his wallet as he paid and the woman, good-looking if slightly dishevelled, looked around in dismay.

'Christ! Greg and Susan! I had no idea they were still together.'

'Who are they?' Ruth asked.

'Greg was at school with us. Then university. He met Susan there. Don't know why he's here – we didn't hang out that much.'

A long gap, then a couple of carloads of people of different ages. One woman with a baby in her arms. Family, Ruth guessed. Their security detail had split. Ben was staying by the gate, Sam went into the chapel. They were trying, Ruth thought, quite hard to be discreet.

'Oh shit.' Andrei threw down the stub of his cigarette and stood on it as the hearse turned into the car park, followed by a limousine. Three people got out of the latter. A middle-aged man and woman, and a younger girl.

'Mr and Mrs Baxter and their daughter Laurie,' Andrei said miserably. 'We'd better go in, don't you think?'

He looked as if he was hoping she'd say no, let's go home. She didn't. They walked side by side along the concrete path back to the chapel and followed the coffin and the family into the interior. Ruth took an order of service from the woman in the cardigan. A folded card with a huge portrait of Peter smiling, but looking slightly drunk. He was wearing a rugby shirt.

'They aren't rich,' Ruth said, almost to herself as they sat down and a tape of one of the 'Enigma Variations', slightly distorted, began to play from the speakers.

'No,' Andrei replied. 'They had to struggle to send Peter to Harrow and he was always a bit embarrassed about it.'

Ruth gave a tiny shake of her head. What possessed people to spend all their money to send their kids to these places? Were they worried they'd be contaminated by contact with poor people if they went to a comp? Probably. She'd had plenty of people look at her like she was a disease in her time. She'd asked once at the wealth management place. They'd murmured something about connections.

'He tried a bit hard, you know? People can smell that. It puts them off. The English boys didn't like me because I was Russian, the Russians thought I was English, so we got together,' Andrei said.

'Where are your friends from the club?' Ruth asked. Other than the two owners of Revolution, and the university friends, there was no one of Peter's age in the chapel.

'They were more acquaintances than friends. Half probably don't know he's dead, and the other half don't care.'

Ruth wondered who'd come to her funeral. It wouldn't be much of a crowd, but she'd have the Cunninghams and Sunny from the solicitors. Megan would come if she knew. This was bleak.

The music faded and a vicar made a short speech of vague generalities. Then the young woman, the sister, Laurie, stood up and read a poem. She read it too loudly and with strong emphasis, as if that would help her get through it. When she sat down next to her parents, Ruth noticed her mother take her hand and squeeze it briefly. Another burst of music and the coffin disappeared. Peter's mother gave a sort of gulping exclamation as it rolled back on a conveyer belt and the burgundy curtains swung swiftly together over it.

The undertakers led the family out. Andrei looked straight ahead, but as she passed, Peter's mother looked at him. Her expression was of bafflement, as if she was observing an alien species from the far side of the universe. Ruth noticed a flush on Andrei's neck. He must have caught it. The rest of the crowd, such as it was, left and being in the back, Ruth and Andrei were

among the last. They moved slowly. There was no mention of a
wake on the programme or during the service, which had to be
a relief. Ruth caught the eye of the security guy. He raised an
eyebrow, she gave a tiny nod. In such a way are plans made, cars
ordered.

They stepped out and turned the corner to the car park.

'You shit.'

The sister. A sort of strangled shout. She was Ruth's age and
dressed the way Ruth used to before Isme came into her life. Hair
a bit frizzy, Marks & Spencer pencil skirt and a slightly over-
washed thin black sweater. A navy coat that didn't go and court
shoes.

No sign of the parents or the limousine. She must have sent
them home then waited for them, well for Andrei. She stepped
up close to him, her fists balled at her side, her body rigid,
face red. Ruth didn't need to look to know the security guys
would be approaching, and she held up her hand. As far as
she was concerned, unless and until this girl struck Andrei,
she could have her say. And even then it would depend how
hard.

'Laurie!' Andrei said, taking a half-step back, trying to make
some space between him and her laser eyes. God, she really hated
him. 'I'm so sorry. I'm going to miss him.'

'Fuck you,' she said. 'What did you do? He was so pleased with
himself these last few months. I knew he was into some shit and I
knew it was to do with you. What did you get him into?'

Andrei cowered. 'I didn't. Nothing at all. You know he always
wanted to work with my father. I . . . I asked Dad to help. We
invited him to dinner and he was wasted before he arrived. I was
trying to get him a proper job.'

She shook her head, violently. 'No. That's bollocks. Peter's been
running side hustles and cons since he was six years old and stole
my piggy bank. You and him cooked up a scheme, didn't you? Was
it drugs again? He bought a Rolex. We're flogging it to pay for the
funeral. And that's *all* he left. Twenty-nine years and all that's left
is a trashy watch.'

She was crying now, but not wiping the tears away.

'He thought earning an honest living was beneath him and so do you! You are toxic and you got him killed. I know it! Who did you con? I hate the pair of you, too pleased with yourselves to earn a living and too stupid to be criminals.'

'No! He was drunk! Michael drove him to the Tube station. Then there was an accident the police said—'

'The police!' Laurie spat it out, then turned away with a gasp, half-sob, half-laugh. 'One morning, *one morning* they spent going through Peter's bank records and searching through his stuff. They found suspicious transactions, forged bank notes! There were fake five-hundred-euro notes in his fucking sock drawer, did you know that?'

'No! Of course not!' He looked around as if searching for inspiration. Damp tarmac. Bins. Grey stone walls. 'It was probably for a joke. A prank or something!'

She was shaking with rage. Ruth remembered that feeling. 'Do you seriously expect anyone to believe that? The police didn't. Then all of a sudden Inspector Brooks gets a call and it's all over. Case closed. Investigation done. They told us about the coroner's inquest an hour before it started and it lasted twenty minutes. You think I didn't notice the high-priced lawyers in the back of the room? Your father's lawyers, I'll bet.'

Andrei shook his head. He looked as if he was about to cry. 'I don't know, Laurie. I don't know. It's not my fault.'

Her lip curled and she stood back. 'You're an idiot, Andrei, and my brother was too. He was an entitled, devious idiot, but that didn't give your family the right to murder him.'

She turned round and walked away through the gates of the car park. Ruth watched her go, the hunched shoulders, the rapid stride. Andrei span round to the nearest security man, Sam.

'Why didn't you stop her? She could have attacked me!'

Ruth answered for him. 'These men are here to guard you from physical threat, not from getting an earful, Andrei. And how would that story play? Bereaved sister manhandled by guards outside her brother's funeral.'

Andrei was shaking again. He took out another cigarette and stuck it between his lips, but he couldn't keep hold of the gold zippo. Ruth took it from him and held the flame steady. He sucked the smoke down in great gulps.

'It was an accident. He was upset after the dinner. We thought Dad was going to give him a job in the business, the security contracts but it . . . it didn't go well.' He sounded like he was talking to himself.

'Shall I get the car, Ms Miller?'

'Yes, thanks, Sam.'

Andrei stared hard at the security man as he stepped back to a discreet distance. 'Why is he asking you? I'm the Shilkov here. He works for me. Not you.'

Ruth gave him back his lighter and checked her phone. 'Yeah, but I'm not the one having a meltdown. What job did Peter think he was going to get? He wasn't an accountant.'

'No. He thought he could get a place with Glenville Solutions. Executive of something.'

The car was approaching with a dignified purr.

'What happened?'

He waved her away. 'Nothing happened. He overdid it again. Got pissed. It was an accident. Fuck, my life sucks. I'm just in hell. After everything I've done for them. I can't believe how they treat me. I'm not even invited to the conference until the evening. I should be meeting people.'

He pulled open the door and climbed in. Ruth went round the other side. She slid in next to him and did up her seatbelt. Andrei buzzed down his window and dropped the end of his fag onto the concrete as the car pulled away.

Ruth watched him. 'You've got a degree and at least one good suit. Why not go out and get a job yourself?'

He shook his head. 'Don't be stupid. Elena and Dad could get me any job in the world, they just don't want to. I'm English, you know. That's the problem. I mean, I speak Russian but I've been here all my life. I'm supposed to be an executive, or manage a hedge fund or something, but they never let me do anything important.'

'I wonder why,' Ruth said.

'I sacrificed my soul for them – my immortal soul to keep their secrets and they won't even let me sit in a room for real meetings with their business friends.'

What did he mean? No. Not that. When they told her her mother was dead, she'd put her hands over her ears and screamed, like she could keep the words out of her head that way. They'd made her listen in the end. For her own good. As if they knew what that meant. 'I'm not your confessor, Andrei.'

He didn't answer and she turned to look out of the window. They passed Laurie Baxter, waiting alone at the bus stop in her bad coat. Andrei caught sight of her and looked away. But Ruth was sure he was pitying himself, not the sister of his dead friend. *Andrei, say something!* Some hope.

Ruth got back to a flurry of panicked calls from the printers. Yes, that paper stock would be fine. Yes, they could courier her round a final version for approval late this evening. Then she went through her checklists and decided, cautiously, that this was probably all going to work. Now back to the emails. Midway through the stack of unopened messages from the morning she found one from Jimmy Reeves. Jane. Ruth put her elbows on the desk and ran her hands through her hair. What could she tell her? She hated Jane, but she had to keep her sweet. If the truth about the trial got out . . . No, Ruth did not think she could live with that. She could tell her what Peter's sister had said at the funeral, hand over the visitor logs. But Jane wanted to know about Korčula, and now Ruth had her copies of the spy diary. Did that give Ruth a chance to bargain? If Jane really wanted it, then Ruth would have to get something in return. Some guarantee that Jane wouldn't follow through on her threat or blow up Ruth's life just for the hell of it. She wished she knew how important Jane was. Important enough to have a traffic warden get rid of her driver outside Suzanne D'Arcy's place so her messenger could make contact. Important enough to have access to Ruth's emails; *Send your usual holding reply.* More than that, Jane had the alpha-dog vibe of a person in charge. Important enough then to squash someone like Ruth and not even break stride. Ruth spent some time working out a time and place to meet. She sent it to Jane and got a confirmation.

Flashes of the trial kept coming back to her. The evenings curled up with Megs eating junk food and watching crap TV. The assurances her identity would be protected. Well, Michael and Jane had both proved what a crock of shit that had been. She had been stupid. She had been young. It had been the right thing to do. It had been a horrific mistake which had landed her in the shit now.

'Funeral went OK?' Elena, leaning against the door of her office.

Ruth nodded and Elena came and sat in her usual chair on the other side of the desk. 'This room is very boring. Yuri has some Chagall prints in storage. We shall hang them up. Let a little of his Russianness seep into you.'

'*Khorosho,*' Ruth said carefully and Elena laughed.

'Peter's sister gave Andrei an earful at the funeral.'

'Tell me.'

Ruth did.

'She said all that to his face? In front of you and the security?' Elena raised her eyebrows. 'She is not *sheeple.* What does she do?'

'I looked her up on the way home. She's a GP.'

Elena harrumphed. 'Ach, Harley Street I could send her rich patients. For a GP, I have nothing.' Her eyes narrowed. 'Why are you grinning at me like a sales person?'

Ruth lifted her hands. 'Just. I mean, she laid into your stepson and basically accused you and Yuri of bribing the police and murder. And you react by wanting to send her business.'

Elena was working her phone with her thumbs again and paused to scratch the corner of her left eye. 'In my business, you cannot keep grudges. Grudges are small. Even big ones are small.'

She sprang to her feet. 'What did we send to this man?' She pushed her phone into Ruth's face. It was an awkward CEO shot.

'Centre Court package at Wimbledon. And one of Yuri's companies sponsored the fete of the school he's trying to get his youngest son into.'

Elena chortled. 'Very good. Maybe not a print. Maybe an original Chagall. But only for looking at in the office. It is still ours. Thank you. And our yacht is coming to London after the conference. Maybe you'll see the Matisse too. I told you I would teach you about business, maybe it is time you see how business is done.'

29

Showtime.

Registration began at 10 a.m. and the first session at eleven. The greeters had the pictures of the attendees on their clipboards and welcomed every arrival by name before ushering them into the wide and high-ceilinged rooms – they must have them reinforced to hold up those chandeliers – to be offered coffee and croissants by white-coated waiting staff. Ruth didn't really have anything to do. It felt weird. She found a table with a dining chair at the edge of the room where she could work at her iPad and be available for any questions or problems, and watched. There were seventy-five people attending, so the atmosphere was intimate, polite, rather than frenetic. Fifty men, twenty-five women. A grand total of seven who weren't white and none of them under the age of fifty. She recognised Tuchman, of course. He was circulating, moving from one island of leather sofas to another, shaking hands with a double grip. One or two of the elder statesmen had their own security teams who took up positions around the walls and set about making themselves invisible between the high arrangements of tropical foliage and huge mirrors. Gold-striped wallpaper. At least it didn't smell of lemon, only bacon and coffee.

'No, I don't want a sodding coffee. Even if it is free.'

A man in a slightly rumpled suit, his grey hair sprouting out wildly round the edge of his head. Ruth recognised him. John Bakewell. Mr Incorruptible. He sat down on the other side of the table and stared around him with a mixture of distaste and nerves. It took him some time to notice Ruth.

'Sorry. You OK if I sit here?'

'It's a free country.'

'Ha! Not if this lot get their chance.' He took off his glasses and started polishing them as if he was punishing them for something. 'Not that it was before really. It's bloody expensive to be free here.'

Ruth started typing at her foldout keyboard again.

'I don't know you. Do you work here?'

She looked at him over her screen. 'I'm Ruth Miller. I work for Elena Shilkov.'

He looked at her iPad with suspicion. 'What do you do for her?'

'I'm her personal assistant on social and charitable affairs.'

'Does that mean you run her troll farm? You the one with the Photoshop skills who posts me into pictures with Hezbollah?'

Ruth folded up her screen. 'No. I didn't know she had a troll farm.'

His shoulders slumped. 'Her, or her boss at the Kremlin. Or one of the libertarian billionaires. Christ, it's like the nineteenth century. The global one per cent screwing over everyone else. Take back control my hairy arse. The nation state only exists when they want to whip up a patriotic Twitter mob.'

She put her iPad in her bag.

'What? Does politics bore you?'

'Yes. It does. I hope you have an interesting day.'

'Why?' He had turned his full attention on her and his expression had become one of keen interest. 'Why does politics bore you? It's the most important thing in the world, the laws we live by and who makes them. What else do you care about, *can* you care about if you don't care about that?'

She hefted her bag over her arm. 'I've never seen it make a blind bit of difference is all. Every break I've got has been from people who stood up to help their neighbours. Whoever was waving their dicks around in Parliament didn't change anything.'

He blinked at her. 'How old are you?'

'Twenty-three.'

He looked not just sad, but winded. 'You're too young to remember. It can make a difference. I swear it can.' Then he got up. 'Sorry love, you're doing your best and I'm a sour old goat and these places make me feel it. You keep your seat, and I'll go listen to what our overlords want us to think.'

That made her smile and she sat down again. He shambled off with a half-wave, just as the doors to the conference chamber were opened and the guests started strolling in for their first session. Ruth could just see the lights on the stage, that classical house logo projected on the back. The armchairs, and the water set out on a table between them. The welcome session with Tuchman and a journalist they were paying ten grand to ask pre-arranged questions but with the air of someone giving a grilling. Hell of an hourly rate.

She took the iPad out again. She never went on social media unless she was looking for the right gifts for the Sir Tobys or researching the people asking for cash. Post an image of yourself on a cruise and you weren't likely to get an envelope of money. For the first time Ruth wondered if Yuri even knew how much money Elena spent on her quest to piss off the Almighty.

She searched Twitter for John Bakewell and the memes flooded her screen. She sat back. Jesus, that was brutal. She clicked on a couple of the accounts to see what else they'd posted. She had read about internet trolls, or troll farms, offices full of people spreading fake news during the whole Brexit thing. These accounts all looked like they were from real people though, proper names and lots of posts about their pets and kids, favourite books. She closed it and opened another search, then spent twenty minutes learning that this was what troll accounts looked like now. So you couldn't tell. Did Elena have a troll farm? Why did she need one? She did all her business in person.

Ruth carried on reading, following links to newspaper articles about the troll farms and who ran and funded them. Some shadowy stuff. Then she saw a name she recognised. Marguerite. Full name Marguerite DeValois, countess, former model, married a racing car driver then divorced him. The laughing woman from the library. The dinner guest. Now the discreet owner of the Online Protection Agency, based in Budapest. She appeared at right-wing populist gatherings all over the world, the same bright smile and smooth flowing hair. She wore it well. One of the articles accused her 'farm' of driving a journalist to suicide. Another talked about her team being staffed by ex-Facebook analysts. Natasha and Katerina had called her Princess Perfect in their spying diary.

At half past eleven she left the hotel and turned up South Audley Street. The high white faces of the buildings looked down on her. Beyond the windows through half-closed blinds or thin net curtains she could see flashes of office life, computer screens and ergonomic chairs, then a stretch of shops with china and art lit with buttery spotlights, the panels of the windows divided by dusky-pink columns. She crossed the road and stepped into the Grosvenor Chapel. It looked a bit shabby from the outside compared to the rest of the street, flaking plaster on the bottom of the pillars, notice boards haphazard with A4 sheets advertising concerts and get-togethers, service times. The inside was lovely though. An arched ceiling, a balcony running round three sides, and a proper pulpit with steps up to it.

She took a seat in the back and waited until Jane joined her. She was in a version of her middle-aged woman disguise today. Businesslike but unremarkable. Ruth automatically searched her for opals. She found them winking from a simple, almost girlish bracelet on her right wrist.

Ruth AirDropped her the list of names from Peter Baxter's last dinner party and told Jane about what she had seen that night and heard at the funeral. Andrei's hints and the list of attendees and speakers at the conference. The MPs and civil servants who had been accepting tickets and hampers from the Shilkovs for years.

Jane looked angry. 'How long have you had this dinner party list? I might not have been so blindsided by this conference if you had given it to me. I have a source in the house and a junior analyst had to tell me Elena had just requisitioned the Dorchester. Humiliating. I need to know this sort of thing straight away.'

'You should have given me an instruction manual like Elena did. I'm gutted you are disappointed, of course,' Ruth said bitterly.

'Who is John Bakewell?'

Jane snorted. 'He's nobody. A fossil. A socialist who came up through the unions. They were a problem for a while but most of them have died off. Have you heard anything more about Milos? Is he at the conference?'

'No. Did you know that James Tranter was murdered while I was in Paris?'

She was reading the names from the dinner party on her phone. 'Yes. One of Elena's security team. He seems to have fallen in with a bad crowd after the attack on the café.' A bad crowd. A familiar story.

'The All Stars?'

'Possible. That would explain why he was in Paris. Our colleagues in France believe it was a professional job made to look like a mugging.'

Ruth blinked and stared upwards at the figure of Christ on the cross in gold which hung above the altar. 'Did Michael Fitzsimmons kill him?'

Jane paused, a light smile on her face as if she was thinking over some secret joke. 'Well, Mr Fitzsimmons was in the city at the time and has a more colourful CV than he lets on. I can't say one way or another, dear, but I'm quite certain that the Shilkovs are behind the killing.'

Ruth twisted in her seat. 'Then arrest them! For God's sake what are you doing?' It came out as a sort of squawk.

Jane looked at her with utter contempt. 'Oh, so *now* you believe in justice. The rule of law?'

'I've always believed in justice,' Ruth replied. She felt too sick and scared for tears. She remembered that winded look on John Bakewell's face when she had said she didn't care about politics. She probably looked the same just now.

'How inspiring. Well, that's not how we work, I'm afraid.' Ruth could feel her eyes on her. 'Is there something else, dear?'

It made her feel ill, dirty, being called 'dear' like that by this woman.

'I think there might be. But why should I give it to you? You say the Shilkovs ordered someone killed. You're forcing me to spy on them. You're asking me to risk my life and offering me no guarantees that even if I do do what you say, you won't destroy my life anyway.'

Jane's voice became more gentle. 'I can see how you might feel that. But I'm afraid this is the nature of blackmail. I know you did what you thought was right, but when you and Megan made that choice, all those years ago, you handed your lives to me.'

Then Ruth knew. She had suspected for a time, but now she knew.

'You did this to Megan too. Oh my God, the spy journal. Megan was spying for you too.'

Jane looked at her sharply. 'There's a journal? You've seen it?'

'Natasha showed it to me. Megs made it like a project for them. There are dates and names, some photographs. How did you make Megan spy for you? What did you have over her?'

Jane studied the polished wood of the pew in front of her, twitched her shoulders while Ruth felt all her hopeful and pathetic excuses collapse around her.

'I didn't "make" her. *She* volunteered. Very keen to do her patriotic duty. Practically bit my hand off on the first approach. Very handy. The Shilkovs aren't stupid. They take their disgusting yacht from one cove to another between Korčula and Dubrovnik and their guests were shuttled out on tenders. Impossible to surveil from the shore. Megan looked like a godsend. She told me she was inspired by the selfless bravery of a dear friend.'

Ruth felt her throat close. 'She told you. Megan told you about the trial herself.'

'Yes. Naive little thing, wasn't she? In spite of everything. I suppose that's what got her into trouble in the first place. She was so eager to talk about this amazing thing you did. Of course, neither of us knew how terribly useful that information would be to me later.'

Ruth's chest felt as if it was about to cave in. She needed to face this. 'Is Megan dead?'

A shrug. 'Probably. It sounds rather like Andrei killed her and the Shilkovs covered it up, don't you think?' Something strange happened to Ruth's vision. Jane's words seemed to take a long time to make sense to her. She was back in the café, her eyes full of sugar and her wounds beginning to pulse with pain among all that smashed luxury. 'She failed to turn up at one of our meetings, and the fallback too. Of course in the circumstances that didn't necessarily raise alarms, but discreet enquiries to some of the crew told us there had been some disagreement between her and Andrei, then she disappeared.'

'And that's it?'

'There was no proof. None whatsoever. Even if it had been strategically sensible to arrest the Shilkovs over Megan's disappearance, we had nothing that would stand up in court. And we needed to know who they were working with.'

'So Megan and I are just disposable?' Ruth was shaking – rage, fear, grief – some poisonous cocktail of emotion in her blood. 'Christ, why am I surprised, we always have been.'

Apart from in the Shilkov house. Ruth thought of the earrings, Elena's applause and her low chuckle of pleasure when she saw the work Ruth had done. How the security team asked her for instructions instead of Andrei, the feel of Natasha's hand in hers. *You are already half me.* No longer replaceable, not disposable. Not just a girl from the agency. Not there.

'Yes. That must be uncomfortable. But you are useful to me now. Get me that journal.'

'I don't know if I can.'

'Find a way!' she snapped. 'Then stay in your job. Enjoy your lovely clothes, tell me everything and make sure the Shilkovs don't find out about our arrangement. That way I'm sure we can have a long and happy partnership.'

'But . . .' Ruth said quietly, 'this has to end. If they have murdered people . . . once you *have* proof . . .'

'For the last time Ruth, I am not looking for proof. I'm not a policeman. I'm looking for information. You don't deal with people like the Shilkovs and their network by blundering in with arrest warrants. Leave that to the grown-ups. Now get me this "spy journal", clean yourself up and get back to it.'

She'd been hoping for a guarantee, some sort of escape route out of the maze.

'I can't. How can you?'

Jane folded her arms. 'Please. You knew when you walked into that house that the Shilkovs were dangerous people. You've read the newspapers. You googled them for about three months solid when you got out of hospital. But they showed you a comfortable room and a pile of money and you shut your eyes to their dark side, just like everyone else in this godforsaken whore-ish city. Perhaps you did believe you were doing the right thing at the trial, but this? You were vain and greedy and this is the life that has bought you.'

30

The rest of the conference went off smoothly. Ruth carried on through it in a daze, which seemed to make the staff of the Dorchester more careful and conscientious than ever. The keynote speaker at the dinner was late, but made the crowd laugh. Ruth couldn't really understand what they thought was funny about his rather shambolic act. It looked as if everyone was in on a joke she didn't understand.

She had seen almost nothing of Michael all day, but he appeared at the dinner wearing black tie, only his relative youth and the earpiece making him look like he didn't belong at one of the flower-drenched tables.

Ruth didn't eat. She remained at the back of the room, watching. Yuri and Elena were both here, near the centre of the room but off to one side as if they were just other guests, luminaries of a certain London social scene, there to make up numbers. Andrei was with them, and another Russian family. All the Sir Tobys and CEOs sat elsewhere. Ruth couldn't stop looking at the Shilkovs. The affection in their faces when they exchanged remarks, Elena's quick laugh and Yuri's indulgent smile. Elena had turned her chair to watch the speaker more comfortably, and Yuri had his arm across the back of it. At ease. Could they really have ordered murder? The man on the security detail? Megan's? Was it possible to do such things and then wander around in the world looking at peace, happy?

'Congratulations.'

She turned slightly. Christ. The tall spidery man from the dinner party. She heard the rich roll of an American accent in his voice.

'I'm Noah Warrington, by the way.' CEO of Glenville Solutions. Another puzzle piece she didn't know how to place. 'I know I'm not on your list. I wanted to attend quietly and I'm afraid we played our little games to get around you. But I did want quite sincerely to congratulate you on an excellent event. Exactly what we were hoping for.'

He looked older, close up. Yuri's age at least. They must have been brought up to think themselves enemies, Ruth thought, this American and this Russian, yet now they were partners, somehow in some way.

'Elena managed all the programming, she and Yuri's people. I just made the phone calls. Sent emails.'

He had a glass of champagne in his hand. He sipped it, his eyes scanning the crowd. 'You should learn to take credit when it is offered, Miss Miller. I am aware of how important your efforts have been to our influence campaign.'

She couldn't reply. He continued to stand next to her as the speech wound on. The cheers increased and the speaker lifted his arms above his head, giving them a full vision of his rumpled suit, then appeared to forget the punchline to his story, which sent the room into gales of sycophantic laughter.

'Why do you do that?' Ruth asked.

'What?'

'Play games. Go round me.'

He shrugged. 'It's a matter of discretion. Elena might trust you, but not all those greeters and flunkies you had to share the guest list with. There was no need for you to know.' He smiled at her again. 'But again, and most sincerely, my congratulations. I think Elena is beginning to see you as a protégé. A remarkable stroke of luck for an ambitious young woman.'

Ruth managed to nod and he bowed slightly and raised his glass before leaving her and melting into the crowd as the speaker stumbled off stage to raucous applause.

She didn't get much time to herself. The other half of the ballroom was opened for dancing, roulette or *vingt-et-un*, and as the guests were ushered through by the staff the dining area was reset into a version of a gentleman's club, the dining tables removed and replaced with the usual leather sofas, glasses and decanters of whisky set on the low tables between them. The smoking terrace, heated and under an awning of course, was opened. The relationship manager came to check each element was as she wanted. Yes. It was all good. The summaries of the sessions, with important quotes underlined and the proper citations given, had been prepared and proofed by Yuri's people during the dinner. Copies were now laid on each table in stiff cardboard folders. The information was also available in electronic form on a flash drive in each folder.

Her duties were almost done. She began to think about going home. Whatever that meant. It was a prison and she was trapped there. And if the Shilkovs found out she was supplying information to Jane Lucas, she'd end up like Megan, like Peter. Panic itched under her skin.

'Penny for your thoughts?' Michael. Most of the other men had undone their ties, loosened their collars, but not him. He had brought her a whisky. She took it and knocked it back. The burn was good.

'No. That's a rubbish deal. People say that, but they never pay up, do they? I bet you don't even have a penny.'

He frowned. 'I don't think I do. I saw Noah Warrington talking to you earlier. What did he want?'

She looked at him. How handsome. How kind and competent he seemed. Had he stabbed one of the old security team before taking her out for her lovely, magical night in Paris? Exhaustion made her honest.

'He wanted to congratulate me. And tell me that Elena sees me as a protégé.'

His mask slipped. For a moment he looked so shocked, grieved, it was as if she had stabbed him. Then he straightened up.

'How wonderful for you.'

'Isn't it?'

Elena told her to go home at around midnight. 'And no work for you tomorrow. Go read a book or whatever people do.'

Yuri had offered his polite congratulations, a handshake. Andrei had asked if she fancied going to Bleeding Heart again. He looked flushed and pleased with himself. He'd got over his grief for Peter, it seemed. She refused.

The doorman summoned her a cab. The days of the night bus were long gone by now. A doorman in grey livery and a top hat summoning a taxi instead. She sat in the back seat staring out of the window, catching her reflection occasionally in the glass. Elena's hair and make-up woman had been given charge of her this evening, and put her hair up. It made her face look longer somehow. She looked away, stretched out her fingers on her lap, thought of the way her heart had stopped when Andrei caught her on the stairs coming down from Natasha's room, when Masha had seen her with the dinner party list in her hand, then of Megan being caught getting the kids to take photos of the guests on the yacht in Korčula with the Polaroid. They were crap spies. They were crap spies and she was going to get caught and killed. She'd have thought with those habits of secrecy learnt in her childhood, with her good memory and 'natural ability', as her teachers had called it, even that bravery everyone had gone on about during the weeks and months of the trial, she might have been able to do this, but on current showing, she was rubbish. Mind you, if someone did find out and murder her, Jane Lucas wouldn't expose the truth about the trial, would she? Cold comfort.

She wrapped her coat around herself as if for warmth but the silk lining suddenly felt like a straitjacket.

'You chilly, love?'

'No, no, I'm fine. Just knackered.'

She saw the back of the driver's head nod. 'We'll have you home safe soon.'

'Thanks,' she said quietly. Not home. Not safe. And the worst of it was she still had no idea why any of this was happening. Some of it she had worked out. Or thought maybe she had. Elena was plotting grandly. Something political because she needed these MPs and lords. Then there was the attack. Every time she thought of it she felt that dragon breath of the exploding grenade.

Elena's security detail conveniently delayed. The men in the attic. *Send her the name.* Elena's attaché case was probably payment to them to tell her who the traitor on her security detail was, then she had ordered Michael to kill him. And he had. It was the only thing that made sense. So those men, the men in the attic, they were the men in the Donald Trump masks? But why had they been targeting Elena, and what had any of it to do with the spidery man at Peter's last dinner, Noah Warrington, who had congratulated her on becoming Elena's protégé? Peace. The man had said that as he unwrapped Elena's scarf from round the bricks of currency. Milos might have helped negotiate that payment – but he had been there in Korčula. What had Peter got to do with it, or a troll farm? Too many pieces and they all felt as if they were from different jigsaws.

'Sorry, love. Did you say something?'

'No. I mean, just talking to myself. I said knowledge is power.'

He indicated left and drew up at the guard post. The guard shone his torch through the window and she put up her hand to shield her eyes. He mumbled an apology and the bollards sank.

'Don't know about that, love. Plenty of stuff I know that I wish I didn't. I go with "ignorance is bliss" myself.'

It made her smile. He drew up in front of the house and she added a tip with the card machine.

'Have you always lived in London?' she asked.

'You'd think it, wouldn't you, listening to me? No. I came here from Southend when I was twenty. My wife is a Londoner. Wouldn't think of living anywhere else, so when I fell for her I had to come. Thanks. That's very generous.' The machine whirred and he passed a receipt through the dividing panel.

'Do you like it?'

'Love it now. Got to love it doing the Knowledge really, it's full of surprises this city. You can have any sort of life you want here.' He was smiling at her now. His head was shaved, and his cheeks stubbled. He wore round glasses and she noticed a half-read paperback on the seat beside him. She recognised it from the books she and her flatmates had in the houseshare. She'd read it herself during her recovery. Some thriller about saving the world from nuclear bombs with a posh hero and a love interest who was a physicist but always wore high heels. 'First six months though – loneliest I've ever felt in my entire fucking life.'

'Sounds about right.'

She opened the door.

'Chin up, love.'

Chin up.

The present from Elena was waiting for her in her room. A jewel box, and inside it a necklace, old, delicate, a mix of sapphires and pearls with a matching bracelet. They were stunning. She'd choose them over Madeleine's confections any day of the week. Elena had known that without needing to be told. Felt it. A beautiful gift, a reminder that her chances of spying successfully in the household for Jane Lucas were about the same as winning the lottery. Elena saw too much, knew Ruth too well. She set them aside and collapsed into bed.

31

Ruth clambered automatically into the shower the next morning and wondered what to do with her day. How many of them did she have left? Maybe she should make a will. She'd been paid her first month's wages after all. Maybe she'd survive to a second pay cheque. Ten grand would make a difference to the Cunninghams.

'Oh, sod this,' she said out loud, getting out of the shower. If she was going to get killed, she was going to try and work out what was going on first. No way she was just going to sit here and see who got her first, Jane or Elena. She might not be able to change it, but she could face it. Whatever she found out had to be better than this. She dressed. A visit to the office and she was out of the house by nine. She took a book.

By early afternoon she was sipping tea in a café on Westbourne Park Road. A man, a spray of acne round his chin and one of those wispy semi-beards, joined her and ordered toast. He unzipped his jacket, pulled out a loose bundle of papers and handed it to her.

'This all of it, Simon?' Ruth said.

'Yes. That's it. Now can I have my money?'

'Calm down, love. I want to make sure it's what I need first. Drink your tea, eat your toast like a normal person.'

Ruth had met Simon as he was coming on for his shift four hours earlier in an alley round the back of the police station – one of the corners where the reluctant and resentful paused for a smoke, waiting till the last possible minute before going into work. No point approaching the bright and shiny lads and lasses who bounced up the steps with a sense of purpose and their tails

wagging. Ruth glanced up at him as he thanked the waitress for
the tea and started crunching his toast. He looked shifty and ill at
ease, a young man, not out of his twenties, with none of the physical confidence Ruth associated with the decent policemen she had
met. She started scanning the photocopied pages he'd handed her
– yes, this was what she wanted, autopsy report, incident report,
thirty or forty pages in total – the complete output of the very
short investigation into the death of Mr Peter Baxter. God rest his
soul, if God had managed to find one.

'Why photocopies?' she said as she folded the sheets together
and shut them in her handbag.

'What?' He wiped crumps off his thin lips. 'Oh, they log printouts from the computer so I had to copy the file off Brooks's table.
He's out at lunch celebrating his new promotion, so I had time.'

His nails were bitten to the quick and his face was hollowed out.
He looked more like an addict than an officer. She took the envelope out of her bag and handed it to him. Five grand in a mix of
twenties and fifties.

He stuffed it into his jacket, eyes darting round the room.

'Mate, don't spend it down the bookies,' Ruth said. He started,
eyes wide. 'Maybe the police isn't for you. Be a plumber or
something.'

'Why do you say that? About the bookies?' His eyes narrowed
again – aggressive, defensive.

'You were too easy to bribe. Odds on you've been spending
money you haven't got and you look like a gambler to me. Get out
of the force before you do something that could really screw
someone up.'

'Yeah, thanks for the advice.' She was pretty sure he didn't
mean that. 'Why you want this stuff anyway? You a journalist?'

Because she wanted to know. Because she needed to have an
idea of what had happened that night. Because if she could put it
all in a line from Megan and her spy games, to the men in the attic
above the jeweller's shop, to the murdered bloke in Paris and Peter
being hauled off after the dinner, the conference and the Sir Tobys,
maybe she'd see where she fitted in. Where Jane Lucas fitted.

Where Michael fitted. Michael – was he just after the pay cheque? Happy to overlook inconvenient truths when it suited him. Plenty of people like that around. And this report now stuffed in her bag felt like a corner piece.

'I'm just a concerned citizen, pet,' she said giving it the full northern and watching his face crease up with mild confusion.

She put a tenner on the table to cover the teas and toast and left without looking back. The phone buzzed. From Elena.

Where are you?

Out for a walk. You need me?

Where?

Hyde Park.

No, need you Saturday now, so take time on walk Have left things on your desk.

Perfect. Ruth headed for the Albert Memorial and found a bench were she could read the papers without having to drink more bad coffee. The bench was shaded by a massive plane tree. When had she last seen real countryside? Out of the bus window on the way down to London, and the view from the M1 doesn't really count as countryside. She remembered getting the bus to Richmond once with Megs in the middle of the trial. Pat Cunningham's idea and they'd both made faces at it. They were town girls. But she'd made them a packed lunch and waited with them for the bus, so they'd had to go. They'd gone to see the castle then taken the rover bus up the dale. That was countryside. Another gift for the Sir Tobys – hunting and fishing weekends. On the estate of someone impressive. Christ, she couldn't stop.

She got out the pages and read. First the emergency call reporting a body by the tracks at 3 a.m. The guy who made the call, head of a maintenance crew walking the line in the early morning hours, sounded in pieces even on the transcript. There were pages of crime scene logs, most of it full of acronyms and technical details Ruth couldn't understand, and a note that the death was being treated as suspicious. One of the first officers had flagged what he thought were drag marks half a mile up the track from where the body was found. Then came the autopsy.

The language was so dry, so technical, it was hard to remember that it was about Peter. Ruth thought of him being bundled into the back of the car, and bundled was the only word that worked really, no matter what she had said to the police. She remembered his angry appeals to Andrei, the spidery man – Noah Warrington, she knew that now – standing with the family and Milos. Had Peter been afraid? Yes. One of Ruth's therapists had once told her anger is just another way of expressing fear, and it was one of those things people tell you sometimes that end up feeling like a key in a lock. A door opens and you understand something, get something about yourself or other people which had been mysterious before. What about drunk? She checked the line on the report about his blood alcohol level. Didn't mean much to her. Something to google, but the report also noted he had cocaine in his system. He hadn't been slurring when he shouted out to his hosts though. And he had sounded desperate. Shit.

Ruth turned the page and saw a sheet of photographs of Peter's body on the slab. The horror was muted by lack of colour and her informer had obviously set the copier to draft to speed things up, but Ruth still felt a foul taste in her mouth. Peter was a lump of meat by the time he got to the mortuary, a vaguely human-shaped mess of tissue. She turned the page. These things had to have some kind of executive summary. *Time of death.* Finally, a fact she could slot into her own timeline of events. Between eleven and half past midnight, just like the solicitors' email had said. So Michael wasn't in the clear. Give me something else. She stared at the pages, started again at the top of the autopsy section. *Cause of death: blunt force trauma.* Peter's skull had been crushed, but as he had been struck twice by trains it was impossible to tell if that had been the blow that killed him. Most of the other injuries were, the report informed her, post mortem. *Stomach contents.* She almost skipped it, her gorge rising again as she read salmon, potato, chocolate of some sort and ... what the hell? *Also discovered in his stomach were two five-hundred-euro notes.*

* * *

Ruth stuffed the papers into her bag, got up and walked through the park all the way to Hyde Park Corner, not really sure where she was going. She turned into the streets north of Piccadilly and found a quiet pub in Shepherd Market. She bought a coke so she could go through the rest of the report with her back to a wall. Five-hundred-euro notes. Like the ones she'd delivered to Madeleine, like the ones she'd delivered in blocks to the shaven-headed guy and his mate.

Was Peter enough of an arse to eat them for show? Like those cocktails with gold flakes in them, or lighting a cigar with a fifty quid note? She could imagine him as the sort of man who would do that. She could imagine him doing it in front of some homeless bloke in Mayfair just for the fun of it. But then eating them. I mean, the gold flakes make your drink look pretty and a burning note will give you a light, but Ruth couldn't imagine eating those notes would be fun. She turned back to the autopsy and tried reading the report again. Something had caught her eye. *Developed bruising round the face.* She sipped her coke and set it down on the table. Shifted it from side to side. Developed bruising. The red marks on his face. Two lines later: *Small cuts on lips and soft palate.*

Oh, Christ. Someone had *made* him eat those notes, and if Ruth was right about the marks on his face, he had been made to eat them in the Shilkovs' dining room. She wanted to stop. She had to stop. But she couldn't take the papers back to the house, not if Michael was searching her room when the impulse seized him. She kept going. Only a few more pages. A report on the visit to the Shilkovs' house, including her statement about what she had seen and when Michael got back. A note that the CCTV cameras outside Ladbroke Grove had been vandalised early in the evening, though a traffic camera on the Kensington High Street recorded the Shilkov car with Michael in it going towards the station and away at roughly the right times. Jesus. Were they supposed to think it was a coincidence that the CCTV was out?

Then a report on the notes found in Peter's stomach. They were fakes. Fakes. Another key turning in a lock. Now a report on the search of Peter's room in his parents' house. She read it carefully. The fake notes there too. Also five hundred euro. Same batch. Special Branch officer on attachment suggested a forger he suspected was active on the Edgware Road. A note to follow up, then the investigation was closed. No further action. Edgware Road. Her trip with Elena after she came back from Paris.

Ruth finished her drink and left the bar, out into the first stirrings of rush hour. Getting rid of the pages took a while. A few in one recycling bin, a few in another wrapped up in *Evening Standard*s and the morning's ragged *Metro*s, more among the fast food wrappers in a bin outside Sainsbury's.

Then as she tore up the last pages and stuffed them into the general waste outside Green Park Tube, about to head towards the Palace, she heard a distant crump, a false note in the music of the city. The world paused as half the people on the street stopped, turned towards the noise, shielding their eyes, and half hurried on, oblivious. Gasps, people pointing, holding up phones, a thin column of smoke, glittering in the low light against a pinking sky to the east, towards Piccadilly Circus. Then the sirens began.

32

People just stopped. Then, after a couple of minutes, as the plume lost its form and began to collapse down into itself, they began to talk to each other.

'What was that?' Woman with short blonde hair in trench coat and summer business dress.

'Some sort of explosion.' Skinny bearded man with a backpack.

'A bomb, at the National Gallery! BBC are reporting it now.' Older businessman, oversized phone in his hand, briefcase at his feet. The smoke was still in the air. People started to gather around him. Someone else got their phone streaming too. Ruth didn't move. Just listened to the newsreader's voice over the tinny speaker.

'. . . an explosion at the National Gallery and we're going to BBC reporter Nayla Hadad live now on the phone from the scene.'

'Hi Brian, yes it's very loud here, but I can just about hear you.' Sirens and screams squelched over her voice. 'The explosion happened approximately three minutes ago. I can't tell you much – obviously the situation is very confused and the smoke is only just beginning to clear, but I think the explosion took place in the Sainsbury Wing of the gallery and . . . all I can say is the damage seems very extensive.'

One of the women watching over the businessman's shoulder started crying. The guy with the beard hugged her. Ruth finally got out her own phone and checked Twitter. Pictures of dust clouds. Tiny videos snippets of running feet and shouting.

'We have no idea about casualties as yet,' the newsreader was saying, 'or the causes of the explosion.'

Her phone rang. Michael.

'Where are you?'

'Green Park.'

'Stay there. I'm coming to get you.'

Ruth looked up as helicopters thudded overhead. 'Don't be daft. Roads will be blocked. I can walk home.'

'Just wait, will you! By the coffee stand. I swear Ruth, if you're not there waiting for me I'll skin you alive.'

'Fine.' She disconnected and stared at the handset. He didn't sound very home counties then. People were beginning to wonder what to do with themselves. Fragments of conversation. 'I'm fine . . . I'll find a bus.' 'I don't know.' 'I'll head back to the office for now.' 'Getting home's going to be a nightmare.' 'Can you pick up the kids tonight?' 'I don't know!' 'I'm OK. I'm OK, baby.'

She saw him before he saw her. He was using his height to look through the crowds. When he spotted her his face flooded with relief. He jogged towards her, then hugged her hard.

'What are you fussing about, I'm fine!'

He was dressed in his Sunday special. Chinos and T-shirt. He noticed her noticing.

'Day off. The family is all safe.'

'I can smell it,' Ruth said. It was true, something acrid in the air, like a bonfire on waste ground. 'Where were you? Why are you here?'

He took a step back from her. 'I was seeing a friend by the river. It's my day off.'

'Yeah, you said.' She was angry with him. She turned away towards Piccadilly and started walking. He followed.

'Where are you going?'

'I want to see it. With my own eyes.'

He put a hand on her arm. 'Why? That's mad. Come home.'

She shook him off. 'No. Why was Peter Baxter forced to eat fake five-hundred-euro notes?'

He was shocked. 'How did you know?'

So he had known that's what happened. 'I bribed a copper to get my hands on the autopsy report. How did *you* know?'

'I . . .'

'Why was Elena targeted? Was it the jewel thieves, the All Stars, who attacked the café shop? Does the Uprising really exist or were they just made up by a troll farm? Did you fucking kill James Tranter on Elena's orders after those goons upstairs at Elena's sent her his name?'

His lips moved, but nothing came out, before finally, 'Did Elena say I did?'

She didn't answer, just turned to walk away again.

'I called you first, Ruth,' he shouted after her. 'When I knew you were OK, I checked in with the team, but I called you first. I care about you. Come home.'

And that was supposed to be enough, was it? That and all his 'trust me' rubbish. Him caring about her, getting soft when he saw a picture of her as a teenager, his cryptic warnings. That was supposed to take the place of actually doing something to help her, of explaining to her when they were part of, of action, was it? Low-cost caring. Concern, that was what they used to say to her, to Megan. *We're concerned.* It had been no use to either of them. Now Megan was dead and Ruth was hanging on by her newly manicured fingernails. She kept walking.

It had been perhaps twenty minutes since the explosion. Traffic was stopped dead and the air was thick with blowing horns. The closer she got to Trafalgar Square the thicker the crowds grew. She started seeing people with dust in their hair, faces dirty. As she watched, a man – dazed, blood trickling from a graze on his forehead – put his hand out to the wall and lent against it. A teenager, her hair plaited with gold thread and oiled on top of her head, stopped and put her hand on his shoulder, steadied his hand so he could drink from her water bottle. By the time Ruth was passing them, the teenager had his phone in her hand and was talking to someone. 'He's OK. Just shook up, I think. I know . . . I know . . . What's your address? Me and my mates will see him home . . . No worries.'

The consistency of the air began to change and the smell of burning grew stronger. Two boys passed her, their arms round each other like they were in a three-legged race, holding each other up. Down Haymarket. Police on motorbikes were rapping their leather-gloved knuckles against car windows, making the drivers pull up over the curb to leave space for emergency vehicles. They blew whistles, blocked turnings on the east side, drove traffic off against the one-way system to the west.

Ruth began to walk faster. She dodged into Suffolk Place then Suffolk Street to avoid the cordon between Haymarket and Pall Mall, then past the statue of a bloke on a horse and down Cockspur Street to take her to the south-west corner of Trafalgar Square itself. Bloody Nelson looking in the wrong direction again. One or two of the police on duty shot her dark looks, but they were too busy clearing a way through the traffic to stop her.

She shouldered her way through the crowd, clustered in the corner and looked. The front of the National – it looked just like the logo for the conference, those high columns with the portico on top – looked undamaged, then she noticed the light bouncing off the broken windows. A bus and three or four cars were stopped, scattered at crazy angles in the road. A taxi cab had gone into a lamp post, bending it over the car as if it was asking for directions from the driver, and the windscreen was a frost of broken glass. A group of school kids, their bright yellow backpacks now grey with dust, were being swaddled in aluminium blankets. A couple of TV crews. Huge trailers on the east of the square marked 'Incident Command'. More police directing traffic, armed officers in baseball caps.

Smoke still rose from the gap between the main building and the Sainsbury Wing. Everyone around her had their phones out. Ruth closed her hands around the yellow police tape and stared. Pulsing blue and red lights. The white stone looked as if a bite had been taken out of it. She looked around. Lots of paramedics, lots more people with silver blankets round their shoulders being led off towards the blue-and-yellow-striped ambulances.

A van drew up and half a dozen guys in what looked like military gear got out. They had dogs with them. Under Nelson's Column a gaggle of press with cameras and microphones crowded round a man in police uniform. He appeared in close-up on the phones around her, but she couldn't hear what he was saying. Then he walked away and disappeared into the back of one of the trailers.

More whistles, the growl of motorbike engines and a limousine flanked by outriders growled up the Mall.

'Who is it?' she asked the man standing at her shoulder who was half a head taller than she was.

'Prime minister. Make for a nice photo op with the ruins and smoke, while he gives us his law and order shtick,' he replied bitterly. 'Fucking idiots, these terrorists. Playing right into their sodding hands.'

'It wasn't an accident then?'

He looked at her as if she were insane. 'The Uprising have just claimed responsibility on Twitter. There was some party on tonight for the toffs, that was the target. They said the bomb went off early.'

Oh yes. That party. Elena had decided she didn't want to go, but a raffle book of tickets had gone to the Sir Tobys and their wives. Fundraising for Venice, restoration of a Canaletto. The Gallery had laid heavy emphasis on the exclusive nature of the occasion. A second limousine pulled up behind the first. The men who got out of it followed the prime minister.

Warrington. When you see a chance, take it.

'Noah!' Ruth shouted, and the spidery man turned towards the crowd, shading his eyes. Then he spoke to a younger man standing next to him before turning back to follow the prime minister again.

The younger man came straight for her.

'Ms Miller? How can I help you?' he said as he reached her and put out his hand. 'I'm Felix Page, Noah's assistant.'

'Elena told me to meet up with you. She wants eyes on what's happening,' Ruth said. He might believe it.

'I don't think that will be possible,' he said, frowning.

'Make it possible, Mr Page.' Helps saying stuff like that if you mean it. Commit. If this was another corner piece, Ruth wasn't going to miss her chance to grab it.

He walked away a few steps and had a short conversation on his phone, then he came back towards her.

'If you'd like to come with me.'

She ducked under the tape and he walked with her, his arm held up stiffly behind her back, not touching, in the direction of the Incident Command trailers.

'Ms Miller, just to keep things simple, Noah and myself are vouching for you as a member of his staff. Do you have any identification with you?'

'I have my passport.' She hadn't put it down since she got it.

'Excellent.'

Ruth was led to the cordon, then once her passport had been checked, up the little flight of steps and into the trailer. It was divided in two. At the far end she could see a set of desks and computers and men and women in uniform wearing headphones. At the closest end was a narrow conference table.

'Ruth, thank goodness you're all right,' Noah said, getting up from his chair and coming to kiss her on the cheek. Then his hand tightened round her arm and his voice changed. 'You shouldn't be here. Elena knows better than this! Why did she send you?'

'She didn't. I lied,' Ruth replied. 'I saw you arrive and I wanted to see what was going on.'

His eyes were flinty. 'This is not a game, Miss Miller. You do not amuse me. You should know Elena's protection has its limits.'

Curiosity and cats.

'Noah?' The prime minister was calling him to the table.

'One moment, please, Prime Minister.' He turned back to Ruth. 'Do you understand, Miss Miller?'

'Yes.'

'Good. Now stay by Mr Page and if I so much as see you look in the wrong direction I will bury you.'

Shit. She had enough enemies already. Stupid, Ruth. Stupid.

Felix beckoned her to stand next to him up against the wall. The prime minister looked at her briefly, then turned back to the other people round the table.

It was only then Ruth noticed one of them was Jane Lucas. She looked at Ruth too, but without a twitch of recognition. Idiot, Ruth. Christ, if Jane Lucas was important enough to be in this room Ruth's worst fears about her power were true. And she'd made another enemy. Maybe she should just throw a rock at the prime minister and have done with it. Get dragged off to jail, claim to be part of the Uprising. Could that be worse? Yes, it could, because of the people in jail who needed to stay there. Who deserved to be there. She felt panic prickle up and down her arms and clasped her hands to stop them shaking.

'Well! What in hell is happening?' the prime minister said. He looked irritated, as if he'd just been yanked out of the shower by the delivery guy or something.

The man who had been briefing the press before he arrived cleared his throat.

'At approximately four thirty-five today an explosive device was detonated in room nine of the National Gallery. Room nine had been closed early so it could be made ready for a sponsors' event this evening. Extensive damage was done to that room and to the two adjoining.' He looked down at his notes. 'Also to the bridge to the Sainsbury Wing.'

'That whole end of the building looks like it's about to fall down!' the prime minister barked. 'And what the hell are you doing speaking to the press before I got here? Not your show.' He twisted round and scowled at one of his aides. 'And tell his office, if I see the mayor down here this evening I'll feed him to my dog. Put up roadblocks if you have to. No way that runt is speaking before me.'

Big words. But Ruth found Jane, sitting there calmly with no expression on her face at all, and Noah with his flint eyes and sallow skin, a lot more frightening.

'The damage is more superficial than it might appear, Prime Minister,' uniform said.

'How many dead?'

'We don't know. If the bomb had gone off during the reception, as the people who are claiming responsibility say was the intention, it would have been a great deal worse.'

'That's what I'm supposed to say to people, is it?' the prime minister said, slapping his hands down on the table. '"Don't worry, chaps, could have been worse"?'

Uniform didn't reply. The prime minister looked at the heavily jowled man sitting next to Jane Lucas.

'What about you Sir Philip? Cat got your tongue?'

Sir Philip looked at the prime minister coldly. 'No, Prime Minister. I am only wondering why that man,' he indicated Noah with a twitch of his chin, 'is in this meeting with his staff when your own home secretary is not.'

'We are lucky to have him with us,' the prime minister said. 'We were meeting in Downing Street when the sodding bomb went off and the home secretary is presumably deciding which heels to wear when she goes for a stumble in the rubble.'

He looked around as if expecting people to laugh. A couple of nervous smiles was all he got. Ruth hardly dared breathe; she was concentrating purely on Jane, the way she was holding herself. Sir Philip is her boss, she thought. That's it.

'Noah, show them what you've got. There's a good chap.'

Noah reached into his coat pocket and produced a single sheet of folded paper. He passed it to the man in dress uniform.

'As a sign of goodwill, and with the blessing of our State Department, Glenville Solutions has been devoting some of its energies to finding the identities of the leaders of the Uprising and the authors of their manifesto.'

Sir Philip stared at him with loathing.

'I was meeting with the prime minister this morning to share with him these names and addresses.' Uniform had unfolded the sheet and was reading it. 'My assistant, Felix, is ready to supply you with the raw intel, and we have summaries of the evidence collected in a form suitable for you to draw up search and arrest warrants with immediate effect.'

Uniform passed it over his shoulder, and another man in uniform took it from him. Felix reached into his pocket and handed the same flunky a dark-green flash drive. He scurried off with it to the computer room.

'I would hope that we'll be receiving copies of this intelligence,' Sir Philip said, his voice dripping with disdain.

Noah smiled. 'I'm sure copies can be provided.'

'Are you checking it now?' the prime minister said, craning his neck to see where the officer with the address sheet had gone. 'I tell you now I'm going in front of the cameras in twenty minutes and I'm going to tell the nasty little jackals there has been a major breakthrough in the investigation.'

'Prime Minister!' Sir Philip said, his face flushing. 'Until our own people have had the chance to verify—'

He cut across him. 'Noah, do I have your word this intel is good?'

'You do, Prime Minister.'

'Good enough for me.'

Sir Philip tried again, but the prime minister turned on him. 'Enough! God, I wasn't on board before, but I am now. You've provided me with nothing but rumours and gossip and the British taxpayers are sick of it. GCHQ is a dinosaur.'

Sir Philip wasn't ready to stand down yet.

'Prime Minister, the legislation under consideration is a threat to the integrity of the intelligence agencies.'

Legislation. That was Yuri's speciality. All those MPs. Security. Tuchman's report and Townsend's rumours. The pieces reoriented themselves.

'Codswallop! You've been riddled with spies since World War Two and now any teenager with a laptop can run rings around you. Signals intelligence in this country is a joke as this afternoon clearly demonstrates. About time the intelligence agencies learnt to take a helping hand from private enterprise, or we're all fucked! This country is staggering into the gutter and you just look down your noses at the only people willing to try to get some value out this hellscape. Sink or swim, people. Sink or swim.'

He seemed to have surprised himself. He looked down at the table again.

Another flunky handed the senior officer a piece of paper.

'The latest casualty figures, Prime Minister.' He glanced at it and handed it over.

'Good. Only two dead,' the prime minister said. 'A cleaner and a security guard. Names: Carmela Blake and Kambili Oni. Check I'm pronouncing that right will you? I always get the stress wrong. Tragic. Tragic. Best of Britain. Multiple wounded . . .' His eyes widened. 'The bastards got a Caravaggio! Damn, damn it! And a Canaletto and two Veroneses. Christ!' He scanned the sheet again and tucked it into his pocket. 'Noah, you can stand behind me with my people as we make the statement. Trading on the stock exchange will remain suspended this afternoon as a mark of respect, blah blah blah. Open as usual first thing in the morning. Anything from the Palace yet?'

'I have the statement here, Prime Minister. It will be posted in front of Buckingham Palace as soon as your remarks are complete and the home secretary is on her way.'

'Good. She can stand next to Noah. Right. Let's get this over with, then I better go visit the wounded. If I meet one bloody protester on the way through the hospital I'll have you all fired. I do not want another lecture about the sodding NHS! Right. Everyone out.'

Ruth streamed away with the rest of the hangers-on and waited, uncertain, at the bottom of the steps. When Noah emerged he left the prime minister to huddle with a couple of his aides, then he looked round, saw her and came up.

'Were you entertained, Miss Miller?'

Damn it, she wasn't going to shrink in front of this man. Standing here between half of the Metropolitan Police and the prime minister's security team was probably as safe as she was ever going to get. But she could smile. She looked him in the eye, took a breath. Play nice, Ruthie.

'A fascinating insight, Mr Warrington. I sincerely apologise for lying to join you. Thank you so much for your role in bringing the terrorists who put me in hospital to justice.'

He rocked back slightly, raised an eyebrow. 'Well I think no one in there recognised you as someone who works for Elena, so you seem to have got away with it. Lucky girl.'

Apart from the woman sitting next to Sir Philip, of course. The one blackmailing her to spy in a house where they didn't just colour outside the lines, they coloured in blood. She kept her face blank.

'Thank you, Mr Warrington.'

He offered her a wintery smile. 'Another of Elena's original creations. Be very, very careful young lady. You are being watched.'

Yup.

Then he walked away to join the group around the prime minister again.

Jane Lucas emerged behind her boss. He looked as if he was on the verge of a heart attack. Jane stared at her, then followed him across the square where a policeman lifted the cordon for them. The sky had darkened, and the first fat drops of rain were spattering the pavement. Most of the ambulances had gone, but the helicopters still swept to and fro over them. Ruth didn't stay for the press conference.

She checked her phone as she walked west from Trafalgar Square. One message from Elena: *OK?* She sent back a 'yes'.

Michael had known that Peter was made to eat a couple of fake bank notes in the hours before he died. She hoped he hadn't seen it happen. He can't have done, it must have been going on while he was still in her room, looking at her photograph. Her relief, realising that, made her feel weak. But he knew about it and hadn't said a word to her, yet he still had the brass neck to ask for her trust. New rule: only trust people who don't ask to be trusted.

33

The only remaining phone box in London. Well, not quite, they were still scattered around stations or left on street corners for tourists, and still filled with cards for girls and sex chat lines. New Bond Street, opposite Cartier and outside Ralph Lauren. The shine and squalor. The rain was strengthening and whipped against the dulled plastic panes in petulant twisting squalls. Ruth fed her money into the slot, picked up the handset and dialled. The paint on the numbers was chipped away, the handset felt grimed with the calls of the lost and desperate, and the box smelt of damp concrete and stale piss.

'Hello?'

'Pat? It's Ruth.'

'Ruth! Oh my lovely, how nice to hear from you! Just let me get settled and we can have a proper chat if you've got a minute. You all right? You weren't caught up in that business today?'

'No, I'm good. And a chat would be great.'

Ruth could hear the tap of the receiver against the big colourful brooch Pat Cunningham wore on her cardigan as she held the receiver to her chest and called off. 'Mike! Could I have my tea in here? It's Ruth!'

Ruth could see it, the little square box of a house in one of the rows in the middle of town. Gas fire lit and kettle always on the boil. The front door opening straight out onto the pavement and the back yard with the shed where they stored their bikes and the bins opening out into the cobbled ginnel where the younger kids played football and bullied and befriended each other up and down the street. Pat settling in her armchair near the fire where she could keep an eye on the telly and who was letting themselves into the hall. Woodchip wallpaper and decorative plates high up on the picture rail. Pat's were all of country cottages. Mike, Mr Cunningham, liked ones with World War Two aeroplanes on them. They alternated all round the room and halfway up the stairs.

'Thanks, pet. I'll tell her. Mike sends his love. Now then, Ruth. How are you? It's ever so good to hear your voice.'

Ruth smiled at the blurring taxi lights going past on the street, the hiss of their tyres as they surged impatiently across the junction.

'I'm OK, Pat. I'm working for this really rich woman in Kensington. She gives me money to send to people who ask for it. Charity stuff.'

Pat let out a long sighing breath. 'I'm not sure as I'd like that, love! How do you decide?'

'It's hard. But I can normally send everyone something. Enough to make a difference, anyway. But sometimes I look them up and realise it's a scam and that makes me angry.'

'I'm sure it would. Is that all your job then?'

Ruth thought of the trips to Paris, the jewels from Madeleine, the conference and the dinners. 'No, I organise social things for her and her business colleagues. Tickets and parties and things like that.'

She could almost feel Mrs Cunningham making a face. 'London! Jess, you know Jess from Grant Street who has the twins, she went down there to visit her nephew. Said it didn't look like there'd even *been* a recession. And the prices. Made me sick just thinking about it. Is it interesting?'

Ruth hesitated. 'I met the prime minister today. Well, sort of. We were in the same room.'

She heard Pat's sharp intake of breath. 'I never. Well. What did you think of him?'

She remembered the red face, the swearing. The sort of cursing she reckoned posh boys did to try and sound frightening. 'Not much, if I'm honest.'

Pat snorted. 'Aye, well. Can't say I'm surprised. You managing OK?'

The rhythms of her voice conjured up the warmth of the room, the carpet patterned with small blue cornflowers and forget-me-nots, the coffee table. Mike got shouted at if he put his feet up on it, but he did anyway. 'Yeah, it was tough at first though.'

Pat's voice became tentative. 'And Megan never showed up?'

'No.'

'I am sorry to hear that, pet. Really I am. Have you made friends?'

Andrei? Elena? Jane? Michael? 'Not really.'

Pat sipped her tea on the other end of the line. She liked it strong, no sugar. It kept her going through the daily challenges of a rotating household of troubled teens, and keeping an eye on her own kids and grandkids. Filling in forms and setting alarms and always on the lookout for bargains, clothes and toys and knick-knacks she'd give to the kids just to make them feel for a moment like they belonged.

'You sound lonely, love. What can I do to help?'

Ruth's eyes grew hot. 'I'm just . . . Pat, these people I'm working for.' How to explain? 'I don't think they are good people.'

Pat snorted, a warm bubble of not laughter but something like it. 'Lamb, they wouldn't be. Not with all that money.'

Ruth could feel the tears on her face now. The fear and sudden cold of the air. Her bravery and resolve all tatters.

'I've always been worried for you, Ruth,' Pat went on. 'You're one of the bright ones, and ambitious too. I always worried it might get you into trouble. Wish I could have kept you at home, somewhere safe. But you are a jittery one. Always away and jumping into the next thing.'

Ruth swallowed a sob. 'I think I'm in trouble, Pat. I don't know what to do.'

'I wish I could give you a hug. Not that you ever were much of a hugger, but sounds like you could do with one now.'

Ruth wiped her eyes on the back of her hand. 'It's good just to talk. Sorry to be such a misery.'

'Don't be daft. Are you stuck?'

'Yeah. And I'm scared.'

There was a long pause and Ruth closed her eyes again, just to hear Pat breathing.

'You know what to do, Ruth. Deep down you do. And it'll be the same stuff that got you into this will get you out. You're smart. You know right from wrong. And you've got a good heart. And you're loyal. That's enough, you know. Remember at the end of the day all that glitters isn't gold. Better to be poor and know where you left your soul when you wake up in the morning than rich and spend all that money to try and forget you ever had one.'

'Maybe you are right.'

'Of course I'm right. Mike! Am I right?' Ruth heard the answer in the distance. Imagined Mr Cunningham at the kitchen table with the local newspaper huffing at the council news. 'You're always right, my queen.'

'See? You can always come home, love. Stay with us till you get settled. Mike will blow up the airbed for you. He's got a foot pump.'

'Thanks. How's the family?'

'Oh Kascee is kicking up rough because she didn't get the part she wanted in the school play, but Samuel's decided he's going to be an engineer. Doing his A-levels and really settling down to it, Chris says. He went on work experience at the old ICI plant and loved it.'

'Tell them hi. Don't tell them I've been mithering on though, will you?'

'Ha! They wouldn't believe me if I did. Tough cookie like you. Just needed a moment to gather your thoughts, didn't you?'

Ruth drew in her breath, slow and deep so she could feel it from her heels to the top of her head. 'That's it.'

'Off you go then. You know what to do, so do it.'

'Thanks, Pat.'

'You need anything else now, do you?'

'No. I have what I need.'

They said goodbye and Ruth hung up the phone. Heard an unspent coin rattle into the returned money slot. She stayed still, holding the receiver, head hanging down. Not really making the decision as much as taking a minute to understand that the decision had already been made.

It took her a couple of hours to get back to the Shilkov house.

With the roads blocked and the Tube suspended, walking back seemed like the best option, but she wasn't rushing. Halfway back she turned into the Swan on Bayswater Road and ordered whisky. Drank it. Ordered another. Drank it too. They helped. Ben on the door must have called in on his radio as she arrived. By the time she got downstairs, Michael was waiting for her.

'Are you OK?' he said. Urgent, taking a step forward then sensing she didn't want the hug, the concern, holding himself where he was. Pat was right, Ruth wasn't much of a hugger.

'Yeah. What's the latest?'

'You heard the Uprising are claiming responsibility?' Ruth nodded. 'An hour ago the police launched a raid in Hammersmith. Latest reports are two arrests and the recovery of some bomb-making equipment.'

She could smell hot metal, taste copper in her mouth.

'Hammersmith? What do your "contacts" say?'

She undid the belt of her Prada trench coat. She needed to clean herself up.

'Nice house. Educated. A couple. Radicalised in 2016 though they'd been active in left-wing politics since 2008.'

Sounded like Noah's information had been solid. Probably more photo ops with the prime minister in the future for him.

'Ruth, what aren't you telling me?'

He was doing the big wide eyes thing. His hands held slightly from his body, palms open. Open, trust-me body language.

'You are either a liar, Michael, or an idiot. And why would I trust a liar or an idiot?'

He took a step towards her, grabbed her wrist hard. Good cop to bad cop. Just like that. 'What are you talking about? I've told you, I've done nothing wrong.'

'We like to tell ourselves that, don't we? Have you checked

exactly how many of Yuri and Elena's former friends and employees are dead or missing? Just you know, out of interest?'

He uncurled his fingers from her wrist, hearing the despair in her voice. 'Ruth, I don't know why you are thinking like that. But for God's sake, if that's what you believe, then I'll say it again: get out. Or would you rather sell your soul for a Chanel bag?'

The last bit came out sharp, a little venom on it.

She smiled. 'Most of my life no one would have thought my soul was worth even a bag for life, love. I'm glad I've upgraded.'

Then she went down to her room and closed the door on him. He didn't try and follow her.

She cleaned herself up, retouched her make-up. Then she changed into fresh jeans and a mint silk top and checked her reflection in the mirror. Yes, she looked like herself. The Shilkov version of herself. She picked up the phone and checked on Elena. All red. But she was in the house. Masha had been taking a coffee tray into the living room as she came downstairs.

For a moment she just stood there in the padded silence of the room, thinking of the Cunninghams, of Megan, of the giddy hungry delight of holding Michael on a Paris dancefloor, then that second as the grenades exploded in the café, the shimmering bright, burning destruction of it. The plume of smoke on the skyline and the way Noah had stared at Jane Lucas's boss. She had already decided, Pat was right.

She left the room and walked upstairs to the ground floor, knocked on the door of the library and went in. Elena was talking on the phone. When she saw who had come in she frowned, said something in French to whoever was on the line and hung up.

'Why are you here, Ruth? The schedule is red.'

'This can't wait.' Elena just stared at her; anger made her face look smoother, tighter, more animal-like. Ruth drew in her breath. Looked her in the eye.

'MI5 have been blackmailing me to spy on you. It started the day of the Restart party.'

34

Elena didn't say anything. Ruth didn't look away, but her muscles tensed, ready to be attacked. Then Elena nodded.

'Come.'

She stuck her phone in her pocket and strode towards the doors at the back of the room. The doors to Yuri's inner sanctum. She pushed them open.

'Yuri, *khochu tebya. Nuzhno eto uslyshat.*'

Ruth followed her. Elena didn't pause in the doorway, just went round behind the huge mahogany and green leather desk and put her arm across the back of Yuri's high-backed chair. Lent her hip against it. Ruth came in far enough to stand in front of the desk. She tried to take in the room. What had she been expecting? Bluebeard's cave? Just another fancy chamber. High windows overlooking the terrace, though Yuri's desk faced away from them. Box folders in highly polished bookcases. Between the windows hung dozens of small oil paintings in thick gilded frames. Dark pictures of fruit, dead game on wooded tables, cracked shellfish, a hare hanging against a plaster wall.

'Tell him.'

Ruth licked her lips. 'MI5 have been blackmailing me to spy on you and Elena. I was approached on the evening of the Restart party. I ignored it, then the same woman cornered me when I went to get my passport.'

Just as Elena had done, he stayed silent for a long moment, then he shut his laptop, opened a drawer in his desk and pulled out a yellow legal pad. He set it on the table and picked up a pen from the holder on his right. A fountain pen.

'Sit down, Ruth.'

The chair in front of the desk was an Edwardian-looking thing, the wood polished to a honey-coloured sheen, the leather seat matching the leather on the surface of his desk. She did as she was told. The last light was behind them now, putting their faces in shadow.

'Tell me everything,' Yuri said. 'From the beginning. Leave nothing out.'

Ruth did. She started at the party, moved on to the meeting on the roof of the passport office, the man pretending to look for directions, the email and the coffee shop. Yuri didn't ask any questions, just took notes on the yellow paper. The only sound was of Ruth's voice and the whispering pen. She gave precise details of the information she had passed to Jane, including the guests at the dinner party and existence of Natasha's spy book, and the information she hadn't – the meeting at Madeleine's. The spy book itself. She went through her meeting with Jane the day before in the church, then she reached seeing Jane with Sir Philip and the prime minister this afternoon, and Noah, and what had been said by whom in the Incident Command trailer.

'Then I decided to come and tell you everything.'

Yuri put out his hand. 'Your phone, please.'

She opened it with her fingerprint and passed it over. They bent their heads over it, scrolling back and forward through her messages, the photos on her camera. Yuri deleted them. 'Elena, I'll leave you to deal with the hard copy of Natasha's school project?'

'*Konechno.*'

Of course. Ruth realised she recognised that one too. How much she had learnt with the Shilkovs.

'Why?' Yuri asked. 'Why did you decide to tell us?'

'I don't trust Jane. And I'm a crap spy. She will blackmail me to get intelligence out of the house until you find out and kill me.'

'So you come and tell us yourself?' Yuri said. His voice was lightly ironic. For the first time Ruth lowered her eyes.

Elena was studying her. 'This is the only card she has to play, Yuri,' she said. 'Ruth is losing the game, trapped. She needs to change things, turn over the playing board, so she does this. It is not about trust.'

Yuri nodded as if accepting the assessment. 'But what do we do with her now?'

Elena turned and looked out into the garden. Yuri appeared to be reading through his notes. His handwriting was very elegant, swooping curls on his ys and gs. Swooping angles to his ts and fs. Ruth wished she had handwriting like that.

'Why not just leave?' Elena said without looking back at her. 'Why not just say "Elena, I do not like it here" and run away?'

Ruth's mouth was dry. 'I tried. I said I'd do that. She said if I did she'd destroy me, that getting an agent of her own into the house would waste time. Even if I managed to hide from her somehow, she could still . . .' Her voice tailed off.

Yuri tented his fingers together. 'What exactly does Jane Lucas hold over you?'

'Yes,' Elena said, her voice dark. 'What frightens so much a girl who picks up a live grenade?'

So Ruth told them that too.

Once she was done, they sent her to her room and asked her – it sounded like a request, not an order – not to leave the house.

Ruth sat in one of the armchairs in front of the fireplace and stared at the wall. She couldn't concentrate on anything, so there was no point picking up a book. The first question, she supposed, was would they kill her now? She had no idea how any of this worked, but James Tranter had betrayed them and he was dead, and Peter had done something with forged money and now he was dead too. Still all too fuzzy. She didn't want to die not understanding.

Ruth began to pull apart what she knew, see if she could work out what it was that had meant Peter had to die. He had run an errand for the Shilkovs, an errand that Andrei should have run, but had passed on to his friend. The police had discovered bundles of fake euros in his drawers, unusual transactions in his bank. Ruth thought of the bricks of notes she had handed to the brothers grim in Madeleine's attic, how the one with the hair had tested them with a pen. An anti-fraud device.

So her guess was Peter had skimmed a pay-off the Shilkovs had made, probably to the All Stars, replaced some of the notes with fakes. The All Stars had taken revenge against the Shilkov family, going after Elena and the girls in the café. Then Suzanne D'Arcy and Milos had brokered a peace. The Shilkovs had made up the shortfall, confirmed it was Peter's scheme and handed him over to the people he'd tried to con. And James Tranter was murdered, the man who had given them Elena's location and kept the security team out of the way. A blood covenant. The jewels to Suzanne had been a payment for putting the All Stars and Shilkovs back in contact and helping them to come to an understanding.

What had Elena paid the All Stars for in the first place? Megan and the kids had taken pictures of Milos and Suzanne in Korčula, as they were meeting with Noah Warrington and the troll farm princess. Her mind skidded sideways. Ruth remembered a book she'd read once about a jewel heist where real diamonds were replaced with fakes. What would have happened to her if she'd tried to pull that with the collars and cuffs from Madeleine? Her throat and mouth grew cold as she imagined being forced to eat cut glass, then being turned out among the wolves. Running in darkness and then finding Milos at the end of a shadowed alleyway. Her hand went to her throat and she realised she was still shaking.

The door opened and Elena came in. She shut it behind her and then sat in the chair opposite Ruth's. She looked older than usual, her skin dry, her eyes without their usual light.

'When are you due to meet Jane Lucas again?' she said, without preamble.

'I don't know.'

'Check your email. She will want to meet.'

Ruth did. Elena was right. Another message from Jimmy Reeves.

'She wants,' Ruth's voice cracked. She took a breath, cleared her throat and looked Elena in the eye. 'She wants to meet tomorrow. At Fortnum's. I'm supposed to email and confirm. She wants the list of Sir Tobys you've helped through Yuri's firm. And the journal.'

Elena looked her up and down very slowly.

'Elena, did you kill Megan?'

No flinch, no shock. Just one long moment of silence. 'How do you think I should deal with spies in my home?'

Ruth couldn't take it any more. She dropped her eyes and felt the tears on her face. Oh, Megan, you fool. Megan had felt she owed the world some brave and noble act because of what they had done and Jane Lucas had manipulated her into believing that spying on a dangerous oligarch and the well-connected criminals he was plotting with was just the thing to get rid of the red in her ledger. And Ruth? Curiosity killed the cat. She had wanted to know what had happened to Megan, and found herself in fairy land. Stayed there, just to see what it felt like to be seen. To be important. And she had found it felt good.

She still hated the phrase, but yes, curiosity had costs.

'But this is a different thing,' Elena continued. Ruth looked up. Elena was staring into the empty fireplace, twisting the chain around her neck through her fingers – it was the same one she had been wearing when she came to Brockley, the one with enamel birds and fruits worked through it. 'You came to me and confessed. That is unusual. Tell me, Ruth, if you were me, what would you do?'

I am on thin ice, Ruth thought, balanced on a knife edge. Choose your words carefully. Her brain rattled with useless clichés. It was hard to get oxygen into her lungs and Elena could surely see her trembling. God, she could feel the ripples of terror under her flesh, trying to make her run, fight, shutting down her brain when she needed to be calm and think. She sniffed, wiped her eyes. Elena watched her, her expression cat-like and still, winding and unwinding the gold links round her fingers.

'I don't know. How can I? I don't understand what it is you are doing, what all the . . .' come on brain, '. . . factors are.'

'Guess, Ruth.' Her voice was arctic.

'OK! I suppose you might think I have a use as a way of making Jane Lucas and her people think what you want them to think. Or . . . I feel as if . . . I feel as if things are at a crucial juncture and they're circling. Sir Philip, the boss of MI5, he obviously hates Noah so I guess that means he is your enemy too. I know he's not on any of the Sir Toby lists. It might . . . it might be useful to misdirect them?'

Elena nodded.

'Correct. You might have a use. Work out this "mis-direct". You are to speak of this to no one else. Not to Andrei, not to Michael. To them you are to be as business as usual. If we decide to tell them, we shall.' She stood up. 'Now go to your work. Another misery box has arrived. Your email is full of sad desperate people. Go make your decisions about their fates. You are still being paid by me, wearing clothes I bought.'

Ruth almost said it to herself. 'Perhaps I should ask them to pray for me too.'

Elena nodded. 'Perhaps you should.'

Ruth returned to her office on automatic pilot and for a couple of hours wrote emails, did her research, refilled the troughs for the Sir Tobys with fresh favours, and stuffed envelopes with cash and prayer cards till she could hardly see straight. A coffee appeared on her table, and a sandwich. Masha must have brought them in and put them there, but Ruth had not really been aware of it.

She glanced at the time on her laptop. Nearly midnight. No word from Yuri or Elena. No visit from Michael. She shut down the machine and returned to her room. Teeth. Pyjamas. Olivia Von Halle pyjamas. She was wrapped in luxury twenty-four hours a day. Under the duvet. The silence of the house cut through her like a scream. What better time to get rid of her than now? She shouldn't have drunk the coffee or eaten the sandwich. In the dark her imaginings multiplied. She was in the back seat of a car, thumping the heels of her hands against the window. She was being pushed, dazed and terrified, in front of a train. Lights and noise. She was wandering through old greenhouses then feeling the cold shock of a stab wound in her stomach. In the half-dream of her terrors she looked up at her attacker. Michael. He had his hand on her shoulder, he pulled back his arm and stabbed again, his expression affectionate and concerned.

'You have to trust me,' he said with each blow.

Ruth woke up again, fully, into the dark, sweat sticking her hair to her forehead. She gathered the duvet in her arms and carried it into the bathroom. Made herself a nest between the sink and the shower on a mattress of thick towels, locked the door and turned off the light. The lock wasn't strong enough to keep anyone out, but if they came for her, she'd know it.

35

Ruth was back at her desk at half past eight. There were shadows under her eyes and her back and hips were sore from the bath-room floor, but she had slept a little at least. It was harder to keep working this morning. She hadn't been expecting to hear anything more from Elena yesterday after she left Ruth's room, unless it was a trip to the railway tracks, but she was due to meet Jane Lucas today. Elena knew that, knew when the meeting was to take place.

When the door did fly open, opening so fast the doorknob banged against the wall, she leapt in her seat. Not Elena. Not Yuri. The girls, Natasha and Katerina.

'Ruth!' They shouted then came round the desk to hug her.

'We just got back from school. Sam drove us,' Katerina said. 'We've got study days rest of this week. Mummy says come to the library now, but that you can't take us out this afternoon because of your appointment. That's sad because we are going to the zoo and we thought you'd like to come.'

Natasha smiled at her. 'You should come anyway. After your appointment. We are going to be there ages and see all of the animals. I like the lemurs best.'

'I like the zebras,' Katerina said, 'because they are like horses, but really very strange horses and that makes me think maybe unicorns exist, because they are just like strange horses too.'

Ruth returned the hugs from her seat.

'Anyway that is what we came to say,' Katerina finished. 'Now let's tell Masha what we want for tea when we get back and we *have* to decide on a film for this evening.'

Natasha added a wave from the doorway, but no one needed

Ruth to actually say anything. Good. Library. Girls told she had an appointment. Maybe good.

Ruth had got used to coming into the library and sitting next to Elena on the sofa as they went through the notes, lists, suggestions and accounts. Today Ruth came in and stood.

She'd knocked of course, heard the *vkhodi*, but Elena wasn't looking at her. Just tapping and scrolling at her phone and frowning. She glanced up.

'Sit. And look up hashtag security on Twitter.'

Ruth did. Her screen filled with a cacophony of voices. A lot of them including pictures of flags and handshakes. The hands, airbrushed and semi-transparent against images of green fields and the tower of Big Ben, were white and male, she noticed automatically. Shirts with cufflinks. James Bond-style watches.

'The opinion formers are using their press packs from the conference,' Elena said. She sounded bored now. 'Many MPs are getting letters. Glenville Solutions has helped track down the dangerous radical left-wing terrorists. Legislation will be passed late next week to open up the part of GCHQ work to private contractors. Everyone is very happy. Apart from MI5 and Sir Philip Mackay.'

Elena didn't look happy. Just tired.

'If all the MPs owe you favours, what does it matter what people think?' Ruth asked. Her own voice sounded flat and exhausted. I am dead or not dead, she thought. I just don't know which yet. I am Schrödinger's Personal Assistant. It felt, weirdly, quite freeing. God, the things your mind does when you're scared. She felt like laughing one second and screaming the next.

Elena shrugged. 'It helps if the people think they are in charge. That it is their, what is it, will.'

'The prime minister seemed very friendly with Noah.'

Elena put down her phone. 'Old friends. They have been meeting in very expensive houses at very expensive parties for ten years.'

Then she put her hand on Ruth's knee, rubbed it as if Ruth was a pet demanding attention.

'You saw Jane Lucas and Sir Philip after the bombing?'

'Yup. He looked like a walrus.'

Elena frowned. Ruth mimed a seal with tusks and Elena laughed and clapped her hands. 'Ah, *morzh*! Exactly!'

I am playing charades with a woman who might order my death this afternoon, Ruth thought as Elena wiped her eyes.

The stroke became a firm pat. Good dog. Out in the garden with you.

'He will be dealt with. Now, how can you help deal with him, Ruth?'

Her one fragile hope was that Elena would let her pass something to Jane, something faked, false narratives and fake news, sand to throw into the wheels of Sir Philip Mackay's machine. That might keep her alive another day, and at the moment that was as far ahead as Ruth could think.

'I thought . . . Jane wants the Sir Toby list. The people who've been taking hard cash via Yuri's people. Suppose I give her some real names, and a few others. Some of the government and civil service people who have refused your . . . favours. If Sir Philip's people start poking into *their* business in the next day or two, they might start seeing things your way, stop supporting him.'

Elena shifted sideways so she could look directly at Ruth and took her hands.

'*Dorogaya*, you came to us. You did a brave and very dangerous thing. But you took a long time, and you lie a lot. You also like having power over these people who think your accent is funny and your home a shithole full of shit.'

She was holding her hands quite hard now. 'You mean you don't know if you can trust me?' Ruth asked.

'Trust is bullshit,' Elena said, squeezing her hands tighter and watching Ruth's face. It hurt, but Ruth wouldn't show it. 'I do not trust anyone. I know where I have common purpose, but the most important is love. Love and fear. You love me a little, you fear me a little. Good. Perhaps I feel the same about you. Now I want to know if that love and fear makes you interesting. Worth growing in my garden, tending like a rose to give me petals and perfume, or if you are ugly and useless weed and should be destroyed.'

She knew what she was doing, the bones crushed each other. Jesus. Keep steady. Do not flinch.

'You are one thing or another, Ruth. Be clever and useful. And I shall feed you. I need to see your nature.'

She dropped her hands. The release in pressure brought a fresh wave of pain. Jesus.

'By their fruits, you shall know them,' Elena said turning back to her phone. 'Now go and prepare.'

Jane Lucas met her in the restaurant at Fortnum & Mason. They probably looked, Ruth realised, like a wealthy woman treating her niece.

Jane looked rattled for the first time since they had met. She was wearing her city executive clothes, complete with the opals in her ears and a high white collar on her shirt, but her eye make-up was a little smudged and she couldn't keep her hands still. Her face might be calm but those other signs betrayed her. Nudging the cutlery one way or another, straightening a knife, twisting her plate so the discreet logo on the rim was at exactly twelve o'clock.

'How the hell did you end up in the command centre?' Jane snapped as soon as she had dismissed the waitress with their order.

'I met Noah at the conference, after that I just bullshitted. No harder than getting into a club underage.'

She gave a small tight shake of her head, irritated. 'He was at the conference? He wasn't on the list of attendees.'

'He just came.'

'Something else you forgot to mention. And how did Warrington get that information on the Uprising? He's just a stuffed shirt! He's donated enough to the president to get a few military contracts over there, but we had no idea he had interests in this country.'

'I heard he and the prime minister were friends.'

She snorted. 'The prime minister has more friends than we can keep up with.'

Ruth said nothing.

'We've had our best people on it ever since the Piccadilly attack and they've come up short. Then he strides in like a saviour, humiliates Sir Philip in front of the PM.'

'Maybe his people are better,' Ruth said. The waitress bought coffee in a silver cafetière. She poured slowly and Jane twitched with impatience till she retreated out of earshot.

'They aren't.'

'Who are these people anyway? The ones who were arrested? What are they saying?'

Jane's lips thinned. 'Three years ago they were perfectly ordinary and distinctly harmless activists.' She gave activists scare quotes. 'Noisy, but not dangerous. Radicalised in the wake of the Brexit vote, it seems. Then they got ambitious.'

Ruth's Welsh rarebit arrived. She wasn't hungry, but had ordered it to annoy Jane and because she had no idea what it was. Fancy cheese on toast. As soon as she started eating it though, her appetite broke out of its terrified stupor and she had to stop herself devouring it whole.

She caught Jane's look of mild contempt out of the corner of her eye. This woman thinks I'm stupid, Ruth thought. She can't help it. She hears my voice and thinks I'm her maid or something. I can use that.

'So they're admitting they planted the bomb? Threw grenades at me in the café?'

Jane tucked a lock of her perfectly grey hair behind her ear.

'They claim to have ordered the attacks and written the manifesto. Those attacks took money and expertise, but they seem to believe, actually believe, the people who did carry them out were simply persuaded to do so because of the force of their infantile arguments.'

'I don't understand.'

'You don't need to understand.'

Ruth's plate was already empty. She reached into her Chanel bag, blood red, and took out a folder of papers. They had taken her hours to falsify, print out and then photocopy.

'These are the people in Yuri and Elena's pocket. The ones that they've been concentrating on recently. The ones I've highlighted,

Yuri has quiet arrangements with their stockbrokers or business partners. They use various shell companies to channel the money. On paper it looks like they've just had a stroke of luck, buying shares in mines just before a new seam of something is found, or bought into a company six months before they get a huge contract from one government or another. It's all just bribes.'

Jane Lucas flicked through the pages. Some nods, some flickers of surprise.

'This is more like it, Ruth. I can use this.'

Good dog. Ruth ran her finger round the edge of the plate, gathering up the last of the sauce on her finger and then sucking it off. She felt Jane's shiver of disgust. Enjoyed it.

'But where is the spy journal?'

'It's gone. I looked under Natasha's bed, but no go. Perhaps she told Elena about it and it got confiscated.'

Jane twisted round, picking her knife off the table with one hand while putting the other round Ruth's shoulders. She pushed it into Ruth's side, enough to hurt, not enough to break the skin.

'Listen you stupid bitch, that spy journal is the whole deal. This shit you've fed me is nothing but innuendo and paper trails. If what you said about the journal is true, it is proof that the Shilkovs and Warrington cooked up the entire scheme together. Got the initial legislation written, and planned to push it through with their opinion-forming conference and a false flag operation which almost killed you and did kill Carmela Blake and Kambili Oni. Your best friend died trying to get me that information, so don't betray their memory or hers. Find it or find me the information another way.'

Ruth wanted to spit in her face. Nice speech, but did Jane think that Ruth was going to believe she cared about any of those people? After abandoning Megan and threatening Ruth with the trial? Now Jane thought remembering a couple of names would convince Ruth she had some noble purpose. No way. Instead she looked away, cringed, *Like a whipped dog* a voice said in her head, with an American accent and a vicious pleasure.

'What does that mean, a "false flag"?' she asked, a little whiny, properly scared.

'It was Shilkov money that paid for those grenades, that bomb. I *know* it. God, I thought she was just running some scheme with Milos and his thugs, then she springs the conference on us and it turns out she and her friends want all of GCHQ to play with. Didn't even see their fingerprints on the legislation.'

Ruth was still twisting away from the knife. 'But why did they throw the grenades at Elena?'

The knife pressed harder, a dull edge but it really was beginning to hurt.

'My guess is Andrei's friend tried to steal part of the payment. The mercenaries thought the Shilkovs were trying to con them and made their displeasure clear. The death of Mr Baxter and the Shilkovs' old security man have been part of the healing process. I want that journal. And I want enough to convince the powers that be of my little theory. The prime minister needs to realise he should trust *us*, not whoever got him drunk on his last free holiday. It's our last shot at keeping hold of this country.'

Great minds think alike.

'Fine! I'll find it. Maybe Natasha just moved it. I'll ask her.'

Jane chucked the knife back on the table.

'Good. See you do.'

She took out her wallet and pulled out a couple of twenties, threw them on the table and left with the folder of papers. Ruth breathed slowly then refilled her coffee cup with an almost steady hand. *Our last shot at keeping hold of this country*. Ruth did not think she was included in that 'our'. She glanced out of the plate-glass windows at the back of the room. Ben, just back from Tenerife, was on the pavement outside. Elena had ordered a close protection team for Ruth today. When Ruth told the waitress to keep the change, the girl flushed to the roots of her hair, and was still thanking her as Ruth got up from the table and shrugged on her coat.

36

Ruth delivered her report to the Shilkovs in Yuri's study. Just like yesterday the light was behind them. She showed them the falsified reports she had given Jane.

Yuri read each of the documents in turn, then put them to one side.

'Good. Elena tells me this was your idea.'

'It's the journal from the boat she really wants,' Ruth added. 'She was nervous when I saw her today.'

'And the journal is gone. Poor Jane.' Yuri said. 'She and Mackay still believe in a world where the interests of one nation are pitched against the interests of another. Cold War thinking. The real battle is and always has been between those who have power and those who do not. It is a great shame.'

He looked up at his wife. Some communication Ruth couldn't understand took place. Yuri nodded slightly.

'Have you seen the dominoes on YouTube, Ruth?' Yuri asked, turning back to her. Those very elaborate set-ups where you push one and they all fall together into a pattern.'

He was actually waiting for her to answer. 'Yes, yes I have.'

'That is the game we play, my wife and I. I am beginning to think you might learn how to play it too. It will be very interesting to see what happens next.'

Elena put her hand on her husband's shoulder.

'The girls want to watch one of those disaster movies tonight in our cinema. Seven p.m. You come too. Be with the family.'

It was an invitation and a dismissal. Ruth stood up. 'Thanks, I shall.'

'And Ruth?' Yuri said. She turned to face him again. 'Keep your phone on you at all times, please. We like to know exactly where you are when we can't see you.'

She nodded and left the room.

Her legs were like water but she made it down to her own room and lay on the bed, staring at the ceiling, knowing that Elena and Yuri, Michael and Andrei were going back and forth above her.

The home cinema was in the other basement with the gym and the family safe room.

Natasha gave Ruth the tour. The safe room was completely bare, its only feature a thick metal door.

'Mummy says we shall never use it,' Natasha said, peering in. 'It came with the house. Masha wanted to use it to grow mushrooms but Mummy said it would smell of shit.'

'Why will you never use it?' Ruth asked.

Elena heard her, approaching down the corridor with a striped bag of popcorn in her hands. 'We will not hide from our enemies like rabbits, will we Natasha?'

'No,' Natasha turned and grinned at her.

'What will we do?' Elena leant forward so she could look her daughter in the eye.

Natasha grinned. 'We will meet them in the hall with baseball bats.'

Elena smiled at her. 'We shall. Now kiss your mother and go and get your snacks from Masha.'

Natasha put her arms round Elena's neck and kissed her cheek then ran at full tilt back along the corridor and up the stairs to the kitchen.

Elena watched her go, then turned back to Ruth.

'Ruth, after the film come to the library. We need your funny brain.' She took a step towards the cinema room – Ruth hesitated. 'Come on. You will sit next to me and share my popcorn.' Her forehead creased with genuine concern. 'You do like popcorn, don't you?'

'Yeah. Of course.'

★   ★   ★

The film was *2012*. Ruth had seen it when it came out, sneaking in through the fire doors of the local multiplex to watch it with her mates. The cinema staff turned a blind eye on quiet days as long as they didn't play up too much. It was noisy, silly, full of earth-quakes and John Cusack outrunning lava flows in a limousine. It also featured an oligarch, an ox of a man, his trophy wife and his twin sons, round-faced and spoilt. Natasha and Katerina found this hysterical, especially as the bull-necked oligarch was called Yuri, and they started calling each other Alec and Oleg after the twins.

A happy family. The girls kept explaining the plot to Ruth to make sure she was keeping up. They did the same for their father. Even Andrei looked relaxed; he made some joke about the storyline and when his father laughed, he blushed with pleasure. Like a proper family, in-jokes and teasing, what Ruth had really wanted growing up. What she got a flavour of in the Cunninghams' kitchen. Her head hurt with it, trying to square this with her own fear. Her funny brain. Yeah.

The film finally ended with the survivors emerging out of a floating ark to admire the remains of the world. Not much left. Elena herded the girls off towards bed, and Yuri got up stiffly from his seat.

'Half an hour, Ruth,' he said as he left the room.

Andrei picked up the empty popcorn bags and threw them into the bin as Ruth checked her watch. Asprey. She should have run on that first day, pawned every brand name they'd strapped her into and buttoned her up in and run for it. She sighed. Michael would have come after her. She'd have been arrested. The second she had signed her name on Elena's contract she was done. A fit of bravado. She hadn't noticed she'd been signing in blood – hers and other peoples.

'Ruth?'

Andrei was watching her. 'Yup?'

'Dad's got me a job in the City. I start next week.'

He looked defeated.

'Lucky you.'

'Hardly!' He ran his hand through his hair. 'It means he and Elena are cutting me out from the firm completely. They don't trust me to do anything important.'

Ruth closed her eyes briefly. 'Why the hell should they? Suck it up, Andrei. You're walking into a plum job with your nice accent and good clothes. Enjoy yourself. Try not to shove it all up your nose and stop whining.'

She picked up one of the kids' popcorn bags and shoved it viciously into the bin.

'I made one mistake!' he wailed. 'I shouldn't have let Peter persuade me into letting him be the bagman, I know that. But we paid for that. It's unfair.'

She was too tired to care any more. She stood up close to him.

'Peter paid, didn't he? He's the one scattered in the garden of the soon-forgotten in Putney, not you. And you knew he was skimming that payment. You took your cut. Christ, you talked about it in front of me in the sodding club! One mistake, yeah sure. But when did you ever do anything right?'

'I got rid of the girl!' he said it in a yell. 'I found the Polaroid camera! I took it off her. I didn't mean to kill her, but . . . Elena just cleared up afterwards.'

The air smelt salty and sweet, stale. In the morning it would smell of lemons and lavender again. Ruth put her hand on the back of one of the cinema seats.

'That girl was my *best friend*, you waste of skin. And you just confessed to murdering her, to *me*, because you're feeling sorry for yourself. Then you wonder why Elena and Yuri don't read you in on their plans?'

His face went blank, his lips slightly parted. 'Does Dad know you knew her? Does Elena?'

Stand on the beach if you can take the freezing grip of the water, and feel the sand loosen and suck and the waves run in and out. Feel the pull of the moon and tide wanting to take you deeper till you are just another scrap of flotsam lost on the sea.

'They know everything,' she said hopelessly, and left him.

*   *   *

Their wants were simple enough. A friend of the man they wanted to speak to, someone who could invite him for a meal without causing suspicion.

'But we must own him, Ruth, or be able to do so,' Yuri said.

Elena wasn't standing at his shoulder this time. She was sitting sideways in a polished wood and green leather chair with high arms, her phone in her hand.

'A full Sir Toby,' she said.

'Who are his friends? I need his school, university, clubs.' Yuri handed her his iPad, the browser open to an entry in *Who's Who*. 'Shall I take this to my office?'

'Do it here,' Yuri said.

She could feel the prickle of sweat on the back of her neck.

'What will happen to him?' she asked, reading through the entry.

'Do you really care, Ruth?' Elena said, quietly.

'I don't know.'

Elena laughed. 'A quiet conversation. An intervention. But what happens after that is up to him.'

Her fingers felt slippery. Sugar and blood. Ignore it. Just survive another hour. Find the right Sir Toby. Ruth went through the names in her mind of the people who had received the Shilkovs' favours, while running through the names spawned by the *Who's Who* entry. She had some choices. This captain of industry who was in the same year at school, this member of the House of Lords who was in two of the same clubs. Both had taken hospitality from the Shilkovs, but had independent means. Not easy to own. She was looking for an Andrei, she realised. Someone who only had a name to trade on.

Elena sighed. What, was she on a clock? Christ. A name to trade on, or a title. She checked the clubs again. Her gut told her Sir Philip Mackay was a snob. Preferred the aristocracy to the oligarchs.

She suggested a name. 'He has the ancestral pile on the Suffolk borders, but he's low on cash. Did a few years in the City, but didn't make enough money to retire in comfort. Has a seat in the

Lords and been very grateful for everything you've thrown his way. Not involved in the conference.'

Yuri and Elena looked at each other. A tilt of the head, a lift of the eyebrows. How long did you have to be married before you got this psychic thing down?

'Good. Arrange it. For Tuesday.' Yuri said. 'And by the way, your trick with Jane Lucas seems to be paying dividends already. She must have got straight to work and they are panicked, blundering. I hear the Services are already losing friends. Well done.'

So I get to live another day, Ruth thought. She went downstairs and to the staff kitchen. No one about. No point thinking about it, no point not thinking. Megan – beautiful, funny, damaged, brave, kind Megan – killed by that weak self-pitying shit upstairs. The waste of it, the shame.

No point trying to fight the current, she'd go with it and either go under or be washed up somewhere else. She went to Michael's room, knocked and opened the door. He was sitting in one of his armchairs. Just like her own. By the fireplace, under the picture.

He stood up when she came in, said her name, but she didn't speak to him, just kicked off her shoes and then crossed to him, held him and kissed him hard. He didn't push her away, ask her what was going on. Didn't ask her to trust him or interrogate her. Perhaps he knew better than her what was coming. He responded, hands in her hair and she pulled his shirt out of his waistband, felt his shiver as she reached her hand up his back, felt his muscles and shoulder blades under the pressure of her fingers.

None of the strange out-of-time frivolity of their first night, none of the companionable intimacy of the night he came home from his family – quiet hunger, resignation and abandonment. An agreement between them to be somewhere else for a time. When they were done she slipped out of bed, dressed and left without saying a word.

37

The chosen Sir Toby was actually a viscount. Samuel Grainger, Lord Poslingford, and he was only too happy to oblige. Eager, in fact. He rehearsed how he would beg his friend to come to his house, convincing details of troubled nephews and bad company. His need for advice. Ruth told him not to overdo it. Masha and Ruth arrived at half past four with crates of ingredients.

Ruth had never been to Suffolk before but she couldn't take in much of the scenery. Her ribs felt tight, bruised, as if she couldn't inhale properly. She'd done another day on automatic pilot, feeling herself falling slowly into darkness. Samuel Grainger's place. A half-timbered building, the plaster a canary yellow, between the black, slightly twisted beams. It looked as if it had sagged into its current position over a hundred years. Like an old relative on the sofa, it seemed both fragile and immovable.

The house was up a long drive, which twisted under oaks between fields of scrubby pasture. Samuel Grainger kept llamas. Of course he did. They had to drive over a bridge to get to the house itself because it had a moat. Of course it did. And, Ruth glanced at her phone, no signal. The security team were already there. A car with two men in it discreetly parked where they could watch the entrance to the long drive. Ruth spotted two more in combat trousers and heavy fleece jackets walking over the sharp scrubbed fields beyond the formal gardens. They seemed to be checking the side roads from the property. Ruth didn't recognise any of them. No Ben. No Michael. They looked like the guys from the attic.

Samuel was there to meet them, his Labradors at his heels. He shook hands with both of them, pumping their hands up and down like he was trying to wrench them off.

'Excellent, excellent. I'll just show you where the kitchen is. And the Great Hall isn't too chilly at this time of year.'

Masha looked round the kitchen and sniffed. It all looked very modern to Ruth. The familiar steel fridges and granite island, twelve-burner stove. They set down their crates and Masha began to unpack, then Samuel led Ruth through a narrow stone-flagged corridor to the Great Hall.

It deserved the name. A double-height room, not much wider than the drawing room and library in Kensington, but the length of both combined. The hall had a table to match, thirty chairs round it, and it seemed to be made of oak as ancient as the beams. Three silver vases were placed along it, brimming with white flowers.

A series of smoky portraits hung round the walls, men and woman in every style of dress from ruffs to twentieth-century business suits. They all had Samuel Grainger's chin.

'Nice,' she said.

'I suppose so. Yes, yes it is. The blooms are from the garden. Elena is free to throw them, of course, but the gardener suggested bringing them in and I thought why not?'

'They're lovely. How many staff do you have?'

'Just Thornton in the garden, and Phillipa and Beth doing the office and front of house. No one here but me this evening though.' A twinge of worry creased his brow. 'That's right isn't it? You wanted to be private?'

'Exactly right, my lord,' Ruth replied. 'I better see if Masha needs me.'

Elena, Yuri and Andrei arrived at six o'clock. At seven the doorbell clanged again. Grainger answered it, while Ruth hung back in the shadows of the entrance hall between the dark wood chests and taxidermy.

'Philip! How was the drive?'

Sir Philip was wearing what Ruth supposed were his casual clothes – a patterned shirt and a jacket, but with his collar open. He grinned broadly and the two men shook hands heartily and slapped each other's backs – the dance of close friends of a particular class and age.

'Fine, Poslingford, fine! Pleasure to escape the city even for an evening.'

'You're welcome to stay, of course.'

Sir Philip shook his head, pursing his heavy lips. 'No, no. With everything happening at the moment . . .'

'But the arrests have been made! A great success! I wouldn't have troubled you with my difficulties if I thought I was taking you away from important matters of state.'

'My dear friend, your call sounded urgent.'

Samuel scratched the back of his neck. 'Well, perhaps, let us say, I was given to understand it was a matter of urgency.'

Sir Philip looked at him, his eyes narrowing. 'What have you done, Samuel?'

Grainger wouldn't meet his eye. 'Nothing, nothing. An opportunity arose to be of help. Build some bridges perhaps. For the greater good.'

He had steered Philip across the hall while they were speaking, and pushed open the door to the drawing room. Ruth saw Elena and Yuri standing by the fireplace, both in evening dress. Philip saw them too, and looked at his host again with an expression of shock and disappointment.

Elena came forward. 'Sir Philip! How wonderful. Champagne. Or do you want sherry? I am told English people like sherry whenever they are in a house more than a hundred years old.'

Grainger stepped back into the hall, and shut the door on his friend, then stared at the heavy oak frame in silence.

'Thank you,' Ruth said.

He started. 'Good God! I didn't see you there. Yes. I suppose.'

Ruth took an envelope from her bag and handed it to him. 'Give this to your broker in the morning. The details of the share purchase as discussed.'

She could have given it to him some other way. Didn't need to be so in his face about it, but she was done with people pretending.

He took it from her. Stared at the envelope.

'You can wait in the kitchen until dinner is over,' she told him. She felt it, a sharp fizz of pleasure. How many hundreds of years had Grainger and his ancestors in their capes and collars and codpieces told people like her to wait in the kitchen. Probably right back to whichever Norman overlord waved around one of those ancient spear things hanging in the Great Hall, she reckoned. It felt good. Let him be told where to sit by a girl half his age with diamond earrings and an accent raw from the narrow streets of Middlesbrough.

'It's all right isn't it?' he said, his blue eyes a little bulbous, a few threads of red across the whites. His sandy hair was still in a sort of long-topped flop. It was beginning to grey, go thin. 'I mean, no harm will come to him, will it?' Do you care? she wanted to ask. Or are you just concerned?

'Just dandy,' she folded her arms.

He backed away. 'Good. Good.'

Then she went to join the others.

Andrei handed her a sherry and she took it without a word, caught Elena's eye and nodded. Sir Philip Mackay was dealing well with the ambush. He was standing to one side of the fireplace under an old painting of some sort of hunting scene. Men and horses charging over fences in their red coats, the fox a few rough paint strokes far enough away from them to make you think maybe the beast was going to make it, find an escape, even with the hounds baying for him through the wood.

'I take it,' he said, looking slowly round the faces, 'that Poslingford will not be joining us.'

Yuri inclined his head – not a nod, an acknowledgement. 'He understands we will be talking business and confidentially.'

'But we're not talking business, are we?' He spat out the words, shaken out of the long stare and chill smile of his class. 'We are talking about the takeover of this country's security by an international elite of special interests. A takeover constructed of bribery, extortion, blackmail and murder.'

Elena shrugged. She was wearing blue tonight, a simple sheath dress which made her look taller, slimmer. 'You say potato . . .'

'I hate that song,' Sir Philip said viciously. 'No one says "potahto".'

Yuri treated it as a witticism, chuckling.

'But Sir Philip, under your leadership the higher ranks of the security system have been systematically purged of anyone who didn't attend the right schools, who don't come from the right sort of families. A little hypocritical, isn't it, of you to start championing the benefits of democracy now?'

Ruth sometimes forgot – her life in the house had always centred round Elena – how fluent Yuri's English was. Just with that slight foreign pronunciation. He sounded like someone in an old film. She wondered if Sir Philip had ever heard Yuri speak before; he looked shocked, but she couldn't say if that was down to the way Yuri spoke, or what he was saying.

He gathered himself. 'The right schools, as you call them, teach certain things that other schools and universities do not. They also instil a sense of duty that benefits every one of Her Majesty's subjects. You cannot compare that to your kleptocratic worldwide thirst for power and wealth. You have billions. When will it be enough?'

Ruth laughed.

'Something amusing, Miss Miller?' Sir Philip said.

She smiled at him. 'Think the fancy sherry went up my nose. Only used to a Bristol Cream at Christmas.'

Yuri offered her a fatherly smile. 'Perhaps Ruth is too polite to point out the irony of what you have just said, given the behaviour of the British upper classes across the world for the last three hundred years.'

Yeah, Ruth thought, my restraint is remarkable. She wanted to laugh again. It was too weird for words, sipping sherry in this house, surrounded by dark wood panelling and over-stuffed armchairs, the hunting paintings and the leaded windows, while these men fought over how to carve up the world, or at least who got to hold the carving knife. Maybe it was shock, this horrible urge to laugh out loud, the effects of ongoing trauma.

She remembered that from the leaflets she'd read and then passed on to Megan. From the sessions with the therapist after the trial – behaviours to watch for, how to ask for help. When did the shock start? Sitting in the study in front of Yuri wondering if she was going to live another day. Imagining Michael coming into her room to murder her that night. Maybe watching the prime minister looking up at Noah Warrington under his messy fringe like a posh girl trying to get a ring off the popular boy. Or maybe the bomb? Reading the autopsy report and picturing Peter at the Shilkovs' dining room being forced to swallow his fake five-hundred-euro notes, watched by his best friend and his best friend's parents in a room with a million quid's worth of art staring down at him. Maybe the moment she had plucked the silk scarf trailing out of Elena's handbag to use as an excuse to ask about her missing friend.

A knock on the door and it opened. Masha in her tightly waisted dress with its full skirt and her blood-red lipstick.

'Dinner is served.'

38

Soup. Chilled. With champagne. Then duck. Ruth wondered if it was all going to waste. Would Mackay consent to eat at the table, would he even dare to? Maybe Masha and Elena had thought of that too. The soup was served from a tureen in the centre of the table, the duck carved on the sideboard and the dark-grey meat with its golden glazed skin passed on warm red-and-blue-patterned china round the table so guests could take as much or as little as they wanted.

Yuri and Elena were quite clear about what they were offering. A partnership. Glenville Solutions would be awarded the contracts to take over certain elements of work previously handled by GCHQ, reinvigorating their ability to deal with identity theft, financial crime, and their capacity to keep a watchful eye on those troublesome individuals who pop up around the world, and at home, from time to time. In exchange, quietly, deniably, information might flow in other directions. To Washington and to Moscow. To keep the capital flowing quietly and without friction across the oceans. Safe from the malcontents. Like Elena had said, it was always about money.

'You can't lean on Europe any longer. America has been recon-figured,' Yuri said as he loaded his fork delicately with glazed meat. 'You both need the Russians, the Arabs, the Chinese more than ever. The leaders may huff and puff at each other, but we all know sovereignty is a worn-out idea. Sir Philip, you have always been paid by your masters to recognise which way the wind is blowing and act accordingly. I'm sure the leadership of MI6 would welcome an improved relationship with my country. I don't understand why now, when your elected masters can see the writing on the wall, you are trying to play the crusader.'

Mackay ate. 'There is such a thing as principle.'

'No,' Elena said. 'Principle is bullshit. There is power and no power. Principle is a little hat those with power wear on their pink bald heads.'

Mackay swallowed, then sipped his wine.

'Miss Miller, you are an Englishwoman. You were nurtured by the state, educated by it. It defended you when you were in trouble, it offered you protection and justice. Do you want to see it sold to the President of Russia and a handful of American billionaires? Do you think murder, slander and bribery the proper way to do business?'

'I'm an Englishman!' Andrei said. 'More English than Ruth will ever be. I don't want to live my life in a nostalgia theme park. The spirit of free enterprise will allow this country to grow, to generate significant inward investment. And the charitable donations of families like mine are having a greater impact on the lives of the poor than any ill-conceived programme of government handouts. At last we have political leadership that recognises the facts as they are.'

Sir Philip stared at him.

'And you promote this grand vision by bombing the National Gallery and a tea shop?'

'Sometimes the herd need to be steered in the right direction,' Yuri said quietly. 'Your organisation and your sister organisations in my own country have always known this. But I shall let Ruth speak for herself.'

So there it was plainly spoken. The whole thing. The bombings had been a false flag operation. Andrei and Peter had almost fucked it up, but peace had been re-established. The Uprising, bolstered and amplified by a troll farm who normally specialised in right-wing memes and race baiting, had talked themselves into taking the fall, and at the same time were making anyone who questioned the shibboleths of late capitalism look like an anarchist. Win–win. Ruth's worst suspicions had been confirmed over duck and roast potatoes and a glass of cold white wine. She felt their attention on her. She looked at Mackay.

'I think if you and the people you serve had given a shit about principles and the right way to do business you wouldn't have welcomed in Yuri and his mates to this country years ago. You made it easy for them to keep what they took in Russia and hoovered up any scraps they dropped from the table. I think if you could afford it, you'd join his club like a shot.'

'So you are without principle too.'

Ruth cut herself another piece of meat. 'I didn't say that, I'm saying I don't buy the idea you have any principles, Sir Philip. So why get uppity now? No one's thrusting you away from the trough. Still room for your nose and plenty of others. Just take it.' A phrase bubbled up inside her. Something from the courtroom, outside it. 'If you didn't want to get fucked, why did you come to the party in that short skirt?'

Elena laughed, then hiccupped into her wine, waving her hand in apology. Ruth ate. Mackay put down his knife and fork and stared at his plate for a long moment.

'And if I don't agree?'

Elena patted her mouth. 'That would be a tragedy, Sir Philip. A sad, unnecessary tragedy.'

Yuri's knife scraped on his plate. Ruth glanced up at Sir Philip. She did not think he looked frightened, just tired.

'Perhaps we can find a way to work together.'

Yuri lifted his glass. 'To a new understanding between our people.'

Mackay pursed his lips and lifted his glass too. Ruth managed to swallow and set about cutting another slice, this duck was her penance. Masha was an excellent cook, but she felt as if she was eating the sins of the world. Our people. They weren't talking about Americans, or Russians, let alone British people. They were talking about the powerful, and that club didn't seem to recognise borders any more.

'What about the woman?' Elena said, putting her knife and fork together. 'The one who was with you when you met Noah and the prime minister the other day?' It sounded off-hand, friendly. 'Will she be ready to work with us?'

Sir Philip twisted his glass from side to side. Shot a look under his eyebrows at Ruth.

'She is a zealous and successful officer, whose integrity in operational matters is beyond reproach.'

Ruth wondered if that was meant for her. He must know that Ruth was Jane's source in the Shilkov house by now. Ruth felt something hard in her mouth, like grit, and rolled it out onto her fingertip. Jesus, it was shot. She deposited it carefully on the edge of her plate. Maybe she belonged to Sir Philip now too. Probably should have thought of that earlier. Shit.

'That doesn't answer my wife's question,' Yuri said politely.

Sir Philip sniffed. 'She does not hold grudges and will do what I ask her to. I assume, given how diligent she has been in her research, she will be well rewarded for her hard work.'

Yuri drank his wine and closed his eyes briefly. 'We do not forget our friends.'

Dinner finished with chocolate soufflé and a bland discussion of the merits of various golf courses in Surrey between Andrei and Sir Philip. Yuri ate silently. Elena didn't even pretend to be listening.

The plates were cleared and Sir Philip complimented them on the meal.

'But now I must leave you. I shall drive back to London tonight.'

He got to his feet and the others did the same. The chandelier above them, made of criss-crossed antlers, cast branching shadows across the table as if they were dining in a great winter forest.

'I want to meet her,' Elena said. 'Jane Lucas. Yuri's yacht will be berthed in St Katherine Docks this week. Perhaps she could come and dine with me there tomorrow. Just us girls.'

Sir Philip nodded. 'I'm sure that can be arranged.'

Yuri opened the door to the hallway and led him out. One of the unfamiliar security guards opened the arched medieval door to the drive. The warm air and smells of a summer evening, cut grass and a distant tang of farmyard shit. A nightingale sang.

Yuri took Mackay's hands in both of his own. 'We are friends.'

'I will tell the prime minister I have reconsidered and am happy to withdraw my objection to the new legislation. I can see how this might lead to a more secure future for us all.'

A new world order. How lovely.

Ruth went to the kitchen to tell Grainger that dinner was over and that his house would soon be his own again. When she came back to the hall, Andrei was standing at the hall table. Her bag was on it and open and her phone was in his hand.

'What are you doing Andrei?'

He started and looked at her, frowning.

'I was looking for a light.'

'I don't smoke.'

'Thought you might have one anyway, given what a useful assistant you are.' He said it with a sneer. 'Your phone is warm.'

Elena opened the door behind him. 'Andrei, there are matches over the fireplace.' Then she stopped, taking in her stepson, the phone and Ruth.

'Ruth's phone is warm.'

Elena put out her hand. 'Give it to me. It is defective perhaps.'

Ruth said nothing, and when they went in to join Yuri in the hunting room until the cars were ready to head home, Elena said nothing either.

But Ruth knew what the warm phone could mean. She hadn't charged it or made any calls since they arrived at the house. The warmth suggested it was being used for something else.

She travelled with Yuri and Elena back to London. The driver was one of the men who had patrolled the estate. No one spoke. Elena folded her coat, Armani, into a pillow and apparently went to sleep. Yuri was reading something on a Kindle, his lined face washed blue, occasionally tapping out notes on the screen with one thin finger. The legislation allowing the partial privatisation of GCHQ probably – he was just checking his truffles were quietly buried in the small print. A careful man.

The late-night streets of London were almost free of traffic and they purred back to the house in Kensington, frictionless. Back at the house, Michael was waiting for them on the steps. Yuri stepped out of the car, offered Ruth his hand. She rested her fingers on his forearm as she stood up from the low back seat. It felt like iron.

'Grainger was an excellent choice,' he murmured, 'and I appreciate what you said at dinner. From a Russian it would have come across as rude, too arrogant. From you it has the authority of an Englishwoman speaking an unpalatable truth.'

Ruth watched Elena climb out of the passenger seat, her coat over her arm.

'His type are not in the habit of listening to people like me, Yuri.'

That wintery smile. 'Perhaps not, but I think they hate foreigners even more than they dislike young women with Middlesbrough accents, my dear. It was only a matter of time of course, but you helped.'

Elena was waiting for them now at the bottom of the path. The car with its mysterious driver pulled away into the night. Ruth wondered if they were All Stars, part of Milos's crew, on standby in case Sir Philip had been unreasonable.

'He knows we can get to him too now, of course,' Elena said, as if she had read Ruth's thoughts. 'He will join in the noise against the Uprising. Use Noah's intelligence.'

'The rich have always been afraid of the poor,' Yuri said as the car disappeared. 'They have so much to lose, and the poor have nothing to lose. It makes them powerful even in their rags. But it makes the rich easy to manipulate too.'

Elena put her arm through his. 'Ah, my philosopher king.'

Yuri bowed slightly acknowledging her and the title. 'I shall leave for Moscow in the morning. Time to speak quietly to our friends there.'

They turned up the path and Ruth trailed in their wake. The phone, the phone. What were they going to do with the phone? Did this new understanding with Sir Philip mean she was no longer of use or of more use than ever? If she turned and ran now, just hightailed it past the security booth and onto Bayswater Road, how far would she get? Not far. She couldn't tell if it was fear or bravery making her put one foot after the other as she followed them up the path.

'Good evening, Elena, Yuri,' Michael said as they reached the steps. He opened the door for them like a butler. 'I hope you had a productive evening.'

Elena chuckled. 'Brother Michael is angry because we used another team tonight. I can tell by his polite voice.' She lifted a hand and patted him on the cheek. 'Yes, Michael, we all had a pleasant evening.'

Then she put her hand into the pocket of her coat and pulled out Ruth's phone.

'This is Ruth's. The battery is warm when she was not using it. Give it to the tech people when they sweep in the morning.'

Then husband and wife passed by him and made their way up the stairs. The second car drew up and turned into the back yard. Masha and Andrei and the crates with the remains of the shot birds, soufflé ramekins and Masha's knives. They would disappear into the kitchen and everything would be pristine again by the time they woke.

'Ruth?'

Somehow she had stepped through the door and it had been closed behind her.

'What?'

He held out the phone. 'Unlock it please.'

She felt her stomach clench with fear. Rested her fingertip on the screen. It sparked into life. That battery was very low.

He swiped the screen a couple of times, pinning it open so all her secrets were at his fingertips. 'And this was fully charged when?'

'Before dinner this evening.'

He paused. 'You geoblocked it.'

'Yes. Yuri told us to. He didn't want anyone knowing where we were tonight.'

They looked at each other for a long moment. 'Good night then,' he said, and put the phone in his pocket.

* * *

She went to her bedroom, but no way she was getting between the sheets. The bathroom wasn't a long-term solution, so she'd ended up making a nest for herself with the two armchairs. The bed was no good. Couldn't do it. The moment she lay down she started to think of someone coming in, that she could be carried off, bundled away before she even knew what was happening.

She curled up and sleep skittered away from her. The Shilkovs had won. They had the government and now the intelligence agencies. Everyone was working for them now. Want to make a living? Get with the programme. She thought of the tech guys coming in the morning. What did they think, sweeping houses for bugs, phones for signs of tampering? Did their job and wrote their reports. On to the next house not thinking about whose secrets they had protected, whose they had exposed. Everything that was supposed to keep people like Ruth safe, like Pat Cunningham and her friends back home safe, it was going to keep the Shilkovs and their friends safe instead and no one cared. Almost no one cared.

The knock on the door came a couple of hours later. Maybe she had been asleep, because it startled her. At least it was a knock, not the door just opening.

'Yeah?'

The door opened. 'Michael.'

She switched on the light next to the armchair and he turned round in the door, surprised at seeing her there in the armchair.

'Can't sleep, Ruth?' He came in and closed the door behind him. She straightened up, took her feet off the other armchair and pushed it away from her slightly so he could sit down.

'I was asleep. Sort of.'

He sat down opposite her. He was holding her phone, but looking into the fake fireplace rather than at her.

'Your phone might have been hacked,' he said carefully. 'There's an app on it, turns it into a microphone then sends the recordings to an anonymous IP address. I've destroyed it. Ported your data over to a new handset without that software.'

'You were supposed to give it to the tech people in the morning.'

'They'll get the new one.'

She drew up her legs under her. 'Does Elena realise you have these technical skills?'

He was staring at her again. In fairy tales it's normally the woman who's struck mute. A quick sigh. 'They weren't relevant to this position.'

'Mostly rotas?'

That wry smile. 'Mostly rotas.'

He has a more colourful CV than he lets on. That's what Jane had said.

Then he reached out and took her hand. 'Ruth, are you a good person?'

Something about the intensity in his eyes made it hard for her to speak now. 'I don't know what you mean.'

He kept hold of her. 'Yes you do. I know you do. I think you are. I think you've done some mad things, I think you're impulsive and touchy and that Elena has got under your skin.' He took a long breath. 'And I think you are afraid. But I think you are a good person. Are you trying, are you at least *trying* to be decent?'

A dozen glib angry retorts bubbled up to her lips and died.

'Yes. I'm trying.'

He nodded. He was stroking the back of her hand with his thumb now. 'And do you have a way out?'

The million-dollar question, the life or death question. Stuck in a dark room but yeah, perhaps there was a glimmer of light showing where the edge of the door might be, if she could just get there in time.

'Maybe.'

He put the phone down on the table next to her. 'Give it your fingerprint.'

She did. He put it back in his pocket.

'The phone got hot because it was searching for a signal to send the data. It uploaded what it needed to from the car when you were on your way back.'

Then he got up and bent over her, putting his hand on her shoulder, his thumb and forefinger circling her neck. With his other hand he stroked her hair back off her face, then he kissed her.

She returned the kiss, feeling the warmth of his fingers, his mouth. He tasted of coffee, and the faint smell of cedar came off his collar, the skin around his neck. Made her think of cool evenings in a desert, cafés lit by paper lanterns, verandas draped with night-blooming jasmine. Stuff she had never seen, places she had never been. She waited for his hands to shift, tighten around her neck. They didn't.

He broke off.

'Goodnight, Ruth.'

'Goodnight,' she replied automatically and he left, shutting the door behind him quietly, as if she were a sleeping child.

39

Michael was gone in the morning. Elena came down to Ruth's office first thing to tell her that, and that Jane Lucas would be coming for dinner that evening on the yacht.

She threw Michael's resignation letter on Ruth's desk. 'He says as he does not have our full confidence, perhaps we should hire another team. These Englishmen. Just because we did not tell him about last night.'

'What will you do?'

She sat down sideways on the chair. 'Hire other people. Perhaps I must use an agency this time. I am not worried. He has made rotas for the week, including the boat, and nobody will be throwing grenades at me today. And tech people say your phone is fine.' She pulled it out of her jeans and pushed it across the desk. 'You will need a new lover though.'

Ruth handed her back the letter. 'Perhaps there's an agency for that too.'

'Ha!' Elena laughed. 'Now say thank you for your present.'

'What present?' She'd thanked her for the sapphires and pearls by text as soon as she'd got them. She was sure of that.

Elena bounced to her feet and closed the office door. Behind it was a painting, a man and a woman floating over a snowy village. 'See! Chagall! Original. Not a print. Maybe when the law passes and Glenville get the contracts we shall sign the picture over to you. Bonus.'

Ruth stared at it. She could feel tears in her eyes. 'It's beautiful. Thank you.'

'*Nichevo*. So this evening you come to the boat too. Jane and I shall have a nice talk together over dinner, then I will call you up for a drink and we shall see.'

Ruth nodded. Her cage was getting more lovely all the time. 'Do you want to use me as a double agent still? I mean, will you tell Jane you know I've been feeding her information?'

Elena clapped her hands. 'We shall see, shan't we? I do not know this Jane. I see her. I speak with her. I make my decisions.'

She closed the door as she left and Ruth covered her face with her hands. Michael was gone. He was gone. Did that mean he had been honest? That he had nothing to do with Tranter's death? Probably. After all, if Elena had trusted him to kill the former security guard in Paris, she would have trusted him to guard them last night. Trusted him to speak to the men in the attic. He had done what he had told her to do a dozen times and got out of here, before he got blood on his hands. And now he was gone and she was here with everything that money could buy and nothing at all.

She wiped her eyes and began to sort through the emails and the latest misery box. Maybe she only had today left, only a few hours. Elena could change her mind. She could find out what Ruth had done. She could find another girl with a talent for gift giving to stuff envelopes full of cash. So if these were to be her last few hours, she would spend them sending some of this blood money to people who needed it, who wouldn't be tainted by it.

Elena drove them herself. Masha was getting the night off and the catering was being handled by the onboard staff, so they were able to take the Porsche. She parked at the very end of Wapping High Street and they walked together into the marina itself. Elena was in her crocodile boots and designer jeans. This was a casual supper after all, not a formal dinner like last night.

They turned the corner. Patches of water filled with boats of all shapes and sizes. Buildings in dark-brown brick, strolling tourists enjoying the long summer evening, no sign of rain today.

Elena led her across a wooden bridge. It reminded her of the Pont des Arts in Paris. Of walking over it with Michael.

'Here!'

The largest ship in the marina, obviously, but Ruth had almost been expecting something the size of a cruise ship. It was steel grey and the windows were tinted. Two women were waiting on deck. Both in white and with their hands behind their backs. Elena took hold of Ruth's hand and jogged with her up the gangplank towards them onto the main deck.

Ruth looked over her shoulder. Sam and Ben were following them discreetly and took positions on the wharf. Elena introduced her to the two women, captain and boat manager, and checked the arrangements for the evening. Caterers were already in the galley, cleaners had been and gone. Security sweeps complete.

Elena clapped her hands. 'Excellent!' Then she glanced at her watch. 'Come, Ruth! I can give you tour before Jane comes.'

The Matisse was in the dining room just off the main deck. It was one of those blue dancing figure ones and the slight movement of the boat made it seem as if they were moving. The table could seat twelve, was set for two.

'Pool on top deck, five bedrooms – no, I mean cabins. Staff quarters. Do you like it?'

'It's amazing,' Ruth said honestly and Elena beamed.

'Did you see the name? It is *Lady Elena*. Perhaps next month we shall take a holiday in her. Take her to the south of France this year. No business. You can come.'

Ruth watched her. No sign Elena thought holidaying in the yacht on which her best friend had been murdered might be a problem.

She strode down a corridor and pushed open a door. Ruth looked past her to see a smaller saloon, windows on one side only, a desk, some armchairs and a drinks trolley crowded with liquor bottles, cocktail shaker, ice bucket.

'This is Yuri's study when we are on board. This is where you will come when I message you. Till then you will wait in a cabin.'

'OK.'

Elena looked at her watch again. 'She is coming now.'

A little further along the corridor was another door, and this time Elena thrust her inside. It reminded her of her room at the Ritz. Maybe they had used the same decorator.

'Bye!' Elena paused in the door. 'Do you have a book to read? There are some over there.' She pointed to a short bookshelf on the far side of the room, then disappeared and shut the door behind her.

Ruth didn't read. She didn't even move until her phone buzzed two hours later. *Come.* So she went.

She knocked on the door and entered. Jane Lucas was sitting with her back to the drinks trolley in one of the armchairs. Jane studied her, a malicious smile twitching the edge of her mouth.

'Ah, Ruth Miller, your faithful assistant.'

'Hello, Ms Lucas. We met after the National Gallery bombing.'

'So we did.'

'Ruth, what do you want to drink?' Elena said, ignoring Jane. 'Vodka?'

'Yes, vodka,' Ruth replied, sitting down as far away from Jane as possible.

A slight tremor in Jane's expression. She had never seen Ruth and Elena together and Ruth's straightforward manner with her boss, her lack of please and thank you, registered and confused her.

Elena handed her the drink, Ruth nodded her thanks and took about half of it in a gulp.

'So you and Ms Lucas have come to an understanding, Elena?' Ruth said.

Elena plonked herself onto one of the other chairs, drink in hand.

'Yes. Jane understands it is better to work with us. She and many of her friends have decided maybe we are not so bad.'

'Lovely,' Ruth said and finished the liquor in her glass. 'A happy ending.'

'You should be careful about who you trust,' Jane said. 'Ms Miller has been passing me intelligence from your house since the week after you hired her.'

So there it was. Elena glanced at Ruth, her expression stony. Ruth's stomach lurched. Jane was useful now, Ruth was not. Jane was at the centre of government intelligence, Ruth was just a flunky and if Jane was now in the fold of the Shilkov influence, Ruth was nothing. Elena had been happy enough to trade bodies to re-establish peace with the All Stars. Perhaps that was why she was here tonight – to form a blood bond between Jane and Elena. They needed something to bind them together, and now here was Ruth – a sacrificial lamb with its wool washed and a bow round its neck, led to the altar.

'Really? And what has happened to that information now?' Elena asked.

'I spent half the day cleaning it all off our system,' Jane said airily, 'according to Sir Philip's instructions. Not a breath of suspicion remains in our files.' She blinked at Ruth. 'I suppose you will not need to worry about the magic "spy journal" any more, dear.'

No, Ruth thought. I have other things to worry about now.

'How did you persuade her to betray us?' Elena said. 'Money?'

Jane rolled her shoulders; she was comfortable again. Her voice sounded like one of the Downton ladies, taking off their jewels at the dressing table and discussing the dinner guests while their husbands undid their ties and dropped their cufflinks into a little ivory pot.

'You must know about the trial?' No reaction from Elena. 'When Ruth was seventeen, she bravely testified against a nasty group of men who had befriended her at fourteen and had then been systematically raping her and forcing her to use drugs for two years. The jury were very impressed at her bravery and the men were convicted. They are still serving lengthy sentences.'

Jane spoke in a sing-song voice. Elena's faced looked carved. It was the look your lover gives you in your nightmares when you are drowning and he won't put out his hand. Ruth shifted her grip on her glass, leaving sweaty shadows of her palms. Jane noticed, enjoyed it. If Ruth ran now, this second, would they stop her? Ben and Sam outside on the wharf would though – Jane and Ruth wouldn't need to lift a finger.

'No,' Elena said at last, slowly. 'That did not happen to Ruth. Those things did not happen to her.'

Jane sipped her drink. 'I can see why you've come as far in the world as you have, Mrs Shilkov. No, none of that happened to Ruth.'

Elena swirled her drink. 'But it did *happen*, didn't it, Ruth?'

One. Two. Three.

'It happened to Megan,' Ruth said quietly. 'Megan Talbot. She couldn't face going to the police herself.'

An image. A flash. Lying on the narrow bed in her room in her first flat with Megan at her side. Megan snotty and weeping, Ruth trying to persuade her to go to the police and the sound of her voice cracking. I can't do it, Ruthie. I can't. I'm scared. It was my fault. Ruth pushing. Megan saying she couldn't remember, was confused, they don't need me. Other girls will come forward. Don't make me. And Ruth felt again her own rage, the phosphorus glare of it. And the solution had been so obvious, so easy, the way things are obvious and easy when you are seventeen years old and there is an opportunity, a golden, unique opportunity to see the people who hurt your friend punished. Justly punished.

'So I went to the police and told them it had all happened to me.'

'And they believed you.' Jane said it with a sneer.

'Everything I said happened, happened . . .'

The feel of Megan's hand in her own. Her own voice saying I'll do it, Megs, let me do it, and Megan's relief. Her gratitude. Her belief that her clever, brave friend Ruth was right. Her faith. It had made Ruth feel six feet tall and the horrors Megan had poured out, Ruth hadn't known the half of it, made her more and more sure she was doing the right thing.

And it had worked. Megan got better after the trial. That was when things started coming together. Sid and his mates were off the street and the compensation money – Ruth gave it to Megan, of course she did – was enough for her to train as a nanny. Of course, it had meant Ruth didn't study for her A-levels, got distracted and missed bill payments, but when it was done the Cunninghams had taken her back into their home for resits and college, got her back on track.

Elena looked at Jane. 'You will make this information public?'

Jane shrugged. 'I will leave that entirely up to you, Ms Shilkov. Personally I think it would be best. Ruth's allegiances shift rather alarmingly. Tell the police the truth now and in future she'll have no credibility, whatever story she decides to tell. She'll be in jail herself.'

'And the men who raped Megan will be free,' Elena said, swirling the last of her drink. 'Megan was your agent too, I think. You have done a good job of putting these damaged girls in my home.'

Jane nodded, a professional compliment. 'She was. You have a weakness for them, Ms Shilkov. Megan wanted to be brave for a good cause, following Ruth's example. She boasted about Ruth, you know. I didn't get very much useful intelligence from her however. Your stepson saw to that. Yes. Sid and his friends will go free – and no doubt receive a great deal of compensation from a very apologetic police force.'

Which was worse? Death, prison, disgrace, the disappointment of the Cunninghams. Ah, but maybe they suspected the truth. Ruth thought she had fooled them at the time, but they knew her, knew Megan. Perhaps they had allowed themselves to be complicit too in service of some higher truth. But Sid and his friends walking free, talking about the injustice they had faced. She had an image of one of them on a talkshow, chatting with a sympathetic host. They'd said all along they'd never met her, hadn't they? But she'd been so convincing, knowing their faces, their likes and kinks, favourite booze and fags, the dates and times and places. Funny brain.

And would the police ever put up a girl like her, like Megan, on a witness stand again after this? No. And that would be her fault. Not just Sid, but the men who would come after him. She had just made the case for reasonable doubt for all of them. Ruth folded her arms around herself. Stupid, stupid, stupid.

'Who knows?' Elena asked, standing and moving to the trolley to refresh her glass. 'Who knows this happened, apart from Ruth?'

'Only me at the moment,' Jane replied breezily. 'But it will be easy enough to prove. I've had a glance through the files. Ruth was such a good witness, and the defence barrister obviously didn't know his arse from his elbow, but a few days of diligent research and Ruth's testimony will collapse in on itself. School records showing she attended on days Sid was supposed to be driving her between men. Meetings with her social workers which show she was making her curfews at her foster placement when she was supposed to be out of her mind on vodka and dope in a backstreet bedsit.'

Ruth just had time to register the knife in Elena's hand. She had picked it up from the drinks trolley. A blade sharp enough to separate delicately the peel from the pith of an orange for negronis and Manhattans. It was antique, had a mother of pearl handle, was part of a set from Mappin & Webb with the shaker and a tiny silver sieve.

Elena sliced Jane's throat open with it while Jane was still smiling at Ruth. Ruth sprang up, stumbling backwards and sideways over her low stool. The blood cast a great arc over the wall of the cabin, spattering on the soft furnishings and the thick carpet, like a sudden summer downpour.

One bright drop of crimson dropped, tear-like, on the hem of Ruth's white shirt.

Jane didn't have time to speak or fight back. Her face changed, shock and then fear. Her hands reached up towards her throat but fell away, the strength gone before she had time to touch the wound. The noise. A low bubbling. Like a ripe fruit bursting, but no groan, no shriek, just the passage of air.

Jesus. No. Ruth's back against the wall, the taste of bile in her mouth.

Elena dropped the knife on the trolley and picked up her glass, tossed off the contents.

'It happened to me,' she said. 'But I think you know that. I told Yuri soon after we met. He had pictures sent to me of their bodies. It was part of his courtship.'

She picked up her phone, unlocked it then threw it to Ruth.

'There is a number in there. Under cleaner. Text them the berth number and tell them twenty minutes. Then go get rid of the staff and security. Everyone gets to go home early. Come back tomorrow.'

She dipped a napkin in the ice bucket and started wiping the blood off her hands.

The phone was in Ruth's hand. She swiped, touched the screen clumsily, couldn't focus. Her fingers moved slowly, like in a dream where you can't hit the right numbers. Her vision swam and her throat closed. The swooping sound of message sent.

'I hope Megan doesn't decide to confess again.' Elena kept rubbing her hands, examining them, rewetting the napkin and rubbing again. She indicated the body – she was a body now not a person – with her chin. 'This will be expensive.'

'Megan's dead,' Ruth said, her head snapping up. 'Andrei told me he killed her, that you cleaned up.'

Elena lent against the drinks trolley. Ruth couldn't look at her without seeing Jane, her head fallen forwards, the gush of blood down the front of her blouse. Elena snorted.

'Pfft! I do not kill stupid children. I paid her off. She is still in Korčula, I think.'

'But Andrei said . . .'

'Andrei pushed her over and she hit her head. He ran away without even checking her pulse. He is like a child. She was already waking up when I went in and found her. But Andrei is an idiot and I like to have him scared and woeful.'

The world expands and contracts. Ruth was scrambled. Megan is dead. She was spying and the Shilkovs killed her. They switched off her mobile and killed her and nobody gave a shit. Nobody even noticed.

'You're a killer, Elena.'

Elena raised one eyebrow. 'Obviously.'

'So why should I believe you?'

'About Megan?' Elena refilled her glass.

'Yes, about Megan.'

'Believe or do not believe. I did not need or want to kill her, so I did not kill her. I wanted those men to stay in prison, so I killed Jane.'

'Peter Baxter, James Tranter. What about the people killed and injured by the bombs?'

Elena screwed up the napkin and threw it onto Jane's lap for the cleaners.

'*Bozhe moi!* Peter stole much of the first payment we made to Milos's friends and replaced what he had taken with fakes. His stupid greed got me and my girls,' she mimed the explosion of a grenade. 'James Tranter drove my children to school each week for a year. And he sold us out for the price of a cheap BMW. Those others? They are on God's conscience. He put them in the shop that day. The cleaner in the gallery? A call on her phone, a chat on the stairs, a dropped mop. A million ways God could have saved her if he wanted. Same with security guard. Fuck God if he's not paying attention.'

She paused, refilled her glass and drank half of it.

'I have a code, Ruth. I am not always sure what it is, but it is a code.'

Megan was alive. Jane was dead. The world tilted crazily sideways. Ruth was losing her grip, sliding off it.

Ruth wasn't sure what her code was either. It had involved lying to the police, the court, the jury in pursuit of justice, so yeah, twisted.

She saw the raindrops on the wall of the phone box, the sound of Pat's voice. The moment she had decided to go to the Shilkovs and confess. The moment she had decided what else to do.

'That's not enough for me.'

'What's not enough?'

'Blaming God. Acting like it's all a game. It's not. This shit you do has consequences.'

Elena frowned. 'OK, then what is enough?'

Ruth swallowed. Decided. Maybe one day she'd get to make a decision slowly, with time to talk it over with people she trusted. Maybe meditate or sleep on it. Not today though.

'Elena. You have to go. Run.'

Elena set down her glass.

Ruth had picked up the phone again after she rang off from talking to Pat. She had made a call and met John Bakewell in the

Swan Inn. She'd downed her whiskies and told him everything. Given him the real files on the Sir Tobys – not the altered ones she'd handed to Jane. Photos of the spy journal, of the Polaroids the girls had collected with Megan, of the dinner party seating plan – copies of everything Yuri had deleted later that evening.

'What?'

Ruth had recorded the conversation at Samuel Grainger's place over drinks and dinner, and the recording had been sent automatically to Bakewell as soon as the phone got a signal again. He gave her the emergency number at the pub. He told her to stay as long as she could. To try and get Elena's phone, unlocked, because that was the last, best piece of the puzzle. Her contacts, her messages, her operations during red time.

But none of that had stopped Ruth loving Elena, it seemed. And she did trust her. She believed Megan was alive because Elena had told her she was.

'I didn't text your cleaner. I texted John Bakewell. Met Counter Terrorism Command are on their way. I gave him everything I have on the false flag operation. On the arrangement with Glenville Solutions. On Peter. Run, Elena. Now.'

Elena picked up the knife and took a half step towards her.

'You have six, eight minutes at the most. And Jane didn't see you coming. I can. And I know how to fight. So go.'

The knife rattled back onto the polished steel of the trolley and Elena walked briskly round the chair where Jane's body was slumped and out into the corridor. Ruth followed her automatically.

She opened a cupboard by the entrance to the dining room and pulled out a leather holdall.

'Give me my phone, Ruth.'

Ruth took a step back. 'Not going to happen. You have less than five minutes.'

'Perhaps I have a gun in this bag.'

'If you had a gun, you'd be pointing it at me.'

Elena hesitated again. They were evenly matched physically and taking the phone from Ruth would take time. She made her decision, lifted her long summer coat from the hook and slipped it on, picked up the bag again, then with one cold look over her shoulder at Ruth, disappeared towards the gangplank onto the dock. Ruth stayed where she was, staring at the curve in the air where Elena had been. She heard her curt command to Ben and Sam to stay where they were, and then her boots on the stone wharf as they faded into silence.

Ruth went into the dining room, then took a seat at the head of the table and waited for the police. Frosted macaroons scattered with gold flakes on the plate in front of her. She ran her finger round the edge of the plate and put it in her mouth. The familiar prickle of sugar. She looked at Elena's phone, the lock disabled, and checked the time she had sent the text. Three minutes ago. Four. The boat was perfectly quiet. Then she heard the first shouts from the dock.

Sam and Ben didn't try and stop them. Immediate and complete co-operation. It was how they were trained. Ruth heard the orders, the warnings of *armed police*. The exclamations and crackle of a radio as they found Jane's body. Heavily booted footsteps in the corridor outside.

The point man, gun raised, in goggles and helmet. Ruth looked at him, lifted her hands slowly above her head. The two men with him scanned the room from behind their semi-automatics. Masked men with guns, Ruth thought. Kinda familiar, really. At least they weren't wearing Donald Trump masks this time. Just breathe.

The point man kept his gun on her while the others checked the doors onto the main deck and gangway.

'Clear.'

'Clear.'

The point man lowered his weapon, leaving it slung from his shoulder, then pushed off his goggles and took off the helmet. She laughed, a short dry gasp. Not sure if she was surprised, relieved or had been expecting it all along.

'Hey, Michael.'

He set the goggles and helmet down on the table.

'Hey Ruth. Where is she?'

'Gone.'

He studied her for a long moment. 'Anyone else on board? Who is the woman in the rear lounge?'

Ruth felt a flash of the moment, the expression on Jane's face, the scarlet. Whited out by her own shock like a detonation.

'I knew her as Jane Lucas. MI5. Worked directly for Sir Philip Mackay. Elena killed her. The boat's captain and a couple of the catering and cleaning team are in the galley below deck.'

He nodded and began to speak into his radio, giving Elena's name and description, last known location, address in Kensington, the registration number of the Porsche. He requested road blocks and alerts at the airport, and as he did, came forward and rested his left hand on Ruth's shoulder. She lifted her own hand and closed her fingers around his.

40

It was dawn before Counter Terrorist Command let her go. Hours of interviews, and not with Michael, going through the events from the bombing of the café to today. Bad coffee in small cups. A cheese sandwich which looked like a seventies serving suggestion. Explaining each day, each action till her memory got foggy. And at the end, that last question again and again.

'Why did Elena kill Jane Lucas?'

To keep my secrets, Ruth thought. 'I don't know,' she said again and again. 'It happened so quickly.'

She had a solicitor. He had turned up at the station at the same time she did, introduced himself as a friend of John Bakewell. He had been sitting next to her taking copious notes ever since.

He clicked his ballpoint. 'Time for a break, I think.'

For the first time the thought occurred. 'I have nowhere to go.'

Sternly paternal. 'We'll sort something out.'

Something turned out to be the nearest Holiday Inn. She showered and crawled into bed and to her surprise, she slept.

Michael arrived mid-morning and offered to take her out for breakfast. They went to a hipster place and though she couldn't face food the coffee helped. She got the first question.

'So, I'm guessing you aren't really Michael Fitzsimmons.' He shook his head and stared into the froth of his coffee. 'So? What is your name?'

He cleared his throat, suddenly awkward as a schoolboy. It was almost endearing. Almost. 'Matthew. Matthew Telfer. Matt to my friends.'

Matthew. It suited him. Ruth repeated it under her breath, trying to make it stick to him.

'Did you know I was Counter Terrorism?' Michael, no, not Michael, Matthew, asked.

She shook her head, studied the haphazard mosaic on the tabletop.

'I hoped you were one of the good guys. Wasn't sure. I just knew that Elena didn't trust you. Then, when you gave me my phone back, I hoped maybe you were doing more than just turning a blind eye.'

He nodded. 'I had everything I was going to get by then.'

'So what happened in France . . .?'

A flash of pain across his face. 'Tranter was living in Paris and I persuaded him to meet me. I said I wanted to talk to him about the Shilkovs as I was now in charge of their protection. Played it bright and breezy. We were going to meet in the early evening. Then I got the message saying he thought he was being followed. Asked me if I'd put people on him. I went to meet him and he didn't turn up, didn't respond to any messages. I thought maybe he'd just bottled it until I saw the report on the news the next day.'

She put her hands around the cup, feeling the warmth.

'Have you read the printouts of my interviews?'

'Didn't need to. I was next door watching it live.'

OK. Is that good or bad? 'So you know about the guys above Madeleine's?'

'Yeah. They sent Elena Tranter's name, and then dealt with him as a favour to her.'

'So much for honour among thieves. He was there with the All Stars, wasn't he?'

Matthew Telfer drank his coffee. 'Some of this is still guesswork, but after he lost his job here it seems he tried to reconnect with them in Paris. But they didn't think of him as one of them. Easy choice to kill him as part of the process of re-establishing peace with the Shilkovs. We think. We have the messages now from her phone, thanks to you, but of course they are coded.' He paused. 'You couldn't have known, or done anything different, Ruth. You did OK.'

Bullshit. There was a lot she could have done differently. She could have thought before signing away her soul to irritate a hand-some arrogant man. She could have resigned the next day. She could have told Elena that Megan was a friend of hers and sent Isme and her fancy dress box packing. She could have walked away a dozen times and gone back to the agency to earn her bread filing and making appointments for self-important executives until something else came up. She had not made good choices. This one she had thought about though. Time to tell the truth.

'Matt . . .'

'It was real,' he said it fast. 'You and me. Everything that happened between us. It was never an operational play.'

'Shit, is that what you call it? "Operational play"? Romantic or what?'

He laughed and she was glad she had got him to laugh.

'Real for me too,' she added and he took hold of her hand. She pulled free.

'Steady on, love. I only learnt your name a minute ago, and I have something else to tell you.'

'I can take it.'

Have to do it, she thought. No choice. 'Elena told me Megan is still alive.'

He looked like she'd punched him in the gut.

'That's why you let Elena go,' he said at last. 'You told her we were coming, and don't tell me you didn't. Shit Ruth, that was our best, probably our only chance of catching her. Knife in her hand standing over the sodding body! She's in Moscow now, you know that? With Yuri. Private jet via Luxembourg. She got there before dawn.'

'I am not going to deny it, *Matthew*. What about Andrei?'

His voice was miserable and bitter. 'He's in Kensington Station for now, but we have fuck all to hold him on. He just needs to keep his mouth shut. But *why* did you warn Elena? I mean even if Megan is alive, and I really hope she is, Elena still ordered Tranter's murder, offered up Peter, paid for the bombing of the National Gallery, murdered Jane Lucas . . .'

She held up her hand. Stopping him. 'That's it. I mean I know the rest, and you're right, of course you are right, but she sort of did that last one as a favour to me.'

'Holy hell, Ruth!' He put his head in his hands. 'OK. Tell me everything.'

And she did.

It was complicated. Ruth wanted to get on a plane, and there were plenty of people who thought she had every right to do whatever she wanted, and plenty of others who thought letting her go as far as the Holiday Inn had been a big mistake. In the end, and after pressure from John Bakewell, the authorities agreed to the trip, but only if Ruth was accompanied by a member of the British police force in good standing to guarantee her return.

'You OK?' Matt asked. His name was beginning to stick now.

They were walking up a steep narrow track which smelt of pine and hot soil. Holding hands. The insects grated in the trees and Ruth could feel the sweat under her hair. Through the branches to her left she could see flashes of the turquoise of the Adriatic. No I'm brilliant, terrible, afraid, angry, over the moon, in pieces. Seemed like too much to say at once, so she went with:

'Yeah.'

Yuri's companies had folded in on themselves in the minutes after CTC stormed the boat, a series of shell companies registered in the British Virgin Islands, Malta and Luxembourg, arranged like petals into a glossy, inflammable whole. Light the touch paper and it's gone. The London employees arrived on Monday morning to find the doors locked and, when the police did get in, the computers were bleached and the safes empty. The employees who tried to sue for back wages and lack of severance pay found themselves chasing ghosts. The dark pearl of Yuri's business, the actual money, the actual files, disappeared into the deep ocean of international finance and the waters closed slowly around them for good.

Natasha and Katerina had been collected from their school by 'an uncle' and flown to Moscow to join their parents. Sir Philip Mackay retired as Director General of MI5 the next day. The legislation to allow for the privatisation of parts of GCHQ was immediately, quietly dropped and two days after the Shilkovs fled, Noah Warrington resigned as CEO of Glenville Solutions to pursue other interests.

The track swung right, through the gap in a low stone wall and into a wide dusty courtyard. A house. Two stories and painted white with a wide wooden veranda the same green as the pines surrounding the yard. A dog, mutt-ish, black and white so it merged into the patterns of light and shade, lifted itself up and barked once. Wagged its tail. To their right stood an open-sided roofed area with a barbecue at one end, crowded with rough tables and benches. Some sort of restaurant.

The house door clattered open and there she was. Cut-off denim shorts and vest top with a man's cotton shirt over the top and a baby on her hip. A great plume of red curly hair.

Matt let go of Ruth's hand and watched as she took a step forward, shielding her eyes from the sun.

'Megs? It's me.'

Megan yelped and ran towards them, holding out her free hand.

'Ruthie! Oh my God, oh my God. *Ruthie!* Oh, I've missed you so much.'

Matt didn't hear any more for a while, just watched as the two women held each other. Then they began talking, quietly, intensely and at the same time.

So Megan had had a baby. He watched as the child was introduced to Aunt Ruth. This might take a while. He went and sat down under the thatched awning. The dog wandered up and pushed its snout, with a sigh, into his hand. He scratched its ears.

They would stay for dinner. Over the course of the afternoon Matt learnt Megan was with the owner of this place, a Croatian named Ranko. He was good-looking, wiry and tanned, with green eyes, and he seemed devoted to Megan. The baby boy was theirs, conceived within a week of them getting together, just a few days after Megan had fled the Shilkovs' boat.

The women sat near him most of the afternoon and didn't seem to mind if he overheard.

'Elena told me I was never to go back, never contact anyone in the UK again. She scared me. I was too scared to call you and tell you where I was, Ruthie,' Megan said. 'First for myself and then for the baby. I thought you'd just forget about me anyway. You were always the clever one.'

'You're an idiot, Megs,' Ruth replied. Maybe in her place, friendless and terrified of the Shilkovs, she'd have done the same as Megan. Told herself a few convenient half-truths and tried to believe them. 'You knew bloody well I wouldn't forget you.'

'Sorry.'

'I know.'

Megan finally got up to help set up the place for dinner and Matt watched Ruth wipe her eyes. Catching him, she shot him one of her flaming 'what are you looking at?' stares. He offered her his handkerchief and she took it.

People started arriving, finding their way up the path on foot or on puttering mopeds. Tubs of ice stuffed with bottles of beer were carried out to the makeshift bar and carafes of red and white wine set out. The barbecue reached what Ranko judged was the right cooking temperature and a couple of young women, Ranko's cousins it turned out, fished tomatoes out of a cool pail of water and started cutting them into paper-thin slices at astonishing speed, still talking all the time. Ruth and Matt took turns with Ranko's family looking after the baby while Ranko and Megan greeted their guests and fed and watered them.

The evening softened. Matt watched Ruth. She couldn't stop watching Megan, and Megan, whenever she passed by, would touch Ruth on the shoulder or arm, as if they were reassuring each other they still existed. Matt stroked the dog and wondered if Ruth would ever love him that much; if, after the cases were wrapped up, he could take a real chunk of leave – should be OK after being undercover for a stretch – and he and Ruth could come back here. He quite fancied learning how to sail. He rubbed his fingers through the dog's soft hair. Swimming every day. Wandering the old city. Getting to know Ruth out of that damned house. Letting her get to know him, Matt Telfer, grammar school boy, career policeman. Mum and dad living in the same council house they'd had their whole life on the edge of Lincoln. He had given his mum the perfume, grabbed from the Paris Ritz gift shop as he raced in sweaty and unshowered at three minutes to eight. She thought it smelt 'off' and gave it to her niece who was absolutely made up.

They had made a mistake, establishing him with a posh cover. He should have gone in as himself. The Shilkovs quite liked the upper-middle-class accent, the Englishness, but they had never trusted him. Ruth though, Ruth they thought they understood.

But then she had given Elena that head start, so maybe in their twisted way they were right to trust her after all. Ruth had her principles, her own way of honouring the contracts she had made and reckoning her debts. He'd have to get used to that.

A burst of laughter from another table. He looked up and found Ruth was smiling at him. He winked at her, and Megan set down another carafe of white wine on the table, then Ranko presented them with a platter of prawns, pink and black from the barbecue and smelling of garlic and lemon. He and Ruth tore them apart with their fingers, wrapped them with flat breads cloaked in the tomato salad. Matt thought of the scallop in Paris at the Ritz with the flower on it.

Megan took the baby to bed and Ruth went with her. They were gone a long time and the crowd began to thin out. Matt checked his watch and started to think about calling a cab and walking down to meet it by the light of an iPhone torch. Getting back to the hotel. Back to bed. The girls came back out and Megan started talking to Ranko. He watched. Ruth returned and sat down astride the bench next to him.

'Hey.'

'Hey yourself,' he answered. She was looking serious. 'What is it, Ruth?'

'Matt, when we get back to London I'm going to turn myself in. For the perjury. Don't try and stop me.' She paused, then stared at him. 'I thought you would try and stop me!'

He filled his wine glass and drank. Thought.

'Nope. I'm not going to do that.'

'Why not? I could go to prison. What about Sid and his gang?'

He drank again. 'Maybe. But I think you talked about it with Megan tonight and she's going to come back with you to the UK and testify herself this time. Also, if you don't, you'll always be looking over your shoulder in case Elena decides to use it against you. And,' he grimaced into the glass, he might have drunk more than he'd thought, 'you'll do it because I was right. You are a good person and it's the right thing to do.'

She looked wry. 'How did you work it out? That Megan had volunteered to come back and testify, I mean?'

'I just saw her talking to Ranko. He's not happy. Wasn't hard to read the body language in the circumstances. See, I'm not an entirely crap spy.'

She didn't answer, just leant forward and kissed him, which Matt supposed was answer enough in a way.

Ruth confessed to perjury and was sentenced to eighteen months, suspended. Sid and his gang were released and then immediately rearrested. Megan testified at the new trial and the jury found them guilty after two hours of deliberation.

Masha and Andrei remained in London. Andrei worked at the banking job Yuri had got him and he was credited with bringing the company a number of valuable Russian clients. Megan declined to prosecute him for assault. His stepmother remained a person of interest in the murder of a middle-aged woman aboard a yacht held by one of her husband's shell companies. The yacht and the collection of artworks it was found to contain were seized by British authorities in spite of protests from the highest levels of the Russian government.

The two leaders of the Uprising continued to insist that the bombings were carried out by their supporters and on their orders.

Their patchy knowledge of some of the operational details of the attack, however, led the authorities to regard their claims as highly dubious. Though support for their manifesto continued on social media there were no further attacks in spite of their frequent calls for them.

Thanks in large part to the generous donations of high-net-worth individuals, the National Gallery was rebuilt within a year. The destroyed paintings were replaced with high-quality projections which occasionally fade symbolically from the walls. A small plaque records the names of Carmela Blake and Kambili Oni. Suzanne D'Arcy and Milos kept their home in London, though they began spending most of their year in Montenegro. The murder of James Tranter in Paris remained unsolved and the verdict on the death of Peter Baxter of death by misadventure was not challenged.

The Russian authorities said the wild accusations of the British police were nothing more than fake news.

Noah Warrington declined to help British authorities with their investigations. Glenville Solutions changed their name to Servictus and continued to work internationally. The parliamentary authority rebuked four MPs and five members of the House of Lords for their failure to properly complete or amend in a timely fashion the register of members' interests. The MPs were all re-elected at the next general election. John Bakewell was not.

Ruth and Matt returned to Korčula to see Megan become Mrs Ranko Novak on their son's first birthday. The baby crowed in Ruth's arms and 'helped' hand out sprigs of rosemary tied with ribbon to the guests. The civil ceremony was in the old town hall, a room of aged, butter-coloured stone set in the walls of the great island fortress. Megan wore a short cream dress and Ranko a new linen suit. Megan repeated her vows in English and halting Croatian, and blushed when Ranko's family applauded. They all took photos on the ancient open-air stone stairs leading up to the old town. The baby seemed to think it was all in his honour and beamed at family and tourists alike.

Ruth wore blue. And the sapphire and pearl set. The reception was up the hill of course, and after the ceremony Matt waved down a taxi to take him and Ruth and two of Ranko's younger cousins to the end of the track. It was while he was turned away, his hand raised to hail one of the passing saloons, that Ruth saw her. Maybe. A woman sitting at a pavement bar in huge sunglasses outside one of the luxury hotels, her hair a thick tumbling gold, a gold chain with winking enamels hung around her neck, her face partly in shadow.

The woman seemed to feel Ruth's gaze and looked up. Picked up her glass and drank. It might have been a toast. It might have been nothing. She set down her glass, stood up and went back into the hotel without another glance.

'Ruth?' Matt had got the cab and the two cousins were already giggling and taking selfies in the back seat. 'Everything OK?'

'Yeah. Miles away.'

Ruth got into the back seat with the girls while Matt slid into the front and gave the driver the address, then they went to the party.

ACKNOWLEDGEMENTS

Many thanks to Nick Sayers for his guidance and patience during the writing of this novel and to my agent Broo Doherty for her encouragement and support.

I am lucky to have a group of writer friends to share the triumphs and disasters which are part of every book. I couldn't manage without them – particularly Robyn Young, Alex Von Tunzelmann and Kate Williams who have an uncanny ability to say exactly the right thing at the right time, and heartfelt thanks to Amanda Craig, Antonia Hodgson, Miranda Carter, Hallie Rubenhold, Liz Fremantle and Laura Shepherd-Robinson for fellowship, support, sanity-checking and gnawing over the day to day business of the writing life.

I am also very grateful for the friendship and advice of Rowan McBrien and James McOran-Campbell. Bonds formed travelling in Russia in the early nineties prove to be enduring. Particular thanks goes to our comrade Philip Worman for a sunny lunch which could power a library of thrillers. I continually rely on the faith and love of my husband Ned, not to mention our long evenings of Negronis and plotting. And the food. Ned and I got engaged in Korčula while at my brother's wedding, so thanks are humbly offered to Charles, Ivana and her family, Phil, Gregory and Ranko for Serbian hospitality on that stunning Croatian island. Also my love and gratitude goes out to friends, family and neighbours in my home town of Darlington, but particularly Emma Tyers, co-conspirator for life.

Though this is a work of fiction it was inspired in part by fact as recorded by some remarkable journalists and non-fiction writers. I'm particularly indebted to Heidi Blake and the team at

Buzzfeed behind the *From Russia with Blood* series in 2017, Misha Glenny's *McMafia* and Oliver Bullough's *Moneyland*. Truth remains stranger and in many ways more terrifying than a fiction writer like myself can keep up with.

THRILLINGLY GOOD BOOKS FROM CRIMINALLY GOOD WRITERS

CRIME FILES BRINGS YOU THE LATEST RELEASES FROM TOP CRIME AND THRILLER AUTHORS.

SIGN UP ONLINE FOR OUR MONTHLY NEWSLETTER AND BE THE FIRST TO KNOW ABOUT OUR COMPETITIONS, NEW BOOKS AND MORE.